Jessica Tre_____ _____terested
primarily in the psycholo_____ may be
hiding things from themsel_____. United
Press International, she published her first book of stories in 1992,
followed by her first novel in 2001 and a second collection, winner
of the Flannery O'Connor Award for Short Fiction, in 2010. Most
of her work is realistic fiction about families. Jessica is a professor of
creative writing at Emerson College in Boston.

IF SHE DID IT

Jessica Treadway

sphere

SPHERE

First published in the United States in 2015 by Grand Central
First published in Great Britain in 2015 by Sphere

1 3 5 7 9 10 8 6 4 2

Copyright © Jessica Treadway 2015

The moral right of the author has been asserted.

*All characters and events in this publication, other
than those clearly in the public domain, are fictitious
and any resemblance to real persons,
living or dead, is purely coincidental.*

A CIP catalogue record for this book
is available from the British Library.

ISBN 978-0-7515-5524-0

Printed and bound in Great Britain by Clays Ltd, St Ives plc

Papers used by Sphere are from well-managed forests
and other responsible sources.

MIX
Paper from
responsible sources
FSC® C104740

Sphere
An imprint of
Little, Brown Book Group
100 Victoria Embankment
London EC4Y 0DY

An Hachette UK Company
www.hachette.co.uk
www.littlebrown.co.uk

To Daniel Johnson—
gentleman, scholar, treasured nephew

Of all the ways to lose a person, death is the kindest.
RALPH WALDO EMERSON

Are You Looking at Me or Not?

The detective was waiting for me when I arrived home from work. He sat in his own Civic, rather than an official police car, on the side of the driveway where Joe used to park. He might have been doing a crossword; I saw him lay down a folded section of the newspaper when I pulled in beside him.

I swore, not at the sight of Thornburgh, but because reporters from TV news vans were also waiting for me, on the street in front of the house. They ran up the driveway with cameras as I parked in the garage and stepped out of my car, but when I held my hand over my face and said that I was sorry but I couldn't talk to them, the detective moved forward and told them in his reasonable but no-nonsense voice that they needed to get off my property.

Then he turned to me and nodded, a variation on an old-fashioned bow. I'd always been grateful for that quality in him, his politeness, the way he treated me with respect back then and didn't—like so many of them—seem to believe that I must have brought what happened to me upon myself. Although Dawn had

1

never been indicted, I knew that a lot of people who hadn't even met me thought I was a terrible mother.

He wore civilian clothes: neatly pressed pants and a turtleneck under a windbreaker. The crease in his pants reminded me of the care my husband had always taken with his own appearance, and I felt a quick jolt, grief and pleasure together, thinking about Joe and the things I loved about him.

What I knew about Kenneth Thornburgh, besides the fact of his kindness, was that he had moved to the Albany area three years earlier—just before Joe died—from a small town across the border in Massachusetts where he had been unable to solve the murder of a fifteen-year-old girl. He saw this as his own personal failure, if you could believe the conclusions drawn by Cecilia Baugh in the feature story she wrote for the local weekly, *The Everton Eagle*, shortly after Thornburgh joined the force. He lived alone in the new condo development across town. After our trial, he suffered a mild heart attack, and since then he did not go out on active calls anymore. Instead, he ran investigations from behind his desk.

"Mrs. Schutt," he told me as we walked toward my back door together, "I'm sorry to bother you." He was the only one of his staff who didn't call me by my first name from the very beginning, from that morning they'd come in to find Joe dead on the stairs and me, with barely a pulse, beaten and bloody across our bed. In the way that matters most, they saved my life, but in another way they destroyed it with the questions they asked before the ambulance rushed me away.

Thornburgh was one of the few people who could look at my face without wincing. The surgeons had done their best, but the scars were obvious, and my features looked as if they'd been pulled apart and rearranged, like a Picasso painting. Maybe in a museum a distorted face is a symbol, but it's become all too clear to me that nobody appreciates encountering one on the street. No symbolism there—it means your face has been bashed in.

My hair had grown back since they shaved it for my brain surgery. When I was young I hid behind my bangs out of a shyness that felt paralyzing sometimes, but as an adult with facial injuries I had a better reason to let my hair fall over my bad eye— the one with the sagging lid they hadn't been able to fix—and the cheek on the same side, the right, which remained slightly uneven, the skin buckled despite reconstruction of the bone. On good days I could almost forget what I looked like, but every time I went out in public, the stares and whispers reminded me.

There was one blessing in it, if you could call it that. For the first time, I understood what Dawn must have felt like as a child, when other kids either leaned in to get a closer look at her lazy eye or turned away because—as Iris would have said back then— it freaked them out. How many times had Dawn come home crying because some classmate had called her a name or, probably not even meaning to be cruel, asked her in frustration, "Are you looking at me or not?"

In the garage I told Thornburgh it was fine, this was not a bad time, and asked if he wanted to come in. In fact, I was glad for the company, however brief it would be. All I had to look forward to was another Friday evening ahead of me with no plans, except to eat a microwave dinner in front of the TV with the dog stretched out beside me on the couch. Besides, I knew from experience how stressful it was to face reporters alone.

I gestured at the door with my chin because I was carrying a potted ficus, which somebody at the office had given up on and put out with the trash. When my friend Francine, the reception-ist, saw me pick up the plant on my way out to my car and I told her I was going to take it home, she warned me that it was too far gone. But this only made me more determined to nurse it back to life.

The detective said no thanks to coming in, it wouldn't take a minute, and then he looked down at his shoes before he contin-ued, covering his mouth with his fist as he cleared his throat, a habit I'd become familiar with during the trial. "I wanted to make sure you heard," he said. "About the appeal?"

"Appeal?" My arms went slack, and he stepped forward to take the plant from me.

"You're not going to tell me you didn't know this was up before the court today, are you?" He pointed his thumb at the news trucks. "What do you think they're doing here?"

I shrugged, feeling my shoulders shake. "I tried not to pay at-tention." I didn't say that I'd purposely left the radio off in my car on the way home—afraid of what it might tell me—precisely be-cause I *did* know what was going on.

Thornburgh said, "Well, you'd have to find out sooner or later. The court granted Petty's appeal for a new trial."

I had not heard the name Petty spoken aloud in months. The sound of it made a ripple rise up the back of my neck.

I put a hand on the car hood to steady myself. "Did they grant it based on the dying declaration?" It always seemed wrong to me that it could be called that, when I hadn't actually died afterward. But it had been explained to me that this was the law.

Thornburgh said, "It was more of the Sixth Amendment thing. The fact that the defense couldn't cross-examine you during the trial, because you didn't remember."

4

I rubbed my forehead as jolts of pain darted behind my eyes. "He's not going to get out on bail, is he?"

"Oh, no. Absolutely not. No way would they give bail for a crime like this." He squinted in his rush to reassure me, and with a thud of dread in my gut I could tell what was coming next. "But Mrs. Schutt—*Hanna*—we want to put him away again as much as you do. Well, I shouldn't say that. Of course you want it more." He coughed gently.

"Who is 'we'?" I said, though I already knew.

"The police, and Gail Nazarian. She's worried he might walk this time, unless they can get a direct eyewitness to what happened."

At the prosecutor's name, my temples folded in on themselves in a full-blown throb. This had been happening more and more lately, and I knew I'd have to mention it to my neurologist during my next checkup. Quietly, to subdue the noise in my head, I told Thornburgh what I'd told him every other time before. "I don't know anything more than what I've said already. I can't remember that night."

It seemed again that he didn't believe me, and for a moment I thought he might say so. Then I remembered that this was more Gail Nazarian's style, not the detective's. "I'm sorry," he said, and he did look sorry. It was an expression I'd seen often during the trial, especially when he had to testify about what he'd seen in our bedroom that morning three years earlier, when my friend Claire called the police after looking through our front window and seeing Joe lying on the stairwell in his own blood.

At the sound of children shouting, Thornburgh looked down the block to a yard near the corner where the Osborne girls, Portia and Rosamund—who were young enough that they didn't even

5

seem to notice the media chaos on their street—chanted an old camp song as they took turns jumping into a huge leaf pile I'd watched their father rake for them the day before. The detective smiled slightly as he handed me the ficus and turned to leave.

"Is there anything you can do to get them out of here?" I asked, meaning the reporters.

"They're allowed to be in the street," he told me, which I already knew. "The only way to get rid of them is if you go down and give them something they can use." When I hesitated, he added, "Want me to come with?" The childlike phrase made me smile, and I said yes before fear let me change my mind. I set the plant on my car and began to follow him toward the curb.

Before we could reach the reporters, my next-door neighbor Pam Furth approached from where she'd been watching everything on the strip of grass between our driveways.

"Anything I can do, Hanna?" she asked, feigning all care and concern. I knew this was for Kenneth Thornburgh's benefit, because everyone knew he was a bachelor and Pam, whose husband had divorced her, made no secret of the fact that she was always on the lookout for a new husband.

I didn't bother to answer her.

As Thornburgh and I approached the street, the reporters began to close in. At the front of the pack I saw Cecilia Baugh, whose face was twisted into an expression calculated to remind me of our past connection, and that she was the one closest to home on my story, since the house she grew up in was just around the block. I looked away from her. Questions were yelled from every direction, all on the order of "How does it feel to hear that Rud Petty will get a new trial?"

"I don't have any comment, except to say I'm confident he'll be

6

convicted again." I spoke slowly, forming each word in my head before I said it.

"Would you mind repeating that, only louder?" someone shouted from the back.

Meeting my eyes and seeing that I was finished, Thornburgh told them, "Give Mrs. Schutt some breathing room, please," and motioned for me to walk back up toward the house. "I'll be in touch," I heard him say under his breath, so only I could hear. "Take care of yourself, okay?"

His words were more than a formality, I knew. I could sense how much lay behind his wish for me—*Take care of yourself*—and I would have liked to show him that I felt it, but it didn't seem like something I could afford. All I managed was "Thank you," and I watched him get back in his car and pull out of the driveway, giving me a gesture that was either a peace sign or half of a wave. I remembered how he'd reached for my hand in the hospital, the first time he came to talk to me there. He'd touched my fingers with the merest hint of a squeeze, which I took to be reassurance and comfort, until he cleared his throat and started asking me to repeat the statements I'd made when he discovered me in our ravaged bed, next to the croquet mallet that had killed my husband and just about killed me.

Before I brought my plant inside, I paused for a moment to listen to the song the Osborne sisters were singing as they climbed to the top of their picnic table, jumped off into the leaves, and scrambled up again. It was a song my older daughter, Iris, had learned years ago at the YMCA day camp we used to send her to, instead of the fancy sleepaway ones—horses, soccer, dramatic arts—her friends attended. We offered to send Dawn to the camp, too, but she said she'd rather stay home. Which I let her do, even

7

though Joe believed it was our duty to push her sometimes. "She needs to get out in the sun," he said. "She's too pale." He was right. Once, a new student in her eighth-grade class asked Dawn if she was an albino.

Apples, peaches, pumpkin pie—those bones gonna rise again! Who's not ready? Holler aye! Those bones gonna rise again. When I was a child I learned the lyrics as "dem bones," but of course that wasn't acceptable anymore, at least in a town like Everton. I wanted to wave at the girls, even though I knew they wouldn't see it from such a distance. Besides, I knew my house was off-limits to the children who'd moved to the neighborhood in the past few years. Though I tried to ignore it, I knew some people called it the Lizzie Borden House.

And even when I was out walking the dog, the kids avoided me, probably in large part because of the way I looked. Maybe their parents had told them to stay away. It still stung, but I was used to it by now. This Halloween, the same as the last two years, I knew I'd end up with as much candy left in the bowl as I started out with.

In the old days, entering the house through the garage, I would have used my key to get inside, then pushed the buttons on the alarm system to disable it when I entered. I would have taken my shoes off by the back door before stepping into the kitchen. When Abby greeted me with her usual tilted-up, black-snouted sniff-kiss and the expression that meant *What are we having for dinner?* I would have measured out her food with a cup from the storage tin in its place under the sink. Then I would have picked up the mail and stacked it in order of importance, bills on top. Living with an accountant had taught me to be organized, to think in terms of "systems" for everything in the house. Though it wasn't my nature,

8

I learned from the beginning of my marriage to sort, check, anticipate, and plan, and it became clear to me quickly why Joe liked to live that way; it made me believe I had control over my life.

But now I didn't bother with systems anymore. I just poured Abby's food into her bowl, letting some spill over, and went upstairs to change my clothes, tossing my blouse in the direction of the hamper. After putting on my jeans and an old sweatshirt that had belonged to some boyfriend of Iris's, I clipped on Abby's leash and patted her flank the way she liked it. It was better for both of us if I walked her before night fell completely, because we were both afraid of the dark. At the window, I pushed a corner of the curtain aside and saw that Thornburgh had been right. After filming my flimsy quote for their newscasts, the reporters had all gone to file their stories.

Our town was the kind Joe never thought he'd move to. His family had been what he called "blue-collar Buffalo" for three generations before him, and even though he was proud to have left the bad parts of his heritage behind—his father's drinking and sarcasm, the dependence on food stamps when his father got fired, hand-me-downs that had already been through two cousins before him—he was also committed to not straying too far from his roots. For a year after we were married we lived in an apartment in Albany, but then Joe surprised me by saying he thought we should start looking for a house, and he named a few of the suburbs. When I asked why, he said it was because of the schools. "They're better out here," he said, as we drove around Everton checking out For Sale and Open House signs. I wasn't even thinking of being a mother yet, but as it turned out, with Iris being born the following year, he was right to settle us into the four-bedroom Colonial at 17 Wildwood Lane.

The houses on our street lay in a staggered pattern across from each other, and Wildwood ended in a cul-de-sac bordering the conservation land known as Two Rivers. This was where my friend Claire and I had always met for our walks on Saturday mornings before that Thanksgiving weekend three years earlier, and where I still took Abby for her exercise twice a day. As the dog and I stepped out the back door and through the garage after Thornburgh and the reporters left, she headed automatically in that direction.

There was no denying it anymore—it was starting to get cold. We hadn't turned the clocks back yet, and technically the sun was still out, but the air held that distinct winter's-on-its-way feel. I was halfway down the block, pulling the hood of the sweatshirt over my ears, when I heard somebody's front door open behind me. I shut my eyes for a moment because I knew what was coming, and I hadn't decided yet how I wanted to feel about it.

Sure enough, Warren Goldman called my name in a low voice, then ran to catch up with me. He hadn't had time to put on sneakers, but came out instead in his moccasin slippers, the soles slapping softly on the sidewalk.

"Hanna," he breathed, trying not to give away that the short sprint had winded him. He needed a haircut; little wings lifted away from his neck in the nippy breeze. He hadn't bothered to grab a jacket, and I could see goose bumps rising on his arms, which were bare beneath their tee-shirt sleeves. The shirt, faded and stretched over his stomach, said THIS IS WHAT A FEMINIST LOOKS LIKE. Reading it I smiled to myself, remembering the party he and his wife Maxine had thrown in celebration of Hillary Clinton's election to the Senate. Joe hadn't wanted to go, saying he wasn't a big fan of the Clintons, but I knew his resistance had

10

more to do with the fact that parties made him uncomfortable, and he hated small talk. I let him think I believed his reason for declining, but I liked Hillary and didn't mind small talk, so I said I was just going over to show my face at the party to be polite, and then I didn't get home until midnight.

I reminded Warren of that party now, and he smiled. "That was a good one," he said. His face sobered. "Remember Maxine got out her guitar?"

I felt guilty, even though I hadn't intended to cause him a painful memory. Warren reached down to scratch Abby behind the ears. Then he straightened quickly, giving out a mild exclamation at the sudden movement and putting a hand on his back, imitating an old man. "I've been meaning to ask you. Do you have plans for Thanksgiving? I was going to invite you over, if you didn't. Our son and his wife are coming." Ever since Maxine died, two years before Joe, Warren had referred to his wife as if she were still alive. Joe considered it creepy, and I knew other people did, too, but I thought it was sweet. I thought it was touching that he honored her memory this way, even though he must have realized it sounded odd.

"I thought I'd try the 'Small and sophisticated' dinner from *Bon Appétit*," he added. "Celery bisque, turkey breast roulade, and pumpkin mousse." He looked at me hopefully, as if he'd been afraid I might turn him down but would change my mind once I heard the menu.

Warren had taken up cooking after Maxine's death. He routinely invited people from the neighborhood to eat with him, and sometimes he brought meals to other people's houses. The sight of the rumpled man in the rumpled clothes carrying a casserole dish was a familiar one on our street. Joe and I had joined him a

11

few times, and after I came home from rehab, Warren had more than once suggested our sharing a meal. I knew he figured it was only natural that two widowed people should do so, but I usually found some excuse to say no.

It had been almost a year since he'd asked, and because I'd been trying to forget how soon Thanksgiving was, his invitation took me aback. I coughed, stalling, trying to figure out how to respond. "I'm not sure," I managed to stammer, as Abby started to whine on the sidewalk between us. I recognized that my answer was what the kids would call "lame," but I couldn't think how to improve it. Just the word *Thanksgiving* was enough to speed up my breath. That and the fact that I'd wondered, over the past couple of years, whether the conversations Warren always initiated—when we were both outside getting mail from our boxes, or unloading groceries—were an effort to, as the kids would say, "hit on me." I couldn't quite bring myself to believe this was the case, because, well, why would he? I'd never been pretty to begin with, and since the attack, I was even less so. I wasn't particularly smart or accomplished, and I didn't have an impressive or lucrative job. Not to mention what had happened in our house three years earlier. Unless Warren was one of those people who got turned on by catastrophe, what could he possibly see in me?

And even if he *could* see something, did I want him to?

"I'll let you guys go," he said, nodding at Abby, who was straining against the leash. "Will you think about it, Hanna? You don't have to give me any notice—we'll be here either way." He put his hand out to touch my arm in good-bye, but I pretended I didn't feel it and turned away.

After our usual loop of the brook at Two Rivers, Abby trotted me back toward home. But halfway down the street she paused, making the low growl in her throat that meant she was scared of something. "It's okay, girl," I told her, trying to sound convincing even though I had no way of knowing if it was really okay or not. Then we heard the familiar sound of Emmett Furth's motorcycle revving up in his driveway, and he sped past the dog and me, coming so close we could feel the wind and hear him whoop as he rushed by us.

"Goddammit," I breathed as he moved down the street, but it must have come out louder than I thought, because Pam, his mother, heard me from the curb where she had dragged out her trash barrel.

"You know he can't help it, Hanna," she chided me.

She'd been saying this for years, that Emmett couldn't help it. When he was an eight-year-old getting into trouble for kinking people's sprinkler hoses and chasing cats up trees, all of us on the block tried to buy Pam's explanation that Emmett had an "auditory processing problem," which was the source of all his troublemaking.

But as he grew older, we became more and more aware that he just chose not to listen to people, including his mother, when they were telling him what not to do. And he couldn't have cared less whether he ruined your yard or terrorized your pet or caused water to back up into your basement. In fact, he always seemed happier leaving destruction in his wake. This was why some people seemed to believe that Emmett, and not Rud Petty, had been responsible for the attack on Joe and me.

I used to talk back to Pam, and let her know when I was angry about her son tormenting Dawn or charging on his bicycle through my garden. But after he set fire to our tree house when he was in tenth grade, I became afraid of him.

13

During the trial, when Rud's lawyer proposed Emmett as a possible alternative perpetrator, he cited the fact that Joe had refused to provide a reference for Emmett after he graduated from high school the same year as Dawn and, instead of going on to college, applied for a job at Home Depot. I remember telling Joe he should just go ahead and do it, for the sake of peace with the neighbors. He didn't have to make Emmett sound like a saint, but couldn't he just say the kid would probably show up on time and not make any trouble? It had been three years since the tree house, I reminded him. Didn't he deserve a second chance?

When I suggested this, Joe said, "He *burned down* our property, Hanna. Do you realize how easily that fire could have spread to our house? If I'd had my way, we would have pressed charges. What possible reason would I have to recommend him for a job?" I quit trying to persuade him, because he was right.

The jury didn't buy the notion of Emmett as a possible culprit, probably because the defense also suggested that Joe might have been targeted by someone associated with Marc Sedgwick, the former superintendent of schools over in Shelby Falls, whom Joe had helped expose for embezzlement and whose case was scheduled to go to trial a few months after Joe got killed. The defense had no evidence of this, and everyone could tell it was just a Hail Mary pass attempting to put doubt in the minds of the jurors. According to Gail Nazarian, Rud Petty's legal team "royally fucked up" by floating both scenarios as possible motives for Joe's murder. She said, "Emmett Furth probably tipped the scales. Without him, we might have ended up with a hung jury."

Though I knew it was silly, I almost felt I owed Emmett a favor for contributing in this dubious way to the fact that there had been a conviction in my husband's death. So when Pam told me now that her son couldn't help it, I only waved at her, and gave her a nod excusing Emmett again, as she turned away from her trash cans and I followed Abby back to our door. I'd fed her but not myself yet, so I settled down in front of the TV to eat a dinner I hadn't had the patience to heat properly in the microwave.

I wasn't nearly as particular about what I ate, after Joe died, as I was when he was alive. After certain things have happened to you, you start to feel as if it doesn't make any difference. No matter how much you want to believe what they tell you, you realize you can't really keep yourself safe.

The news was about to come on—pirates, suicide bombs, drunk drivers, and stocks going down the drain. Before I could hit the Mute button, I heard the teaser to the top local story: "New trial on tap for so-called Croquet Killer." Even though I warned myself not to, I found myself peering at the screen, squinting to distort the image a little, when Rud Petty's photograph came on.

How was it possible that after all he'd done to destroy me and my family, my instinct at seeing his picture was to think *That's a good-looking man*?

And could I really blame my daughter, who was so much younger than I, who considered herself ugly and who'd had no romantic experience before him, for wanting to believe that he was in love with her?

After finishing the tepid mess its package called a stroganoff, I picked up the phone to listen to my messages, already knowing, because of what Thornburgh had told me, that at least one of them would be from Gail Nazarian. And there it was, along with requests from still more reporters. I ignored those, and was jotting myself a note to call the prosecutor back (maybe the following week, after I'd figured out how to say, once again, that I couldn't help her), when I heard a rap at the back door and saw her standing there, peering at me through the pane. It was too late to hide and pretend I wasn't home. I had no choice but to go over and let her in.

"Ow, shit!" she said, reacting as the door I held open gave off a static spark. She shook her hand a little and added, "I know you don't want to see me." In her other arm she clutched a leather briefcase to her side so tightly it might have been a tourniquet preventing her from bleeding all over my floor. "I came by because I thought you might hang up on me if I just called." She tried to say it in a joking way, but humor was not one of her strengths.

I resisted the temptation to tell her she was right. Once she'd failed in her effort to persuade the grand jury to indict Dawn in the attack against Joe and me, I tried to warm up to her because she was working to send Rud Petty away. But I couldn't, mainly because I knew Gail believed Dawn was guilty. She did everything she could to get her bound over for trial, but there wasn't any physical evidence against Dawn, and she had an alibi.

I tried to make my voice light, so she could take what I said as a joke, too, if she wanted. "Don't you have anything better to do on a Friday night than harass crime victims?"

"Sorry," she said, sweeping past me into the kitchen, but of course she was not sorry at all. "You really should give me your cell phone number. I might need to get in touch with you immediately sometime, like I did today."

"I don't have a cell phone," I told her. I knew she'd think I was lying, but I didn't care.

Most of my friends just thought I was a technophobe. The truth was that I didn't have a cell phone because I grew up with a father who flinched every time the phone rang in our house.

16

Later, after he was convicted of fraud and a few other "legal infe-licities" (his lawyer's words), I understood that this behavior was related to the fact that he lived in constant fear of being found out. Though all of that was a long time ago, I never got over the impulse to cringe at the sound of a ringing phone. So I stuck to my old-fashioned landline at home and used caller ID to screen any calls that came in.

But I wasn't about to explain any of this to Gail Nazarian. "I know why you're here," I continued. "Ken Thornburgh just came by to tell me about the appeal."

"I was surprised you weren't there in the courtroom to hear it yourself." Though Abby was sniffing at the hem of her brown skirt, the prosecutor didn't reach down to pet her. Gail Nazarian had always looked like my idea of a female lieutenant, with her severe style of dress—always the same cut of dark-colored suit— and the way she didn't let her hair, which I noticed had grayed somewhat since the end of Rud Petty's trial, wave around her face as it wanted to. She was short and plump, with stubby limbs and a lean in her walk that made me think one leg might be longer than the other. Her eyes appeared black, and they moved in her face the way a bird's eyes move, darting sharply to both sides above a beak poised to sense the slightest threat at any distance.

"I didn't have any reason to be there," I said to Gail.

"You don't care that he got a new trial?"

"Of course I care. It's just that I knew I'd find out sooner or later which way it went. The last thing I wanted was to be in the same room with him again." I scooped some more food into the dish for Abby and felt happy, as I always did, to see her eat with such appetite. For months after the attack, while I was recuper-ating in the hospital and she went to a foster home, she ate too

17

little and lost too much weight. Now she was almost her old self again, give or take a few creaks that were part old age, part leftover trauma.

"Well, I came in person," Gail told me, drawing out her enunciation as if she were speaking to a child, "and on a Friday night, to let you know that I have every intention of putting Rud Petty away again, this time for good." She would have kept talking, but I held a hand up to interrupt.

"Just a minute. Can you tell me what happened in court?"

She sighed in the weary manner I became used to during the trial. *If you had been there yourself,* the sigh said, *I wouldn't have to explain it to you.* "It was a little complex, in terms of the legalities. But basically, the judge ruled that because of the medical witnesses the defense put up, the nods shouldn't have been let in."

The Nods. It was a phrase coined by Cecilia Baugh, in that national crime tabloid she freelanced for, to describe in a kind of shorthand what happened when the police found me beaten in my bed that November morning. I had appeared to implicate both Rud Petty and my daughter when Ken Thornburgh questioned me, before the medics sped me away. My testimony about The Nods hadn't been heard by Dawn's grand jury, but the judge at Rud Petty's trial allowed it under the "dying declaration" rule, which basically says that when you think you're about to die, you have no reason to lie about who tried to kill you.

But now the appeals court said The Nods had to be thrown out and the trial started over, apparently because—since by the time the trial started, I couldn't access my memory of that night—Rud's lawyer hadn't been able to question me about them.

My chest knew what the prosecutor was asking of me before

she even spoke the question, and the knowledge squeezed my lungs to the point that my next few breaths came out in a pant. For three years, there had been no reason for me to try to remember the attack. Not that I had tried; to be honest, I didn't *want* to remember. Who in her right mind would?

"I still can't testify," I told Gail. "I don't have anything for you to use."

She was silent for a moment, and I remembered the way she had, in the courtroom, often allowed herself to pause when she was questioning defense witnesses, not because she needed the extra time, but because it made them nervous; you could see it in their eyes. Even with her own witnesses—including the state police investigator who took the stand to confirm that our alarm system had been disabled by someone who knew the code and then smashed the keypad to make it look like a random break-in—she came off as somewhat hostile. When Warren Goldman testified for the prosecution that he'd gotten out of bed at two o'clock on the morning of the attack and thought he'd seen Dawn's Nova parked in our driveway, he went on to explain that he'd had insomnia since his wife, Maxine, died. But Gail cut him off. "We're only interested in what's relevant," she said.

In my kitchen she shifted from one foot to the other, and for some reason this simple movement triggered a feeling of dread. "I know you want to protect your daughter, Mrs. Schutt," she murmured. "I get that. If I were a mother, I'm sure I'd do the same thing."

"But I'm not 'doing' anything," I told her.

She looked at me long and hard. I could tell she didn't believe me. "There's something else you should know."

There it was, that chill to my neck again. I filed this in my

19

mind as another thing to mention to the neurologist, although I guessed it wasn't actually a physical symptom.

"They found a cell phone on Rud Petty," she said. "He hadn't made any calls yet, so they couldn't track any numbers. But— well, like I said. I thought you should know."

She wasn't telling me this because she thought I cared what Rud Petty did with his time at the correctional facility in the northern part of the state. She wanted me to think that it was possible it had been Dawn he was trying to contact. "How did he get a phone?" I asked, to distract myself from the panic I felt gathering in my belly and threatening to break out. "I thought that wasn't allowed."

"It isn't. But lots of things happen in jail that aren't supposed to."

"Well. It's a good thing they found the phone, then."

She sighed again, this time so quietly I assumed she hadn't meant for me to hear it. Then I watched her decide to take the plunge and come right out with what she was thinking. "You aren't worried he might try to get in touch with your daughter?"

"He won't," I said, loud enough that I hoped I might persuade both of us. "She doesn't want to hear from him. Anyway, even if he tried to, what difference would it make? He's in jail."

"You're a fool if you think he can't get you from there."

I swallowed the urge to ask what she meant by "get" me. I didn't say anything as I watched her face and tried to figure out how much she was thinking about her own reasons for wanting another conviction, and how much she was thinking about me and my safety. She asked, "Where is she, anyway?"

"I'm not sure." This was true only in the sense that at that very moment, my daughter might have been inside her apartment in Santa Fe or out of it. But I didn't have to tell Gail Nazarian that.

"If I find out you're holding something back, I won't be happy," she said, this time making a point of pushing Abby's snout away. "Look, I don't actually need you to tell me where she is. My staff can find her. My staff could find the tooth fairy if they wanted to. But it would be better for everyone if you cooperated with us."

"I am cooperating." My hope was that if I spoke as calmly as possible, it would infuriate her into leaving. But no such luck.

"We need one of you on that stand," she said. Then, after a dramatic pause for effect, she added, "Just keep in mind that we always have the option of trying again to indict Dawn." She took a step back to watch my reaction.

I tried not to let out the gasp I felt. "You can't do that."

"Of course I can. It's not a question of double jeopardy—she never stood trial."

"So," I said, wondering even as I spoke whether I should continue, "you're threatening me?"

She shrugged. "I wouldn't call it that. Just passing on information. Letting you know what our options are."

When I didn't say anything further because my brain had gone on the blink, she thanked me in a tone that said the opposite of what her words did, and told me to call her, please, if something changed—if I remembered anything, *anything*, that might be of use. "The case might depend on it," she said. Pointedly, she propped her business card against the salt shaker on the table. I had a half dozen identical cards scattered in my junk drawer.

I told myself she was exaggerating. I didn't doubt for a minute that Rud Petty would be found guilty again, purely on the evidence that had been presented the first time around. He'd had a motive, he'd had access to the alarm code, his prints were on the

21

weapon. They had a nearly perfect match from a shoe print in our bedroom to a shoe they found in his closet when they arrested him. I reminded myself that the prosecution didn't need me, even if I *could* testify.

Gail Nazarian seemed to intuit what I was thinking, and she wasted no time in attempting to set me straight. "It's all circumstantial," she said. "They can explain everything away. You know that." Her tone implied that she was sick of repeating herself. "The fact that he knew about the code and the key only means Dawn told him about them at some point—it doesn't necessarily have to do with that night. His prints on the mallet could have been left over from the wedding. Even the shoe print isn't a hundred percent—you saw how hard his lawyer worked to prove it could have come from a different pair.

"I watched the jurors when Thornburgh gave his testimony about you identifying Rud," she went on. "I'm telling you, that's what swung them. Without that—and we *don't* have that now—I can't make any promises." She paused again to allow the weight of her words to sink in.

Since I didn't have an answer for this, I said instead, "What makes you think I'd work as a witness, anyway? You know his lawyer will get experts to say my memory can't be trusted."

"Well, we'll get experts who say it can." She said it with enough confidence that I was tempted to believe her.

I asked when the retrial was likely to be, and she said she wasn't sure. She'd need time to prepare the case, but Rud's attorneys would push to have it start as soon as possible—late winter or early spring.

"But it's over," I said, recognizing how weak it sounded, my effort to convince myself.

"No," she told me. "It isn't."

Then she was gone, still clutching her briefcase, which she'd never loosened her grip on during the whole time we spoke. I watched her get into her Volkswagen, and before turning the key she sagged in her seat, leaning back against the headrest. But she allowed herself only a moment's break before sitting up and starting the car with a ferocious gun to the gas, as if there were something under the pedal she wanted to destroy.

Inferences and Conclusions

Sensing my distress after the district attorney's visit, Abby pointed her nose in the air to ask if she could help. Rubbing between her ears, I glanced at the clock and saw that it wasn't even seven yet. I could already tell that the anxiety triggered by the news of Rud Petty's appeal, and the appearance by Gail Nazarian, might overwhelm me. The only solution, I knew, was to get out of the house. Promising Abby I wouldn't be long, I drove to the mall.

I had to do this sometimes, make myself go out in the world, because otherwise it would have been too easy to just sit inside, behind the curtains, and hide. The mall had become my default destination because it held good memories for me—browsing with my daughters for back-to-school clothes, shopping with Joe for the girls' birthday and Christmas presents, strolling through the garden exhibit sponsored by the Horticultural Society every spring.

For the first few months after I returned home from rehab, I found myself at the mall almost every day. I could sit concealed on one of the couches behind a grove of fake trees in the atrium, observing without being observed. The bustle of people going about their lives reminded me of when I had been one of them, and it gave me hope that I might become a normal person again. (If the members of my trauma rehab group had heard me think this way—about not feeling "normal"—they'd have snapped my head off. *You are normal, Hanna*, they'd say, and I'd tell them *I know*, because that's what they'd want to hear. But I didn't really believe it. Inside, I was still waiting to feel normal again. Not like some person who'd gotten her head smashed in with a croquet mallet by her daughter's boyfriend. How normal would that make *you* feel?)

My first stop, as usual, was Lickety Split. As I stood in line, the tired-looking mother in front of me looked down at her daughter, who appeared to be about four, and said, "Sophie, stop arguing with me." Without missing a beat, the child replied, "I'm not arguing with *you*, Mommy. You're arguing with *me*," and her mother, realizing that I had overheard this exchange, smiled as she caught my eye. She did a fairly good job of not reacting when she registered my twisted features. I smiled back at her, but by then she'd bent down with a sudden and intense interest in finding out what flavor her daughter wanted. I tried hard not to understand that she was doing her best to distract the child from also noticing my lopsided face.

My breath snagged on the sharp but familiar pain of feeling shunned as I took my peppermint cone back out to the atrium and ate it as I walked. Ever since the attack, ice cream had given me a headache—brain freeze, I knew it was called—but when I came to the mall I always ordered something at Lickety Split anyway, because it allowed me to feel nostalgic for all the times I'd taken Dawn there as a reward after her appointments with the vision therapist in Schenectady.

25

All through elementary school, she had held out one hope—that when she turned twelve, we would allow her to get surgery on her lazy eye. The doctor had told us that twelve was pretty much the cutoff for surgery to do any good, and I knew that over the years, she'd held that birthday in mind as a kind of deadline, after which she would either finally have a shot at being normal or be consigned to the nickname of Fish Face forever.

But Joe was against Dawn having the operation. When she was first diagnosed he did a lot of research, and he said that since her amblyopia (he always insisted on calling it by its clinical name, because he said there was nothing *lazy* about it) was in fact a problem of the brain rather than the eye muscle, it was wiser to go the route of occlusion and vision therapy. Occlusion meant putting a patch over the good eye, so the weak one would have to work harder and, if the process succeeded, develop improved sight. Vision therapy involved exercises to strengthen the way the two eyes worked together, with the aim of helping them converge.

Surgery has only a cosmetic value, Joe explained to Dawn and me, as she approached her twelfth birthday and made her last bid for him to approve the operation. It doesn't actually help the vision, he said. An operation might fix the eye temporarily, but the odds are in favor of it reverting to its amblyopic state, maybe even worse than before.

At the time, Joe didn't want to make a big deal out of his primary objection, which was that according to what he'd learned, it was possible for someone who'd had the surgery to go blind eventually. He told me he couldn't stand the idea of her not being able to see. I thought we should tell Dawn, so she'd understand we weren't denying her what she wanted without having a good reason. But he worried it would upset her too much.

So we just told her we thought it wasn't a good idea. The only benefit is in appearance, Joe repeated to her, as if using different words this time would somehow make it less hard for her to hear. Dawn didn't point out what I knew she and I were both thinking, which was that when you are a twelve-year-old girl, appearance is all that matters.

When we sat her down in the summer before sixth grade to give her our verdict, she looked at me with a plea to persuade Joe otherwise, but (it pains me to remember) I looked away. When she finally got the message that she wasn't going to convince us, she mumbled, "Thanks anyway" and went up to her room.

It was the "Thanks anyway" that killed us. Joe and I sat for a few minutes in silence before he said, "It isn't supposed to be this hard." I realized then that he was doing what he did for a living—thinking like an accountant, calculating what the return on our investment, as parents, should be.

Hoping he could make it up to her somehow, he went upstairs and told Dawn, through her closed bedroom door, that for her birthday the following weekend, she could bring twelve of her friends out to dinner—one for every year of her life—to celebrate the occasion. When no response came from Dawn's room, Joe added, "We can go to the Schuyler House," making the fiasco complete.

As soon as I heard him say it, I groaned to myself. Dawn didn't have twelve friends, or even half that many. How could he be so oblivious as to not know that? Had he completely forgotten what had happened only the year before, when the popular kids invited Dawn to a party they fabricated solely to humiliate her? It was a rare failure of judgment on his part.

I knew Dawn had to be shocked by his extravagant offer—

twelve dinner guests, and at the Schuyler House, no less. I waited for her to choke out another "Thanks anyway," but instead I heard her draw in a deep breath before she opened the door and told him, "Daddy, that's so nice of you. Are you sure? That would be great." I realized then that she couldn't bear for her father to understand that she was a loser (or, to use Iris's word for it, a freak).

I don't believe I'd ever seen Joe more shaken than when I told him what a mistake he'd made. He went back up to her room and tried to undo it—"I've been thinking about it, and maybe it would be more fun to have a smaller group? Or even just invite one person, like Monica, to make it really special?"—but by then, I knew, she had committed herself to the charade. Up until the night the party was scheduled, she allowed us to hold a reservation for sixteen people at the Schuyler House, even though Iris informed Joe and me that we were, as she put it, cracked. "There aren't even twelve kids who know her *name*," she told us. "This whole thing is pathetic." Shortly before we were due to leave the house for the restaurant, Dawn told us that it was a bummer but she'd just had a bunch of phone calls and it seemed that everybody besides Monica, her donkey-voiced best friend since nursery school, had come down with something. They wouldn't be meeting us at the Schuyler House after all.

"You've got to be kidding," Iris said, laughing outright at the blatancy of her sister's lie. "The phone hasn't rung once."

"Stop it, Iris," Joe said sharply, and looking chagrined, Iris cut off her smile. Dawn said she wanted to go to Pepito's instead, and I knew she'd chosen our favorite Tex-Mex place in the strip mall to reduce the expense for Joe and because she felt unworthy of a place as nice as the Schuyler House. The five of us sat at the round table in the corner, where we all pored intently over the menu far longer than necessary, because nobody seemed to have anything to say that was of interest to anyone else. Iris told a series of jokes about beans and what they did to you, until Joe made her stop. At the end of the meal Monica eagerly thrust Dawn's present at her, a set of *Enchanted Forest* books. I could tell it made Iris want to roll her eyes, but she refrained. Then she held out a wrapped package herself, which Dawn seemed apprehensive to open, and it made me sad to realize she could believe her own sister might try to mock her by way of a gift.

Inside was a cosmetic bag containing tubes of concealer, eye-liner, lip gloss, and blush. "Oh," Dawn said, literally backing away from the collection of items I'm sure she thought could have nothing to do with her. "Thanks, Iris, but I don't think so."

"Why not? I'll teach you. It's easy." Iris waved at her own face to illustrate. Then as now, she wore hardly any makeup because she didn't have to, but when you looked closely you could see that her eyes were dramatized by liner and shadow, her cheekbones heightened with a ruddy powder glow, and her lips drawn into a magenta heart.

"You're both too young for that," Joe said, but all we women ignored him, as he must have known we would. Dawn thanked her sister and set the present aside. I suspect she felt ashamed, thinking that Iris had given her the cosmetics because she wanted a prettier sister, and I didn't blame her, because of the way Iris taunted her sometimes. But I could tell this was a benevolent gesture on my older daughter's part. I don't know whether she ever gave Dawn the lesson she planned to, but I never saw Dawn wear any makeup until she left for college and met Rud Petty.

After the gift-opening, the restaurant's host, Kwan—who had been given the heads-up by Joe when we came in—brought out a flan with a candle in it for dessert, leading everyone in the restaurant in a round of "Happy Birthday." Iris hid her face, Dawn blushed, and Monica broke out in her familiar, unaware bray. I think we were all relieved when we could step outside, into the cool September air, and call the party over.

Later that night someone left a package wrapped in festive paper on our stoop, addressed to Dawn. I found it when I went to get the newspaper in the morning. I was about to bring it upstairs to her when something told me that I should check it out first. Sure enough, the shoebox inside the wrapping contained pellets of dried dog poop. I flushed them down the toilet, threw away the box, and went out to run my errands.

I remember thinking, when I opened the "present," *What did she ever do to them?* At the time, I told myself, *Nothing*. I told myself that it was no different from when I was in school, except that back then, there seemed to be a more laissez-faire approach to ostracizing the kids Iris referred to as "fringies"; you were only ignored, not included in invitations, passed by in the hallways as if you were invisible. Nobody delivered poop to your front door in the guise of a birthday gift. I told myself that this generation had just upped the ante.

Yet even as I tried to believe this, I understood that it went deeper than mere scorn. Whoever had done it—and there was probably more than one of them—was afraid of Dawn. Why? Afraid of what? But I couldn't allow myself to wonder, because I couldn't allow myself to understand that I was afraid of the same thing.

Of course I didn't tell Dawn about the delivery to our doorstep, and I never mentioned it to Joe. Though I am ashamed to say so now, I just wanted that unpleasantness to go away.

Once we nixed the idea of surgery, I expected Dawn to rebel against the vision therapy Joe wanted her to do instead. But she was too good a girl; if we told her to do something, she did it. Sometimes I wished she *would* put up a fight, the same way when she was a child I wished she would rip off the patch and refuse to wear it, because it would have been easier to feel angry than sorry for her.

So once a week I took her to Dr. Diamond's office in Schenectady, where she repeated the exercises designed to help her eyes align. Her eyes hurt at the end of every session, so early on, I decided to take her for a treat after each visit. I thought she deserved a reward for working so hard, and I felt guilty. I knew I should have realized something was wrong even before the amblyopia got diagnosed in a test her teacher recommended because she noticed Dawn squinting all the time. Even though I was a nurse, I hadn't seen a problem in my own daughter. Well, I didn't want to.

If Iris had been the one to develop a lazy eye in grade school, she would still have been as popular as she always was—I have no doubt of that. Either she would have found some way to laugh at herself, or her classmates would have felt sympathy for her. Knowing Iris, I'm sure she would have turned a lazy eye into something cool.

But even without the eye problem, Dawn would not have been a pretty girl like her sister. It hurt me to acknowledge this because I knew she was all too aware of it, and because she looked like me: we both had mouths that were too small, noses that were too flat, and hair too thin for us to be called anything but "nice-looking" at our best. Though I knew like any other parent that I wasn't supposed to have favorites, and that if I *were* going to have a favorite it would make sense for it to be the attractive, more promising child (as it clearly was Joe's, even though he tried not to show it), Dawn had my heart because as a kid I had also been nervous, not cute, and insecure.

When she began wearing the eye patch in second grade and kids called her Squint and Fish Face, her normal expression became one of defensiveness, almost a scowl. She walked around looking as if she expected to be made fun of, as if she hated people already because she knew they were laughing at her.

Even though when Joe and I discussed our younger daughter's unhappiness it was always in the context of the eye condition, I'm pretty sure that separately we both understood it was more than that. I know I did. Even in kindergarten, before we were told about the amblyopia, she didn't seem to fit in with the other kids. When I'd go to birthday parties to pick her up, I'd find her sitting in a corner, staring across the room where everyone else took a whack at the piñata or played musical chairs. When I asked her why, she said those things weren't fun for her. What *is* fun for you? I asked, but she always shrugged and said she didn't know. As she grew older, and especially after her diagnosis, she made more of an effort to join in, which Joe and I were glad to see because we thought it meant she was finally "coming out of her shell," as we put it to each other. Maybe she'd just felt overwhelmed before, we theorized, being in Iris's shadow. Maybe now she'll find out what she likes to do, and she'll get some confidence, and the other kids will come around.

But it didn't happen that way. She didn't enjoy any of the classes we signed her up for—since Iris took tennis and violin, we tried karate and the recorder with Dawn, but she couldn't have cared less about either—and Joe and I figured it was probably worse to force her to continue when she had no interest.

The only thing she wanted to do was use her crayons in coloring books; it seemed to give her pleasure to show us how well she could stay inside the lines. Joe asked if she didn't want to draw her own pictures—I knew he was trying to encourage her to be more creative, and not just fill in what somebody else had put on the page—but Dawn said no, she liked it when the picture was already there. This was okay in kindergarten, of course. But as she grew older, the other kids began to whisper and laugh. The same teacher who'd told us she thought Dawn needed an eye exam also said to me that maybe we should have her "see someone," though she didn't elaborate on what kind of "someone" she had in mind. "It just seems like there's something missing," she said, and my stomach fell to exactly the same spot it had when, years earlier, I overheard Peter Cifforelli ask Joe if he was sure I was "enough."

Whatever kept me from telling Joe about the dog poop kept me from telling him what the teacher said, too.

By the time she was in middle school, she was begging me every day to pick her up from school instead of making her take the bus home, because that was when the teasing, led by Emmett Furth, was the worst.

But I couldn't pick her up, because of my job. Besides, Joe would have said I was giving in to the bullies. He would have been right, but I still wished I could do it to save Dawn that heartache.

So because I felt guilty, and because I knew how much she'd had her heart set on the surgery she thought would cure her of being different, I took her out for ice cream. The trips were our secret, because Joe didn't like the girls eating too much sugar. When Dawn started to gain weight in eighth grade and Joe asked me why I thought that was, I pretended not to have any idea. But to Dawn I said that maybe we should cut down on the Lickety Split visits, which had started to make my waistbands tight, too. That was when she came up with the idea of getting a dog, and Abby replaced Sonic Sundaes as her primary comfort.

At the mall, after leaving the ice-cream store, I found myself in front of the display window at Sports Authority. I must have been standing there for a few minutes without realizing, because I'm a slow eater, and my cone was almost gone. I went inside and browsed through a rack of sale jerseys: Rodriguez, Jeter, Canó. When the college-age salesman asked if he could help me, I pulled my hair over my bad eye and said no, I wasn't looking for anything in particular.

I walked toward the back of the store, ignoring the colorful croquet sets—FUN FOR THE WHOLE FAMILY!—and picked up a baseball bat, which I carried to the counter. "For my granddaughter," I told the salesman, though of course he had not asked me who the bat was for.

"How old is she?"

"Two and a half."

He smiled. "This one might be a little big, then."

"That's okay. She'll grow into it." I signed the receipt quickly, then turned to leave; he had to call me back to hand me the bag with the bat sticking out. Immediately I felt silly about the purchase, but I didn't have what it took to say I'd changed my mind.

As I left the store, I thought I felt someone watching me, and turned to see a young man who looked to be about college age, though his face was so vacant he did not fit my idea of a college student. He stood to the side of the store, slurping soda through a straw from a cup the size of a bucket. He was on the short side, and thin, with reddish hair that curled down around his neck. It would have looked pretty on a girl, I thought, but it only made him appear sloppy, as did the low-slung jeans he wore with a chain hanging from the belt loops across the front. His untucked tee-shirt displayed a cartoon of a joint-smoking Cat in the Hat.

When he caught me looking back at him, he seemed to choke a little on his drink. I told myself I was just being paranoid. I reminded myself that people often stared at me because of my mangled face. This felt like more than that, but I decided to put it out of my mind. When he turned and walked off in the other direction, I tried to laugh at myself.

Outside Blue Moon, the boutique for teenage girls, I paused to remember all the times I'd taken Iris here over the years, when my role was to stand at the cash register and remind her that I couldn't buy all the clothes she'd chosen. She'd sulk and negotiate, and in the end she usually wore me down and brought home more than I knew Joe would have allowed if he'd been there. I went in and moved some hangers, pretending I was shopping for a daughter, and couldn't help eavesdropping on a conversation between two girls who didn't even look old enough to be in high school. "I wish I had it in me to break his heart again," one of them said to the other, and I smiled to myself.

Then, looking up, I froze as I saw Emmett Furth through the display window. He stood with two of his friends, watching the girls inside browsing the racks. It struck me as creepy, since Emmett was twenty-one now and the girls just teenagers. But he had always been immature. Remembering how he'd scared Abby and me during our walk less than an hour before, I wondered if he'd followed me to the mall, before I realized that it was just a coincidence; even Emmett Furth had better things to do than that.

I tried to escape the store without his noticing, but then I saw one of his friends pop him on the shoulder and point at me. In a voice loud enough for everyone around us to hear, the friend seemed to enjoy himself as he drew out the chant that was all too familiar: "Lizzie Borden took an axe . . . gave her mother forty whacks."

Emmett looked over. When he saw it was me, he locked us in a gaze so tight I was afraid I might sink to my knees. My tongue went sour and I coughed. He turned his back and resumed joking with his friends, but not before I thought I saw him flick two fingers from his forehead in my direction, a signal of some kind.

A signal of what? I couldn't be sure. I tried to convince myself it was a greeting, but that wouldn't be like him. And it felt more ominous than that.

For a panicked moment I lost my vision, and then it came back alternating between blurry and black. Feeling a cry in my throat that I knew better than to let out, I rushed to the nearest mall exit, which was not the closest to where I'd parked. As I stumbled across the lot toward my car, I could feel my head pounding. The plastic bag with the baseball bat banged against my knees. *Just get home, just get home*, I told myself, using the words as a mantra to focus my attention through the pulsing ache. Pulling up to my house, I felt the heat of relief spread through me, both because I'd arrived safely and because there were no reporters confronting me as I went inside. Even though I knew it wasn't good for her I let Abby have a piece of leftover pizza from the fridge, because I knew she'd love it, and love me for it, and I felt like being loved just then. Then I sat down at the kitchen table, drawing deep breaths and pressing my fingers into my temples.

The only time I'd ever had an actual conversation with Emmett Furth was fifteen years earlier, when he and Dawn were in first grade. I was working at the medical office part time back then, and once a week I went into the school as a parent volunteer. Though at the time I liked to believe that my motivation for visiting her classroom was a pure desire to contribute, to do my share, I understand now that I was also trying to figure out what made my daughter different from her sister and other kids, even at the age of six, aside from the lazy eye. What caused the other kids, including sometimes her own sister, to call her—in addition to all the other nicknames—Ding-Dong Dawn.

When I went in that day she was sitting by herself on the padded window seat, her knees drawn up to her chest as she looked out at the empty playground. I wanted to go over and ask why she wasn't working in her book, like everyone else, but the teacher intercepted me and said that Emmett Furth needed help with his reading comprehension, so I gave up trying to catch Dawn's attention and went over to pull out the little chair at the little table in the corner where Emmett was sitting.

Back then what set him apart from the other kids, besides his behavior, were his buzz cut and his granny glasses with violet-tinted lenses. I'd always assumed the glasses were Pam's mistake, but one day, probably wanting to assure me she'd had nothing to do with them, she told me that Emmett had refused even to consider any glasses other than the purple ones. By the time he got to middle school he'd switched to contacts, and he looked just like any regular troublemaker. I was secretly sorry to see those glasses go.

As silly as it sounds, the memory of those glasses was the main reason I'd never been able to take Rud Petty's attorney very seriously when he suggested it might have been Emmett who came into our house that night and attacked us in our bed.

In the classroom that day I tried to smile at him as I sat down, even though he had already made a reputation for himself—at such a young age—as a neighborhood pest. But he was in no mood for preliminaries, or maybe it was just that he felt embarrassed when he recognized me as one of the ladies whose yard he'd trampled on his bike. In any event, he ignored my smile and got right down to business. The instructions were for him to read passages aloud to me from the workbook, after which we would look at the comprehension questions together.

Craig and his father bought a bird feeder. They studied their backyard to find a good place for it. When the feeder was set up, Craig filled it with birdseed. Then he and his father began watching the feeder every morning.

"Bird feeders are stupid," Emmett said, after reading the story. "They can just eat nuts from the trees."

I wasn't sure if I was supposed to engage him in conversation, so instead I just pointed at the text and, as the directions instructed, asked him which sentence described what most likely happened next, based on the paragraph we had read. "A., Craig and his father will eat the birdseed."

"Ha!" Emmett liked this answer. "They're gonna eat the birdseed!"

"B., Craig and his father will watch the birds eating. C., Craig and his father will knock the bird feeder to the ground."

"They kick it, they punch it, they knock the stupid thing over!" He rose up in his chair and gave the air two fierce jabs with his fists, so hard that his glasses almost fell off.

Eventually I got him to settle down, and I pointed again to the choices on the page. "So, Emmett. Which is it?" He sat there for a long time, looking at the options. I tried not to fiddle with my pencil or shift in my seat. I could see that Dawn was still looking out the window, and I made a mental note to ask Joe that night whether we should bother scheduling another conference with her teacher. Finally, Emmett said, "I don't think it's any of those. A cat might come over and scare the birds away. That, or squirrels might jump up and eat all the seeds."

Those things could happen, I admitted. But I reminded him that they wanted him to pick an answer from the list.

"No." Emmett was firm in his refusal, and I remember thinking that as exasperating as he could be, part of me admired the way he stuck to his guns. "These are stupid questions, anyway." He pointed to the workbook, where the words *Inferences and Conclusions* danced in jazzy letters across the top. "How can you know something's gonna happen until it does?"

The bird feeder example in the workbook reminded me of my own garden, where I had spent so many of my best hours. When we moved into our house before I became pregnant with Iris, the backyard was overgrown and ugly because the previous owners had let it go. But within a few seasons I'd transformed it into the green and blooming sanctuary my mother had always dreamed of cultivating herself. She never got the chance, because when my father moved us to Manning Boulevard, he insisted on hiring a gardener. As much as my mother had always told him she wanted to work in the dirt herself, I don't think he actually believed her. She died before I met Joe, but I still liked to imagine that her spirit was in the air around me as I dead-headed my begonias or pruned my roses or fertilized my rhododendrons. Often, I paused on my knees just to turn my face up to the sun and breathe. Though I had been brought up going to church, working in my garden was the closest I ever came to what felt like God.

Especially when the girls were younger, we ate dinners outside in the summer. Joe had never grilled before we moved to the sub-urbs, but he took to it right away. He loved to cook up a bunch of kebobs, different kinds of meat and vegetables in colorful com-binations. Sometimes they were too fancy for Dawn and Iris, so he'd throw some hot dogs on the grill for them. One of my favorite memories is of the time Joe put one end of a hot dog straight into Abby's mouth, the other in his own, then raced her as they both ate toward the middle until their noses touched. Especially because it was so out of character for their strict and sanitary father, the girls both laughed so hard they almost fell together off the bench.

I'd always kept two bird feeders in the garden, one in a log-style and the other a netted onion bag filled with suet pudding. After Joe died, the police claimed the log feeder as evidence. I don't know why they thought the attacker might have left fingerprints on a bird feeder, but I guess they were covering all their bases. As it turned out, the only fingerprints they found on it were mine.

When I came home from the rehab hospital in March of the following year, I didn't have the heart or the energy to tend to anything but getting myself out of bed every morning. That fall when Rud Petty's trial started, I thought about trying to divide and transplant some of my perennials, but I just couldn't seem to take the first step out the back door. Slowly, over the next months and through the winter, the garden faded into an ordinary yard. Where once the view from my kitchen window had been one of my greatest pleasures, eventually I kept the blinds closed even during the daytime, so I didn't have to be reminded of how com-forting it had once been.

* * *

When Dawn called from Santa Fe the morning after my trip to the mall, I asked her, "Wait a minute, what day is it?" before she could even start talking.

"Saturday," she told me. "I know, I'm early. But I didn't want to wait until tomorrow."

Since she'd left for college, we'd always spoken on Sundays. When I was growing up on Humboldt Street, my father had drummed it into my head that Sunday was the time for long-distance calls, because the rates were cheapest then. Of course that didn't matter anymore, and all Dawn had was a cell phone, but I liked the comfort of our routine. Dawn seemed to, too. It was another thing we shared, while Iris called any time she felt like it.

Dawn said she'd just wanted to hear my voice. She added, "All of a sudden I'm afraid of wildfires," and I remembered, as I did every week, her tendency to jump from one subject to another without warning; you had to stay on your toes. "It's like something's creeping up on me from behind."

"It sounds awful," I said, though I hadn't seen anything about wildfires on the news and wasn't exactly sure what she was referring to. Then I blurted what had been at the front of my mind since I'd received the information the day before. "He won his appeal. He's getting a new trial. You know that, right?" I knew I did not have to identify who "he" was. Saying the name, I knew, would cause a cold clash of cymbals at the back of my neck.

"Well, yes." Dawn's voice flickered briefly.

The district attorney had intimated that Dawn had been in touch with Rud Petty, but of course I knew better. "How'd you find out?" I asked.

41

"Peter called."

I was glad she couldn't see how I winced at the name. Peter Cifforelli had been Joe's best friend from Buffalo; they'd gone to college together there, then both moved to Albany for graduate school, Joe in accounting and Peter in law. Peter and his wife, Wendy, became engaged within weeks of when Joe and I did, and the four of us all became friends. At least, that's what I thought, until the day Peter invited everybody to his apartment to watch the Super Bowl and I overheard Peter ask Joe in the kitchen, when neither of them knew I was approaching, "You're sure about Hanna, right? You're sure she's—*enough*?" For a moment I thought I'd missed a word—*smart* enough? *Good* enough? *Pretty* enough? But then I realized he'd just said *enough*, which could have covered all three of those things and more. Instead of waiting to hear how Joe would answer him, I made a point of walking into the kitchen to refill a bowl of chips. From that day on, I both despised Peter and worried that he was right. But I vowed to myself I'd never show those feelings, and I never told Joe that I'd heard what his best friend asked him that day.

Joe always referred to Peter and Wendy as "the Darlings," but I couldn't bring myself to do the same. Still, our families remained close all the time our children were growing up, celebrating birthdays and holidays and graduations together, and one year we shared a vacation rental in the Outer Banks during the kids' spring break from school. (One of the things I had been shocked to learn, during Rud's trial, was that Dawn apparently told her dorm mates at college that among the property she would inherit someday was a beachfront estate on the coast of North Carolina. It shocked me not only because of the lie itself, but because that vacation had been a disaster, and I couldn't imagine she

42

had any good memories of it; it rained almost every day, and the Cifforelli kids and Iris ganged up on Dawn in every game they played.)

Peter was the first person Iris called after the police notified her, by phone, of the attack. He and Wendy arrived at the hospital—where I was in surgery and expected to die—before Iris and Archie could drive there from Boston. Later, Peter said he would serve as Dawn's attorney, if she got indicted and her case went to trial. When he offered to do this, I didn't know whether he believed she was guilty of helping to kill her father but also entitled to the best defense she could get, or whether he thought she was innocent. I was afraid of what it would mean about me if I even asked the question. In the end it didn't matter, because she was never tried.

You'd think the fact that he was willing to fight for Dawn in a courtroom would have erased my bitterness toward Peter, but it hadn't.

"They're not letting him out, are they?" Dawn asked me. They were almost the exact words I had used when Ken Thornburgh informed me about Rud Petty's appeal.

"No," I said. "I mean, they say not. Gail Nazarian came over last night to try to get me to testify."

"But you said no, right?" She spoke so emphatically into the phone that I had to hold the receiver away.

"Right." I reached down to work Abby's hair with my fingers under the table, where she always sat when I talked on the phone. When she gave a little groan I knew I'd pulled too hard, and I apologized by rubbing the scar on the soft spot between her eyes. "But I changed my mind. I'm going to try."

It was one of those times you say something you hadn't

planned on, but the minute you hear it in your own voice, you know it's true. I realized then that my mind had been working on the decision, even without my being aware. I believed Rud Petty was guilty, and I couldn't take a chance on his being acquitted this time. Short of someone else showing up to say they'd been in our bedroom that night three years earlier and witnessed what happened to us—and short of Dawn remembering something new that might be of use to the prosecution—I knew it was up to me, despite the warning that kept flashing somewhere below my heart.

Besides that, I had my daughter to protect, since the prosecutor had threatened to try again to indict her if she couldn't get either of us to take the stand. But I decided not to mention that to Dawn now.

She took in a stuttered breath, and I was reminded of the old days when she used to have asthma. "I don't think you should do that to yourself," she said in a hollow voice. "After everything you've been through—it could traumatize you all over again."

"It would be worth it, if that's the only way to keep him in jail." *And if I can prove your innocence once and for all.*

I tried to sound braver than I actually felt. We'd had a woman in my rehab group for a few weeks who was standing at the bus stop one day when the memory of her rape as a teenager flooded over her in a rush. She was so undone that the police had her admitted to a psych ward, and she never came back to the group.

Dawn sighed. "Don't let them bully you, Mommy," and although I should have known better, I felt a rise of happiness, because it had been so long since I'd heard that word. Of our two daughters, Dawn was the only one who ever called me Mommy. She continued long after most of her friends had abandoned it; she seemed to understand that it made me feel good, and it created an intimacy between us that I regret to say I never felt with Iris.

"I'm not," I told her. "Gail Nazarian is just doing her job. She doesn't want him set free."

Dawn made a noise, but I couldn't tell what she meant by it. Then she said she had to get ready to go to work. When she first moved out west, she was always vague when I asked her what kind of job she had, using words like *temp* and *provisional* and *in training*. I thought it must come from embarrassment, so I'd stopped asking. She'd dropped out of college after the attack and never returned, as far as I knew, so I didn't see how she could be making all that much money, whatever she was doing. "I'll call you back," she told me, and I said okay, even though I didn't know what more we had to talk about.

I assumed she just said it for a way to end the conversation— that she didn't mean it. But inside of an hour, I saw her number pop up again on caller ID.

"I thought you had to go to work," I said.

"I called in sick. Mommy, I've been thinking. I want to come home for a while. If you're really going to do this—try to remember what happened—I don't want you to be alone."

"I'm not alone. I have my group," I told her, not yet allowing my mind to register her sentence about coming home. I would have added "and Iris," but I stopped myself because I knew it would hurt Dawn to hear her sister's name.

"But they're not your family." Dawn took a breath. "Besides, you'd be doing me a favor. I've maxed out my credit cards." On the pad I kept next to the phone, I wrote *max*. Later I would wonder who Max was. I'd been more forgetful than usual lately. I wasn't even fifty yet, but I had some residual damage from the

45

attack. Not as much as some people who'd been through similar things—God knows I heard their stories over and over again in my group—but I could tell I wasn't quite the same as I used to be. I'd pick up the phone and forget who I was calling. I had trouble finding the right words. And names of people—often, I had to go through the alphabet to help me remember.

Probably taking my silence for hesitation, Dawn added, "They're really cracking down on credit these days," as if I might not be aware how far the economy had fallen during the past few years.

It took me longer than it should have to realize that she was serious about coming home, and I was afraid to feel too hopeful. *Now is when I should tell her what Gail Nazarian said about indicting her*, I thought. But I didn't; I was afraid Dawn would back away from her offer, and I couldn't take that chance.

The idea of her returning made me happier than I'd been in a long time. Already I was imagining that we could re-create the comfort of those days before she went off to college, her final year of high school, when Joe was working so hard on the Marc Sedgwick case that he hardly ever made it home for dinner. Back then, it was just Dawn and me in the house or the garden much of the time, both feeling safe—secure, not afraid of saying the wrong thing or making a mistake—in the connection between us. Neither of us ever said anything about the fact that at the end of the summer she'd be leaving. It was as if we both understood that to mention it would cause it to come sooner, and make the separation worse than we already knew it would be.

I missed those days, the last good ones. And now the prospect that we might have them back again gave me such a rush that I had to put a hand on my heart to settle it. I found my voice and told her, "Of course you can come home, honey. You never have to ask."

She fell all over herself thanking me, and said she'd never forget it. Her gratitude made me feel good, as if I were finally giving her something she really wanted. We'd always had enough money—more than enough, by a lot of people's standards—but Joe was reluctant, because of the way he had grown up, to spend it on things he didn't consider necessities. So we didn't give the girls the trips to Disney World they asked for, or the fancy jeans. Living in Everton, they felt deprived, and I didn't blame them. Joe and I had words about it, but what could I do? I know I should hesitate to admit it, but the way my mother raised me was that you let your husband take care of the finances. Even though both our paychecks went into the joint account, I just didn't think to fight him too hard on it.

"I can be in charge of suppers," Dawn continued through the phone, and I held back the first thing that popped into my head: *Kentucky Fried Chicken or Hunan Wok?* Then I reprimanded myself, *Maybe she's learned to cook. Don't be so critical.* It was what Iris used to say to Joe all the time she was growing up: "Don't be so critical." I could tell this bewildered him, and hurt him a little, too. When he replied, "I'm not being critical; I'm teaching you to have standards," I knew he wished he'd had a father who'd done the same for him.

He'd never been as tough on Dawn as he was on Iris; he was satisfied to let our older daughter be his protégé and leave the younger one, who had less on the ball, to me. I know that's an awful way to say it, but it's true.

Dawn said, "I can be there by Halloween."

I glanced at the calendar on the wall, a giveaway from the local

47

fire department. In the old days, I used to buy myself a calendar from the Horticultural Society every year, and I kept all our appointments and plans on it, but at this point there wasn't much to write down. I figured the freebie was good enough.

Halloween was a week and a half away. "You can be here so soon?" I asked.

I could almost hear her shrugging over the phone. "I don't have much to take care of before I leave here."

"Do you think your car will make it this far?" I was thinking of all the problems she'd had with the old Nova over the years.

She paused for a moment. "I think so. I got a new one."

"And you can fit everything in it?"

She answered, but I wasn't really listening, because I'd flipped up the calendar page. In a month it would be the third anniversary of Joe's death. Would Dawn and I observe it in any way? Or would we let the date pass without mentioning it, afraid that if we started talking, we might not stop in time?

I told myself I didn't need to worry about that now. I thought of what Barbara, our counselor, often told those of us in the rehab group: "When you can afford to put off something you know is going to be painful, go ahead and wait until you think it might be easier for you to handle. You've all earned that right." To Dawn I said, "It'll be good to have you home, honey," and hoped nothing would happen in the meantime to change her mind.

After I got off the phone, I realized it had probably been silly of me to ask Dawn if her car could contain everything she planned to bring with her. How much could she own? I thought back to when Joe and I were first married, and the little apartment we rented on South Pearl Street, not far from the state Capitol. The only things I brought to our first home together were my clothes, the battered set of pots and pans my mother had cooked with all her married life and refused to replace when we moved to Manning Boulevard, and the notebooks I'd kept in college. Joe didn't have much in the way of possessions, either. For the first few months, we ate our meals at a card table, sitting on folding chairs, and watched TV on a couch we'd salvaged from the curb. Or, on warm nights, we sat on the stoop outside our building, drinking Cokes as we watched state workers stream out of the legislative buildings and made up nicknames for them (Botched Haircut, Sad Lady, Bow-Tie Bob).

I wish I could say, as people do sometimes, that those were the best days of our early marriage—that we hadn't needed material things to make us happy, and that love alone was enough. The truth is that even though we did love each other, it only got better and easier when Joe started to make more money, and we had the freedom to buy and do the things that made our everyday lives more comfortable. Like being able to keep the heat on high enough to stay warm—which was a big deal, because the apartment was drafty—and go out to dinner and the movies, and even, occasionally, to the symphony.

I had never been a fan of classical music and I knew nothing about it, but Joe had started listening to records when his family's TV broke, just after his twelfth birthday, and his father said it would cost too much to replace it. At first Joe was furious (he was old enough by then to understand that his father would always choose beer over the family TV) but later he would say it was one of the best things that ever happened to him. His mother began bringing albums of Beethoven and Brahms and Mozart home from the library, and Joe took them to his room at night, after dinner and homework, and lay on his bed and listened. It was an old turntable, and the needle was in bad shape. So one of the first things we saved for together, after he got the job at Stinson and Keyes, was a Sony hi-fi stereo system, which we set up in the bedroom so Joe could listen to music while I watched TV in the living room. If I had to go into the bedroom for something while he was lying with his eyes closed, I tried to do it quietly so that I had a moment or two, before he realized I was there, to watch him take in the music with an expression on his face that suggested he would have to turn it off soon because it was too much, too beautiful to bear.

After returning from rehab, it took me a month or so to work up my courage to put any records on the stereo system, which Joe had maintained all those years by bringing it in for service at a specialized electronics store in Albany (even as we matched the girls' savings to help them buy CD players for their bedrooms). At first, I started playing albums that hadn't held any particular meaning for us—ones we had rarely if ever listened to together, and nothing remotely classical. In rehab, I had managed to keep myself from breaking down in grief, because I didn't want anyone else to witness it, and when I got home—precisely *because* no one else was there, and my emotions scared me—I continued to resist feeling everything I knew lay beneath the visible scars.

But one day in late spring, returning from a walk with Abby, I surprised myself by deciding to put on Bach's Mass in B Minor while I made my tea. Almost as soon as the first chords sounded, Abby's ears pricked and she raised her face in excitement. It was this—the dog's recognition of Joe's favorite music, rather than any particular memory of my husband himself—that caused me to burst into tears as the kettle blew.

But it was a good pain I felt that day. If it hadn't been, I would have taken the needle off the record too quickly, risking a scratch, and put the album away in a place that would be easy to forget. As it was, I sat on the love seat next to Abby, closed my eyes, and let the music choke me while through the window I felt the sun, weak but steady, struggling to break through the clouds. I felt myself transported, with a rich and wistful sweetness, back to the years during which this house had held us all safe.

Remembering this, I looked at Abby a few minutes after Dawn and I had hung up and said, "Come on, girl." I knew that if I enlisted her in what I had to do next, she wouldn't let me back out. She followed on my heels as I climbed the stairs toward the master bedroom, which I had shared with Joe for more than twenty years. I hadn't stepped across the threshold since the attack almost three years earlier. In many ways, I knew, it was kind of nutty to have a room in my house I never entered or even allowed myself to look into. It felt like a device in a soap opera or a bad haunted house movie: *And now we return to* Don't Go into the Bedroom.

But I'd gotten accustomed to it, and I didn't actually think of it as space that wasn't being used; to me, it was more as if the house just ended at that door. I rarely if ever tried to imagine what lay beyond it, in the form of the redecorating Iris had supervised while I was away in rehab. I paid a housecleaning service to come once every two weeks (an indulgence I never would have considered while Joe was alive), so they went in there, but I'd asked them to make sure the door was closed each time they left.

As hard as I'd always thought it would be, it turned out to be that easy. I just opened the door and walked in. I'd anticipated that my first feeling would be fear, but instead, as I stepped into the room I'd slept in for so many years, it was a sense of euphoria that came over me, in waves so strong I had to put my hand up to my mouth. A conquering. A triumph. I thought of something one of the physical therapists at the rehab center used to say all the time, when I told him I couldn't do what he asked of me: "You *got* this."

To think of it that way, of course, was sad and silly: all I'd done was walk into a room. Somewhere inside myself, I knew that. But for those first few moments, celebration swam through my bones.

Iris had told me she changed the room entirely, and she was right except for one thing—the placement of the bed. There wasn't much she could do about that, given the location of the windows; the headboard had to lie between them against the far wall, the foot catty-corner to the bathroom door.

But the furniture and colors were so different that it didn't feel like the same space at all. Iris had thought she was doing me a favor, but as I stood there trying to recognize anything familiar, I felt an overpowering desire to have my old room back. *Our* old room—mine and Joe's. It had been simple when he was alive, and things didn't necessarily match—the bureaus, the bed, the bookcase—but that didn't bother us. We hung photographs of the girls on the walls, and the shelves held souvenirs from places we'd visited as a family: Plimoth Plantation, Sturbridge Village, Fort Ticonderoga. Joe loved historical re-creations, and though Iris became bored on these trips once she outgrew the novelty of wearing a rented Colonial dress and bonnet, Dawn, who was always eager to please her father, lingered with him as long as he wanted in the blacksmith's shop or the apothecary or the textile mill. Once, she got called up from a crowd of children to try her hand at running the loom in prerevolutionary Williamsburg. I still have the photograph Joe took of her that day, flushed with excitement at having been chosen, sticking her tongue through her teeth and squinting in concentration as the weaver guided her hand. She focused on her task so hard that you can't tell, from the picture, that something was wrong with her eyes.

On the bedroom floor had lain a faux Oriental rug from Joe's parents' bedroom, which we took from the house in Tonawanda after they died. It was worn through in spots, but we never thought of replacing it.

The room had been nothing fancy. But it reflected who we were, and what we loved together.

Iris had bought a plush comforter and bedding set I never would have chosen for myself, in green and violet complementing the soft rose paint of the walls. Thick carpet covered the entire floor. Bright floral prints faced out from ornate frames. She'd installed a chaise longue next to the closet, across from a flat-screen TV.

The last thing Joe would have wanted in his bedroom was a television. And a chaise longue wasn't my style. Iris had decorated the room more in line with her taste, not mine. But she knew this. I understood that after all that had happened there, she thought a complete makeover was for the best. She also thought she was preparing the house to be sold, so it made sense that she hadn't tried to create a space I'd spend any time in.

I walked to the window and looked out, went into the bathroom, opened the medicine cabinet to its empty and pristine shelves. It was clear nobody lived here. But my husband had been mortally wounded a few feet away from where I was standing, and I waited for it to rush over me—a flood of memory, a flashback that knocked me off my feet. I'd counted on it. It had never occurred to me that going into the bedroom might not bring back, in more detail than I could handle, the events of that night.

53

I'd expected to feel panic because I thought I would remember. Now I felt panic because I did not.

But: "Be careful what you wish for," my mother used to remind me, along with "Pride goeth before a fall." I should have known that the ease I felt was too good to be true. I was only a few feet from the door—I remember thinking the words "home free"—when a shadow passed above my head and I ducked, crying out, before realizing there was nothing there.

What was it, then? A vision so vivid I thought it was happening at that moment, instead of three years before. Was it a hand, a wrist, an arm? I couldn't tell, but whatever it was contained a mark. Black figures pressed into white flesh, dark ink on pale skin. The picture evaporated as soon as I tried to read it. Words? Numbers? Both?

It was gone. Holding my breath, I ran the last few steps to the door, yanked it open, then slammed it shut behind me. I sat on the top stair and shivered, despite the warmth of Abby's breath as she laid her chin on my knee.

The experience was almost enough to make me abandon my resolution to serve as a witness in the new trial. But I didn't want to give in to the fear I'd experienced in the bedroom. I didn't want to be that weak. The only conclusion I could draw was that I'd seen a tattoo, and Rud Petty didn't have one. So either I'd made a mistake—hallucinated somehow, conflated a more recent and random image with what I'd actually observed that night—or I was remembering something that could be important to the case.

Joe and I knew Rud Petty had lied about the burglary in our house the day after Thanksgiving. That, on top of the overwhelming circumstantial evidence, was why I and most everyone else, including the police, suspected him in the attack.

But what if he had only committed the burglary, driven Dawn home, then gone to his own apartment for the rest of the night, as he'd always claimed? I could barely bring myself to consider that this might be true, because I'd spent three years thinking it was all behind me. Three years hating him and what he'd done to my family. But I couldn't help what came back to me. Somebody else—memory experts, the jury—could decide if it was real.

Not wanting to lose my nerve, I found Gail Nazarian's card and dialed her office. Since it was a Saturday, I'd expected to get voice mail, but she picked up in person. Recovering from this surprise, I stammered that I just wanted her to know I was on board; I would do everything I could to be able to testify. "My daughter Iris knows someone who could hypnotize me," I told her, thinking it might be a way to find out the truth about that night. I wasn't ready yet to let on that I might be starting to doubt Rud Petty's guilt; my experience in the bedroom was too fresh, too unsettling to trust.

I thought the prosecutor would be impressed by my resourcefulness, but instead she shouted, "No!" into the phone before making an obvious effort to dial down the volume of her voice. "No hypnosis. It can get very dicey in court, and they may or may not allow it. We can't take that chance. Promise, Hanna?"

She had never called me by my first name before, so I knew she was pulling it out now to show how serious she was. I said yes and told her I had to go, though there was really nothing else waiting for me except the question of how to make myself remember—in enough detail that it would hold up in court, and clear my daughter's name for good—the worst night of my life.

Psychological Impact

I didn't tell anyone at work that Dawn was returning, even though I had friends there who would have been interested—who would have cared. As it was, Francine startled me when I arrived on Monday and she said, "Hanna, you okay? I heard," and at first I thought she meant she'd heard about Dawn's phone call, but then I realized she was talking about Rud Petty's appeal.

When I was in the rehab hospital, I never thought about going back to work when I recovered. But after I'd been home for two weeks, and realized how shaky I felt with all that unstructured time, I called Bob Toussaint, who'd been my boss for almost fifteen years. He understood that I didn't need the salary as much as I needed the work itself again. Joe had seen to it, with his usual conscientiousness, that I'd be taken care of if something happened to him, even with the economy as uncertain as it was; I would still be okay, according to Joe's friend and colleague Tom Whitty, who'd taken over the accounts.

What I craved was the contact with patients and the camaraderie our office had always shared. I didn't want to put Bob in the awkward position of having to turn me down about actual nursing, because there was no question that the skills I'd once prided myself on had been diminished by my injuries in the attack. It wasn't hard to convince him, though, that I could make myself useful, especially with the walk-in patients at our clinic—instructing people how to fill out forms, helping elderly patients in and out of their paper gowns, preparing children for their shots. It made me feel good to soothe patients who were worried about a medical visit, and it made the doctors' jobs easier. Once he saw that I had made a niche for myself, Bob was more than happy to keep me on. Though my job title was appointment liaison, everyone in the office referred to me as the concierge.

It wasn't that I didn't trust Francine or the other people I worked with. But I knew what their reaction would be if I told them Dawn was coming back to live with me, and I wasn't sure how I'd deal with it. Start crying? Get defensive and snap at them? I didn't feel up to any of those things.

I thought about skipping my rehab group the next day, because I knew I couldn't get away with not talking about it there. But if I missed the session, there'd be a follow-up call from Barbara, the group leader, and I'd have to explain. I didn't feel like explaining, so in the end I drove as usual to Pine Manor, where the joke was that there weren't any pine trees around and not a whole lot of manners, either.

We called the group Tough Birds. Officially TBI stood for traumatic brain injury, but one of the other group members, my English friend Trudie, had dubbed us Tough Birds Inc. early on, and we all preferred that. If you had told me three years earlier that I'd want to spend a couple of hours every two weeks in a hospital basement with people who had traumatic brain injuries—

who complained about hearing themselves say things like "Button the shoelace" and "What time does it cost?", how they couldn't calculate the tip in restaurants, and how little things made them fly off the handle—I would have said you were nuts. Of course, I wasn't one of them then.

When it was my turn to check in at the beginning of group and I told everyone that Dawn was coming home to live for a while, I could feel the tension spread among our little circle of dented folding chairs. Nelson, our only male member, twirled his gray ponytail around his finger and said, "Just be careful out there." It was his stock line, which he'd picked up from some TV show, and it usually meant he was finished listening to one person and ready to move on to the next.

"How did you come to that decision, Hanna?" Barbara asked, leaning forward the way she always did to show she thought something one of us said was important. She was an intense, big-boned woman with frizzy hair that looked windblown even when she was indoors, and huge glasses that came into and went out of style in the eighties. We had all learned that every time she pushed the glasses up on her nose, she believed she was on the trail of something psychologically significant. She pushed them up on her nose now, when she asked me this question.

One of the things we were working on, as a group, was iden-tifying our own thought processes when it came to decisions. We were supposed to slow ourselves down—because a lot of us tended to act impulsively—and force ourselves to make active choices, instead of just going with the first thing that came into our heads.

I told Barbara I hadn't had to make a decision, because Dawn was my daughter and I loved her. (I would have said it was a "no-brainer," but we had banned that phrase from the group.) "We were always close," I said. "You know I've been lonely. Why wouldn't I want her home with me?"

When no one answered—I knew what they were thinking—I got up to go to the refreshment table. Trudie and I were the only ones who ever contributed anything; I always made a batch of my mother's oatmeal crinkles, and Trudie always picked up a can of Hawaiian Punch, which made everyone laugh the first time because they'd expected something more decorous from the British lady.

At the table, I turned my back to the group and picked up a cup with trembling fingers. Trudie came over and led me by the elbow into the hall. "Are you sure about this, Hanna?" she said, in her accented murmur.

Trudie was much younger than my mother would have been if she were still alive, but she reminded me of her, nevertheless with silver-white hair that always grew too long before she got it cut, and the sweaters she wore even when it was hot out. For as long as I could remember, my mother had suffered a perpetual chill, and when I learned that Trudie did, too, I felt an immediate connection to her. Though of course I knew better, I sometimes chose to believe, when I needed to, that in my friendship with Trudie it was my mother showing up, all these years after her death, to bring me a little peace.

Before I could answer Trudie's question, Barbara stuck her head into the hall and asked us to rejoin the group. I started back in, but not before Trudie caught my arm at the door and whispered, "Just because you give birth to someone doesn't mean you owe her for the rest of your life. For God's sake, Hanna—if anything, she owes *you*."

But Trudie didn't have any children; her husband had died young, and she had never remarried. What could she tell me about being a mother?

———

As much as I would have liked to use the phone to tell Iris that her sister was coming back, I knew I had to do it in person. I called in to work the next morning and told Francine I needed the day off, then put Abby in the hatchback and drove out to the little town where Iris and Archie lived, though at the end of the summer he'd moved out, renting an apartment a few blocks from the house they'd bought near the hospital where he worked as a physician in the endoscopy department. Iris had just started medical school at BU when she became pregnant, but then took a leave of absence after Joe and I were attacked, convincing Archie to accept a job offer in western Massachusetts so they'd be closer to me. We'd all expected her to return to her studies by now, but I'd learned the hard way not to bring it up, because when I did, it made her angry. "What am I supposed to do, commute back and forth to Boston with a kid?" she'd snapped the last time I asked.

I worried that she was depressed, still suffering the emotional effects from what had happened to Joe and me. She'd never lost the weight from being pregnant, and had gained even more in the years since. I wouldn't have been surprised to learn she was over two hundred pounds now, and it worried me. If she'd come into the medical office for a checkup, we would have considered her obese.

I knew Archie was worried about her, too. Not just because she'd gotten so heavy, but because she seemed to be trapped inside herself. She couldn't get out of her own way. From the time she was old enough to walk, I had never seen my older daughter look as if she didn't know which direction the next step should take her. But now she had been this way for the past three years. She lost track of important papers, forgot appointments, spent too much time in bed—the opposite of all the things she had learned from and observed in her father, and chosen as the way to conduct her own life. Archie moved out because he was desperate to jog her out of this altered state; he believed that a separation would be the "bottom" she needed to hit before she came to her senses and rescued herself. But he'd been living in the apartment for a couple of months now, and it hadn't happened yet.

I loved my son-in-law, and I knew Iris appreciated the fact that he was so like Joe in his attention to discipline and detail. Every time Archie played a game of Scrabble, he snapped a photograph of the finished board, and kept the photos arranged chronologically in a notebook. His books, CDs, and DVDs were all alphabetized. Those slightly obsessive personality traits Joe and Archie shared, which could be endearing, had a flip side in the form of the high standards they set for other people as well as for themselves. Iris had always thrived on trying to meet and exceed those standards. But after her father died, she seemed to lose her motivation. Even though I understood why Archie thought she needed to be jolted back to reality, I hoped he wouldn't give up on her too soon.

The colors had peaked earlier in the month, but the trees on the turnpike still held most of their leaves, and the day was glorious: warmer than it should have been for the season, the sun misting off the mountains and looking like white breath from the sky. Such sights reminded me why it was that people loved to be alive, and for fleeting moments that made me want to cry, I was grateful I could still feel like one of them.

Crunching leaves under my wheels as I pulled into the driveway at ten thirty, I half-hoped I might find Iris sitting outside on the stoop with Josie. It made me smile to imagine my granddaughter running to the car to greet me.

We had a routine for when we came together at the beginning of a visit. She would raise her arms, I'd pick her up so that her legs straddled my waist, and she'd place a hand on each of my shoulders to steady herself. Then she'd lean in, close her eyes, and reach out to begin touching the damaged side of my face, starting with the forehead—where the skin met in a seam, having been sewn back together—and working her way down to the edge of my eye socket, the uneven cheek and mouth, and ending with the chin, the one part left intact by the surgeries. It was as if she were a blind person trying to "see" my features with her fingers. I don't know why she did it that way, with her eyes closed, but I didn't want her to think I minded, so I never asked. When she had finished going down the side of my face, she always opened her eyes and said with satisfaction, "It's Grandma," as if there might have been some question—as if it had been her job to identify me.

I looked forward to the ritual. But today they were not outside to greet me on the stoop. And when I walked Abby up to the front door and rang the bell, nobody answered. I tried a few more times, and then, since I could see Iris's car parked in the garage, I leaned on the buzzer for a good fifteen seconds before finally hearing movement inside the house. She appeared with a wailing Josie wrapped around her leg, and through the bubbled glass of the foyer window, before she realized I could see her, I caught a look of annoyed dismay on my daughter's face.

"Oh, Mom, sorry—I thought we said more like noon," she said. "The house is a mess. But come in."

I'd told her I'd be driving out after breakfast, and she had said that was fine. But I bit back the temptation to remind her of it. In the old days, before Joe died, she would have said the house was a mess and it wouldn't have been true. Iris had either inherited or over the years come to imitate her father's preoccupation with orderliness; I could never have counted how many times, during dinner, one of them would get up from the table to straighten a frame on the wall by moving it so slightly that Dawn and I couldn't tell the difference.

But after her father's death, the Iris I'd always known just fell to pieces. It would not be an exaggeration to say she had become a slob. I stepped into the foyer over a pile of laundry that had apparently been tossed down from the top of the stairs.

She came toward me and I waited for a hug, but instead she reached to brush the hair back from where I always let it fall to conceal as much of my face as I could. "I wish you wouldn't do that, Mom. It just draws attention to it. Anyway, you have nothing to be ashamed of—nothing to hide."

"Easy for you to say." Even through my irritation over her saying I'd come too early, I marveled for perhaps the thousandth time at how beautiful this child of mine was, with her thick brown hair that managed to hold both wave and gloss even when she hadn't washed it in a few days; the shape and tone of her face, which was an appealing median between circle and oval, with Joe's dark intelligent eyes and a complexion that had always been smooth no matter what she ate; and perhaps most prominent, a proud set to her shoulders it was impossible not to notice. The pounds she'd put on had not traveled to her face, and even the extra flesh she carried around her hips, stomach, and legs she managed to pull off with confidence, almost as if she had decided to become overweight on purpose. On her, it almost looked fashionable. Though I know how crude it sounds, what I thought sometimes when I looked at her was *How did* she *come out of* me?

I'd recognized early on that Iris belonged to one set of the female population, Dawn and I to the other. In addition to her striking looks, my older daughter was athletic and graceful; from the time she could barely walk, we noted her quick reflexes and eye-hand coordination in almost everything she did. When Dawn was almost three, she still couldn't catch the biggest Nerf ball lobbed directly into her arms from six inches away.

Until her amblyopia was diagnosed and we understood that it was at least in part a problem of depth perception, I thought Dawn just took after me in her lack of physical grace. "She's a klutz like me, isn't she," I whispered to Joe once, and he shushed me, worried the girls might overhear. Too late he added, "Hanna, you're not a klutz." Even though most of the kids at school understood that Dawn's problem was at least partly physical, it didn't keep them from hooting every time she dropped her tray in the cafeteria.

When they were little, I encouraged my girls to play together. It was foolish of me, but I thought that maybe some of Iris's physical talent would rub off on Dawn. Either that or Dawn would learn more about how to move, from watching her sister. I taught them games I remembered watching other kids play through the window on Humboldt Street. My mother wouldn't allow me to join them, saying she was afraid I'd get hurt, but even then I sensed that she was also saving me from the humiliation of losing constantly. I protested, knowing we both

64

understood I was doing it because it allowed me to pretend I didn't see through her.

Ring toss, beanbag toss, hopscotch, jump rope—Iris and Dawn loved it all. When I showed them the three-legged race, wrapping their inside legs together with an ace bandage, they hopped around the house or the garden shouting, "Look at us, we're the same person!" There was no sound I treasured more then, or even now in my memory, than the sound of them giggling together as they tried to move in unison, then fell to the floor or the grass in a half hug, half wrestle before finally rolling apart to their separate selves. Eventually, Iris tired of it and preferred spending time with her friends, and I remember how sad I felt the day Dawn appeared in the kitchen dragging the ace bandage behind her, asking her sister to play We're the Same Person, and Iris said it was too babyish for her.

Iris played on almost every girls' sports team at least once during her four years in high school. The corkboard in her bedroom still contained all her varsity letters. She kept up her exercise in college and after her marriage, until Joe and I got attacked in our bed. It hurt me in an almost physical way now, to see how she'd let her body go.

It was a little early to tell yet, but it seemed that my granddaughter was going to take after her mother more than she would Dawn and me; she could sink the ball into the child's-level basketball hoop in her bedroom just about every time. But now she was still clinging to Iris's leg, and Iris said to her, "Can you stop crying, sweetie? Look who's here."

Josie took a step backward and shook her head. "It's the dog," Iris explained to me. "She just decided she's afraid of them."

She had always called Abby "the dog," the same way Joe had.

They were not animal people like Dawn and me. Sometimes they tried to humor us, but more often we could tell they just thought we were silly, spending so much affection on a creature they believed it wasn't possible to have a conversation with (despite the fact that Dawn and I—and even Abby herself—tried to prove to them otherwise).

With Josie retreating, poor Abby cocked her head at me with a question on her face, as if she knew we were talking about her. "Do you think you could put her back in the car for a while?" Iris asked. "Until Josie calms down?"

"I'm not putting her in the car." I tried not to show how the suggestion rankled me. "She was just cooped up in there for more than an hour. Josie, honey, come here and say hi." I picked up Abby's paw to wave it at my granddaughter.

But Josie pulled back even further and started to shriek. I bit my lip and said nothing, directing Abby to a corner of the living room, while Iris soothed Josie and set her up in front of the TV, which was already on, with a snack dish of salt-free, fish-shaped whole wheat crackers. (I knew these were for my benefit. I knew that the cupboard contained packages of Oreos and Chips Ahoy, which Iris broke into when she thought Josie wasn't looking—Josie had shown me her mother's stash once when I babysat—but I'd never confronted Iris about it.)

Iris looked at me. "I don't always have the TV on, you know."

"I didn't say anything!"

"I know what you were thinking."

There was nothing I could say to dissuade her, mainly because she was right. Using the TV as a babysitter, especially this early in the morning, was not something I would have expected of her. But then, we'd all changed from the people we used to be.

Iris sat down across from me, and I saw that her face had softened. "I'm actually glad you came a little early, Mom. I've been wanting to talk to you," she mumbled, and her words filled me with dread.

I wanted to say, *Can't we just have some time first? Can't I just sit here for a minute and catch my breath? Can't we talk about something meaningless, like the weather* (in the past few years, I'd come to appreciate the relief in chatting about meaningless things) *before I have to hear something that's going to change my life?*

Because I could tell it was going to, from Iris's tone.

"I have something to tell you, too," I said, hoping that if I stalled long enough, she would forget what she wanted to say.

Her eyes narrowed. "What?"

But I faltered suddenly. "You first." Maybe I'm wrong, I tried to tell myself, as I braced for whatever she was going to drop on me. Maybe it was good news, not bad. "You're not pregnant again, are you?" I asked, actually daring to think for a moment that I might be right.

"God, no!" She was so startled that she dropped a handful of crackers on the floor, where Abby sniffed at them before turning up her nose. "You think I'd make that mistake again?"

"Mistake?" I looked over at my granddaughter, who appeared mesmerized by a cartoon.

Iris said, "I mean the mistake of not telling you right away. I would never take the chance of you having an accident on your way here. If I were pregnant, I'd tell you on the phone as soon as I knew." Her tone was accusatory even though it had been her own decision, the first time around, to save the news of her pregnancy as a Christmas present for us. As things turned out, with Joe dying

67

over Thanksgiving, he never found out that he was going to have a grandchild.

She was about to tell me something I did not want to hear. I felt this with as much certainty as I'd ever felt anything; I could tell with a thorn in my chest that the bomb was about to fall and there was nothing I could do to stop it. She said, "Archie and I are talking about things. We want to make this—*us*—work."

When she paused, hesitating about how to proceed, I told her through the thudding in my heart that I was happy to hear it. She gave a tense smile and said, "The only thing is, he's going to be interviewing at UCSF when we go out there next month. They told him that with his training, he has a good shot at one of their clinic jobs."

It took me a moment to understand that "SF" meant San Francisco. "You're going to his parents' for Thanksgiving?" I said, though this was not the question I intended to ask.

"Oh, Mom." Another sigh. "You know we are. It's the only time we see them all year. Archie was going to just take Josie by himself, but now that we're talking the way we are—well, it made sense for us all to go out together."

"I know, but"—the real question made me sway, inside, for a moment—"when will I ever see Josie if you live out there?"

Iris leaned forward in an attitude of aggressive enthusiasm, the force of it causing me to sit back in my own seat. "That's just it. If we did this, we'd want you to come with us. Move somewhere else, start over. Watch Josie grow up." She scrutinized my face carefully for a reaction.

I felt totally blindsided, to the extent that my vision actually blurred for a few seconds. "I'm not really a California person," I stammered. It was the first thing that occurred to me, although even as I said it I knew how weak an excuse it was. What I sensed inside me was panic, starting in my center and working its way up to my throat.

I could not imagine leaving. None of my friends or family seemed to understand how I could bear to continue living in that house, which was how they always referred to it—as "that house." When it was time to make plans for me to leave rehab and I told the members of Tough Birds that I was going back home, I heard some of them suck in their breath with shock. Trudie said, "You can't possibly be serious, Hanna. That's just out-and-out masochism."

Iris felt the same way. She didn't use the word *masochism*, but she'd told me before that I must be living in an extreme state of denial. "Like your delusion that Dawn had nothing to do with it," she said, and I reminded her to please not say things like that to me again.

But not only could I bear it, I *wanted* to live there. If it bothered me to remain in the house where Joe had been murdered, it was far enough down inside me that I didn't notice it. Couldn't any of us be killed, anywhere at any time, by a fiend like Rud Petty? Did the fact that Joe died there mean I had to give up all the good memories I had of our life together on Wildwood Lane?

It was true that sometimes when I was going up or down the stairs, I thought of the trial testimony—Kenneth Thornburgh talking about how Joe was found on the landing, where he had dragged himself up again, bleeding "profusely" from his head, after somehow making it down to the kitchen with a crushed skull and attempting to unload the dishwasher. Though I think this detail seemed odd to other people, it made perfect sense to me, knowing Joe, that even through the shock of such severe injury, his instinct was to put things in order and follow his routine. The police speculated that he probably tried but failed to take his tee-shirt off in the bedroom, intending to put on clean clothes when he got up. He had only enough strength to lift the shirt halfway. When they found him, his belly was exposed. Joe would have hated that. He was always a modest man, so that kind of information made me cringe on his behalf.

But hearing about it at the trial was kind of like listening to other people tell you their dreams. You follow the plot, but it isn't as if you've had, yourself, the experience they're describing. It isn't *your* dream.

If I were to have sold my house and moved to another one, what would I have had left? Photograph albums, yes, and the mementoes I'd saved in boxes in the attic—the report cards, the Brownie sashes, the ornaments made out of cotton balls glued to egg carton cups. But the rooms themselves were what had contained us all those years, shaped us into a family.

What I remembered were Christmas mornings, when the girls thundered downstairs to open their stockings before it was light out; the "fashion shows" they put on for Joe and me when they were little, modeling their outfits for the first day of school; tears (mostly Dawn's) over homework at the kitchen table; science projects being planned and constructed on the counter, which was also the place where I left out oatmeal crinkles to cool after they baked, letting the girls think they fooled me when they took cookies from the sheets and tried to rearrange the remaining ones so I wouldn't notice; Saturday nights, before Iris began going out with her friends all the time, when the four of us (well, five, if you counted Abby, which of course we did) took our habitual spots on couches and pillows in the family room and watched movies, sometimes all of us falling asleep until somebody's snore or sigh or fart woke us up, laughing; the blizzard we had in October one year, when we lost power and spent most of two days reading to one another from our favorite books in front of the fireplace; later, after both girls moved out, the suppers Joe and I ate together, often on TV tables in front of the news, not because we didn't care to talk to each other but because we had already said so much of it, and were content to hear, together, what was going on in the larger world.

I could name such memories all day. Times like these were what made us a family. If I was grateful for anything about the attack I suffered, it was that it failed to erase any images from before that night. The house was the only thing I had left of when we were an *us*. And even though *us* had been shattered, I couldn't bring myself to let go of how much the house meant to me.

Besides, I'd been advised that people wouldn't necessarily be lining up to buy property where a murder had occurred. The Lizzie Borden House. In real estate terms, 17 Wildwood Lane carried the stigma of "psychological impact."

There was a more practical reason, too. The house was paid for; Joe had taken out mortgage insurance, which I didn't know until Tom Whitty told me after Joe died. With the economy in such rough shape and the housing market so bad, it wouldn't make sense to try to sell it at what I would get for it now.

Sitting across from me after proposing that we all move to the opposite coast, Iris seemed to read my thoughts. "It's not like you're underwater, Mom. And you have plenty to live on. Even if you sell it for less than you want to, it's still cash in your pocket. And you'd be doing it for a good reason." When she saw I still struggled with a response, she pulled out her last card. "We'd probably look for a place with an in-law suite, so you wouldn't even have to buy anything."

Beneath the anxiety I felt as she spoke, I recognized how touched I was that she and Archie had thought this so far through, making a provision for me in their plans. But then it occurred to me that she was likely doing it more for her father than for me; I was sure she'd made some kind of promise to him after he died, whether she knew it or not, to take care of me in his absence. It was why, after the attack, she'd persuaded Archie that they should move from Boston to the Berkshires, closer to where I lived.

But she couldn't ask Archie to keep his own life on hold forever. I understood that. And I also understood that she herself probably relished the idea of moving as far away as possible—at least geographically—from the event that had destroyed us as a family.

"Let me think about it," I said, though in fact I had no intention of doing so. I felt as if I were being abandoned, or at least forced to choose between two options I didn't like. And despite knowing that it was perverse of me, and wrongheaded, I said, "I'm not sure it's a good idea. Dawn might want to move back home someday." In that moment, I'd decided not to carry out my plan to tell Iris that Dawn was, in fact, coming back to Everton. As glad as I was to hear that Iris and Archie were talking about reconciling, I needed time to absorb the idea that they were probably going to leave and take my granddaughter with them.

I'm not proud to remember the satisfaction I felt at the expression I saw in my older daughter's eyes at that moment. Then I watched her brow wrinkle in suspicion, as if she had figured something out. "You said you had something to tell me, too," she said.

"*Is* she coming home?" I also heard the words she wasn't saying: *Are you* crazy?

"Of course not," I said, answering the unspoken question as much as the one she'd actually asked. In the back of my mind, I told myself that I'd figure out, later, how to escape this lie. For now, it was what I needed.

"I thought it might make you happy to hear I've decided to testify at the new trial," I said. "If I can get myself to remember." I hadn't intended to mention it, during this visit—I figured there was plenty of time. And probably, without realizing, I wanted to preserve the option to chicken out.

But I was proud of myself for my fast thinking in presenting this as the reason I'd come to see her. For a moment, I saw a flash of doubt in Iris's face, as if she thought I might be playing some kind of trick. She'd wanted so much for me to take the stand, during the first trial, that when I couldn't do so, it created a strain between us. Not one that we ever talked about, but one we both felt, and one that charged every interaction we'd had since then. Now she got up and came over to hug me. "Thank God," she said. The relief in her voice scared me a little. What if, after really trying, I still couldn't produce anything reliable for Gail Nazarian to use? "Mom, it's the right thing."

I felt uneasy for a moment, because her words implied what I'd always guessed, that she believed I was somehow *choosing* not to recall the events of that night. During the first trial and maybe even still, she believed as the prosecutor did that I was only pretending not to remember anything, in an effort to protect Dawn. But I didn't feel up to arguing with her now. "I don't know if it'll be that easy," I told her. "I get bits and pieces in my head sometimes—"

"You do?" She looked surprised. "Like what?"

I shrugged. "I don't know. Flashes of things. Noises, a few shapes." I had decided not to reveal yet, to anyone, the disturbing possibility that I had remembered a tattoo. "That's the problem; I can't tell what they are. I couldn't get up there on that stand today, if they asked me to."

She put her hands on my shoulders and looked me squarely in the eye. "Whatever it takes," she said firmly, "you do. Archie can hook you up with that woman at the hospital who does hypnosis—you just say the word."

I didn't tell her that the district attorney had forbidden this, or that I wasn't sure I believed in hypnosis. All I said was, "Maybe. But I want to see if I can do it on my own first." Casting about for a way to change the subject, I let my glance fall on the framed photograph at the end of the mantelpiece. I tried to look away before Iris noticed, but it wasn't in time.

"What are you looking at?" she said.

"Nothing."

"Bullshit." I put up my hand to shush her and looked over to see if Josie had heard the word, but my granddaughter was still riveted to the TV. "You're looking at this," Iris said, grabbing the frame and shoving it under me, so that I had no choice but to see it. "Every time you come here, you look at this picture, and every time I know you want to say something to me, but you never do."

"I don't know what you're talking about," I said, but even to me the words sounded like another lie.

"Say it, Mom. Say what you want to say when you see this picture." She wasn't backing down, even though she could no doubt see what it was doing to me. I made a few more mumbles— nothing that made any sense—and finally, when I felt angry enough, I said, "Fine! What do you think you're doing, putting this on display like that?" I stopped just before adding, *What's the matter with you?*

The photograph was from Iris and Archie's wedding: the bride and groom flanked on one side by Joe and me, and on the other by Dawn and Rud Petty. Having gotten me to say what she wanted to hear, Iris moved to replace it carefully on the shelf.

"I keep that picture there because it's my wedding day, and the truth is that Rud Petty was at my wedding. Just because I wish it weren't true doesn't mean I can change the facts." She lifted a finger to brush Joe's framed face with her fingertip, and I knew we were both remembering that day, though from different angles and with a different combination of feelings. She must have misread something in my face then, because she went on to say, "What, Mom, you think I should Photoshop Rud Petty out of the picture? Maybe I could bring Dad back to life while I'm at it. As long as we're going to live in fantasy land."

She had never learned the phrase her father used, *lacy eye*, when he believed I was trying to make something prettier than it actually was. It originated the day we brought Dawn to the ophthalmologist to hear his diagnosis, knowing what he would say even though I harbored a hope that we might be wrong and he would tell us it was just a temporary condition that would go away on its own. During the drive to the doctor's office, Dawn nattered away in the backseat, not seeming to notice that Joe and I barely responded to her; it was as if she were in her own little world, a phrase we had used about our younger daughter in the past with amused affection, but which was beginning to seem less and less amusing—and scarier—as time went on and she didn't outgrow it.

75

After the doctor had examined her, Dawn sat in the corner of the office looking at a baby's book that was far too young for her—I think it might have been *Goodnight, Moon*—while I tried to keep my fists unclenched in my lap. Next to me, Joe asked the doctor questions and took notes. A few times I looked over to see whether Dawn was listening, but she seemed oblivious, turning pages and murmuring the words of the book to herself under her breath. When we got back into the car to return home, I asked her, "Honey, did you understand what the doctor said?" and I saw Joe glance in his rearview mirror to check her reaction, while I turned in the seat to look at her.

She returned the look with a happy expression, which puzzled me. "Of course I did," she said. "I'm not stupid, you know."

"Of course we know you're not stupid, honey," I told her, but she didn't reply, and I wasn't sure she'd heard me. When we arrived home, she got out of the car first and ran toward the house, where my friend Claire had stayed with Iris. Curious, we followed close behind her. "Guess what, guys!" she called out, letting the screen door bang behind her. "I have a lacy eye! This one!" She pointed up to the left side of her face, and I had to open my mouth to take a breath then, feeling a punch in my chest.

Iris began to say something, but I shook my finger at her and, uncharacteristically, she paid attention to my message and stopped herself. I knew she had been about to correct her sister, because we'd already let her know what was going on—what we knew the doctor would confirm at the appointment.

Joe took Dawn by the hand and led her into his study. Leaving Iris and Claire in the kitchen, I moved to the study door, where I could hear Joe and Dawn's conversation without their knowing I was there.

Joe said, "It's not a 'lacy eye,' Dawn." He had never been one to call me or our daughters honey or sweetie or anything other than our names. "What the doctor actually said was 'lazy eye.' It doesn't mean your eye is actually lazy, or that *you* are. But you can't go around thinking it's something it's not."

"I do so have a lacy eye," Dawn said quietly. "That's what the doctor said. I heard him."

"You heard what you wanted to hear," Joe told her, and I could tell that he was trying his best to be gentle, "but that's not what it is. You have to call something what it really is, in life. You can't just pretend it's something better because you want it to be. Then you're just fooling yourself, and that's the worst thing you can do."

"Worse than somebody else fooling you?" I leaned forward, impressed by her question. Though she was only six and had never seemed all that reflective, it sounded as if this was something she might have thought about before now.

"Yes," Joe said, "because somebody else fooling you isn't necessarily in your control. But fooling yourself is."

She said okay and asked if she could go, and he said yes, but that she had to give him a kiss first. I heard a big smack, and then she ran from the room. I waited a few moments, then asked him from the door how everything had gone. "Fine," he said, turning to some papers on his desk. "I think she got it." I could tell he was pleased with himself.

But the next morning, when I walked Dawn and Iris to the bus stop, Dawn ran ahead of us to tell Cecilia Baugh, "Guess what? I have a lacy eye! This one!" And she pointed.

Iris looked up at me, exasperated. "What a moron," she said, but I shushed her and said I'd better not hear her using that word again.

Standing in her living room now, next to the picture of Rud Petty, I was grateful that Iris had never overheard her father accuse me of "lacy eye," because she was angry enough that she probably would have thrown it in my face, along with accusing me of living in "fantasy land."

"That's not what I'm doing, Iris," I said quietly.

"This picture is precisely why"—she gestured at it again—"you *have* to remember. Look at what we had, before she did what she did." She pointed, and though I didn't follow her finger, I knew she was referring to the way Joe supported the two of us on either side of him, her and me, his hand pressing separate messages into our chiffon-covered backs. In her maid-of-honor dress Dawn stood on the other side of Archie, so that no one from our immediate family was touching her. Was it possible that she'd felt rejected, somehow, within the family celebration? In the photograph she looked a little lost, or hurt, but I thought maybe I was just being too sensitive on her behalf. After all, on her other side—at the edge of the family—stood Rud Petty.

And back then Dawn had made no secret about the fact that as long as she had him, she had everything she needed.

I didn't stay long, after we argued over the photograph. It seemed to me that Iris felt as relieved as I did when she and Josie walked me out to the driveway. Upset as I was about our quarrel, I didn't notice that during the time I'd been in the house, the sky that had been so bright when I drove out had turned overcast, and the air was heavy with about-to-spill rain. I was just getting my keys out when a tremendous crack split the sky, and shutting my eyes tight, I pitched myself to the ground; later, Iris told me it looked as if I were trying to crawl under the car.

"Mom, what are you doing?" She was scared, I could see that, at the same time trying not to show it because Josie was standing beside her.

"What was that?" I asked, still keeping my eyes closed.

"Just thunder." She knelt beside me. "Open your eyes."

I got up shakily with my daughter's help. "I thought...it sounded like—" I said, but I couldn't finish.

"Are you remembering something?" Despite my distress, I could see she was excited. "Did you just have a flashback?"

I brushed off my hands and felt for the keys I'd dropped. "No," I said, though I wasn't sure of that at all. The sound *had* set off a memory of some kind, but it made me feel so sick that I didn't want to pursue it.

"Come back inside," Iris urged, but I insisted I was fine. Reluctantly, she let me go.

I'd only pretended not to be able to identify the sound that had sent me to the ground in terror. And it wasn't thunder. It was the sound of a croquet mallet hitting something as hard as it could.

A Gesture of Modesty

I drove straight home from Iris's and gave Abby a walk. As much as I wanted to lie down when we came inside, because of the headache that had been escalating steadily since we'd started the trip back, I went to the computer instead. I'd had an inspiration about another way I might recall what happened that night, so that I could finally get it over with, be able to testify, and dilute the memory of the power it had held over me for so long. Now that I had the image of a tattoo, which meant that Rud Petty might *not* have been involved after all (making it even easier to prove to everyone that Dawn was also innocent), I needed to do everything I could to learn the truth.

I didn't use the computer very much anymore—only for e-mail and occasional online shopping—because it strained my eyes to look at the screen. But I managed to find, without very much trouble, the archives from the Albany newspaper that had covered the trial. Since I'd been unconscious in a hospital bed for three weeks after the attack, I missed all of the immediate news stories. After that, I made a point of avoiding them. It had oc-

80

curred to me, driving home on the turnpike, that making myself read the details might unlock something in my memory that the district attorney could use.

Most of the first articles I found were only brief, factual accounts—things I already knew—and not likely to offer any insights. I clicked through months' worth of articles, feeling that I was getting nowhere. Finally I paused when I reached a longer feature that had appeared a year earlier, on the second anniversary of the attack, under the headline

MYSTERIES PERSIST IN NIGHTMARE SUBURBAN KILLING:

Everton, N.Y.—When Hanna Schutt failed to show up for their weekly walk on Saturday morning of Thanksgiving weekend two years ago, Claire Danzig knew something was wrong. Unable to reach her friend by phone, she drove to the home Mrs. Schutt shared with her husband, Joseph, on a street in this oak-shaded suburb of the state's capital. Approaching the house, Mrs. Danzig found a dirt-encrusted key in the lock of the front door, and looking through the entry window, she saw Joseph Schutt lying in copious amounts of blood on the stairway landing.

Claire had never told me what that day was like for her, and I couldn't bring myself to ask. Because she was a good friend, she visited me at the hospital and accompanied me on my first trips out to the supermarket and the library, the pharmacy and the post office—places I had to relearn to negotiate, with my not-quite-up-to-par brain. Sometimes we went to a movie together, sometimes a dinner out. Gradually, though, the visits diminished, until we rarely even talked on the phone anymore.

It devastated me to lose Claire. We'd known each other since nursing school, and she and her husband, Hugh, had followed Joe and me to Everton to start their family. Although occasionally we went out as a foursome, we mostly did things in pairs; Joe helped Hugh with the financial paperwork when Hugh opened Caprice, the bakery and coffee shop at Four Corners, and then they took to scheduling weekly racquetball games. Outside the office, Claire and I often made plans to go to garage sales or movies or the book discussion group at the library.

It's probably fair to say that Claire's sensibility and mine were more aligned than even mine and Joe's. Once, we signed up together for a yoga class at a new place in town called Namaste, but we got ejected the first night because we caught each other's eyes as we struggled our way into the Downward Dog pose, set each other off laughing, and couldn't stop. When Dawn started kindergarten, Claire recommended me for a part-time job in Bob Toussaint's office, where she worked. After she retired early, a couple of years before the attack, we began walking our dogs together at Two Rivers on Saturday mornings, as a way to make sure we had a regular time to see each other and to pick up our continuing conversation wherever we'd left it off. The things we talked about seemed so important then: Should I think about reducing my hours at the clinic? Should she and Hugh spend all that money on a new garage? We sat with our faces turned up to the sun, taking our friendship for granted because we didn't know any better, not anticipating—because who would?—the tragedy that would separate us in the end.

Especially after Dawn left for college, the walks became a highlight of my week. But those days were gone now. Claire would never have said so, but I knew it was difficult for her even to look at me, because it reminded her of the horrific discovery she'd made that morning. Though the surgeons had worked for hours restoring most of the sight to my damaged right eye, the skin around the socket was misshapen, and one side of my mouth sagged where the mallet had split open my lip. On the rare occasions we sat across a table from each other, Claire tended to focus her gaze on a point at the side of my face, rather than directly into my eyes. And I could never quite ignore knowing that she was looking forward to the relief of being able to leave.

The last time she'd come over, I could tell she had something to say. When she finished her tea, she put her cup down with trembling fingers, and I tried desperately to think of a way to avoid hearing whatever it was. "Hanna," she said carefully, in the tone I'd learned to pay attention to over the years. "You can't sit there and tell me you honestly believe Dawn had nothing to do with it, can you?"

"Yes, I honestly believe that."

When she didn't answer, I took a deep breath and added, "I know you've always thought she was involved somehow. I get that you think there's something I'm not facing up to." I could feel her skepticism in the air between us, and I knew that whatever I said, it would not convince her. Still, I went on.

"But I know her better than anyone, Claire. The way you know your kids. A mother *knows*." When she remained silent, I felt anger rise in my throat.

"What kind of mother do you think I am, anyway? You think I could raise a murderer?" It was the sentence I'd wanted to spit

83

at someone since I woke up in the hospital and, through Kenneth Thornburgh's sympathetic questioning, realized that the police suspected Dawn of some involvement in the attack. I'd expected the words to taste vile on the way out. Now that I'd forced them into the air, I felt disappointed that there wasn't more relief in releasing what I'd wanted to for so long.

Claire looked away. "I'm not saying she swung the mallet," she murmured, and I tried not to grimace at the image. "I'm not saying it was her idea—in fact, I'm sure it wasn't." She didn't sound sure, but I tried to believe her anyway. "But Hanna, don't some of the things still bother you, that came up in the grand jury? The stuff about the alarm being disabled by someone who knew the code? How the spare key was in the front door? And what about the dog?" She knew that the mention of Abby—the question Gail Nazarian had raised about why the dog hadn't barked, if the intruder was a stranger—would hit home with me, so she saved it for last.

She was waiting for an answer, but I couldn't think. "Don't you understand," she continued, "that that . . . *animal* convinced her to help him kill you because he thought Dawn had a big inheritance coming? And that's not even me talking. That's evidence from the trial."

I said, "That wasn't why."

"See? You said Dawn didn't do it."

"She didn't. I meant—"

She waved my words away before I could finish. "We both know what you meant."

Though I knew it was a losing battle, I fought on feebly. "You're forgetting something. She had an alibi. There was no physical evidence, or are you forgetting that, too? Trust me, they wanted to indict her. You remember Gail Nazarian; she was out for blood. If she could have done it, she would have." My heart was beating too fast again. "Rud Petty was enraged because we caught him stealing from us, right after his father caught him forging his name on a loan. He couldn't get away with his usual act, fooling people into thinking he was a good guy when really he's a sociopath. And he couldn't allow us to live knowing what we knew about him." During the trial and after he had been convicted, I'd read books, when I could stand to, about personalities like Rud's. They described him down to the minutest detail: the charm, the grandiose and unfounded ambitions, the expectation that other people would take care of him, especially financially. And the complete lack of a conscience.

When I look at the accumulated details in retrospect, it couldn't be more obvious. My daughter fell in love with a madman, and the consequence was fatal.

"I'm worried about you, Hanna," Claire said.

"There's nothing to worry about. And it's not your business."

The moment the words were out, I wished I could take them back. From the look on my best friend's face, I could tell I'd said more than I should have. But it was too late. Claire closed her eyes for a moment, and I could only imagine what she was telling herself inside. A few minutes later she said she had to be leaving, and we hadn't spoken since then.

I tried not to be sad about it, but it didn't always work. Some nights, I just lay in bed and cried, using Abby as a pillow behind my head. She never seemed to mind the way I shook against her, or the fact that my tears slid into her hair. I'm sure she didn't feel it—the vet said she had a little paralysis left over from the attack. We were two damaged bodies in the bed together, and it saved me, because if I had to be alone on those nights when I started thinking about Joe dying, and the trial, and the fact that I couldn't be a real nurse anymore, and *what now*, I don't know how I would have survived.

Mrs. Danzig summoned the Everton police, who arrived at the house within minutes along with emergency medical technicians. Before allowing in the medics, who would determine that Joseph Schutt was dead, the officers searched the home to make sure it was clear of danger. In the basement, closed off from the rest of the house, they found the family dog, a mixed breed whose legs had been struck so hard that she was unable to stand.

Reading this, I felt a twinge of discomfort, but I couldn't tell whether it was a memory or the same pain I always felt when I thought about what Abby had suffered that night.

In the upstairs master bedroom, officers encountered a scene so gruesome that police lieutenant Kenneth Thornburgh, a 25-year veteran of crime scenes, described it as "the worst I've ever seen, by far." Lying across the bed was Joseph Schutt's wife, Hanna, who had been bludgeoned in the head so fiercely that one eye was shattered. The officers' initial impression was that she also was dead, but then they realized that, remarkably, this severely injured woman was attempting to pull her nightgown down over her body in a gesture of modesty.

I had absolutely no memory of doing this. I sat back from the computer and closed my eyes, trying to summon even a glimpse of the self-consciousness I might have felt, despite how wounded I was, hearing the policemen's steps on the stairs. But again I came up with nothing. Though I knew the article referred to me, I felt as removed as if I were reading a description of some other woman who'd suffered things I couldn't imagine, in some other part of the world.

That Hanna Schutt survived the attack upon her and her husband that night is, even medical experts agree, nothing short of a miracle. And what followed remains one of the most intriguing puzzles in the Capital District's criminal history, in part because—at least in the opinion of some circles—it has yet to be solved.

Pulling aside the bedsheets to make way for the medics to evaluate Hanna Schutt's condition, Lieutenant Thornburgh uncovered a bloody croquet mallet, later determined to be the murder weapon taken from the croquet set stored in the family's garage. Believing that the victim was on the verge of death, he bent down to ask if she could hear him. When she nodded, he asked her if she had seen who had attacked her and her husband. Again she nodded. "Was it a stranger?" the lieutenant said, and she shook her head from side to side on the bloody pillow.

When asked, "Was it Rud Petty?" Hanna Schutt nodded "with as much energy as she could muster," the officer said in his later testimony.

Sensing the urgency of the situation, Thornburgh
did not stop there. "Was Dawn here too?" he asked,
referring to the Schutts' younger daughter, and Mrs.
Schutt appeared to give one last nod before beginning to cry so vigorously that it was feared she
might choke to death. The medic attending to her
during the lieutenant's questioning confirmed the
officer's account of the exchange.

When I heard this testimony in the courtroom, I had no idea
why I would have nodded in answer to the questions Thornburgh had asked. My best guess was that when he leaned down
to whisper to me, I may have heard him say Dawn's name, but
not the context of the question. I might have thought he was asking something like *Do you remember your daughter Dawn? Do you
want to see her?* and I nodded, the way any mother would.

This solution didn't explain why he hadn't also mentioned Iris,
but I figured that the detective didn't know, at the time, that I had
another daughter. Dawn would have been fresh on his mind because he'd met her only hours earlier, when he came to investigate
the burglary at our house.

"The Nods," as they were referred to by a local
tabloid reporter throughout the trial, became the
cornerstone of the prosecution's attempt to indict
Dawn Schutt on charges of murdering her father and
attempting to murder her mother. District Attorney
Gail Nazarian contended that although Rud Petty,
Dawn's boyfriend, had actually wielded the croquet
mallet, Dawn helped him gain entry to the locked

```
house and did nothing to stop him from committing
the brutal attack.
```

I closed my eyes again, hoping that the phrase "wielded the croquet mallet" would conjure up some image of the killer raising his arm high above Joe and me, then bringing it down hard. For a moment I thought I could hear it, the crack—just as I had heard it when I left Iris's house—and I braced myself, thinking I had remembered something about that night.

But then I realized that the image of the sound came, most likely, from the reception in our garden after Iris's wedding, when Rud took it upon himself to teach Kirsten Danzig and the other kids at the party how to whack the ball through the wickets. Still, I felt encouraged. Exposing myself to the news story seemed to be prompting my memory in the way I had hoped.

```
Rud Petty claimed that he was alone at his apart-
ment, three hours downstate from Everton near the
campus of Lawlor College, where Dawn Schutt was a
student, when the assaults occurred. But the jury
convicted him largely based on the discovery of a
print matching a shoe police took from his closet,
and the fact that no one could confirm his al-
ibi. (His fingerprints were also found on the murder
weapon, but the defense had been able to prove that
their client had previously handled a croquet mallet
belonging to the set in the Schutts' garage.)
    The jury also believed Petty had motive to kill
the Schutts, who had accused him earlier that day of
stealing from them while a guest in their house.
```

A further motive police cited was Petty's reported (and inaccurate) belief that Dawn Schutt
stood to inherit a significant amount of money in
the event of her parents' deaths.

The biggest surprise of the trial for me had come the afternoon
three of her classmates from college testified about how often
Dawn bragged about coming from money that would all be hers
one day. Of course it disturbed me that she'd had to create such a
persona for herself, and tell such lies, once she left home and went
off to school. But I knew it was necessary for the kids to be on
the witness list, because it reinforced the prosecution's contention
that Rud Petty had plenty of reason to kill Joe and me.

At trial, the judge allowed police to testify about
Hanna Schutt's apparent implication of Rud Petty in
the attack, under the "dying declaration" exception
to the hearsay rule. In this exception, the testimony of a victim who is unable to testify in court
because of death or, as in the case of Mrs. Schutt,
disability may still be included in the prosecution's case against the defendant.
    Because the only pieces of physical evidence
against Dawn Schutt were hair, fingerprints, and
fibers taken from her parents' bedroom, which could
have been left there at any time she lived in the
house, the grand jury declined to indict her. Though
forensic investigation revealed that both Joseph
and Hanna Schutt suffered defensive wounds to their
hands and so likely did see their attackers, the

district attorney was able to present nothing other than her mother's nod to place Dawn Schutt at the scene.

Without realizing, I looked down at my hands and turned them palms up. The mallet had left no lasting marks in the flesh, and by the time I'd woken up in the hospital, the sting it must have delivered had disappeared.

Medical witnesses for the defense claimed that due to the severe nature of her injuries, Hanna Schutt could not have understood what she was doing when she appeared to answer Lieutenant Thornburgh's questions. In addition, Dawn Schutt's roommate testified that they were together in their off-campus apartment the entire night in question.

Nevertheless, questions remain. The key found by Claire Danzig in the Schutts' front door, the morning the attack was discovered, was the spare key the Schutts kept hidden in a flower box outside the house; someone with this knowledge of the family's habits, prosecutors told the jury, would have had to instruct Rud Petty as to its location. The keypad to the home alarm system was smashed in, but police determined that this was an effort to conceal the fact that someone who knew the code had used it to deactivate the alarm.

As I'd told Kenneth Thornburgh, Dawn had always had trouble remembering the code, even though it was simple: 768*. She

91

couldn't keep track of the order of the numbers, and she always thought the star came first.

Within minutes of police discovering her near death in her blood-soaked bedroom, Hanna Schutt was rushed to Albany Medical Center, where she underwent twelve hours of emergency surgery. For the next three weeks, she remained in a medically induced coma, from which she awoke just before Christmas. When the district attorney received permission from her doctors to conduct "a gentle interrogation" regarding her statement to police about her daughter's presence during the assault, Mrs. Schutt appeared to have virtually no memory of the events that occurred that night.

Appearing before the grand jury, Dawn Schutt testified that after storming out of her parents' house when they accused her boyfriend of stealing from them while he was alone in the home the day after Thanksgiving, she and Rud Petty drove straight back downstate to the town of Van Dyck, where Ms. Schutt was a student and Petty worked as a veterinary technician. Because she had promised to spend the evening with her roommate, who had remained in their apartment over the holiday, Ms. Schutt parted with Petty at his apartment, and did not see or speak to him again that evening.

Ms. Schutt and her roommate, Opal Bremer, ordered take-out Chinese dinners from a nearby restaurant, and then watched two consecutive Alfred Hitchcock movies before going to bed, according to the testimony of both women. The next morning, Ms. Bremer got up before Ms. Schutt, to go to her job as a waitress at a local pancake house. Ms. Bremer said she knew that her roommate was still in bed when she left the apartment because she could hear Ms. Schutt snoring, a condition she shared with her father because both suffered from asthma and sinus trouble.

This testimony of Opal's had surprised me at the time, because it had been years since I'd heard Dawn snoring when she slept at home—in fact, her symptoms seem to have disappeared almost magically when she turned twelve, the same year she wanted to have her eye corrected. The pediatrician told us this sometimes happened with asthma, and while he couldn't consider her cured, we could say she was in remission. I reminded myself that she'd been away for more than a year by the time of the attack, so if her breathing difficulty had returned to trouble her at night, I might not have known it.

After Hanna Schutt was rushed to the hospital, state police in Van Dyck located Dawn Schutt in her apartment. A "Be on the Lookout" advisory had been issued for her, based on what police took to be her mother's identification of her attackers. State police informed Ms. Schutt of her father's death and her mother's injuries. They said she seemed to exhibit no reaction to the news, but they also acknowledged that such a response was not inconsistent with shock.

93

Officers did not immediately inform her that they believed her mother had identified her in the attack. Ms. Schutt said that she wanted to drive herself to the hospital, but instead police escorted her on the three-hour trip in an official police vehicle, activating their lights and siren when necessary because they had been told it was likely that Hanna Schutt would die during surgery.

Testifying to the grand jury charged with determining whether Dawn Schutt should be bound over for trial, state trooper Ned Cushman said that during the trip upstate, his passenger had seemed particularly preoccupied with the condition of the Schutt family's dog. "She didn't ask me one question about her mother," Cushman told grand jury members. "She just kept wanting to know, was the dog okay?"

This hurt, at first, but then I remembered that Dawn had always had a stronger connection to Abby than any of us. It made sense to me that in order to distract herself from sinking under the weight of Joe's death, and the fact that I might be dying, too, she'd focused on Abby's injuries instead.

The trooper added that as she voiced her concern about the dog, Dawn Schutt appeared to experience trouble breathing. She asked if the police car was outfitted with an inhaler, and when told it was not, she began to have what looked like a panic attack, Cushman said.

94

An inhaler. Something about these words made my own breath catch on something sharp in my chest, and for a moment I thought I might scream out. I closed my eyes. *An inhaler.* What was it those words stirred up? I had been around inhalers since I began dating Joe. When it became clear that Dawn also suffered from asthma, we always had inhalers on hand for both of them. They had become part of our routine as a family, though once Dawn seemed to outgrow the need for the medicine as an adolescent, it was only Joe who kept one with him. As far as I knew, she hadn't even gotten a refill on her prescription before she went off to college.

The mention of an inhaler was significant somehow. I knew that, but I didn't know why. If only I could concentrate a minute or two longer, I felt sure it would come to me.

Some have speculated that Hanna Schutt did remember what happened that night, and feigned memory loss in order to protect her daughter. Whether she actually suffered from amnesia or only purported to, the loss of Hanna Schutt as a witness to the attack that nearly killed her was, in the estimation of legal scholars and lay trial followers alike, a major factor—if not the key factor—in her daughter's escape from prosecution.

"It's sad," commented a neighbor of the Schutts, speaking on the condition of anonymity. "She obviously can't bring herself to see what's right in front of her."

I resisted the impulse to put my hands over my face. I'd always known that the district attorney, Iris, and members of Tough

Birds believed I was faking my memory loss, but I didn't realize the news coverage had also suggested it. No wonder people seemed to think I was so pathetic, if they didn't outright scorn or hate me.

And who would that neighbor have been? I was sure it was Pam Furth. The next lines reminded me why she was so eager to point the finger in my direction:

```
Police briefly investigated a young man who lived
in the neighborhood in connection with the attack,
but no charges were brought against him. Though the
case against Rud Petty was almost entirely circum-
stantial, the district attorney's office said it was
confident it was prosecuting the right person for
the crime.
```

My focus blurred, and with it went whatever had been sparked by seeing the words on the screen. Feeling an almost unbearable pressure inside my head, I switched off the computer and rushed to lie down, but not fast enough to beat the pain.

Lots of Love

Though it was the *last* time I'd seen Rud Petty before his arrest that the prosecutor cared about, I had no trouble remembering the first time I'd seen him, or the way Joe and I learned about the new and powerful force—in the form of an older, handsome boyfriend—that had entered our daughter's life. Our introduction came during the weekend of Iris and Archie's wedding. We would have preferred to meet him at a time other than such an intimate family occasion, but as it turned out, we didn't have much say about it.

We first heard Rud's name during the spring semester of Dawn's freshman year, when she called to tell us that she wouldn't be coming home to live for the summer after all; instead, she'd found a job tutoring incoming students at her college, a private school downstate that made a point of appealing to "alternative" applicants. Though Dawn had wanted to live at home and go to the state university as Joe and I had, she didn't get in. At first, after receiving the rejection (which I thought she seemed almost happy about, though it took me a while to believe my own perception), she said she'd just keep living at home, get a job, and try again the following year. But Joe persuaded Dawn to apply to Lawlor, which surprised me (and Dawn, too, I know) because it was so expensive. He didn't want her to take a year off, he told me, or to live at home—he thought those things would make it too easy for her to slide into an inertia she might never shake.

Lawlor had rolling admission, but Dawn said she didn't want to apply to some place she'd never seen. So Joe and I drove her down the Saturday after she'd gotten the "no" letter from SUNY, and though she tried not to show it, I could see she was impressed (it was impossible not to be) by the cozy green campus, the two-story aquarium in the student center, the plush dorms, and the fact that students were encouraged to design their own majors. When she got her acceptance letter, she was torn; she was pleased that she'd been invited somewhere, but she said she didn't know how she could ever leave me. Though I knew it was the wrong thing to feel, I couldn't help recognizing in myself a certain degree of pleasure when I heard this. On a Saturday at the end of August, she spent the morning sobbing before we virtually forced her into Joe's car and drove her down to her new dorm.

But over Christmas we gave her a car of her own, the used Nova, and it seemed to inspire a fresh independence in her. In March she called to say that although she'd originally planned to come home for the week of spring break, she'd decided to stay on campus and catch up on coursework instead. Then, at the end of the semester, she called to tell us she'd be spending the summer at Lawlor tutoring new students. Of course she'd be home for the wedding in June, she assured me—and maybe another weekend or two, here or there, before then. Then I thought I heard her hesitate before she added, "I have to separate from you, Mommy. Stand on my own two feet."

I tried not to let her know how upset I was by her news. I'd been so looking forward to her return for the summer that when she told me her new plan I said I was proud of her, but I had to hang up soon afterward. "She's not coming home" was all I managed to say to Joe, at first, and then, after a short cry, I repeated the details of our conversation. "I know I'm supposed to be glad she wants to grow up. But it feels awful."

Joe had a different intuition, and it turned out he was right. "There must be a boy in the picture," he said. Though he tried to hide the disappointment in his face, I could hear it in his voice. Sure enough, in the next call, Dawn began mentioning Rud. Not a lot, in the beginning—she said she'd met someone, an assistant at the veterinary clinic in town, when she brought in the kitten she and her roommate Opal had been keeping illicitly in their dorm room before they moved together into an apartment off campus after Christmas break. Now she and this guy were having fun together, "just hanging out."

Gradually, during phone calls and e-mails, we learned more. Rud wanted to be a vet himself someday; Rud called her Kitten—wasn't that sweet?; Rud treated her like a queen. *He's also very good-looking,* she wrote, *which I know doesn't matter, but wait till you see him. He looks like some kind of god.*

"A god?" Joe said, reading the message over my shoulder. "I don't think I like the sound of that." He asked if he could sit down at the computer, and I watched his fingers twitch over the keyboard before he tapped out, *Looks can be deceiving! LOL, your ordinary-looking dad.*

"Why did you sign it 'Laugh out loud'?" I asked him after he pressed Send, and he said, "What?" and I said, "LOL." He looked confused and said, "That doesn't mean 'Lots of love'?" My heart split open for him then.

We asked Dawn when we'd have a chance to meet her new boyfriend, and she kept giving excuses about why they couldn't drive up some weekend. *Rud works crazy shifts at the vet clinic*, she said. *I think you're all just going to have to meet him at the wedding*. This took us aback, but there didn't seem to be any way to avoid it.

Iris was none too happy about the plan. She hadn't wanted Dawn to be her maid of honor in the first place, though she gave in to Joe on that when he told her how good it would make her sister feel to be asked. But adding a complete stranger to the mix put Iris's nerves over the edge. "You guys haven't even met him?" she said when we told her Dawn would be accompanied by a guest. "What if he's some kind of nut?"

"She says he's not," Joe told her. "And apparently he looks like a god."

"Oh, boy." Iris groaned. "I wonder what he wants."

"Iris," I said, in the same scolding tone I'd used when the girls were children. "That's not nice." I wasn't prepared to tell her she was wrong, though, so I changed the subject to something I was more sure about—what the tent was going to cost for the reception in the garden, or which photographer was going to give us the better deal.

Iris wasn't the only one who wasn't keen on including, in our family celebration, someone who was unknown to everyone but Dawn. It wouldn't be the same as when she'd brought her friend Opal up to visit for a few days during their winter break; Opal came after Christmas and left before New Year's, so her visit didn't intrude on the family holiday, and she was a girlfriend, not a boyfriend, which of course made a huge difference.

And with Opal, we felt that we were providing a haven, an oasis of sorts, for someone in distress. Since they'd met as assigned roommates in September, Dawn had been telling us about her new friend's struggles with depression. There were times when, if Dawn didn't cajole Opal out of bed, she would remain there all day, missing classes, not showering or eating meals. Joe and I felt proud of Dawn's concern and compassion, though we made her promise us that taking care of Opal wouldn't interfere with her own studies.

When we met Opal at our house in December, we liked her right away. She may have suffered depression, but she could hide it completely when she decided to. A theater major, she was a deft mimic, and kept us laughing with impressions of professors and other students; she also did a Sarah Palin that rivaled Tina Fey's. It seemed that being around us helped give Opal a respite from what she referred to breezily as "the wim-wams," a paralyzing despair that could overtake her without any warning and freeze her in her tracks.

She made us feel good when she said how nice it was to be around "a normal family." Before Dawn had left for college, it was rare for her to have a friend over, because she didn't have many in the first place. Joe and I were glad Dawn and Opal had become close. It confirmed that maybe we were right in hoping Dawn had finally "come out of her shell," to use our old phrase, now that she was out on her own.

But we'd never expected she'd start dating so soon. A visit from Dawn's new boyfriend, on the occasion of a family wedding, would have an entirely different feel to it. But Dawn promised that Rud would fit right in.

"He really wants to meet all of you," she told me on the phone a few days after saying she wanted to bring Rud as her guest. I saw right away that she was doing what Joe called "chunking," breaking down a big task into manageable pieces, instead of tackling the whole thing at once. It was what he had always recommended to the girls when they were doing their homework. "His family has all these accomplishments, but they aren't very close, and I think he's kind of jealous that mine is."

"Where's he from?" I said, catching myself before asking what I really wanted to know, which was "What kind of accomplishments?" As I spoke I was folding laundry, balancing the phone against my ear.

"Nashville." She paused, and I imagined her smiling as she prepared to deliver the information she knew would impress me. "His father's a head of cardiac surgery and his mother's a civil rights lawyer. And he has a brother who just graduated from Yale."

"Wow." I gave the word more inflection than I felt, because I knew she was looking for a particular response, one that would translate into my inclination to like her new boyfriend, to approve of her selection, and (though this made me sad) to feel impressed that such a man had chosen *her*. I smoothed my hand over a tee-shirt the girls had given to Joe on a long-ago birthday, which read DAD—THE MAN, THE MYTH, THE LEGEND. He used it to sleep in; it was the shirt he was wearing when he died, and it became a piece of evidence during the trial.

"Actually, there's something else you should know." Dawn took what sounded like a deep breath of courage on the other end of the line. "Rud's a little older than me. He's been out of school for a while."

"How much older?" I knew that if she was making a point of

telling me this before I met him, she thought it was a big deal; telling me was a way of making sure I wouldn't say anything when I saw them together and embarrass both of them.

"Well. He's twenty-seven."

"Twenty-seven!" I couldn't help it; the words exploded out of my mouth. "You're kidding, right? You're not even old enough to drink yet."

"Legally, you mean," she said, and I knew that she was trying either to buy time or to distract me.

"Yes, legally. What's a twenty-seven-year-old man doing with a college *freshman*?"

"I'm a sophomore now," she said, though her voice receded with each syllable. Then, as if from nowhere (and after we hung up, I realized that he must have been standing right beside her, making some kind of gesture to feed her confidence) she added, "Look, Mommy—*Mom*—this is who I'm going out with. I mean...I'm not just going out with him, I *love* him." Her voice trembled, and I realized that she might not have even known this until she said it out loud.

As worried as I was about what she was telling me, I also felt a thrill for her—my shy, uncertain girl—that, if it was actually true, she'd discovered what it was like to be in love. I tried to focus on my excitement for her, because almost immediately I located another feeling underneath that one, which I wasn't proud of, and which I tried not to notice. It was the same feeling that must have prompted Iris to ask, "What does he want?" I don't know what it would have been called—suspicion? doubt?—but whatever it was, it didn't feel good to identify in myself.

Joe grumbled a bit, and I knew it was because the prospect of Rud Petty's presence at the wedding, this element of the unknown, made him feel less in control of the event than he would have liked. But there was so much to think about and so much to do, in preparation for the day, that we didn't spend too much time fretting about or even discussing it. When the subject of meeting Rud did come up, we even began to treat it in a light-hearted way. "I don't know what a god eats," I'd say, looking over the menu supplied by the caterers. "How tall do you think the god is? Where should the god sleep?" Though we were smiling as we said most of these things, the last question caused us to look at each other and realize that we were both mentally kicking ourselves, because it hadn't even occurred to us to consider whether we should allow Dawn to share a bed with Rud in our home. Whenever Iris had brought Archie to visit before they were married, we let him stay in her room, but that was because they were both out of college and, to use her words, practically living together.

Dawn still seemed, at least to Joe and me, like a child who needed protecting. When we talked about it, Joe wanted to make a point of telling Dawn on the phone before they arrived that Rud would be sleeping in the guest room, but in the end I convinced him we didn't need to say anything; we'd let it work itself out. He grumbled about that, too, because that wasn't his style—he *liked* to work things out, which was what made him such a skilled accountant—and I'm sure he was imagining a confrontation that would end in tears and maybe even a tantrum on Dawn's part. He told me I'd be responsible if she and Rud made a scene. I let him say what he needed to, in part because arguing wouldn't do any good, and in part because I knew he was as anxious as I was about the profound changes occurring in both our daughters' lives.

Dawn and Rud were supposed to come up on Thursday, the

day before the rehearsal dinner and two days before the wedding itself. I'd told Dawn that we could use her help, but the truth was that we just wanted that extra time to get used to Rud. Iris had been with us all week, looking after last-minute things, and Archie arrived on Wednesday. We thought we'd have Thursday together as a family, but that morning Dawn called and said they'd be delayed because Rud had been asked to work an extra shift at the clinic; would it be okay if they came tomorrow instead? I didn't see how I could say, "No, it's not okay," although when I hung up and gave the news to Joe and Iris, they just looked at me as if to say *We should have known; you should have let us handle it.*

Dawn and Rud didn't arrive until late that Friday afternoon, only a half hour or so before we were scheduled to leave for the rehearsal dinner with members of the wedding party, the Darlings, and Claire and Hugh. I remember being surprised that Rud sat in the passenger seat while Dawn was behind the wheel, but I thought that maybe they'd split the driving duty. (As it turned out, Rud said he had an injury that made driving painful. The next day, when Joe asked him for some help adjusting the lattice bower we'd rented for the ceremony, Rud told us he wished he could, but he'd hurt his back earlier in the week lifting a Saint Bernard onto the operating table. Later I'd learn that this was a characteristic common to people like him: they'll do anything to get other people to make life easier for them.)

Joe and Iris and I went out to greet them in the driveway. When Rud emerged from the car, he didn't step out of it so much as unfold himself. Though Dawn had told us he was tall, neither Joe nor I was prepared for him to be quite *so* tall; Joe, who stood about five feet ten, had to tilt his neck up slightly to say hello as Rud shook his hand. (At the trial, I would learn that he was

105

just shy of six and a half feet; this came out during the forensic discussion of blood spatter and the investigator's estimate of our assailant's height.)

In addition to being tall, he was slender, so his body type was the exact opposite of Joe's. And his curly, full hair was dark, whereas Joe's was thinning and sand-colored-collapsing-into-gray. Rud did not wear glasses, as Joe did, and his skin appeared blemish-free. Joe had recently suffered a flare-up of his rosacea, and still showed a peppering of red spots on his face.

If you'd ever seen my husband on the street, you'd have said he was as average as it was possible for a man to be—on the short side, glasses, gaining a little bit around the middle with each year that went by, despite the regular racquetball games he played with Hugh Danzig. When we met, he was twenty-four years old and his hair had already begun to thin. He'd had asthma since he was a child, so his breath often sounded loud and labored, even when he used the inhaler he always carried with him. The condition tended to act up especially when he felt stress, which also manifested itself on his skin in the form of adult acne and sometimes even hives; because of his sensitivity, he kept himself out of the sun, so if he wasn't speckled with red bumps and blotches, he appeared washed out and pale.

Another man might have felt threatened by the superior physical specimen that was Rud Petty, but Joe had always had a quiet confidence in himself, which was one of the first things I noticed and admired. I remember him telling me he thought it was a waste of time to compare himself to other people. "What good would that do me?" he asked, though I knew he didn't expect me to have an answer. It was another example of the way he tended to view things in terms of their cost-effectiveness.

In fact, he took what other people might have perceived as shortcomings, and mined them for their humor. In bed, whispering, he used to call me Cara Mia, which was what the character of Gomez called his wife Morticia on the old *Addams Family* TV show. Growing up, I'd had a crush on Gomez, the actor John Astin, because of his smoldering good looks: his mustache, his dark eyes flashing with passion for Morticia, that goofy-eyed smile that still managed, on him, to be debonair.

Debonair was not the word that came to mind when you looked at Joe. But he knew this better than anyone. So when he took my arm and began kissing it up and down the way Gomez romanced Morticia, and I giggled, we both knew it was not because it tickled, but because he was making fun of himself. I loved him for not trying to be anything other than what he was.

Joe never told me exactly what his first feeling was upon being introduced to Rud Petty by our younger daughter, who offered her boyfriend up to us with a flourish of her hand, almost as if she were unveiling a piece of art she wasn't sure we would have the sense to appreciate. "This is him," she said, simply, implying that his name didn't matter as much as the fact that she had a *him*.

Rud shook my hand first, giving me a deferential nod and the smile that, although it appears in my nightmares to this day, made me understand in an instant why Dawn was so smitten. It was a wide and ready smile, accompanied by a gaze so direct that I had to break it, and look away, after a few seconds.

Then he turned to Joe. "Mr. Schutt, it's an honor," Rud said, and even in those few words it was possible to detect the southern accent that seemed a partner to the smile—conscious of its allure, but careful not to overdo the charm.

When he looked beyond us at our house, I saw a question

in his face I didn't identify until that night, as I went over the events of the hours before. The house was not what he'd expected. He'd thought it would be bigger, grander, more ornate. More *impressive*—like the house my father had moved us into on Manning Boulevard before he got arrested for stealing money from people who thought he was their friend. I saw Dawn notice Rud's hesitation, too, and she leaned in to murmur something to him. At the time, I thought I hadn't quite caught what it was. But that night in bed, as if the words had just been waiting for a quiet time to make themselves known, I heard them again: *They don't like to show off.*

It was only a fleeting display of doubt on Rud's part; he shook it off almost before I noticed, and I put the moment out of my mind. When Rud was introduced to Iris, he picked up her hand and kissed it, and though I knew she had been prepared to criticize their being so late and arriving on top of the rehearsal dinner, her demeanor shifted gears swiftly upon receiving the kiss, and the look she shot at her sister—surprised, humbled—must have been priceless to Dawn.

The only one who didn't seem intimidated by Rud, or even slightly awed, was Abby. When Dawn's car had appeared in the driveway she trotted out with us to greet Dawn as she always did, but Rud got out first, and Abby gave a couple of quick barks—the signal she used for strangers—before Dawn came around and bent to embrace the dog's head. "What's the matter, girl?" Above her, Rud smiled and tried to explain away the dog's reaction.

"She must smell death on me. I had to help put a dog down this morning—same breed, in fact." Only later, after everything happened, would I remember him saying this, and realize how odd it was, because Abby was a mongrel and not any singular breed. It was an awkward moment, with Abby growling low in her throat at my side, and Rud failed to save it when he laughed a bit too loudly and promised he'd take an extra-long shower before dressing for dinner.

Since he and Dawn still had to get ready, we told them to meet us at the Schuyler House, while we went on ahead. I could tell by the way Iris looked at Rud that she didn't like or trust him. It would never have occurred to her, I knew, that her mousy, lazy-eyed little sister could show up with a date who was better looking than her own husband-to-be. Though I would have liked to think that both my daughters were more mature than that, I knew that Rud's appearance, the kind of impression he made, upset the status quo between them. The disruption was something I'm sure Dawn celebrated; she'd probably been fantasizing about it for a long time, without actually daring to believe that the fantasy could come true.

When Dawn and Rud did arrive to join us at the table, after appetizers but before the main course and toasts, I noticed the expressions that passed among our guests—the bridesmaids in particular, who began to chat him up before he had even taken his seat next to Dawn. My friend Claire made an elaborate show of catching my eye, though I chose not to try to figure out what she was trying to communicate. I could tell that instead of minding or resenting the attention Rud received, Dawn seemed to enjoy and encourage it. A few times, looking across to where she sat talking so animatedly to some of the people who wouldn't have given her the time of day in high school, I didn't recognize her; that is, I knew it was Dawn who occupied that seat, but the girl I saw chatting away without reservation, laughing and touching Rud's arm in a gesture reminding everyone *He's mine*, was a Dawn I'd never seen before.

When she'd gone off to college, Joe and I tried to suggest that Lawlor could be a fresh start for her, but she seemed afraid to expect too much. In that first week after we dropped her off at the dorm room she had been assigned to share with Opal, she called every night, and I steeled myself each time I answered the phone, thinking she would say she wanted to come back home.

But she didn't. After that week, the phone calls subsided. She and Opal adopted a kitten, and at first I was naïve enough to think that having a pet was what had eased her homesickness—when, really, it was Rud Petty. She met him when she took Bella in to get spayed. Later she told me how lucky she felt, because Opal had been planning to take the cat to the vet, but on the day of the appointment it was one of those mornings she couldn't get out of bed. So Dawn skipped her first class of the day and set off for the animal clinic, smuggling Bella out of the dorm in her sweater.

When I imagine what happened during that first meeting, I see her blushing and stammering as the handsome vet's assistant examines Bella and assures Dawn that the kitten will be just fine when she comes back to pick her up later in the day. How will she be paying for it? he asks, and Dawn tells him she has the use of her parents' credit card. Joe *had* given her an extra card on our account, though he made sure she understood that it was strictly for necessities and emergencies. I'm sure Dawn told herself that Bella's spaying was a necessity.

And that's where it started, I'm sure. When she came to collect Bella, and paid the fee with the card, Rud asked if she might want to go to dinner sometime. I'm at a loss to imagine quite how, during those next few dates, Dawn allowed him to believe the things she apparently did—primarily, that she had a trust fund and that her family held a large estate that would all be hers someday. Or half hers, if you considered that she'd have to split it with her sister. I wouldn't have believed any of this if it hadn't come out in court through the testimony of other students at her school, who had heard Dawn say similar things—that Joe flew a private jet, that my father had been a millionaire, that we owned a villa in Turks and Caicos. (The day I heard that, I had to look up Turks and Caicos on a map.) I'm sure she wanted desperately to be liked, and didn't think enough of herself to believe this would happen if she didn't embellish who she was.

When she was in the fifth and sixth grades, Dawn had kept a diary in one of those old-fashioned black-and-white-speckled notebooks, and one day I went looking for it in the dresser drawer I knew she kept it in. I justified this by telling myself that it was parents' prerogative to check up on their children to make sure they were okay.

I anticipated finding a litany of misery—details of the mocking that Dawn had suffered on any given day, along with notations of how it made her feel. Instead, flipping the book open to a middle page, I came across a list of girls' names that sounded as if they came straight out of a soap opera—Cecilia Devereaux (if I had not fully realized, before, how much Dawn idolized Cecilia Baugh, I understood it then), Blair Cartwright, Gisele Forbes—each one practiced multiple times as signatures, in the most elegant handwriting Dawn's mediocre cursive skills could manage.

A few pages later I saw another list, under the heading "Things to Come True by 25 y.o. Or Else!"

1. *Gorgeus—on 2 mag. covers at least (5 better)*
2. *Famous—movies OR write books about vampire trapped inside body of wheelchair girl.*
3. *Tall guy with good hair to marry—looks good in sunglasses.*

I never did see Rud Petty in sunglasses. But I am sure he looks good in them.

I didn't tell Joe about the notebook when I found it. Instead I reminded myself that it was normal for a teenage girl to daydream, which is how I thought of it even though my skin had prickled when I heard a psychologist on a talk show describe children who took on "fantasy personas."

While it could happen to adults as well, the psychologist said, teenagers were more likely than anyone else to suffer from this "syndrome." "They think they're not going to make it through life the way they are naturally, so they have to invent the person they'd like to be." The psychologist was a woman my age, and I tried not to look at the TV screen as she spoke—I think I was cooking at the time, so that I could pretend I had the program on only as a background to the real task at hand. Still, I remember turning the sound up with the remote. "It's a matter of survival for these kids—or at least, they think it is. If this happens to your child, you want to pay attention. It can be a sign that he or she is losing touch with reality."

When I heard this, I remembered a day from the year Dawn was in kindergarten. I picked her up and strapped her into the booster seat in the back of my car, wondering what it was that made her even more quiet than usual. When I stopped at a light, she mumbled something I didn't hear, and I asked her to repeat it.

"I said, I don't belong to this family," she said, looking out the window.

112

"You mean you feel like you don't belong *in* this family?" I thought maybe she'd started to notice that Iris, who'd always been so attentive as a big sister, was starting to pull away from Dawn as she met more kids her own age. Or was she picking up on the differences between herself and her sister in appearance, sociability, intelligence, and just about every other thing that (perhaps she was beginning to understand) mattered?

We were still halted at the red light. Dawn turned from looking out the window and met my eyes in the rearview mirror. Though it would be another year before she was diagnosed with her amblyopia, I should have noticed something funny about her left eye, but I did not.

"I'm living in the wrong house is what I mean," she said to me calmly. "You and Daddy aren't my real parents. Iris isn't my sister."

The light changed and I drove on, knowing I should ask her what she meant. But I didn't. *Probably just the standard "I'm really a princess" fantasy*, I remember thinking. *Better to leave her alone and let her enjoy it.* Why press reality on a five-year-old if she wanted to pretend for a while?

The "fantasy persona" she inhabited when she was older—that of a young woman who came from wealth, and who was accustomed to a life of luxury—was almost certainly the one Dawn presented to most of the people she met when she went to college (as far as I could tell, the only exception was Opal). The students who testified about the lies she'd told provided ample evidence of that.

We didn't know it at the time, but at his trial it became clear that when Rud Petty accompanied Dawn to Iris's rehearsal dinner, he thought he was carrying an heiress on his arm. The whole evening, Dawn just *shone*. If strangers had walked in and been asked to guess which young woman at the table was scheduled to walk down the aisle the next day, they probably would have pointed to the maid of honor.

I saw Claire watching the whole scene with an expression that I took at first to be amusement, before I recognized it as concern and decided to look away. Iris and Archie went off with some of their college friends after the dinner, while Rud and Dawn returned with us to the house. I tensed as we all said good night, expecting an argument from Dawn about where Rud would sleep, but when Joe carried Rud's bag down the hall and deposited it in the guest room, Rud shook his hand and thanked him, saying he'd be happy to make pancakes in the morning, if we didn't mind turning the kitchen over to him.

Kissing me good night outside her bedroom, Dawn whispered, "Mommy, isn't he great?" and because I felt relieved that the evening was over, I was more effusive than I might have been otherwise.

"He's perfect, honey," I told her, of course having no idea how those words would come to haunt me in only a few months.

The next morning, Joe was up before any of us. While most of the time he did his best to avoid eating sugar or even having it in the house, when he felt nervous he went overboard in the other direction, so I wasn't surprised when he went out early and returned with a box of pastries from Caprice, telling Rud, no offense, he'd let him make pancakes next time, but this morning was his treat. I watched Dawn beam when her father mentioned a "next time" for Rud, and as Joe held the box open to her, she shook her head and said she thought she'd have a boiled egg instead. Rud gave her an approving look, and it was the first time something bothered me about him; she seemed to be saying it to him more than the

114

rest of us, and I sensed it had to do with her wanting to keep her weight down to please him. I checked to see if Joe had also noticed, but I knew it was a sign of his anxiety that he was digging into the first of two cherry Danishes with a look of agitated bliss on his rash-pocked face.

Shortly afterward, the people Iris and I had hired—caterers, florists, hairdressers—began arriving, and the house erupted in activity. At the height of it, I noticed that Abby seemed more excited than usual, and looking closer, I saw that she was drooling, which was not like her, even on a particularly hot day, which this was not. Her movements appeared uncoordinated, as if her mind were having trouble telling her body what to do. Beneath her coat, it seemed as if she might be suffering muscle spasms.

Actually, I wasn't the one who first noticed the dog's apparent distress—it was Rud. "Does she always do that?" he asked me as I passed through the living room. He pointed at where Abby lay, in her favorite patch of sunlight beneath the kitchen window.

"Oh, my God." As I approached Abby and put a hand out, she gave a groan as if to ask, *Aren't you going to help me?* I called for Joe, but before he could get there, Rud was kneeling beside me, touching the dog's flank.

"I think it's poison," Rud said, keeping his voice low. "Wait here with her. I'll be right back." Then Joe was beside me, and, my voice shaking, I told him what Rud had said.

"That's crazy," Joe told me. "Poisoned with what? How?" When Rud returned carrying a bag he'd retrieved from the trunk of Dawn's car, we made room for him at Abby's side. "We don't keep chemicals where she could get to them," Joe said to Rud. "Do you think we're crazy? It's not poison. It must be some kind of disease."

115

"It's poison," Rud said quietly, in such a way that it came across without showing disrespect to Joe's claim. "I've seen it before, trust me. Did she go outside today?"

Joe and I looked at each other. Usually I took Abby out for a walk in the morning, but this morning I'd been too preoccupied, so Joe had clipped her leash to the run in the backyard. "Emmett," we said simultaneously, as Rud began rummaging in the veterinary bag. Joe added, "I'm going to kill that kid," and he creaked to a standing position, aiming himself toward the back door and the Furths' house.

As angry as I also felt at Emmett, I told Joe to wait. "Not now," I murmured, nodding at Abby, who whimpered in protest as Rud's hand clamped something inside her mouth. "Abby needs us. Besides, if we go over there and accuse Emmett now, he'll ruin our day."

"Well, shouldn't we at least call the vet?"

"It looks like we don't have to. Rud works in a vet's office; he knows what he's doing."

Behind him, Dawn sneaked up and put a hand on Rud's shoulder. He yelled and threw her hand off with a violent yank of his arm. For a moment Dawn stood stock still, looking as if he'd smacked her, and Rud apologized. "Sorry, Kitten," he said, reaching to pull her toward him. "You know I don't like to be surprised like that." I tried not to notice that the way he embraced her didn't look natural. It looked as if someone had ordered him to strike a pose of a loving boyfriend.

"What's going on?" she asked, seeing that we were all gathered around the panting dog. I knew it took a lot for her to do that, because what she'd been hoping for was that we'd all say how beautiful she looked. She'd been with the bridesmaids upstairs in

116

Iris's bedroom, which had been turned into a pre-wedding beauty salon, having her hair and makeup done for the ceremony. In her cornflower-blue dress, with her hair shaped into an updo, she did look as nice as I'd ever seen her, though *beautiful* wasn't the word anyone being honest would have used.

Rud tried to make up for his outburst by telling her she was a babe. Before Dawn could respond, Abby's breath as she lay at our feet became more and more agonized, and for a few horrifying seconds, it sounded as if it might stop altogether.

"Wait!" Dawn took off like a shot—or she tried to, anyway; even love can't cure clumsiness, and she had to kick off her shoes after only a few steps, because she wasn't used to wearing heels. As I bent down to rub Abby's forehead, and found that this soothed her breathing to a slower pace, we heard Dawn upstairs in our bedroom overhead, then the sounds of her clumping back down the stairs to us.

"Here!" she cried, thrusting something at Abby's face, and I saw that it was Joe's inhaler she was pressing up against the dog's mouth. Abby reared her head back to get away from it, and Joe reached to grab Dawn's arm.

"Are you crazy?" he screeched at her. It was seldom that he ever lost control, so when he did, he sounded like a different person.

"What?" Dawn said. I thought she might have been frightened by her father's reaction, but she seemed only confused.

"That won't work on a *dog*! What's the *matter* with you?"

At first I thought he would apologize right away, especially because Dawn looked so stricken. When he didn't, I thought she might allow herself to feel anger.

But instead, what showed on her face was a measure of mortification I'd never seen there before. Not when she came home

117

crying that the kids were making fun of her lazy eye; not when Cecilia Baugh tricked her into going to a party that didn't exist; not when Emmett Furth called to ask her to the junior prom and for a split second she thought he was serious, before realizing it was a prank

"Sorry, Daddy," she mumbled, and I could see that he was about to tell her he was sorry, too, when Abby began choking again as she tried to take in air.

"Thank God we have Rud here," I said, to change the subject, and I knew Joe was feeling the same dismay I felt when Dawn betrayed her anxiety by kneeling to bite her boyfriend's shoulder as he bent over the dog. He showed us a pill in his hand, then forced it into Abby's mouth and held her snout up so it would go down her gullet.

I asked him what the pill was. "Charcoal. We need her to vomit." Rud spoke calmly. "Is there a place I can be alone with her, somewhere out of the way? I'll take care of her." Seeming to forget that he'd told us he had a back injury and couldn't lift anything, he bent down to gather Abby up in the rug she lay on, and followed Joe down to the basement. A half hour later, while Joe and I were dressing, Rud came back upstairs and said, "She's okay. She got rid of it all. Whatever that kid Emmett fed her, it did a number on her gut. You should take her to your vet for a follow-up this week, but the worst is over."

To show my gratitude I went to give him a hug, noticing how tense his body was in receiving it. I backed away quickly, and Joe shook his hand. We passed the next few hours in the pleasure of knowing that our older daughter was marrying the man she loved—and whom we loved for her—under a sky that was bluer and brighter than she'd dared to wish for. Walking in front

118

of her sister down the garden aisle toward the bower of red and yellow roses, Dawn seemed to have regained her composure. She smiled at Joe and me going by, and I know we both felt glad of it. When Iris and Archie exchanged their vows, Joe reached down for my hand and squeezed it, and though I tried not to, I felt myself shudder with sobs.

After the ceremony, we all posed for pictures. When the photographer called for the family to come up, I saw Dawn grab Rud's hand as she pulled him toward the newlyweds and Joe and me. I watched Iris start to protest, but then she relented as she caught the expression on her sister's face—pleading as if to say, *Do this for me, okay?*

The reception began with laughter and dancing under the tent for the grown-ups, while the children played at the side of the yard, near the maple where the tree house used to be. Even after all these years, you could still see traces of black in the branches where the fire singed the bark. I didn't know exactly what was going on until I ventured over, beyond the actual perimeter of the garden, to take a look. Someone had taken out the croquet set from the garage and arranged the wickets around the yard, and the kids were having a field day with it, smacking balls without any idea, it seemed, that the goal was to send them through in a certain order.

The croquet set had never been opened from its original package, though it had sat in the garage for more than twenty years, since the day Joe's parents drove out from Tonawanda, shortly after we moved into the house, and gave it to us as a housewarming present. I was pleased when Joe pulled off the paper wrapped sloppily around the bulky gift, even though I could tell he was wary of doing so. His father was already on the third Genesee

Cream Ale of the six-pack he'd brought with him and insisted on drinking from the can, despite the mug I'd put in the freezer to frost for him.

"That's so nice!" I exclaimed when the croquet set was revealed, aware of adding heartiness to my voice as I tried to defuse the tension I felt mounting in the room. Joe's mother, who like my own didn't speak much when her husband was around, smiled wanly and said she hoped we'd enjoy it.

Joe thanked his parents, and I saw that he wanted it to end there. But, of course, it didn't. "You're moving up in the world, son," his father said, gesturing around him at our new four-bedroom house with hands scarred from years of work accidents at Lackawanna Steel. He never held a steady job after the plant let him go when Joe was in junior high, and those hands never healed. "We couldn't just give you any old thing. You're a king now. You should be playing the sport of kings."

"You don't need to be a king to play croquet, Dad." Joe had considered not answering, I knew, but then couldn't resist. "I think you mean polo."

"Whuh-oh! I stand corrected." His father rubbed those gnarled hands together as if Joe had given him something he'd been waiting a long time for. "Far be it from me to try to educate Mr. Graduate Degree, hunh, Tilda?" He looked to his wife for affirmation, and Joe's mother flushed.

"It doesn't matter," she said, wringing her hands in her lap, and I passed the plate of deviled eggs so she'd have something else to do with them. She took one and in a desperate whisper added, "It doesn't matter, Len." Years later, after they were killed together when a snowplow didn't see their car around a high bank and carved into their Cutlass, it took me longer than I would have

120

liked to shake the memory of her saying, "It doesn't matter, Len," as if she would have given all she had to make him stop needling their son about his success, and just have a nice visit for a change.

At Iris's wedding reception, Rud Petty had appointed himself in charge of the croquet game. I walked over to see him encouraging the kids gathered around him to swing away at the heavy, colorful balls. Claire and Hugh Danzig's daughter, Kirsten, hung on his every word; it was obvious she had a crush on him.

Standing behind her, he wrapped her small fingers around the top of a mallet. "Pretend this is someone you hate," Rud told her, pointing down at the orange ball in the grass. "You gotta smack it like it did something bad to you." To illustrate, he whacked the ball and sent it flying into the Furths' backyard as Kirsten squealed with delight. I had to step in and ask him not to be so "enthusiastic"—I chose the word carefully—and seeming abashed, he apologized and laughed at himself, saying he must not know his own strength. Kirsten glared at me.

When Gail Nazarian was preparing for the first trial, I told her about Rud playing croquet with the kids at the wedding, thinking that it might be helpful to her case—the fact that I'd witnessed Rud swinging the mallet with such force. Instead, she cursed. "That's not something we can use, but it *will* explain away his fingerprints on the murder weapon. I'm going to have to tell his lawyer." Though I realized I couldn't have been expected to know this, I felt like an idiot for mentioning it.

To my surprise, because Dawn had stuck so close to him during the rehearsal dinner, she wasn't with her boyfriend while he hung out with the children at the reception. Seeming to enjoy the fact that Iris's popular friends now accepted her as one of their own, she was dancing the Electric Slide with them. I nudged Joe

121

to get his attention, and nodded over to where our perpetually awkward daughter was actually *shimmying* to the beat.

By the time most everyone had left and we went to bed, it was after two in the morning, and all I wanted to do was sleep. But I could tell from the familiar wrinkle between his eyebrows that Joe was pondering something. "What?" I said, and he shook his head, the way he did when he wasn't yet ready to commit to an opinion.

"I'm just thinking about the dog," he told me, and I felt a start of guilt, because I'd forgotten about Abby. Rud had promised us, after the poison scare, that he'd check on her periodically in the basement, where Abby lay recovering all day and avoiding the hectic happiness within and outside our house. Once Rud had told us she'd be all right, I'd focused on other things.

"We'll deal with Emmett tomorrow," I said sleepily, turning on my side.

"I don't think Emmett did it." When Joe said this, I turned back, realizing that his tone contained something important. "I think it was Rud."

"What are you talking about? Rud's the one who saved her." But as I registered Joe's words, my stomach contracted with the fear that comes with suddenly understanding something you'd rather not.

"I know. But that's my point. What better way to ingratiate yourself with your girlfriend's family than to save their dog from dying?"

The idea was absurd, I remember thinking. And yet. "I can't believe he would do a thing like that," I said. "We don't have any reason to believe that's what he's like. Do we?" Without wanting to, I remembered the question Iris had asked, when we told her how Dawn described her new boyfriend. *What does he want?* If I had been honest, I'd have to admit it had remained at the back of my consciousness ever since.

Joe said quietly, "I'm a fraud examiner, remember? I can spot it a mile away."

What he said worried me, because back then it *had* seemed that poisoning a dog was out of Emmett Furth's league. He may have burned down our tree house, but he'd never caused any physical harm that we knew of, even to an animal.

The idea that the real culprit could have been Dawn's boyfriend, with whom she seemed to be in love, was too disturbing for me to entertain for very long. "Why would he need to do that?" I asked Joe. "Why wouldn't he think we'd like him enough as he is?" Next to me in the bed, he shrugged, but I could tell he was ruminating. "That would be really..." I wanted to dispel the idea from the air around us, but couldn't bring myself to fill in the blank with *sick* or *cruel* or *crazy*, so I let the line trail off in the air between us.

"Do you think she told him she has money, or something?" Joe whispered after a moment. What he wondered, as we all did, was what a man like Rud Petty would see in a girl like Dawn.

"Even if she *had* told him that," I whispered back, "why would he..." Once again, I couldn't finish my sentence. I wasn't sure what the words should be.

We could still hear the sounds of the caterers outside, dismantling the party and cleaning everything up so that in the morning our house and garden would be restored. Joe clicked off the light, and I felt relieved that he wasn't going to say anything more about the possibility that Dawn's boyfriend had poisoned our dog. By the time I fell asleep, I had come up with a good explanation. But when I woke in the morning, I couldn't remember for the life of me what it might be.

123

Chicken of Everything

Five days after Rud Petty won his new trial, Dawn arrived around dinnertime. I'd taken the day off from work because she'd told me she'd be home in time for lunch, but as it turned out I needn't have done this, because when she drove up in a car crammed with boxes, giving a little beep to announce herself, it was after six o'clock and already dark.

When I heard the horn, I felt my throat constrict a little, realizing that along with my joy and anticipation at having Dawn home, I was nervous because so much had happened since we'd lived in the house together. Then I reminded myself that this was *Dawn*. There was nothing to be nervous about. I threw on my jacket and went straight out to greet her in the driveway.

I expected her to be driving the old Nova. It was the car she and Rud Petty had come in to visit us for Thanksgiving three years earlier, and it was the car Warren Goldman testified he'd seen in our driveway the night of the attack, which made sense to me because Dawn had told us she often lent it to Rud, and I assumed he'd borrowed it to drive back up that night and take out his rage on Joe and me.

But instead she was sitting in what appeared to be a Corvette, black with a moon roof. The "gotcha" light Joe had installed when we moved in, which used to turn on when it detected motion near the house, had long since blown (I hadn't replaced it, because what was the point?) and I've never paid much attention to cars, but I know a Corvette when I see one. My first thought was that it didn't look like a car any woman would choose. Joe would have been appalled to have something so expensive sitting in his driveway; it didn't look like the kind of car owned by someone who had maxed out her credit cards. Which reminded me, before I pushed it out of my mind, that I had no idea how Dawn had been supporting herself since she'd moved away.

I resolved not to ask her about the car, at least not immediately. When she stepped out, I hugged her hard. "You made it!"

"Hi, Mommy," she said, smiling somewhat warily as she pulled back to look at me. It was the closest we had been to each other, physically, since she'd come to visit me in the hospital a year and a half earlier, when I'd had an operation to relieve the pressure on my brain. It took me a moment to realize that something was different from then, and a moment more to understand what it was. In her appearance, that is.

Her left eye, which had been corrected during the surgery we finally let her have when she was fourteen, had begun to stray outward again. Realizing this, I felt myself start, at the same time knowing I shouldn't show it. There was plenty of time to ask her about it—how long it had been happening, whether she'd had it checked out. Though I'm pretty sure I managed not to reveal my surprise and the dismay I knew she must also have felt at this development (which she'd been warned about but was sure would not happen to her), I felt the shock register down to my fingertips.

And to her credit, she didn't exhibit any visible reaction when she studied my face, either, despite the fact that I'd had another cosmetic surgery since she'd seen me last. Then again, maybe Bob Toussaint was right and my face was, in fact, "adjusting" in an effort to return to its original state. He was my friend as well as my boss, and as a family practitioner he had no expertise in such things, and it had occurred to me more than once that he was only trying to make me feel better by suggesting that someday I might look like myself again. But I didn't care; his speculation gave me hope.

I had never thought about it this way before, but now I saw that the trauma of that night had made Dawn and me mirror images of each other—her lazy left eye across from my injured right.

In the chill of the autumn evening, she wore a thin tee with her breasts straining beneath the slogan THIS IS NOT THE LIFE I ORDERED, and a too-short denim miniskirt with her bare legs jutting down into a pair of plastic sandals. The clothing was entirely wrong for an October night in the Northeast, but that didn't bother me as much as the fact that she seemed to have returned to the exposed, trying-for-sexy style she developed during her time with Rud, instead of sticking with the plain and almost prim outfits she'd worn—because his lawyer told her to—every day to Rud's trial.

A car beeped its horn as it passed us, and I saw Pam Furth craning to identify my companion before she turned into her own driveway. Even through the dark, I thought I could read her astonishment at the realization that Dawn had dared to come back home.

I rushed Dawn inside, despite the fact that it was too late—Pam had seen her. I knew Dawn hadn't noticed. I sat down at the kitchen table and indicated she should do the same, but she said she needed to stand for a while, she'd been sitting so long in the car. She began nattering—the word Joe had always used for what Dawn did when she was nervous. She talked about the different kinds of hand dryers in the bathrooms of all the rest stops she'd encountered on her long drive. She began describing a segment of a radio program she'd heard about the opening of a bird sanctuary in the next county over. "Maybe we can go sometime," she said. "I like birds, I decided. You do, too, right, Mommy? Maybe you can teach me how to bird-watch, sometime."

Though I tried to resist it, I couldn't ignore the fact that she was starting to sound like Ding-Dong Dawn. I was about to interrupt her when she said, "This is harder than I thought it would be." Her voice wobbled, and for a moment I thought she might be sick. "It's been a long time, you know?"

Only then did I realize that she had not, in fact, been inside this house since the day of the attack. That Friday, the day after Thanksgiving, someone stole the only halfway-expensive and portable things we had in the house: the Celestron telescope Joe had inherited from his grandfather; the Pentax binoculars Joe had given me when I said I might want to take up bird-watching; an engraved crystal obelisk Joe had been awarded at his firm's accounting dinner earlier that year; and most distressing to me of all, my mother's diamond ring, which she gave to me when she was dying.

I first met Kenneth Thornburgh that day, when he responded to our call to the police station regarding the theft. Twenty hours later, after he had questioned Dawn's boyfriend in connection with the burglary and she and Rud left in a huff, the officer returned to find Joe dead on the staircase and me nearly dead in our bed.

While I was in the rehab hospital and Gail Nazarian tried to convince a grand jury to bring her to trial, Dawn stayed with Peter and Wendy Cifforelli in Clifton Park. The first option had been Iris and Archie, but they refused. There was no question of her living alone in the house on Wildwood Lane during this time, because although the trauma-cleanup people had completed their work, the renovations Iris ordered had only just begun. Not to mention that Dawn said she had no desire to go anywhere near where her parents had been attacked.

I was relieved that she continued to stay on as Peter and Wendy's guest even after the renovations were done and I returned home that March, after the grand jury declined to indict her. Dawn was steadfast in her defense of Rud's innocence, and I was sure he was guilty; with that between us, we could not live together.

The fact that Peter allowed her to stay with his family during the trial made me think he believed she couldn't have been involved in the crime against Joe and me, which did soften my feelings toward him a little. Wendy drove Dawn to court every day, and kept her company on the other side of the aisle from where I sat next to Iris. In the courtroom, Dawn and I mostly avoided each other. As long as she continued to defend her boyfriend, I could not speak to her. Occasionally our glances met by accident, and she was always the first to look away.

The day after Rud was convicted, Dawn took off to drive west, having packed only the belongings she'd had with her at the Cifforellis'. I'd expected she would want to come home and pick up some more clothes and any other items she might want to take with her, not to mention say good-bye to Abby, but she passed on my offer. We parted outside the courthouse, exchanging a hug that would have felt awkward even if the photographers hadn't been surrounding us as they always seemed to be. She'd get in touch when she landed somewhere, she said. She was determined to start over where no one knew her.

It was a month before she told me she'd settled in Santa Fe, and a few months after that before we resumed our weekly phone call routine. I worried about her constantly during that time, even though I drew some measure of comfort from the Tough Birds telling me that if something bad had happened to her, I would have heard. Several times I offered to pay her way home if she wanted to come and visit, but she always put it off, and I told myself she just needed to be on her own for a while, come to terms with what had happened to our family, and establish herself as an adult.

I got used to the distance between us, but it never became easy. I just assumed that one day we'd be as close again as we'd once been, and that day seemed to come when she called after Rud Petty won his appeal.

But it hadn't occurred to me, when she asked if she could return, that this would be her first trip in almost three years to the house she'd grown up in. The last time she'd come home, she and her boyfriend entered as invited guests and sped away in the dust of disgrace.

I could hear Abby scratching at the door between the basement and the kitchen, where I'd put her at Dawn's request. Sensing the desperation in the sounds, I asked Dawn if it was okay to let her in.

The dog's name caused Dawn's eyes to dim. I reminded her that Abby wasn't used to being shut up, restricted from the rest of the house, and that I didn't want to leave her down there, where she had suffered so horribly once, for too long. Dawn hesitated, then nodded, and watched as I headed down to the basement to open the door allowing access to the kitchen.

"Abby! Hey, girl, it's me!" Dawn said, too brightly, when she saw her old pet. Abby wasn't young anymore, and the pain in her injured hip made it difficult for her to climb steps. At night, I had to lift her onto the bed with me.

Dawn crouched on one knee and held her arms out. "Come here, girl," she said in an unsure voice, but Abby—who in the old days used to knock Dawn over with excitement—took a step back toward me and gave a whimper. The sound, and the sight of the dog retreating, pulled my stomach taut.

"It's been three years, remember?" I told her. "She's gotten used to being an only child." I tried to smile, but I could tell from how tight my face felt that it wasn't working.

Abby slunk out of the room and groaned herself down onto the rug in the front hallway. Dawn and I looked at each other, neither of us seeming to know what should come next. I had never felt so awkward and foreign in my own home, not even on the day I returned, after months in the rehab hospital, to unfamiliar, refurbished rooms.

Thinking all this made my legs tremble, and I sank into my chair at the kitchen table. Dawn took her place across from me. At this table she and I had struggled together over her math homework, on those nights when Joe was working late and Iris was out with her friends; both of them would have been able to help more than I could, but Dawn and I usually managed to come up with answers to the problems on her worksheet, and it made us feel good, like a team—even though we usually found out the next day, when she took the homework into class, that our answers were wrong.

This same table was where we'd built a gingerbread house from a kit one Christmas, then left it too close to the edge of the table and came down the next morning to find that Abby had knocked it to the floor. On one of the stools at the counter was where Dawn liked to sit and tell me about her day while I put supper together. During her last year of high school, with Iris away at college and Joe spending long hours working on the Sedgwick case, it was often just the two of us for dinner. It was usually something easy and quick on the nights I worked, but on weekends, I liked to look up my grandmother's old recipes and make meatballs and gravy or beef stroganoff with dumplings or potatoes and fish. Neither Joe nor Iris had an appetite for Swedish food; they were sometimes successful, and sometimes not, at hiding their distaste when they found out I was cooking one of these meals for dinner. But Dawn always seemed to like them.

"I'm starving," she told me. "I haven't eaten since this morning."

"Why?"

She shrugged. "I was saving my appetite. I thought you might have made some cinnamon rolls or something."

Cinnamon rolls were her favorite. On Sunday mornings when the girls were little, I made them for breakfast. When Dawn got to high school and began drinking coffee, she and I would have the leftover ones after she came home and before dinner, the way my mother and I—before my father was arrested, and before she got sick—had often enjoyed a snack together (usually tea and her famous oatmeal crinkles) when I got home from school.

"Oh. Sorry. Actually, I don't have much food in the house right now." What I didn't add was that I'd planned to go to the grocery store after she arrived, because she'd told me to expect her around lunchtime, but that in the end I waited for her all afternoon because she hadn't called to tell me she'd be late. "Do you want to go to Pepito's?"

Dawn gave a start, and I could have kicked myself. Aside from the specific painful association she would have to that particular restaurant—the default location of her sad twelfth-birthday party—she was probably also realizing (maybe for the first time since she'd suggested coming back to Everton) that even though it had been three years, she'd still be recognizable to anyone in this town who was aware of what had happened in our house the night of the attack, which was pretty much everyone. Not a day went by that I didn't catch someone giving me a long look across a store or a parking lot—*Is that who I think it is?*—and although I had grown used to it by now, Dawn had been able to remain anonymous out there in the desert.

The last time she and I had been in public together was outside the courthouse the day she left town, directly following Rud Petty's verdict. He had not blinked an eye when the jury pronounced him guilty. As the guards led him away, he looked not at Dawn, but at me. Letting that seductive smile of his rise to his lips, he pointed at my daughter, then at me—drawing a sinister line between us—and raised his eyebrows. At the gesture, I felt a chill down my back, and it didn't go away until, that night, I piled my bed high with every blanket in the house.

"Never mind—we can just call for some pizza," I said to Dawn, now, but she shook her head bravely and told me Pepito's would be fine.

"I have to get it over with sooner or later, don't I?" she added, as we got into my car and I began the familiar drive toward the center of town. I wondered if Everton looked any different to her now that she'd been away. But for some reason, I felt shy about asking her even a question as simple as that.

Pepito's was tucked away in a corner of the shopping plaza where, when the girls were little, we always went to Woolworth's to buy their school supplies. The owners were a Korean couple named Kwan and Sook Dhong, who originally opened a Korean restaurant but switched to Mexican when the citizens of Everton proved slow to welcome Asian cuisine. The Dhongs' timing was off, though, because the year after they reopened as Pepito's, three Asian places—two serving Japanese, and one a Cambodian menu—took root in town and became popular dining spots, because by then people had come to sense that the more foreign the food, the more fashionable.

Nobody seemed to mind that there wasn't an actual Pepito in the place. Sook, the wife, turned out to be as good a cook of Mexican food as she was of Korean, and that kept people coming in. Kwan worked as the host and waited on tables. Probably because Kwan always showed such an interest in us, as he did in everyone who came to the restaurant—he was known for remembering things people told him, from visit to visit—I had not been able to bring myself back there since the attack.

So, after we parked and began walking across the lot toward the restaurant, I braced myself for—what? Someone to shout at us? That wasn't typical behavior for Everton, but given some of the experiences I'd had since the trial (once, standing in the checkout line at the Target in Shelby Falls, two towns over, a woman recognized me and started shouting that I needed to ask God's forgiveness for raising a monster for a child), I knew I should be prepared for anything.

I was relieved when we made it safely to the restaurant's front door and stepped into the foyer under the same four dusty piñatas that had been hanging from the ceiling for years. Dawn used to be afraid of them—the papier-mâché rooster, donkey, crocodile, and macaw—long past the age I would have expected this of her. Iris used to laugh at the way her little sister would cling to me and whimper when she saw the fake beasts hovering overhead. "Baby," she'd say, gesturing at Dawn. "You're chicken of everything."

But tonight Dawn didn't even look up as we stepped inside. Instinctively I pulled my hair across my face and shrugged my jacket collar up, hoping Kwan somehow wouldn't notice how different I looked from the last time he saw me. For a moment it seemed as if it worked: when he peered out from behind the host's station and saw that it was us, he gave a startled exclamation with a smile, and I allowed myself to hope that perhaps Dawn's return to town might not be as difficult as I'd expected.

My relief didn't last. When I came closer, Kwan tried to hide a wince when he got a better look at me, then asked why we hadn't come in for so long. To Dawn he added, "Dad outside parking?"—to which, in order to save her, I murmured some vague reply—and I realized that by some fluke, Kwan had missed learning what had happened to us. Maybe he didn't watch the news, or maybe he didn't listen to gossip in English. In any event, he appeared oblivious to the reason my daughter and I might be wary of being seen together by people who had known us before the crime. After he said how glad he was to see us—"Better late than never"—and showed us to a booth, I saw, over Dawn's shoulder, Sook taking her husband aside and speaking urgently in his ear, gesturing without subtlety in our direction. I tried to concentrate on Dawn instead, because I didn't want her to know what was going on. But when Kwan came back to take our orders, it was obvious that something had changed. His face had collapsed; he didn't meet our eyes as we chose our entrees, and didn't give his customary smile as he jotted the order down on his pad.

"I guess Sook must have given him the heads-up back there," Dawn said, without looking toward the kitchen. "Do you want a glass of wine? I'm going to have one."

I shook my head, surprised she would ask me this because she had never known me to take a drink. We gave Kwan our orders of Chablis and seltzer and spent the next few minutes crunching on tortilla chips, neither of us seeming to know what to say. I thought Dawn might ask about her sister, but she didn't. I wanted to bring up the subject of Iris because it was so painful to me that my daughters didn't speak to each other, but I had no idea how Dawn might react.

Into the silence she started to speak, then stopped herself. We both laughed a little, trying to ignore our mutual discomfort. Finally Dawn ventured, "So, how's work?"

"It's fine," I said, grabbing at the life raft she'd thrown out, and I told her the story of what had happened in the clinic a few days earlier, during our urgent care hours, when an eighty-seven-year-old man brought in his eighty-five-year-old wife because, as he told the intake nurse, "her heart doesn't sound right." When the nurse tried to determine exactly what he meant—did the man have a stethoscope, and know how to use it?—she finally figured out that he was talking about something more intuitive than that; he and his wife had lived together for more than sixty years, and in that time he had come to believe that he was attuned not only to the rhythm of her respiration when it was healthy, but also to the vibrations sent out by the pulsing of her heart.

135

The woman presented no symptoms, and seemed a little embarrassed by the fuss her husband was making. Bob Toussaint, the doctor on call, was dubious; I could tell from the way he shook his head when the nurse handed him the intake sheet and explained it to him.

And yet within five minutes of his entering the examining room where the woman and her husband were waiting, Bob called for an ambulance to rush her to the medical center. "We've got a rupture!" he shouted, ignoring our usual rule about letting people in the waiting room know anything about what was going on behind closed doors.

As it turned out, the woman had suffered an aortic aneurysm, but there were no external signs of it until the aorta ruptured, just as Bob was about to send her home with her husband, whom he assumed was either suffering from dementia or just seeking attention by inventing an emergency.

They managed to get the woman to the hospital in time to save her, and there was no doubt she would have died if the husband hadn't brought her in to us when he did. Bob Toussaint was so shaken by how wrong his assumptions turned out to be that he got someone to cover the rest of his shift. "I'm still amazed when I see something like that happen," I told Dawn, "even though you'd think I'd be used to it by now."

"Used to what?" She had picked up a crayon from the container at the side of the table and, bending over the connect-the-dot puzzle on her paper placemat with unsettling intensity, begun drawing lines between the numbers. When it came out to show a picture of a cheetah, she sat back and looked down at it in satisfaction, and I tried not to think *What's the matter with you?* because of course the puzzle was for children.

"I don't know what you'd call it," I answered, feeling a little annoyed that she needed to ask. Hadn't she been paying attention? "A sixth sense or something that people have, when they love each other."

She was quiet for a moment, then set the crayon back in its slot. "It makes me sad."

"Why? It had a happy ending."

"I mean about you and Daddy." She rubbed her arms as if to warm them, and I realized I should have offered her a sweater to wear over her skimpy tee-shirt. "It makes me sad that you'll never get to grow old together, like those two."

"Oh. Well." I took a big sip of my water and coughed on it when it went down the wrong way. I hadn't expected that the subject of Joe, and what had happened to him—to us—would come up so soon. And I thought I'd be the one who would have to broach it. "Well, we might not have, anyway. Anything could have happened. A car accident, cancer. And with Daddy's asthma, who knows?" I shrugged and tried to form my face into an expression that said *It doesn't matter now anyway,* but I could tell neither of us believed it.

Beside the table, Kwan appeared with our dinners. Dawn turned her face up to offer a warm smile, which Kwan failed to acknowledge or return. His hands were shaking so much that I had to reach up to take my plate from him.

Dawn made a delicate stab in her quesadilla. "I know I fucked up, Mom," she said. It was so quiet I almost missed it, and the curse word sounded completely alien coming out of her mouth. She used to turn red if someone said "chicken breast" in front of her. I could only assume the swearing was Rud Petty's influence, like the clothes she was wearing; both were habits she'd held onto from the time she spent with him.

I started to tell her she was wrong, but she wouldn't let me. She took a hard swallow of her wine. "That's what this is partly all about, moving back in. If you start to remember what happened, and you have a hard time, I can be there for you. I can at least start to make up for—everything." Another swallow as she looked away from me, her eyes sweeping the room.

"You don't have anything to make up for, honey." What I really meant was that of course what happened *couldn't* be "made up," by anyone, but saying this wouldn't have done either of us any good.

Barbara, my rehab counselor, sometimes urged those of us in Tough Birds to focus on our sensory images when we wanted to redirect our attention, so I forced myself to find the scent of Dawn's shampoo in the air between us, remembering with a quick glide of joy how good it had always felt to have her so near, how familiar. And how I'd always loved the fact that I didn't have to try to be anything other than what I was, with my younger daughter. Was there a better definition of love than that?

"Well," Dawn said, "you're nice to say so. But I know Daddy died, and you got, you know"—she gestured at my disfigured face—"because of me. Because I brought Rud into our lives." Her voice faltered a little on the name Rud.

Not an hour since she'd arrived home, and here it was—the subject of her old boyfriend having won his appeal. And the fact that, depending on the outcome of the new trial, he could walk out of prison a free man.

I wasn't prepared to tell her about the vision I'd had in the bedroom—the raised arm with a tattoo—and the small doubt it had planted in my mind about Rud's guilt. It still seemed more likely that I was mistaken than that the police and the jury had gotten it wrong, so until I could put more of the picture together, I wasn't telling anyone.

"But you always said he was innocent," I reminded her, looking down at my plate.

"I know. But I knew the truth all along, I think. I just wanted to believe something else, so I did." She drained her wineglass. "Hasn't that ever happened to you?"

I set aside her question because I was still trying to catch up with the first thing she'd said. I hadn't expected such a confession, and I wasn't sure how to respond. For the past three years I'd tried but failed to convince myself that, from the perspective of time and distance, Dawn must have come to see the truth of the situation—that as a vulnerable college freshman away from home for the first time, she'd fallen victim to a sociopath who managed to convince an unconfident and homesick young woman (who he believed, because she led him to believe it, stood to inherit a fortune) that he was in love with her.

I sat back in the booth, waiting for the relief her words should have given me. Instead I felt something so sharp inside that I wondered if a tortilla chip had gone down the wrong way.

"But you can't testify to that, right?" I thought of Gail Nazarian and how much she wanted Dawn's help in the new trial.

"No." She started to scowl—I could see it forming—but then she seemed to realize that a different expression was called for, and rearranged her features to show regret. "I don't know anything more than what I told you already, Mommy. He dropped me off at the apartment after we left that day, after you and Daddy accused him, and I spent the night at home with Opal. I don't have anything they can use."

I felt a spark in my gut at her mention of the burglary that

139

had occurred at our house the day of the attack. Was it possible she really still believed that someone other than her boyfriend had committed *that* crime? I almost put the question to her, but at the last minute I remembered my resolution to keep things neutral, at least on her first night back. Trying to sound casual, as if I were just following the flow of the conversation, I asked, "Do you think you'll be going down to see Opal anytime soon?"

Her face darkened further, though again I wasn't sure she intended for me to see it. "We're not in touch with each other," she said, and it appeared to me that she chose her words carefully. "We had kind of a falling-out after the trial."

"You mean you haven't talked to her since then?" I felt shocked, because the two of them had been so close as roommates, and it would not have been an overstatement to say that if Dawn herself had been brought to trial, her future could have depended on Opal Bremer. Opal told Peter Cifforelli she was prepared to testify that she and Dawn had stayed up until two o'clock on that Saturday morning three years earlier, watching a Hitchcock marathon on TV. She would have provided an alibi to mitigate the prosecution's circumstantial case against Dawn, which consisted primarily of the burglary earlier in the day, the disabled security alarm, and the fact that our hidden spare key had been used to enter the house that night. There was Warren Goldman's testimony about seeing Dawn's car in the driveway in the early hours of the morning, but when he'd also had to admit on the stand that he took sleeping pills sometimes and might have done so that night, the defense called in experts to say his cognition could have been impaired.

"You know Opal," Dawn said, and I sensed that even saying

140

her former friend's name caused her distress. "She was always a little unstable. It's hard to be friends with a person like that."

"Well, I think it's a shame." I could tell that neither of us was quite sure which I was referring to—Opal's state of mind or the fact that she and Dawn had lost contact.

I was about to say how much I'd liked Opal, the time she came to visit us at Christmas, when Dawn put her fork down and asked, "Are you still keeping that headache log?"

This was my neurologist's idea; he had suggested I keep a record of how often I got the headaches, how bad each was on a scale of one to ten, and whether they were accompanied by what I had described to him as "flashes"—little jolts of vision, like tiny electrical seizures in my brain. Sometimes they seemed to be about nothing in particular, and other times I thought they might be glimpses of what had happened in our bedroom that night.

I had mentioned the headaches to Dawn, but I left out the part about the flashes. I hadn't even told the people in Tough Birds about those.

"It comes and goes," I told Dawn. "I can go whole weeks without feeling anything. Then, bam! it'll come up and hit me, like somebody split my head open." Even as they came out, I couldn't believe I was actually uttering those words. Splitting my head open was exactly what Rud Petty had done, and Dawn's hand jerked a little when she registered what I'd said. I raised my own hand above the table as if I could pull back some of the sting with my fingers.

Luckily, Kwan chose that moment to come by and ask if everything was okay. With too much energy, we both told him that it was. Quietly, I told Dawn that I appreciated her concern about my health.

141

"Well, I just want you to be all right." She seemed to be measuring what to say next, though when she decided, her voice didn't fully commit. She opened and closed her fists on the table before me, and I sensed that she was gathering something—courage? But why? It made me feel sad that she might be nervous about anything she had to say to her own mother.

"How are you going to make yourself do it? Remember that night?" She wasn't looking at me, having picked up the crayon again and begun scribbling on her mat.

I shrugged, not wanting to admit I hadn't made much progress. I said, "Iris thinks I should get hypnotized," then looked for Dawn's reaction to hearing her sister's name. She was running her tongue over her teeth, a leftover habit from childhood that reappeared when she was tense. What did she have to be tense about in that moment, I wondered?

Seeming to ignore my mention of Iris, she said, "That lady neurologist testified you would probably never get those memories back."

"But the doctor for the prosecution said it was possible. I don't know. Maybe the neurologist's right, and it got knocked out of me forever."

"That wouldn't be so bad, would it?" Dawn said. When I looked up to see what was in her face, she added, "I mean, if you don't remember, you can't have *bad* memories, right? I think I could go for that." She smiled, but a shadow crossed her eyes.

Grateful to have been handed a task, I picked up the check holder Kwan left at the edge of the table and stuck my credit card in the slot. In the old days, Joe used to take care of the check, adding the amounts in his head to make sure there was no mistake. I had never been good with numbers, and it would have

142

been impossible now for me to figure out if they were right, with what the trauma had done to my brain. For big things like taxes and the fund Joe had set up for me in the event of his death, I depended on Tom Whitty. But for smaller things like restaurant tabs and retail transactions, I had to trust that most people were honest, and that if mistakes got made, things pretty much evened out in the end. It was just easier that way.

As we were putting our coats on, I saw that we were being approached by a middle-aged man who'd been sitting in a far booth across from a woman I'd assumed to be his wife.

"Is that you, Dawn?" he said, drawing near.

"Oh, shit," Dawn muttered. An instant later—shifting so fast that I could barely follow it—she turned up a face that was bright and welcoming. "Mr. Cahill!" Her middle school English teacher seemed hesitant about what to do next, putting his hand out tentatively for her to shake, but she hugged him instead. I saw that this startled Art Cahill, and startled his wife, too. He pulled her forward and introduced her to us. When I saw that both of them noticed and then made an effort to avoid looking at Dawn's lazy eye, I knew it wasn't only my own perception that it had begun moving outward again.

"Yes, of course," his wife said, though her words might just as well have been *I know who they are, you idiot.* She gave me an expression I'd seen in town before—a combination of pity, repulsion, and fear. The pity and repulsion said that although she felt sorry about what I had been through, she wasn't prepared to absolve me of responsibility for it. The fear came from not understanding how it could have happened. I shrank under her glare.

Art Cahill had gained weight and lost hair since I'd seen him last, during Joe's and my meeting with him in his office almost

143

ten years earlier. A few weeks into her sixth-grade year, he called us into his classroom to tell us he thought Dawn was depressed. "I checked with her other teachers, and they all say she doesn't seem engaged in her classes," he told us, as Joe sat next to me tapping his fingertips on his knees. I knew the gesture sprang from resentment at this other man for trying to give us information about our own daughter.

A moment followed during which we all realized that the teacher was weighing whether he should say the next words, and he made the wrong decision. Lowering his voice as if inviting us to make a confession, he asked, "Everything okay at home?"

"Of course everything's okay!" Joe exploded before I could send him a message to take it easy. He didn't lose his temper often, but when he did, it was usually because he felt threatened. I could tell he believed that Art Cahill was challenging his competence as a father.

"This has nothing to do with home," Joe went on, and I was relieved to hear that already his tone had come down a notch. "It's about her eye. It's about other kids calling her Spaz and Fish Face." From the side, I could see the vein in his temple twitching. "I mean, how would *you* like that?"

Another person might have backed off, but Mr. Cahill continued pressing. "She's had the lazy eye for years, though, right? Why would it be affecting her mood all of a sudden now?"

"Amblyopia," Joe said, irritably. "Not 'lazy eye.' There's nothing lazy about it." But I knew he didn't say it because he actually cared to educate Art Cahill about the correct term for our daughter's condition. He already felt like the villain in our decision not to let her get the surgery over the summer, and he didn't want to give the English teacher any more ammunition if he saw it that way, too.

144

Joe rose then to indicate that the meeting was over, and I knew he was wishing that the teacher would, by way of making small talk, ask how Iris was doing. Joe liked nothing better than to brag about our older daughter, who'd skipped a grade and excelled at everything she tried, and part of me would have liked to do this, too. Didn't Iris's success mean that, as parents, we were doing something right?

But it would have been disloyal to Dawn, under the circumstances, so I knew we both believed it was just as well that Mr. Cahill didn't ask.

Driving me back to the medical office before returning to work, Joe seemed subdued.

Murmuring into the steering wheel, he said, "You understand why I didn't want her to have the surgery, right?"

"Of course," I told him. *Now ask me if I agree with you.* I wished he would add, but he didn't.

"She hates me, doesn't she?" he said. When I heard that, I felt the anger slide right out of my heart.

"Of course not," I said, although *I hate him* were the exact words Dawn had used.

When Mr. Cahill leaned close to speak to us in Pepito's, I saw that his pupils were so dilated that his eyes appeared black, and I remembered that the kids used to call him Mr. Kay-Pill. "I've told you that Dawn wrote one of the best papers on Emily Dickinson I've ever received from a student," he said, addressing both his wife and me. In fact, this assessment about the paper Dawn wrote for him, when she was in sixth grade, was part of the letter he wrote and intended to send as a character reference to the grand jury. Peter Cifforelli had to tell him that there was no such thing as a defense in the grand jury; he could submit the letter only if

145

the case went to trial. In the letter, Mr. Cahill left out the fact that Dawn was in English R as opposed to S; *R* denoted "regular" (although the kids of course said it stood for "retarded"), while *S* meant "seminar" (or "snobs") and was for the more advanced students. Iris had been an S student all along. When Dawn entered middle school, we hoped that she could manage S, too. But it didn't take long for us to realize that this was aiming too high.

In the restaurant, Dawn mumbled "Thank you" to her old teacher. I could tell she wanted to leave, and I tried to move us toward the restaurant exit, but Mr. Cahill didn't seem to want to let us go. He asked Dawn what she'd been up to the past few years.

She stared at him blankly. Feeling alarmed, I stepped in to say, "I think she's still a little tired. She had a long drive here from New Mexico."

"Oh, really?" He cocked his balding head. "What were you doing out there?"

"What do you mean?" She asked it as if she couldn't make sense of the question.

"Um—for work." The Cahills glanced at each other. I wondered if one or both of them might be thinking *Ding-Dong*, with the same singsong inflection all the kids used to use.

I waited for Dawn to give them an answer, because I'd been wondering what her job had been, too. Instead she said, "I like a look of agony," and a rope yanked through my stomach as Gwen Cahill gasped, "*What?*"

But her husband let a smile cross his lips as he picked up my daughter's prompt, a look of conspiracy passing between them. "'I like a look of Agony,'" he intoned, "'Because I know it's true.'"

"Oh, my God," his wife murmured. "It's a goddamn poem."

She turned away to exhale so loudly we could all hear it, and I felt the same relief.

Dawn gave what she probably thought was a surreptitious tug on my sleeve, though it was clear to me that both Cahills saw it. He put his hand up as if to halt us and, leaning closer even though there was nobody else around to hear him, said, "I never got a chance to tell you, and I shouldn't mention it now because it's all supposed to be a secret. But my brother-in-law was on your grand jury." He looked at Dawn blurrily, and if I'd doubted before that he was under the influence of something other than Mexican food, I didn't doubt it then.

If it had been me he tried to focus on, I would have taken a step back. But Dawn didn't. She looked right at him and said, "So?"

I could tell Art Cahill had expected a different reaction. He seemed to lift himself up out of his shoes in an effort to emphasize the importance of what he had to say. "So, maybe it's possible I had something to do with the fact that you didn't go to trial. They needed a certain number of votes to indict. My brother-in-law was all set to vote yes, but I might have persuaded him otherwise."

A small smile flickered at the corners of his mouth. His wife looked disgusted by the fact that he had divulged what he did, though the content of it was obviously not news to her.

"You're right. You shouldn't be telling us this," I said.

"I just wanted Dawn to know how much I believe in her. Somebody who loves Emily Dickinson that much, a soul who loves poetry like that—no way that person could have been in-volved in, in what she was accused of." He stumbled a bit over the last phrase, making me realize he had probably thought better at the last minute of saying the word *murder*.

I'm sure he thought Dawn would thank him again. Even

though I was aghast at the turn the conversation had taken, I thought she might, too. Instead she raised her eyes in an expression of—defiance? Anger? Shame? I couldn't tell. "They didn't indict me because I was innocent," she said. "You had nothing to do with it."

The smile vanished from Mr. Cahill's face.

"And I never really did like Emily Dickinson," Dawn went on. "I just picked her because the poems were so short."

Mr. Cahill caved forward a little and gave a gasp. He looked and sounded as if someone had let the air out of him.

"She's tired after her long drive," I told the Cahills again. "I'd better get her home." Without looking back, I steered Dawn toward the door and out to the parking lot.

The air was frosty, containing that hard winter bite. She looked up at the sky and murmured, "It's dark so early."

"It'll be worse in a little more than a week."

"Why?"

"Daylight Savings ends then." Was she really that unaware?

"Oh." She smiled feebly. "Well, can't see." It was a phrase we'd learned as a family on one of our historical visits; the guide had told us that people worked in the cotton mills from before sunup to after sundown—"from can't see to can't see."

Then it occurred to me that she hadn't forgotten about the time change. She was just trying to distract me from the discomfort I'd felt during our encounter with the Cahills. I said to her, "That wasn't like you. What was that all about?"

She shrugged. "I don't know."

"He thought he was telling you something you'd want to hear." I paused before adding, "You jumped all over him."

"I did not." She spoke calmly, directing her words at the wind-

148

shield rather than across the seat to me. A few more minutes passed before she murmured, "He always liked me. But he shouldn't have."

"Why do you say that? A lot of people liked you."

"That's not true, Mommy. But it's nice of you to say." She took a deep breath, then added, "I know I was a loser all my life. Until I met Rud." She mumbled toward the window of the passenger seat. I wasn't sure I'd heard right, so just in case, I asked her to repeat it.

"I said, *until I met Rud*," she echoed herself, louder, turning so that I could make no mistake this time.

The sound of his name on her lips halted my hand as I went to shift. "Dawn," I said, intentionally lowering my own volume in an effort to slow my heartbeat, "Why are you bringing him up now? And in that tone?"

"What tone?" It was the thing that had always angered Iris most about Dawn. *She pretends she doesn't understand what you're saying, when of course she does.* I used to defend Dawn, telling Iris that her sister was just a slower processor than some people. I borrowed the word *process* from Pam Furth, even though I scorned it when she used it to describe Emmett. "You make her sound like a Cuisinart," Iris said—clearly pleased with her own witticism, which made Joe chuckle before he realized he shouldn't have— "when really she's just being a pain in the ass."

I shrugged at Dawn now, trying not to let the motion go out of control the way it wanted to. "I don't know. Wistful, or something." It was all I could do not to tell her about Gail Nazarian's visit, and her suggestion that Rud and Dawn might have been in touch with each other. It was another question I couldn't ask because I did not want to hear the answer.

149

As we drove toward the parking lot exit, Dawn looked out the window and said, "Hey, remember?" She pointed at Little Folks, the store where we had bought her first training bra together. It was a rite of passage Iris had not let me be a part of; she'd gone shopping with a group of friends for her first bra, without letting me know what she was up to. When it came Dawn's turn, I offered to drop her off at the shop if she wanted to browse by herself, but she said she wanted me to be there, and I knew she was telling the truth. Afterward I took her to Lickety Split to celebrate, and she told me I was her best friend. Though I know it was wrong of me, I felt gratified hearing it, even as I felt sad for her. I couldn't help loving, that day, how much I knew she loved me.

Now I followed her gaze to the lighted bank kiosk we had to pass before exiting the plaza. "I meant to ask before, do you think I could borrow some money, just until I find a job?" she asked. "I'll pay you back, I promise."

I told myself that I shouldn't be surprised—after all, she'd mentioned that part of her reason for moving home was financial. As I went to open the car door, she said, "Do you want me to do it? It's so cold out. You could just tell me your password, and I'll get it myself."

I felt a chill that had nothing to do with the temperature outside. Insisting to myself that she just wanted to save me the trouble, I told her I didn't mind doing it and stepped out of the car. When I returned with the cash, she kissed me on the cheek and tucked the wad into her pocket without looking at it. We were halfway home before somebody coming the other way flashed his lights at me, and I realized we'd been driving dangerously in the dark.

Eye of the Tiger

Arriving back home, we saw someone standing on the front stoop, and I tried not to let on to Dawn how apprehensive the unidentified shadow made me feel. Then we recognized Cecilia Baugh, with a reporter's notebook tucked under her armpit as she blew into her hands to keep them warm.

"I'm freezing my butt off," she said when we got out, in the tone of someone who'd had an appointment and been kept waiting for hours.

"What are you doing here?" I asked her, as if I didn't know.

Cecilia answered me with the same eerie calmness she'd possessed since she learned how to speak. "I know you don't like me, Mrs. Schutt. But I heard Dawn was home. And I wanted to talk to you both."

I bit back the question *How did you hear?* It had been only a few hours. Then I caught Cecilia's glance falling on the Furths' house next door, and remembered Pam's slow drive-by when Dawn first arrived. I remembered that Pam and Cecilia's mother played Bunco together. There was a light on in the kitchen, and I wondered if Pam was watching my exchange with Cecilia the way someone else might watch a soap opera.

Cecilia said, "We're working on a story about people besides Rud Petty who might have killed your husband. We're not getting very far on the Marc Sedgwick angle, but a lot of people seem to like Emmett Furth for it." Now she inclined her head toward Pam's house.

If I had been fond of Cecilia, I might have smiled at the way she used the lingo from TV cop shows, as in people *liking* Emmett for the crime. I also understood then that if Pam had been the one to notify Cecilia of Dawn's arrival, she had no idea that the story Cecilia planned to write might suggest that her son was to blame for the attack against us.

Looking at her, I couldn't help seeing—along with the adult reporter I would not invite into my house—the four-year-old girl, with black pigtails long enough to sit on and the bearing (even back then) of someone who knew she was admired, who used to come over to play Chutes and Ladders with Dawn on the days I picked them both up from preschool. If Cecilia ended up with a bad draw from the card pile, she always managed to convince Dawn that she should get to choose a different card. I used to listen to her say things like "It's not fair, because you're taller" and "Since we're playing at your house, you should let me go again," and I'd want Dawn to stand up to her and say, "That doesn't make sense" or "That doesn't matter," but I stayed out of it because of Joe's belief that kids should work things out for themselves.

"When you say 'we,'" I asked, "you mean that *Bloody Glove* website, don't you?" Cecilia was still in college, majoring in journalism at the university, but she freelanced for the town newspaper and, more recently, the sensationalistic online tabloid that was

152

trying to give *The National Enquirer* a run for its money. Somehow, she'd convinced them that she had an "in" on what had happened in our house three years earlier.

"Maybe." She shrugged and smiled, and I had to look away because I hated her so much. She went on: "Some people seem to think Emmett's a distinct possibility. If the defense can put enough doubt in the jurors' minds, they think Rud Petty might get off."

Until now, Dawn had remained in the darkness behind me. But now she stepped forward and said, "Hi, Cecilia," in a fawning tone that made me want to shake her.

Cecilia gave Dawn a smile she would never have wasted on her five or ten years earlier. "Hi, Dawn. You look great," she said, and then I wanted to shake *her*. I watched her glance narrow as she peered closely, without wanting to be caught doing it, at Dawn's face; I could tell she was noticing that the operation to fix the lazy eye was coming undone. Surely sensing an advantage, Cecilia continued to press. "I was hoping you'd be willing to sit down with me to talk about the tree house."

Behind me, I heard Dawn make a noise. "No," I told Cecilia. "We have no desire to talk to you about the tree house or anything else." I could feel Dawn begging me silently not to mortify her.

"Okay, Mrs. Schutt." Cecilia closed her notebook. "I understand. I'm sure I can get what I need from somebody else." She leaned around me as I moved in front of Dawn to try to protect her. "What do *you* think, Dawn?"

Dawn looked at me, and I could tell she felt trapped. "You don't have to answer any questions," I told her.

"But why not?" Cecilia pointed her pen at me. "Is there something to hide?"

153

In a faint voice, Dawn said, "Emmett didn't do it." Probably without realizing, she gestured at the bedroom window above us behind which the attack had taken place. "It was Rud Petty."

"And you know this how—did he confess to you? Are you going to testify?"

Cecilia and I both watched as Dawn shook her head.

"Then you can't be any more sure than anyone else, right? Did you know Emmett was arrested two weeks ago for breaking and entering? A house over in Shelby Falls?" I could tell how much Cecilia enjoyed telling us this, so I tried not to let her see my surprise.

"Breaking and entering isn't the same thing as murder," I said.

"True. But the homeowners in that case caught him and called the police before he could do anything. Who knows what he was intending?" Her eyes were sly.

I said, "I think you'd better go now."

"Mom," Dawn whispered desperately. "Mom."

Cecilia turned and made as if she were returning to her car, which was parked at the curb. Then, as if she'd only just in that moment thought of something else, she turned and called out, "Oh, I almost forgot. Do either of you want to comment on the vandalism?" She gestured toward the driveway.

At first I had no idea what she was talking about. Then, through the darkness, I saw that someone had used blue spray-paint to write KILLER! on the passenger door of the Corvette.

Dawn stared at the car, then held a fist up to her forehead and pressed it into her skin. "But I was found innocent. What's wrong with these people?" she said, sounding not indignant but hurt.

As at the restaurant with the Cahills, I knew there was no point in correcting her. The grand jury had not ordered her bound over for trial, but that was not the same as finding her innocent.

"You sprayed that on there yourself, didn't you?" I said to Cecilia. "To stir up drama for your story, because there isn't any. Who else could it be?" I looked around us at the empty street.

"Of course I didn't." She gave me a look that said she pitied the fact that I could actually think such a thing. "It might be some random Halloween prank. Or maybe it was him," she added, nodding at Emmett Furth's house.

I spit out a curt "No comment," before I hurried into the house. If I'd had a stone in my hand, I might have thrown it at Cecilia's car as she pulled away.

Dawn waited until we were back inside before she said, "You didn't need to be like that," and the fact that she didn't express any anger made me feel more of my own.

"Yes, I did. I did need to, Dawn."

She said, "But she's an old friend of mine," and I thought she was going to cry.

It took everything in me not to remind her what Cecilia really was.

In fifth grade, every student in Mrs. Karp's music class had to sing "God Bless America" in front of the rest of the class. I couldn't imagine sitting there and listening to twenty-one renditions of any song, let alone that one with all its opportunities for missed notes, but that's what Mrs. Karp and every kid in Dawn's class had to do on the Monday after the February break. I don't know when Dawn practiced, or if she did, because we never heard her singing at home before that Monday night, when Mrs. Karp called to say that she understood Dawn was shy, but did we think we could convince her to sing the song in the school's upcoming Spring Showcase?

"Spring Showcase? I'm not familiar with that," I said.

"It's the new name for the talent show," she told me. "They don't want kids who decide not to participate to feel untalented." She went on to say that in class that day, Dawn had nailed the song, to the extent that many of the other kids sat with open mouths as they listened. When she finished, there was that stunned silence that usually precedes a standing ovation. "She shocked them. Shocked me," the teacher said. "You know, I think it would be really *good* for her to perform. She'll bring the house down. She's gifted, Mrs. Schutt."

On the other end of the phone, I didn't know what to say. Finally I managed to mumble, "You're kidding," and when I realized how negligent it made me sound as a parent, I thanked her and said I'd do what I could to talk Dawn into performing. When I told Joe about it that night, he expressed the same skepticism I felt. "Is this the teacher who drinks?" he said, and I told him no, that was the music teacher at the middle school.

We went to Dawn's room together and told her Mrs. Karp had called, and we asked her if she'd mind singing something for us. She blushed. "I can't do it in front of people," she said.

But she'd done it in front of her whole class, we pointed out.

"It was part of my grade. I had to." Her voice tightened and I realized how stressful it must have been for her to do this. I could tell Joe understood it, too. I was going to leave it at that, and drop the idea of her signing up for the show, but Joe had different ideas, more in line with the music teacher's. He told Dawn he understood how difficult it might be for her, but that he thought it would be a big step; if she could force herself through that anxiety and perform onstage, it would do wonders for her.

I remember that this was the exact phrase he used—"It would do wonders for you." I know he really believed it, and risked putting that pressure on her only because he wanted so badly for her to have the new and unfamiliar experience of succeeding at something, especially if it could be witnessed by the kids who made a habit of teasing her.

I watched the moving complications in her face as she struggled with how to respond. She did not want to do anything onstage before an audience, that much was clear. And yet I knew she did not want to disappoint us. Finally, she said she'd think about it, and we left her to go to sleep. In the morning, at breakfast, she said she'd decided to give it a try. Iris started to say something, but I gave her a warning look. At school Dawn told Mrs. Karp to put her on the program, and the teacher called to thank us, saying she was thrilled.

We waited to hear Dawn practice, but she never did. On the night of the concert, she let me curl her hair and zip up the new dress Iris had helped her pick out. Joe drove us all over to the school in silence as we took our cue from Dawn, who, it seemed, was too nervous to do her usual nattering. I dropped her off at the music room with the other kids, most of whom—including Cecilia Baugh, dressed in a black-spotted leotard for her jazz dance interpretation of "Eye of the Tiger"—did double takes in surprise at the sight of her. I pretended I didn't notice, and tried not to make a big deal out of wishing Dawn luck before I left her behind (feeling her eyes bore into my back as I did so) to take my seat with Joe and Iris in the auditorium.

It probably goes without saying that it was a disaster. It would have been better if she had just chickened out before she even got onto the stage, but as it was, she emerged in her assigned place on the program, after Graham Tompkins and Lyle Kroke performed the "Who's on First" comedy routine. She walked to

157

the microphone, and I felt my stomach constrict as the spotlight fell on her. I could tell by the way her bad eye twitched and flickered how scared she was. Mrs. Karp began playing the music on the piano, her big face beaming encouragement at Dawn. Dawn opened her mouth, and I held my breath waiting for the first note, but instead she turned and threw up, onto the floor of the stage behind her and her own dress. A murmur passed through the audience; I heard "Gross," "Eew," and "Poor girl." Dawn rushed off the stage and out the exit, and I knew she'd be running toward the car. Joe began the grim passage out of our row, and Iris and I followed, but not before I caught sight of Cecilia Baugh behind the curtains at the side of the stage, her face showing disgust and a triumphant fascination. I knew they could never return to the friendship they'd had once, after that. Standing along the wall, Pam Furth tapped my arm and said, "Oh, dear, Hanna," and I heard the tone of false sympathy in her voice. In the car, Dawn apologized to all of us, and even though we all (including Iris) said she had nothing to be sorry for, I knew we didn't convince her.

A few weeks later, Dawn came home one day looking uncharacteristically happy, and I felt wariness spread through my blood. At dinner she filled us in on the reason for her mood: Cecilia Baugh had invited her to a party.

"She's having it at Hot Wheels," Dawn told us, her face so animated that for a moment she almost looked pretty. I smiled to encourage her to continue, even though I could feel a stitch starting in my side the way I did when I tried to run too fast with Abby—a warning to slow down or stop or, in this case, be cautious of my daughter's exuberance.

"Cecilia Baugh does *not* want you to come to a party," Iris said to her sister, in the same emphatic tone she had begun using on all of us as soon as she hit puberty. "Dawn, you can't be such a sucker when you get to middle school. You just can't." Though I knew she was speaking partly out of protectiveness and for Dawn's own good, I knew it also embarrassed her to have a sister people considered a dunce. I shivered inside at the harshness of her message, as I could tell Dawn did.

"And she's *not* having a party at Hot Wheels. You *know* that's a place for little kids. Like, little." Iris put her hand out beside her chair and leveled it at about three feet. "This is a setup, Dodo."

"Don't call me that," Dawn said, lifting her chin in a feeble attempt at defiance.

Joe's eyes met mine, and I knew he wanted me to step in. When I answered him by looking away, he cleared his throat and said, "Are you sure, Dawn? Because Cecilia seems like she's changed a little, to me. She wasn't very nice after—" Mercifully, he stopped himself before mentioning the Spring Showcase fiasco. "Why would she all of a sudden decide she wants to be friends again?"

"Because she feels bad! She said so!" Dawn threw her napkin on the table, and for a moment I thought she would get up and leave, but instead she put her face between her hands and stared down at her plate. I saw her jaw trembling. "She knows she's been a jerk. Now she just wants to go back to the way things were."

"I think it sounds great, honey," I said. Around me I felt darts of disbelief and resentment coming from Joe and Iris. "It sounds like fun."

"All the popular kids are going to be there." Having calmed herself down with this reminder, Dawn put her napkin back on her lap and began eating again.

159

Of course, Joe and Iris had been right in their suspicions. Dawn told me the details later, when she could bear to talk about it, during one of our ritual bath-time discussions. But even before then I knew the truth, and on some level she must have known it, too, but like me, she chose to ignore her better judgment in favor of the wish that Cecilia Baugh really wanted to atone for her previous acts of unkindness. When I dropped her off at the rink, I asked her if she wanted me to wait for a minute, and when she said, "Why?" I realized there was no reason I could give her, so I drove away and watched her enter the building in my rearview mirror, feeling my heart miss a beat.

The only parties being held at Hot Wheels that day were for a seven-year-old girl named Anna and a six-year-old boy named Jake. Shortly after she went inside and asked to be directed to Cecilia Baugh, Dawn heard herself being paged over the rink's loudspeaker, and summoned to the front desk. She identified herself and was told she had a phone call. Later, when I asked her if she knew who it was going to be on the other end of the line, she told me no, and though it occurred to me that maybe she just felt too sheepish to admit that she'd known what was coming, I was afraid it was true—she'd picked up that phone completely unaware of what she was about to hear, despite the fact that she couldn't find the party she'd been invited to.

Of course, it was Cecilia. "We changed our minds, Upchuck," she said, and Dawn, hearing other kids' laughter in the background, understood finally that she should have listened to her father and her sister—it *was* all a setup. But she wasn't fast enough to disconnect before she heard Cecilia add, "We decided not to have the party in a place nobody would be caught dead in after third grade, and we decided only to invite people who aren't,

160

like, total tards." This line was followed by louder snickers from behind her. Then Cecilia said, "I can't believe even you were stupid enough to actually *go* there, Ding-Dong"—before somebody urged her to "Hang up already," and she did.

Dawn didn't ask if she could use the phone at the counter again, to call me to come get her, and she didn't go to the pay phone in the corner. Instead she waited there for three hours, until the fictional party would have been over, and came outside to meet me at the time we had arranged. Even then, she didn't tell me what had happened. I asked her how it had gone, and she told me it was fun—more fun than she'd expected. But her lips were shaking, and that was how I knew the truth.

When we got home she went up to her room and shut the door, and I assumed she was taking a nap. That night at dinner, speaking with more energy than usual, she told us all about the party: how thirty of the most popular kids in her grade had been there, how roller-skating was actually a lot easier than she'd expected, how surprised she was that some of the kids she'd thought were the meanest were actually pretty nice.

I should have just called her on it then. But I thought she'd feel less ashamed if she came to the conclusion by herself to tell us what really happened. "I'm glad you had a good time, honey," I said.

"Oh, my God." Iris stood up and carried her plate to the kitchen, then grabbed the phone and went out to the garden. I knew that Joe would have liked to do something similar, but he didn't let himself.

Dawn looked down at her plate. "Can I be excused, please?" She smiled in both our directions, but couldn't look at us.

Joe and I sat without speaking for a minute or more, waiting until we heard the closing of her bedroom door. "How can you continue to do that, Hanna?" he asked, and immediately I felt defensive.

"How can I do what?" But we both understood I was stalling.

"Lacy eye," he said as he rose from the table, using the words that had become a code between us. I wanted to tell him that wasn't fair, but I couldn't because I knew better. He put a hand on my shoulder, and though I knew he meant it as a sign of support, I shrugged it off and left the room so he wouldn't see me cry.

Before Cecilia brought it up during the conversation on our doorstep, it had been a long time since I'd thought about the night the tree house burned. Joe had built it for the girls when they were eleven and fourteen. When they were younger it would have been the perfect thing, but at that point they were too old— at least, Iris was. "You have to tell him, Mom," she said, after Joe announced his plan. We'd all watched a movie one Friday night that featured kids who had a tree house in their backyard, and it put the idea in Joe's head. Once an idea got in there, it was almost impossible to get out. Iris knew this as well as I did, yet she insisted I try.

But I couldn't bring myself to discourage him—he was too excited. And Dawn was, too, though I couldn't tell if it was for her own sake or her father's. Claire's husband, Hugh, and Peter Cifforelli and Warren from across the street all offered to help, but Joe wanted to do it by himself. He bought a book of instructions and supplies from Home Depot, and spent an entire weekend banging wood into the maple tree on the line dividing our property from the Furths'. He told the girls the "unveiling" would be after dinner on Sunday, and he persuaded me to serve the spaghetti at four thirty, which let me know how much he had invested in this project and the girls' reaction.

I watched them both slow down and then stop as they approached the rope ladder hanging down the trunk. Remembering the movie that had inspired the project, I knew they thought they should be seeing a proper wooden stepladder leaned at just the right angle for them to scale without any effort. As it was, though Iris gamely began climbing and pretended she enjoyed the challenge, Dawn hung back and hesitated in following her sister. It occurred to me that she might be right in this; she was so uncoordinated that it didn't seem it would take too much for her to lose her grip on the rope and fall backward onto the ground.

Once Iris reached the top, she found another obstacle to her appreciation of her father's gift. Instead of a wooden door with a window (the one in the movie had a pretty rainbow-colored sun catcher hanging on it), this tree house's entryway was an old burlap blanket Joe had nailed in place. "I didn't want to put a door in," he told me, when he saw I had a question about it. "This way there's ventilation, and they can never get stuck inside."

I'm ashamed to say I wondered if those were the real reasons, or if it was just too difficult for him with his limited carpentry skills to figure out how to fit a door. *It's kind of ugly*, I wanted to say. Couldn't he see that? On top of which, once you were inside the house, the heavy blanket made everything darker than it would have been otherwise. There was a small window on the back wall, but it was covered in plastic rather than glass, so you couldn't see out clearly.

The tree house in the movie had had carpeting, comfy beanbag chairs, and even its own little TV, on which the movie children played video games. There was a soft-light lamp on a table in the corner and a fan for when the weather got hot.

Joe's house had a bare plank floor and no electricity. When we were all standing inside and he held the blanket open so we could see better around us, the girls' expressions were dubious, though they both tried to hide it for Joe's sake. "Cool, Dad," Iris said. She went to the plastic window and looked out, and I saw her lip tremble.

"I love this!" Dawn put her arms out on either side and twirled herself around, and I had to catch her before she fell. "Just think of the things we can do up here!" It was a line Joe himself had used when he described to them his plans for the house. He envisioned kids playing board games and telling secrets. A space for rainy-day reading. They could even spend some nights out here if they wanted, he'd told them. Before construction, Iris had half-heartedly thought she might have an outdoor sleepover, but now I knew she was reconsidering; she was not a flashlight or sleep-on-a-wood-floor kind of girl.

Only after we'd all navigated the ladder backward, down to the ground again, did I notice what Joe had painted over the burlap doorway, and I pointed it out to Iris and Dawn: FORT SCHUTT. Cool, Iris mumbled again.

Joe didn't seem to notice their lack of enthusiasm. Over the next few days, when they got home from school, I encouraged them to go out and play in the tree house, but there was always some reason for staying inside or going over to someone else's. I admit I lied to Joe; when he got home and asked if they'd gone out there, I told him yes. But it was the end of the school year, I reminded him, and things were busy. They were doing final projects and studying for exams. I was sure, I said, that when summer came, we wouldn't be able to get them to come down for meals. Of course I knew this wouldn't happen, but it satisfied Joe in the short term.

Summer came and went, and as I suspected, the tree house got used only a few times. Used a few times, at least, by the children it had been built for, and those were short, mercy visits: Iris and two of her softball teammates went up one day with a tube of frozen chocolate chip cookie dough and copies of the high school yearbook, planning which boys to stalk; Dawn and her friend Monica struggled up the ladder with a box of Monica's model horses and then called me in to watch an impromptu round of jumps and dressage. In both cases, squadrons of daddy longlegs in the corner chased the girls out, and they tumbled recklessly from the tree with disgusted squeals.

After they stopped using the house altogether, Emmett Furth claimed it as his own. I don't know exactly when he started, but it was at the end of the summer, after his father moved out, that I noticed the sign over the door had been amended to read FART SCHUTT. One night I caught sight of him hopping down from the tree in the dark, and when I opened the back door and called, "Hey!" he only scurried fast into his own yard. Climbing up the rope ladder, I could smell the cigarette smoke that had been trapped inside the house, and when I pulled the blanket back I saw butts littering the floor, along with matchbooks from Pepito's, candy wrappers, empty chip bags, soda and a few beer cans.

Without telling Joe about it, I cleaned the place up and went over to confront Pam. At first she denied it had been Emmett who'd made the mess, but when I said that maybe the police would be interested in asking him a few questions, she conceded that her son might have "checked it out a few times" and said she was sure we could settle it ourselves.

165

"What do you expect? A teenage boy looking for a place to himself, and that house just sitting there empty all the time. Right next to our property. That's what they call an attractive nuisance, you know." She made it sound as if it had been our fault, but then she must have remembered what I said about the police, and she pulled back.

"He's not a teenager." For some reason it gave me satisfaction to correct her on this. Both Emmett and Dawn were about to start sixth grade.

"He might as well be. I don't know what I'm doing with him, Hanna." For a moment her face caved, and I didn't know how to react to this uncharacteristic display of vulnerability. "Ever since Paul left...I just have no idea."

I wanted to sympathize, but it felt wrong, in light of the reason I had come over. Still, I wish even now that I'd managed to murmur something supportive before I asked her to please just keep Emmett away from our yard. Her tone got snippy again as she said, "I'll talk to him about it. You don't have to do anything. Your girls can have their tree house back again." This last line was sarcastic, of course. She knew they never went up there.

I didn't see Emmett in our yard again after that, and throughout the fall I made it a point to climb up the ladder several times to conduct random spot checks. I always found the floor bare except for dead bugs, and the smell of smoke was gone. I didn't bother during the winter, because it was so cold. When spring came, Joe went out to make sure snow hadn't weakened the maple's branches, and announced to the girls that the tree house seemed "shipshape." They pretended to be happy at this news, but as far as I knew, neither of them ever climbed that ladder again.

It was three years later that Emmett burned the house down,

on a morning before school in the middle of January. Joe was in the shower when I smelled smoke, looked out, and saw the tree on fire. I called 911 and then, yelling at Dawn to stay in the house, I ran out to make sure that nobody was in danger (already I suspected Emmett, and I was afraid he might not have escaped in time). There was a book of Pepito's matches on the ground, where he must have dropped them after he lit the fire and ran off. But for a combination of reasons—the memory of his violet-tinted glasses in first grade; the way his mother had allowed me to witness the distress she felt at being a newly single mother; the fact that I believed he had burned the tree house down by accident, and not out of malice—I put the matches in my pocket and didn't mention them to Joe, who threw on his robe and came running as soon as he heard Dawn shouting at him through the bathroom door.

I persuaded Joe not to give Emmett's name to the police. Though they determined it was arson, there was no hard evidence of who might have done it—I buried the matches deep under our garbage—and they made no arrests. Though I didn't know how, it seemed obvious to me that Emmett understood the role I had played in concealing his guilt. After that, it seemed he bothered us less frequently.

By then he'd grown his hair long, in the style that had been popular when his mother and I were his age. His name appeared in the *Eagle's* police blotter for sneaking into the house of a neighbor on the corner and stealing her anxiety meds. He shoplifted beer, and when he was old enough to ride a motorbike, he got into trouble racing other kids on the bypass. I saw Pam crying outside on her back stoop more than once, and although I felt the impulse to go out on some pretext and find a way to comfort her, I refrained. She'd have seen through it; contrived friendship was the worst. So I stayed in my house and pulled the curtain to give her privacy, and called myself content with our détente.

After Cecilia left, having gleefully pointed out the graffiti on Dawn's car, Dawn and I began carrying in the boxes from the Corvette. When they were all stacked on the kitchen floor, she picked one off the top and began slicing it open.

"Careful with that," I told her, wincing at the sound of the blade through the tape.

She tsked away my warning and began digging through bubble wrap. Then she pulled out a clothing box wrapped in a shopping circular and said she had a present for me.

Somewhat uneasily I pulled the tissue paper aside to find a leather jacket, the kind of thing I would never wear. It looked like the female twin of the jacket Rud Petty had worn to our house when they came for Thanksgiving three years earlier, and I could tell it was worth a lot of money. "How did you get this?" I asked, before I realized how it sounded.

"I bought it. What do you *think*?" She was trying not to sound insulted, but she didn't succeed. I thanked her and put the jacket on, letting her admire it and pretending not to have any idea that once I hung it up in the hall closet, she would be claiming it as her own. What I really wanted to do was suggest that instead of having borrowed money from me, she should have sold the jacket. But again I held my tongue.

"Thank you, honey," I said.

"I'm so glad to be here," she murmured, coming over to hug me. As soon as we touched each other, a spark erupted between us and we both pulled back.

"What happened to the humidifier?" She sounded annoyed.

"It died. I have to get a new one." I tried to ignore realizing that I was just as glad the hug had been interrupted. *It's only natural*, I told myself, hoping to believe it. *It's been a long time*. But this line of thinking didn't feel good, so to distract myself I suggested we bring the boxes upstairs. In front of the closed door at the front of the hallway—the master bedroom that had been Joe's and mine—Dawn paused and set down her box.

"Do you ever go in there?" she asked.

"I hadn't, in a long time. But I tried it the other day. I thought it might help me remember."

Her face widened. "So did it?"

I shook my head.

"Well, that's good," she said, with what sounded like relief. "I wanted to be here when you started trying to do stuff like that."

Rather than take either of the girls' bedrooms when I came back from rehab, I had made the old guest bedroom, at the end of the hallway, my own. I assumed Dawn would return now to the room that had always been hers, but at the doorway, she hesitated and asked, "Mind if I use Iris's instead?" I shrugged and said it was fine, though I knew Iris wouldn't have been happy about it if she'd known. When Dawn saw I was surprised by her request, she told me it was because she wanted to start over—her old room held too many sad memories.

When I heard her say this, I felt a guilty start. Of all the times I'd spent with her in that room over the years, one in particular rushed back at me. It was the day I learned, firsthand, that what the fifth-grade music teacher had told us was true: the daughter Joe and I considered our graceless one had in fact been endowed with a glorious voice.

We'd never had any indication that she had the slightest interest in music at all.

169

Iris had always sung along with me in the car—our favorite was Billy Joel's "Scenes from an Italian Restaurant"; she could blast out the whole Brenda-and-Eddie saga perfectly at the age of four—but Dawn had never seemed interested. I always assumed it was just another thing she didn't want to do next to her talented sister.

Though Joe had always played down Mrs. Karp's enthusiasm, I believed what the teacher said, even though I had yet to hear my daughter sing. I believed it because my own mother had a beautiful voice, though the only people who ever heard it were my father and me. She'd be folding the laundry or stirring something on the stove, and the sound would start low as she hummed at first; then she'd work her way up to a full-throated version of "Yesterday" or "Hey, Look Me Over," which was her favorite because she'd heard Lucille Ball sing it in a musical the one and only time my mother had ever been to New York City, on my parents' honeymoon.

She waved it off when we tried to compliment her, especially if it came from my father. Ordinarily he was quiet and a little gruff—"the Swedish way," my mother used to call it—but when my mother sang, it was as if she woke up the looser, more generous part of him, the part that wanted to have fun. I remember once she was passing through the living room with a basket of clothes and my father got up from his chair to toss the basket aside and pull her close to him. My mother was so startled she almost stopped singing, but then he danced her over the old, bare rug and they finished the song—"And look out world, here I come!"—as a duet.

All of this was before he concocted the scheme that would undo us as a family. I am sure of this because the memory takes place in the dark and stuffy house on Humboldt Street, where we didn't always have enough money to pay every bill at the end of the month, but where my father still knew how to smile. A year or so later, after he started taking the money he knew he would not give back and we'd moved to Manning Boulevard into what my mother called, not happily, "the mansion," she must have sensed that he was in an even more sour mood than usual, and she tried to reenact the playful scene I could tell they had both enjoyed so much when he let the laundry fall and took her by surprise in a waltz across the room. She put a Frank Sinatra record on the fancy new hi-fi and tried to pull him up from his chair in front of the fancy new TV. "Let's show her how it's done," she said, daring to let a sultry tone slip into her voice as she gestured toward where I sat pretending to do my algebra homework when really I was watching *Happy Days*.

But not only did he not comply with her invitation, he shook her hand off his arm and told her not to be stupid. Not long after that he was arrested, and I never heard my mother sing again.

And I didn't hear Dawn sing until she was fifteen. When I did, it was by accident. In January of her sophomore year, I learned from a notice in the *Eagle* that it was the week of auditions for the high school's spring musical, a production of *A Chorus Line*.

A year earlier, Joe had changed his mind and consented to let her have the operation on her eye. He was impressed because Dawn had taken it upon herself to do her own research, and he wanted to reward her initiative. She presented him with entire studies contending that the surgery typically made "a significant difference" in a teenager's social development and, more important to Joe, that the procedure had progressed to the point that it was less likely to lead to a worsening of the amblyopia, or to blindness, down the road.

Dawn was determined, when we took her to Boston for the operation that summer, to leave all the teasing behind her once she got to ninth grade, and to do her best to follow in her sister's popular footsteps. But after all that hope she'd invested, the surgery hadn't done anything she'd wanted it to, in terms of the way other kids treated her. She looked different, but everyone acted the same way they always had. The night before classes started, I suggested we go to Blue Moon (where she usually felt too intimidated to try on any clothes) so she could pick out an outfit, and though she tried to hide how she was feeling at breakfast the next morning in her new blouse, I could see how hopeful she was. She went to the bus stop with straight shoulders (a first), but when she came in the door at three, they were back to their usual sag. "Cecilia said I can have all the operations I want, but I'll still be a loser," she said, and my heart folded in on itself as she went up to her room with Abby following at her heels.

So it would never have occurred to me—or to anyone, I'm sure—that Dawn might be contemplating an audition for the school play. I found out the day I got home early from a dentist's appointment. She didn't know I was there. I admit it: I sneaked in on her. Wednesdays were usually my long day at the clinic; Iris was away at BU, where she'd been accepted into its accelerated undergraduate and medical degree program; Joe was still at work. Dawn would have had every reason to expect she'd be alone in the house until five thirty or quarter of six, but I got home a little after five. Even before I heard the music coming from upstairs, a different vibration I felt as I stepped into the house—having nothing to do with sound—kept me from calling out that I was home.

Abby didn't come to greet me, so I knew they were both up in Dawn's room with the door closed. Usually that meant they

172

were together on the bed. If I knocked and then stuck my head in, Dawn always seemed to be scrambling for whatever textbook was nearest, and I always sensed she was trying to hide the fact that she'd just been lying there, looking at the walls or the ceiling as she stroked Abby's head.

This day, I took my shoes off at the bottom of the stairs, walked up quietly, and stood outside the room, humming in my own head the familiar tune of "What I Did for Love" coming from the other side of the wall. I remembered how I'd felt hearing the song onstage when we all went to a regional production of *A Chorus Line* a few summers earlier in western Massachusetts—the catch in my throat as the character Diana sang that poignant line "Wish me luck, the same to you," which was so moving to me that I found myself humming it for months afterward, even when I wasn't consciously summoning the words. Sitting in the audience between my daughters, I could tell that Iris was embarrassed by my emotion, while Dawn patted me on the arm and leaned close to whisper, "Me, too, Mommy."

Standing outside Dawn's door, I realized that it was an a cappella version of the song I was hearing; it sounded so rich and polished that I assumed, without thinking about it, that she was playing the CD soundtrack I'd purchased during the show's intermission. I knocked as I always did, but she must not have heard me. When I opened the door, I saw her standing with her back to me, watching herself in the bureau mirror as she finished singing with a flourish. For a disorienting moment, I lost track of which daughter I'd walked in on; her voice was so confident, and her movement so graceful and un-Dawn-like, that it seemed impossible I had the right room.

But of course I did. On the last note, she noticed me behind her and cut herself short, giving a little cry and wrapping her arms around her middle as if it needed protecting.

"My God, Dawn," I said, still shocked by what I had heard. "That was *you?*"

"What do you mean?" She pulled a sweater around her and gave me a look that was a mix of suspicion, resentment, and—this is the hardest part to remember—hope.

"What do I mean? That was incredible."

"You're just saying that." But I saw the ghost of a smile as she reached down to scratch Abby between the ears.

"I'm not just saying that. Why would I? Besides, we told you what Mrs. Karp said, way back in fifth grade. 'Gifted.' That's the word she used."

"They say 'gifted' about everybody, Mommy. It doesn't mean anything." But there was the smile again, with more body this time.

"Dawn. *Really.* That was beautiful." Then I identified, creeping into my heart, a feeling I wish to this day I had rejected, refused to recognize, been able to ignore: dread.

Of course I loved the idea of Dawn standing up in the auditorium for her tryout, bowling over Cecilia Baugh and everyone else with the sounds I had just heard, and even more I loved the vision I had in that moment of her inhabiting the stage on opening night and shocking everyone with her rendition of that song.

But (this is the part it hurts so much to acknowledge) as excited as I felt by that prospect, I felt the dread even more powerfully, remembering the night in fifth grade when she fled the stage in chagrin. There were still kids, five years later, who called her Upchuck when they passed her in the halls.

Even more painful to remember than the feeling of apprehension itself is the moment I realized that Dawn could see it in my

174

face. I tried to erase it, and to sound only enthusiastic when I asked her, "Are you going to try out?"

"I don't know. I was thinking about it." But her posture had deflated, and she flopped down on the bed.

"You should!" When she winced, I told myself to scale it back. "I mean, why not?"

"Because I might get up there and puke, that's why." A wry twist of her mouth. "Don't tell me you're not thinking the same thing."

"That was a long time ago. You didn't know how to manage your feelings."

"Oh, like I know *now*." But she was still smiling, the way she might have if we shared a private joke. "I don't think so, Mommy. It's too much like a dream. Standing up in front of all those people? Singing? It isn't me."

"But it *would* be you. That's the whole point."

She clucked, waving away what I had intended, too late, as encouragement. The moment when she thought she might achieve her dream had passed, and we both knew it. Even now, thinking about it, I feel shame burning in my chest. I'd done my best to convince myself it was Dawn I was trying to save from repeating the humiliation she had suffered the first time. What I find too much to let in, most days, is the possibility that I was also trying to save myself.

After we returned from Pepito's and I told Dawn she could move into Iris's old room instead of her own, I said good night, because waiting around for her all day, and feeling anxious about it, had made me tired. The baseball bat I'd bought on impulse at the mall had rolled out from under the bed, still in its bag from Sports

175

Authority, and I pushed it back under with my foot, thinking what an irrelevant purchase it had been and still not understanding why I had made it. I lay in bed with my legs bunched up so that Abby could spread out as usual across the bottom of the mattress, but I couldn't relax enough to fall asleep. I wasn't used to having another person in the house, especially at night. In the next room I heard Dawn unpacking. She kept moving around for another few hours, until finally—when my bedside clock read after twelve thirty—the house grew still. "Thank God," I sighed to Abby, who sighed back in agreement and shifted beneath my feet.

I'd never had trouble falling asleep, and once I did, I seldom woke up before morning. My mother had always told me I slept the sleep of the dead. But tonight, with Dawn on the other side of the wall between us, I lay there letting my fingers fuss with the edges of the quilt my mother had not quite managed to finish before she died. Throughout the night, I kept jerking awake in a sweat, panicking, certain each time—even though I knew I had only dreamed it—that I'd heard footsteps on the stairs.

Uneasy Lies the Head

The day after Dawn's return was a Friday. If it had been any other day, I would have stayed home to help her settle in. But Fridays were our busiest time at the walk-in clinic, and on top of that it was flu shot season, so they needed me. Though I didn't say anything to Dawn about it, I hoped she would go out and get some groceries, but when I got home the cupboard was empty and she was lying in front of the TV, asleep. We ate canned soup and peanut butter and jelly sandwiches for supper, then sat together in the family room and watched reruns of *Law and Order*. Abby lay not next to Dawn, as she used to, but at my feet at the end of the sofa.

As glad as I was to have her back home, I found myself feeling anxious as the weekend approached. I'd grown used to those long quiet stretches, with no one but Abby around, and even though it was *too* quiet sometimes, I knew it would take some time for me to adjust to having someone else in the house.

I also had to get used to the sounds of Angry Birds on Dawn's cell phone; she played it almost constantly as she sat in front of the TV, clucking in a level of frustration that puzzled me because, after all, it was only a stupid game. I could tell she was also sending text messages, and when I asked her who they were to, she looked taken aback, as if she hadn't expected me to be savvy enough to understand such a thing. "Nobody. Somebody in New Mexico," she said, but her tone warned me not to pursue the question further.

On Saturday morning I asked her if she wanted to help me run some errands. "You could be my helper," I said as a joke, but when she didn't smile, I remembered that it was Iris, not Dawn, who had taken such pride in being my "helper" at the grocery store when the girls were little. She ran around the aisles retrieving cereals and soups, racing back to present the items proudly for my inspection before plopping them into the cart. Dawn sat in the cart's front, facing me, sometimes whispering to herself with a faraway look on her face. When I asked her if she wanted anything in particular—just to get a response out of her—she shook her head, but often, as we wheeled our bags out of the store, she would start wailing because I hadn't bought the mac-and-cheese she liked or the chocolate milk or the chicken tenders that were, depending on her mood, the only thing she would eat.

Now Dawn just said no thanks, she didn't want to go to the supermarket, she was tired. *From doing what?* I felt like asking, but I didn't.

At Price Chopper, I ran into Pam Furth coming the other way down the Baking Needs aisle. By the time I realized, it was too late to turn around and pretend I hadn't seen her. I smiled and tried the fake "Hi, how're you doing?" pass-by greeting I had polished and perfected with people I knew less well over the past three years, but of course she wasn't going to let me get away with that.

Leaning toward me over her cart, she said she couldn't help noticing that Dawn had come back home. I said yes, and that I was glad to have her. I tried to move on then, but Pam had positioned herself at such an angle that I couldn't get by. "It doesn't make you nervous?" she said.

"Nervous? Why would it make me nervous?" I knew why she'd asked, but that didn't mean I had to accommodate her nosiness.

Even Pam Furth didn't have the nerve to name what she had referred to obliquely—the fact that, like so many other people in town, she believed Dawn was somehow guilty in the attack against her own parents. I leaned over my own cart, and I could tell she was almost licking her chops at the idea that I might be about to take her into my confidence. Instead I said, "Listen, Cecilia Baugh mentioned something about Emmett being arrested for breaking and entering. That must be disappointing. I thought he was over that phase?" I used "phase" deliberately, because it was Pam's favorite word when referring to her son, even now that he was twenty-one years old.

It was obvious how shocked Pam was to hear that the daughter of her Bunco friend had betrayed her son's latest trouble to me. "That was a trumped-up charge," she said, nearly shouting the words, oblivious to the woman behind her who wanted to get at the chocolate chips. "He had permission to go into that house. From their son. The parents just didn't know it."

"Oh," I said. "Well, I know how hard it is when everybody thinks one thing, but you know the truth is something else." I jiggled my cart to show that I wanted to move on.

She narrowed her eyes as if she understood I was speaking in a code she hadn't cracked yet. Then, when she got what I was saying, she looked at me with a new and different expression, and let me pass. It might have been respect I saw, or sympathy. I couldn't be sure. As I wheeled my bags out of the store a few minutes later, I wondered whether what she'd said *had* been true: that Emmett's arrest was the result of a mistake or miscommunication. He'd stayed out of official trouble the past few years, as far as I knew, but on the other hand, he was still living in his mother's house and didn't appear to be able to hold down any job for very long. His manner and appearance gave the impression that he didn't care about anything except riding his motorcycle. The innocence I remembered from that day in first grade had long disappeared from his face. I understood how Dawn, especially after her history with him, could have believed once that he might be guilty of assaulting Joe and me. And she had an investment in believing it, just as Pam had an investment in believing that her son's arrest had been "trumped up."

After putting my groceries in the car, I went to the hardware store, bought a humidifier, and headed home. One of the employees had loaded the box into the trunk for me, so I hadn't realized how heavy it was, and in trying to lift it out I almost dropped it. Cursing under my breath and keeping the box pressed between my thighs and the car, I tried to calculate the chances of Dawn hearing me if I called. Figuring that she wouldn't, I thought about shoving the box back into the car, but then I worried about breaking something. I craned my neck to look over at Warren's; why couldn't this be one of the times he noticed me in the driveway and came running? But his car was gone.

"I could help you." Emmett's voice startled me, and the sound, along with his sudden appearance behind me when I hadn't heard him approaching, made me jump.

"Oh, God. You scared me."

"Sorry." He didn't actually seem sorry, but then, how would I know? I hadn't had a conversation with him in a long time. He was taller than I remembered; in the past few years, I'd seen him only from a distance or on his motorcycle. His hair was un-combed, his shirt crooked, and he looked as if he might have just gotten out of bed. "Here, I'll do it," he said, reaching for the box. I smelled cigarette smoke on him, and maybe pot, but also the unmistakably sweet aroma of Lucky Charms.

I saw no choice other than to step aside, and in fact, I was grateful for his help. But as I watched him hoist the box out of the car, my eyes fell on the back of his right wrist, where MATT. 7:7 was etched in a black crescent.

I must have gasped, because he looked up surprised and set the box down. "What?"

"Nothing. Just—I didn't know you had a tattoo."

"Oh, that." He gave a small, sheepish smile. "That's old. From when I went through a Jesus phase." He lifted the box again and carried it on his shoulder toward the door. I ran ahead and opened it for him, so he could set the box on the kitchen floor. From the TV room, I heard the sounds of a football game.

"How old?" I asked Emmett.

"Me?" He raised his eyebrows. "Same as her." He jerked a thumb toward the next room, and I knew his mother must have told him about seeing Dawn in the driveway the night she arrived.

"No, I mean the tattoo." Though I tried to hide it, I had to lean against the counter because I felt slightly breathless, even though I hadn't been the one to exert myself on the way in.

"Oh. I don't know. Senior year." Before Dawn went off to col-lege. Before she met Rud Petty. Before someone, who might or might not have had a tattoo, attacked us in our bed.

181

He shifted from one foot to the other. "I could apologize," he said, gesturing again in Dawn's direction. His tone was so low I could barely make out the words.

"For what?" My voice cracked.

He shrugged. "You know. For everything."

Was he really seeking forgiveness for teasing Dawn, for burning down the tree house, for riding his motorcycle too close to Abby and me? Or was it just a way of throwing me off the scent, in case—now that there would be another trial—I had joined with those who believed Rud Petty's conviction had been unjust?

I didn't know how to answer, and I'm not sure I said anything. I expected Dawn to come into the kitchen when she heard me talking to someone, but then I figured she'd seen Emmett through the window and decided to ignore the fact that he had accompanied me in. I thanked him for carrying the box, and he gave me the same two-fingered salute he'd shown me at the mall the night Rud's appeal was announced. This time it reminded me of those old sailor cartoons: *Aye-aye, matey*. More comical than sinister. Still, watching him walk back across the driveway and into his own house, I locked the back door, something I never did during the daytime.

I went into the TV room, where Dawn sat in front of a college football game. She said, "So you let *him* in, but not Cecilia?"

"He was helping me with the humidifier."

"I could have done that."

"Well, you weren't there." I didn't say what I was thinking, which was *You weren't paying attention*. Then I worried that my tone had been too harsh. Nodding at the TV, I said, "I didn't know you were a football fan," and she shrugged.

"There's a lot of things you don't know."

"Like what?" I asked. She shrugged again, switching to the home shopping channel.

I left the room, unpacked the box from the hardware store, and set up the humidifier, taking my time because I knew what my next task would be. I'd had a Bible once, but gave it away after my father was arrested and my mother died. Switching on my computer, I searched for "Matthew 7:7" and found "Ask and it will be given to you; seek and you will find; knock and the door will be opened to you." I remembered the words from going to church as a child. They were familiar; I had probably found them comforting back then.

It didn't seem to me to be something a murderer would choose as his mantra. But then, what would I expect? A pentagram or 666? Some other sign of the devil?

I tried to divert myself from these new thoughts, because I didn't want to acknowledge what they meant. Before having the vision of a tattoo in the bedroom that day, I'd never considered the possibility that it was anyone other than Rud Petty who came into our house that November night. But now I couldn't prevent the series of questions buzzing through my mind almost faster than I could keep up with them.

Why hadn't there been any blood (or any other evidence of such a vicious assault) in Dawn's car, if Rud had driven it back up to our house that night and cracked our heads open? Had Warren Goldman been mistaken, confused by a dose of Ambien, when he said he'd seen her car in the driveway in the early morning hours? If it had been Emmett who broke in and struck us with the mallet, he could have just gone home afterward, cleaned himself up, and gotten rid of his bloody clothing (and any gloves he might have used), at his leisure. Couldn't he? By the time the police made their perfunctory search of his house, based on his flimsy police record, whole days had passed since the attack.

But if it had been Emmett, *why* would he have done it? It didn't seem that Joe refusing to give him a job reference was reason enough, but how could I know what went on in a murderer's mind? I'd always thought that Emmett and I had an understanding, based on the fact that we both knew I hadn't implicated him, as I could have, in the tree house arson. Of course, I had no way of truly knowing if he was grateful to me. Maybe I read into his attitude what I wanted to see. Maybe whatever had motivated him to burn down the tree house was the same thing that sent him into our bedroom that night. Impulse. Misplaced rage. Hatred of Dawn, for whatever reason; maybe he recognized in her the "offness" that reminded him too much of the offness in himself. And maybe, though we'd ended up privately accusing Rud for it, Emmett had been the one responsible for poisoning the dog, too.

For the rest of Saturday I kept myself busy, doing my best to escape the memory of Emmett's tattoo and what it triggered inside me. With Dawn still ensconced on the couch in front of the TV, I filled a bag with old clothes for Goodwill and asked her if she had anything she wanted to donate, but she said no. Standing in front of the hall closet, seeing the leather jacket she'd given me, I was tempted to put it in the bag, too. But I decided not to, because I didn't want to hurt her feelings.

Passing by Iris's old bedroom, the one Dawn was using now, I hesitated, wanting to look inside. If the door had been pulled shut, I would not have entered. As it was, it stood a few inches ajar, so telling myself that Dawn would not have left it that way if she didn't mind it being opened, I pushed it aside slightly and

184

held in the exclamation I felt rise in my throat, in case she could have heard me from downstairs.

Everything of Iris's was gone. Or, rather, it had been shoved into the closet, which I could see because it contained so much stuff that the closet door wouldn't shut; moving into the room, I saw that all the clothes, jewelry, photographs, and other mementoes Iris had left behind when she went off to college, and still not reclaimed, had been dumped anywhere they would fit (or not fit, as it turned out)—the closet first, and then under the bed.

The shelf above the window, which had contained Iris's athletic awards, was bare except for the sole trophy Dawn had received in her lifetime: the one for entering a single race on her fifth-grade Field Day. PROUD PARTICIPANT, the trophy's plate said, under the gold-colored plastic figure of a runner in midstride. All the kids had received them, which Joe thought was absurd. I told him it was supposed to help with their self-esteem. He said, "Nobody feels good about getting an award they don't deserve." Dawn's race required her to run seventy-five yards with an egg balanced on a spoon. Of course she dropped it a few feet from the starting line. Cecilia Baugh won all the sprints.

On top of the anxiety I felt in the wake of seeing Emmett's tattoo, the memory of that egg-and-spoon race distressed me as much if not more than the fact that Dawn had dismantled her sister's once-sacred space with such apparent indifference, such disregard.

I went back downstairs and waited until a commercial came on, then said carefully, "You didn't need to throw Iris's things all over the room like that."

"They're not all over the room." She said it as if she'd known she'd have to correct me on this and had practiced her answer. "Besides, anything that's still here, she doesn't want. Right?"

185

Of course this wasn't necessarily true, but I didn't see how it would do any good for me to say so. I held my tongue and asked if she wanted to take a walk with Abby and me. Dawn said it was too cold outside, and reminded me that she was used to the heat of the desert. I found myself on the verge of apologizing for the weather, until I realized how ridiculous that was.

She didn't leave the house the entire weekend, and complained about the shocks we both still kept getting: "That humidifier isn't doing a goddamn thing." She didn't bring up the graffiti on her car, either, or what she was going to do about it. I averted my eyes from the word *killer* every time I took Abby out.

She slept late her first few days home, but on Monday morning she came down as I was eating my cereal and sat across from me at the table. I told her to pour herself a bowl, but she said she wasn't hungry. When I finished and got up, she said she'd changed her mind, and I realized she wanted me to serve her. Joe would have told her to get her own breakfast, but I figured it was no big deal to throw some milk and cereal in a bowl. Still, it would have been nice to receive a thank-you.

I looked out to the driveway and the defaced car. "That paint isn't going to come off by itself, you know," I said. I had meant to conceal my annoyance, but it came out in my voice.

"I know." Dawn got up from the table, leaving her empty bowl at her place, and shambled back upstairs.

Exasperated, I went out and began wiping at the spray-painted word with an old towel dipped in nail polish remover. I was making some headway, but not much, when I heard Warren Goldman's door open, and he crossed the street carrying a stained rag and a container labeled RUBBING COMPOUND in Magic Marker. He wore flannel pajama bottoms and a parka, and his hair hadn't

186

been combed. "I've been waiting for somebody to do something with this," he said, pushing his glasses up straighter on his face. "I didn't want to impose myself. But this stuff should do the trick." Stepping back, I watched as he ran his rag in a circular motion, pressing hard into the car. The blue paint began to come off, and I heard myself saying "Thank God" under my breath.

"Wait!" The back door slammed, and Dawn bolted out of the house with uncharacteristic speed. She hadn't bothered to put anything on over her nightclothes, a pair of sweatpants and a tee-shirt that said I'M WITH MUGGLE, left over from her infatuation with the Harry Potter series; besides *Twilight*, they were the only books I ever saw her read that hadn't been assigned by a teacher. "Stop! What are you doing?"

Warren halted in his rubbing motion and took the rag away. He'd managed to erase the first three letters, so that LER! was all that remained. "Just thought I might be able to help," he said, stepping away from the car and giving her a smile that made me remember how he had always gone out of his way to be nice to Dawn, ever since he and his family moved into the neighborhood when she was two. It might have been because Warren and Maxine's son, Sam, had been born with only three fingers on his left hand, which caused him to be mocked and ostracized by kids like Emmett Furth. I think Dawn's lazy eye always made Warren feel sympathy toward her.

In fact, when she was about nine or ten, Dawn developed a downright crush on Warren. She told us as much one Saturday morning, looking out the window as he washed his car. "I like his curly hair," she told us, looking pointedly at Joe, whose own hair—what he had left of it—was straight and wispy. In fact, it would not be going too far to say that his style was pure comb-over.

187

"Isn't Sam the one you're supposed to have a crush on?" I said.

"Sam's weird," she said, dismissing him with a wave of her cereal spoon. Joe and I looked at each other, and I knew what we were both thinking, though of course we would not say it: *But Dawn, you're weird, too.*

Whatever positive feelings Dawn had once held for Warren were not in evidence now. Probably, I thought, it was because Warren had testified at Rud's trial about seeing Dawn's Nova parked in our driveway the night of the attack. "I don't need your help," she said to him with a bitter tone in her voice, "and be careful with my car. It's a Corvette, you know."

I was glad to see that though Warren wanted to smile, he held it back. "Yes, I know," he said, making sure to survey the car with an appreciative eye. "It's a beaut." After a moment during which none of us spoke, he said, "That's why I thought it would look better if we cleaned it up. You think?" After another moment, Dawn nodded, then turned to head into the house.

"Say thank you," I called after her, as I'd done when she was a toddler. And as she'd done back then, she said the words half sincerely, without looking at the person they were directed to.

Warren set back to his task, and I told him I was sorry.

"No need to apologize, Hanna." He rubbed a few more minutes, his breath coming out in white ribbons of exertion. "You didn't mention Dawn was coming home," he said then, and I remembered our conversation the day the reporters had come to get my reaction to Rud Petty's appeal.

"I didn't know. It was kind of sudden."

"Ah. Well, that explains it." He was almost finished. I could see only the faintest trace of the original blue now, and nothing of the ugly word that had been sprayed across the door. He was sweating; drops slid down the sides of his face. "We should give it a wax at some point, but that should do it," he said, and impulsively, gratefully, I reached up to hug him and kissed one of his damp cheeks. He looked surprised, but then broke into a grin I hadn't remembered seeing since before Maxine died. "I should have offered my services sooner," he said, and we both blushed.

"I can't tell you how much I appreciate this. How much *we* do—both Dawn and me." I blushed some more, thinking I'd made a fool out of myself with that last part, considering the way Dawn had acted toward him. But if Warren was thinking the same thing, he didn't show it.

"Well, I've had some experience. When Maxine went to her protests, she sometimes came back to find her car had been—decorated." He smiled, perhaps remembering some particular message his wife had driven home from some rally. As long as I'd known her as a neighbor, Maxine had been an activist. I had a sudden vision of her setting off for one of her demonstrations against the invasion in Iraq: a slightly squat, round woman with her silver curls tucked under a red beret, waiting on the porch to get picked up by fellow sympathizers and driven off to Syracuse or New Paltz or Plattsburgh, where they would lock arms at busy intersections and chant "U.S. Out Now!" She always brought a tambourine to bang for good measure.

I told Warren I wanted to invite him in for coffee but that I had to get to work. He said of course, he'd take a rain check, and we both turned away. But then I heard him turn back and add, as if it were an afterthought, "So what are you going to be?"

Even now, it's hard for me to describe my reaction to this. Of course I heard the words, but I didn't understand them for another few seconds. I felt to the center of my being that he had asked me a profound question I should be able to answer. But I had no idea how.

"I'm sorry—what?" I said, my lips fumbling even those few syllables.

He seemed to recognize the anxiety his question had provoked, and he raised a hand to indicate that he hadn't intended to touch a nerve. "Halloween," he said, waving vaguely in the direction of the Furths' front stoop, where Emmett had hung a mannequin by a noose. The figure wore a white shirt covered in fake blood and a Hannibal Lecter mask. The first time I'd walked to the driveway and seen it out of the corner of my eye, I cried out and stepped back before realizing the person was a fake. "I was just asking what you were going to be for Halloween," Warren elaborated, when I didn't show any hint that I grasped what he was saying. "It's a stupid question at our age, I know. I was just trying to be cute." He smiled and blushed again.

"Oh. That's today? I didn't even realize." It was true; since Dawn's arrival, I'd lost track of the dates. Warren had made it almost back to his porch when I called, "Thanks!" after him, and he raised his hand again in a wave without turning around to look at me. I'd made a fool of myself again.

I was unprepared. At the clinic, I was the one who'd originally suggested that everyone in the office wear some form of costume on Halloween, even the doctors. I remember the year Bob Toussaint came in dressed as a pirate and made the mistake of using his fake hook to lift a stethoscope to a three-year-old girl's chest. It took me fifteen minutes to calm her down, but even after Bob took the hook off, she wouldn't let him near her—we had to call in one of the female interns, who was dressed as Snow White, instead.

I stopped at the drugstore to see what they had left in the

190

way of costumes. It was slim pickings, but I managed to find a cheap-looking tiara and a blond wig, and when I got to the office I fashioned a wand out of tongue depressors taped together with aluminum foil. All morning I went around saying to people, "Your wish is my command."

"It's good to see you back in the spirit, Hanna," Francine said. She had to keep reaching up to adjust the moose ears over her head. "Hey, how's that plant doing?" When I looked at her blankly, she said, "The one you were so sure was worth saving?" I realized she was referring to the ficus I'd picked up from the trash the day Ken Thornburgh came to tell me that Rud Petty had won a new trial.

Once I'd brought the plant in that day and set it down in the dining room, which was hardly ever used, I forgot about it completely. "Mommy, this plant has had it," Dawn said the day after she moved in. She picked it up and laughed a little to show me how bad it looked. "Could it *be* any deader?"

"Just throw it away, would you?" I said, and she carried it out to the trash barrel in the garage. I didn't want to look at it, remembering how I'd told Francine I would bring it back to life. That used to be my specialty, when I had my garden—my friend Claire always said that if my thumb were any greener, I'd be a Martian.

I didn't feel up to telling Francine the truth. "Still working on it," I said.

Just before lunch, I did a double take when I saw who was waiting for me in the clinic's examining room: Gail Nazarian. "What, are you stalking me now?" I said, hoping she'd take it as the joke I halfway intended.

To my relief, she smiled—only slightly, but it was more than I'd ever seen her smile before. "That's a good look for you," she said, gesturing at the tiara on my head. "'Uneasy lies the head that

191

wears the crown,'" she added, and I couldn't tell if she was showing off or trying to say something to me. When I responded by pulling off the tiara and throwing it on a chair, she sighed and said, "I do have a medical reason to be here. But yes, I'm trying to kill two birds."

I looked at her closely, without wanting to let on that I was doing so. Her face appeared as unreadable as ever; I saw no signs of illness or distress. "What can we do for you?" I asked.

"It's a urinary tract infection. I get them sometimes. I just need a script."

"You couldn't call your own doctor?"

She shrugged. "Like I said, I had another reason to come."

"Okay," I said, pretending to make a note so I wouldn't have to look at her. "Shoot."

"First, I wanted to say how happy I was to hear you're going to testify," she said. "I wanted to make sure you knew that. And we want to help you, if we can." I guessed that by *we* she meant the people in her office—who, I remembered, could find the tooth fairy if they wanted to.

"How?" I asked. From her briefcase, she pulled a folder and held it out. I didn't want to take it, but I also felt as if I had no choice. "What's this?"

"It's a copy of the interview police did with Dawn when they brought her in the morning after the attack. After they took her to the hospital, once they knew you'd survived the surgery." She hesitated. "It's not easy reading. But I thought it might nudge your memory."

"I don't see why it would." Without looking down at it, I set the folder on the counter behind me.

"Now the second thing: I don't understand why you didn't tell me your daughter was home." Those bird eyes bored into me; I felt them even when I looked away, realizing how similar this conversation was to the one I'd had with Cecilia on our doorstep the night of Dawn's return. I also understood suddenly that Cecilia, trying to create the best news story possible, must have been the one to contact Gail to tell her that Dawn was back. "You know I want to talk to her."

"Why? She doesn't have any more information than she did before." For a moment, because I missed it so badly, I was tempted to feel the kind of intimacy I used to share with Claire when we went for our Saturday morning walks with the dogs and talked about the things we told only each other and no one else. But then I remembered that Gail was a prosecutor, not my friend, and where I had been leaning toward her, I drew myself back.

She gave me a long look, and since I knew I was being tested, I made sure to hold my ground, even though I was squirming inside. *But why?* I asked myself. *It's the truth.*

"And I still don't understand why you don't just call me when you want to say something," I told her, hoping to deflect the intensity of her gaze, "instead of coming in person."

"I guess I have an inflated sense of my own persuasive powers." She gave a rueful smile.

"And if it does have to be in person, why here, instead of my house, like last time?"

The smile vanished so fast it made me breathless. "I didn't want to show up when Dawn was around. Mrs. Schutt, we have reason to believe you might be in danger."

"From Dawn?" I laughed. "That's ridiculous."

"From Rud Petty." She slid awkwardly off the examining table and went over to her briefcase. "I can show you the cell phone

193

records, if you want. He's been in touch with one of his cousins, a real lowlife who's already been in and out of jail twice and he's not even twenty."

"I don't want to see whatever you have there."

She must have heard how much I meant it, because she put the briefcase down. "We think he might be using the cousin to talk to Dawn."

"Of course he isn't. Why would he be talking to Dawn?" I could tell that my voice was scaling upward and louder, but didn't seem to be able to rein it in. "Even if *he* wanted to do that, she doesn't want to talk to him. She's finished with all that. She's trying to start over."

Gail Nazarian gave me a dubious look. "Did you tell her you were planning to testify in the new trial?"

"I mentioned I was trying to remember what happened." She made a face as if to say, *See?* "Why?"

"Because that would be information we don't want getting back to Petty. Especially before you've actually remembered anything."

My mouth betrayed me; I could feel it forming words I didn't want or intend to speak.

"What?" she said, noticing. Her voice took on an excited edge. "You *have* remembered?"

I shook my head, in part because it had begun to hurt, as it always did when I felt a conflict brewing inside.

"Then what?" She wasn't going to let it go; it was probably one of the reasons she'd made it so far as a prosecutor.

I hesitated. "You're sure Rud Petty did it, right?"

"Of course we're sure. Why would you ask me that?"

"I just wondered if you really had everything you needed to clear Emmett Furth."

The bird eyes widened. "You'd better tell me what you're talking about."

I told her about the memory I'd had in the bedroom, and about seeing Emmett's tattoo when he helped me carry the box in over the weekend.

"You're sure the arm had a tattoo on it? The arm from that night?" she asked, and I said I was, even though I wasn't, because she seemed skeptical of what I was saying. Even though I felt skeptical myself, I didn't like that she doubted me.

"Okay. Well, thanks. That's useful," she said, not sounding at all as if she meant it.

"Are you going to follow up?"

"Sure. That's my job." I could tell she was less than thrilled by my report; she'd gotten her hopes up, I'm sure, that I remembered Rud Petty committing the crime.

To change the subject, I asked, "Do you really have a UTI, or are you making it up?"

"It feels better now. Probably just a false alarm." She put her blazer on slowly, giving me a suspicious look, and said she wanted me to come down to her office sometime soon, preferably later in the week, to discuss my testimony.

Then she added that if I wanted, her office could offer me protection.

"I don't need you to protect me." I opened the door and had to stop myself from pushing her out. When she was gone I sat down hard, crushing the fake crown. Then I got up and carried the folder she'd given me out to the shredder behind Francine's desk, intending to destroy whatever was in it, but at the last minute I withdrew the papers from the machine and stuck the whole folder into the bottom of my bag.

The Truth Is Out There

When I got home expecting to find Dawn in front of the TV, I was surprised to see her standing at the stove, cooking something I couldn't identify. "I'm making Tuna Helper," she said, with far more pride than should ever be attached to that sentence.

"I thought we were out of tuna." I leaned over to pet Abby, who always perked up when I walked in the door.

"We are. I'm just making the Helper." Dawn laughed, and her hyper cheeriness made me feel wary.

I asked, "Have you been in touch with Rud Petty?"

Her too-big smile collapsed. "Why would you ask me a thing like that?"

"You haven't had any contact with him since the trial, right?" I didn't know if she would hear, as I did, that I was begging her to convince me.

Her lips were as pale as her face. "I can't believe you would even ask me that, Mommy." She put a hand up to her chest as if something hurt her there. "I mean, what are you saying?"

I opened my mouth and then closed it again without speaking. I was hesitant to mention what Gail Nazarian had told me about Rud Petty being found with a cell phone, or about her cautionary visit to the clinic that day. "I don't know," I faltered. "You were just so close—back then."

"Well, of course we were. I loved him." Though she stirred the noodles vigorously, I didn't necessarily detect any anger in it. "But how could I possibly be in touch with him? I've been two thousand miles away." She set the spoon down straight on the counter. If Joe had been there, he would have told her to use a napkin. "Besides that, why would I *want* to?"

"I meant by phone," I told her, not answering the second part of her question.

"People in jail don't get phones."

"A pay phone, I mean. Can't they do that?"

"How am I supposed to know what goes on in *jail*?" If her tone had been indignant, I would have been tempted to think she was feeling defensive. Instead, she just sounded puzzled about why I would be asking her these things.

We sat down to the noodly glop, and I pretended to like how it tasted. I took a long sip of water and decided I might as well ask the other question that had been on my mind. "What about Cecilia?"

"What about her?"

I could read in her face the answer to my question. "You called her, didn't you?"

"No." She leaned back and glanced away from me, and anyone could have seen that she was lying.

"Dawn."

That was all it took, my murmuring her name, for her to

implode the way I'd witnessed so often over the years, the crumpling-up of her reddening face before tears blasted out of her eyes as if they had a volition of their own. She nodded violently, thrusting her hands up to her face. "I'm sorry! But you don't understand. She's changed, Mommy."

"Just tell me you didn't let her into the house, after I specifically asked you not to." I kept my voice as steady as possible.

Dawn shook her head with so much vigor her hair whirled around her head. "No. I would never have done that, knowing how you felt. I met her at Caprice. We had scones and lattes. It was nice, like we were friends or something." The wistfulness in her voice threatened to scrape another layer of hardness from my heart, but I didn't let it.

I set my fork down, hoping to give the impression that I was resting between bites rather than that I found the dinner inedible. "She can't be trusted."

"God, Mommy. All you ever do is see the worst in people." Dawn rose abruptly and clattered her plate into the sink. I was so taken aback—it was so unlike the Dawn I had always known for her to say something like that to me, let alone throw down a plate—that I didn't manage to respond before she flounced into the family room, where I heard her flipping through TV channels and playing Angry Birds on her phone in a way that would have driven Joe crazy. I was used to it by now.

When the doorbell rang a few minutes later, I picked up the bag of peanut butter cups I'd bought at the drugstore that morning. I brushed my hair over to hide my face as much as possible (the last thing I wanted was to scare away some little kid) and thought, too late, that I should have bought a pretty mask in case somebody rang the bell seeking candy.

As it turned out, I needn't have worried. Standing there were not any children I didn't recognize, but Iris and Josie, whose sturdy little torso was wrapped in a cube of yellow foam rubber. "Trick or treat," Iris said, nudging Josie, who turned suddenly shy and concealed herself behind her mother's leg.

"What are you doing here?" Hearing the question land in the air between us, I recognized how ungracious it sounded. But as glad as I was to see them, my heart froze in anticipation of the confrontation that was no doubt about to take place.

"Nice to see you, too, Mom. Josie wanted to show you her costume."

"Oh. Good! It's a—is she cheese?" My brain seemed to have frozen, too. I had no idea what my granddaughter was supposed to be.

"No. SpongeBob." Iris carried Josie beyond me into the living room, then set her down and began shrugging off her jacket. When she saw that I looked at her blankly, she added, "Square-Pants?"

Now I saw that the block of yellow encasing my granddaughter showed a face of blue googly eyes and a pair of buck teeth hanging down from a grin, and I vaguely remembered watching the cartoon with Josie once when I was babysitting.

"SpongeBob—of course you are!" I picked her up so that she could go through her routine of feeling my face, but she must have sensed the tension in my body as I held her, and for once she didn't lift her hands.

I could tell that Iris was a little angry and a little hurt, on her own behalf and Josie's, at my lukewarm reception. "You could at least pretend to be excited. We drove all this way." She wore a stained Snoopy sweatshirt over a sloppy pair of jeans. Looking at her, I wondered if she'd gained even more weight in the short time since I'd seen her last.

"I *am* excited. I'm just surprised, that's all." I set Josie down again and tried desperately to think of a way to prevent my daughters from facing each other. "Do you want to go out trick-or-treating on my street?" I asked, motioning to the door they had just entered and reaching in the closet for my own coat, but it was too late as I heard Dawn coming in from the other room.

Josie had been in the middle of reaching for the bag of candy I'd set down on the table, but she paused abruptly at this new person's arrival on the scene. It almost looked to me as if she noticed a resemblance between her mother and the stranger, though it was rare for anyone to take them for sisters without knowing it was the case.

Before I could offer any words of preparation, Iris said, "You've got to be fucking kidding me. What the fuck is this?" It was a measure of her shock and consternation that she said the word twice in front of Josie.

"I was going to tell you," I said, feeling myself retreat from the force of her spit-out ire.

"Oh, my God." Dawn had stopped short when she realized who it was she'd heard me talking to, but now she moved closer to peer at Iris with her eyes slit, as if she didn't trust what she saw before her. "You got *fat*." Her voice contained a mix of alarm and fascination.

"Shut up." Iris reached for a peanut butter cup and opened the package with a savage rip. I thought she might just stuff it whole into her mouth, but instead she seemed to catch herself at the last moment, and handed it down to Josie instead.

"Is there any way," I said weakly to both my daughters, "that this could be not awful?"

"I don't see how," Iris said. "Considering she"—she hesitated, glancing down at Josie, and tried to rein in her voice—"considering she's responsible for Dad's death. And would have been responsible for yours, too, Mom. I don't understand how you can even let her inside this house."

"I didn't kill anybody," Dawn said, and I saw her shoulders form the familiar slump she had always worn when around her pretty sister.

"Somebody got killed?" Josie's mouth opened to show half-chewed chocolate.

Iris glared at Dawn. "Never mind," she told Josie. "We don't listen to her."

Dawn had knelt to bring herself to eye level with her niece, whom she was seeing for the first time. "You must be Josephine," she said softly. "I'm your Aunt Dawnie." Josie's eyes furrowed with suspicion, and it pained me to realize that Iris might never even have told her daughter that she had an aunt. If she had, she would not have used the name Dawnie, which I'd never heard before. "Did your mother ever teach you to play We're the Same Person? Want me to show you how?" She put her hand out toward Josie's, and for a moment it seemed that my granddaughter might reach out, too.

"Hey." Iris yanked Josie back within her reach. "You"—she pointed at her sister—"stay away from my kid."

Well, I thought, *at least this time it's out in the open.* The last time my girls had been in a room together was a year and a half earlier, when I'd had surgery to relieve the pressure on my brain caused by the blunt-force trauma in the attack. Iris left Josie at home with Archie for a weekend while she made the trip to Albany for my operation and to make sure I got settled in at home afterward.

Without telling us beforehand, Dawn flew in from New Mexico just for the day, having booked a return flight for that same night. She hadn't been in touch with either Iris or me, but she said Peter Cifforelli had informed her that I was having the operation, and she wanted to be there. When she appeared in my room at the hospital after the surgery, I thought Iris might walk over and strangle her. Instead she said to her sister, "You have one hell of a nerve," and left the room. I could tell she wanted to give Dawn a shove on the way out, and stopped herself only because she knew it would upset me.

That day, Dawn struck me as paler than usual, and unhealthy, and I was about to ask her about it when she reached down, grabbed my hand, and held it up to her face. "Iris still thinks I'm guilty, doesn't she?" she murmured.

My chest puckered from the inside, and I tried to tell her it wasn't true. But we both knew I was lying. Dawn gave me a quiet little smile and said, "It's all right. Someday she'll know better." I tried to apologize for the way Iris had acted, but Dawn just told me to "Ssh, ssh, Mommy," and she even stroked my forehead, the way I used to do to them when they were children. Then she asked about Abby, and I told her the dog was doing okay. But when I tried to elaborate, she held a hand up to interrupt me. "I can't hear about what's wrong with her," she said. "It's too painful." It took me a moment to comprehend what she'd said. Touching the gauze at my temples, I was confused, because a moment earlier I'd felt so hurt on *her* behalf, but now I wanted to say, *More painful than the fact that I'm lying here with this bandage on my head?* The

202

phrase Ding-Dong Dawn sang through my mind, and the words of Dawn's first-grade teacher came back to me in an unwelcome flash: *It just seems like there's something missing.*

She stayed at the hospital for an hour or so, sitting beside me, neither of us talking much, and then she said that for the sake of peace in the family, she thought she should leave. She was scheduled to take a plane back to Santa Fe in a few hours.

"But it's such a short visit," I said. I was tired and wanted nothing more than to sleep, but I thought I should at least pretend to object.

It was fine, Dawn said—she'd just wanted to make sure I was okay. Of course, I was anything but okay, but I knew what she meant, and I let it go. She left before Iris came back, and nothing was said about the fact that she had been there.

Since I'd wished more than anything, growing up, that I had a sibling—especially a sister—I'd always regretted that my girls stopped being close around the time Dawn's eye problem was diagnosed. Once they both moved out of the house, I thought they might find their old connection again as adults. But Rud Petty had made that impossible.

Standing in the living room now, I hoped that I might still have some authority when it came to the two of them. "Iris, Dawn came home because she's sorry about what happened. And I invited her." I did my best to sound convincing, but I could see the flare in Iris's nostrils as I spoke, and knew what I'd said hadn't been enough. "She wants to—what do you call it?—make amends."

Iris snorted. "Amends, right." She ventured closer to her sister, and I was surprised to see that Dawn managed to hold her ground without flinching. "How do you think you're going to do that?"

At the end of her question the words trailed off, and she leaned more closely to study her sister's face. "Your eye's pointing out again," she said, and though I wanted to believe it was sympathy I heard in her voice, I was afraid it was only the same fascination Dawn had felt in calling Iris fat—with maybe a little triumph thrown in.

I had explicitly avoided asking Dawn about her eye since she'd been home, even though of course I'd noticed the same thing Iris was seeing now. The "lazy" eye, operated on seven years earlier, was reverting to its amblyopic state. I held my breath, wondering how Dawn would answer.

"It is not," she said, in a tone I tried not to recognize as hatred. "What's wrong with you people? My eye got fixed. Or did you forget that?" She made a dismissive sound between her lips, as if to say she wouldn't have expected anything else of us.

Iris and I looked at each other. I begged her with my expression to let it drop, but when she turned back to Dawn, I knew there would be no such luck. "I don't know what planet you're living on," she said to her sister, "or what mirror you're looking in, but that eye"—she held a finger up to Dawn's face—"is pointing out again. Not as bad as it used to, but it's on its way."

"You're just saying that because I said you were fat," Dawn said, then pounded up the stairs to her bedroom and slammed the door.

The sound made Josie run to her mother, and Iris drew her up in the best hug she could manage for a child wrapped in foam rubber. Then she turned to me. "How *could* you?"

"I was going to tell you when I came out last time," I murmured. "But you were talking about moving to California, and that hurt."

"But I asked you to come with us!"

"And now you know why I can't."

"The idea of the two of you in this house together makes me physically sick." Without even seeming to realize, Iris ate one of the peanut butter cups Josie had opened, then reached for another before swallowing the first. I looked away from the smears around her mouth as she spoke. "It's not safe."

"Of course it is. We're fine." My voice trembled.

"Mom, I'm worried about you."

"There's nothing to worry about." I paused, hearing Dawn stomp out of her bedroom and into the upstairs bathroom. "It would probably be best if you take Josie and..." I trailed off before saying *leave*, but it was clear Iris got the message. For a moment, it looked as if she might cry, but then she allowed anger to fill that space. She scooped up Josie and muttered, "This isn't over," as she carried her daughter out to the car.

Only a minute or two passed between their departure and the sound of Dawn clomping back downstairs. She had on a pair of pajamas Joe and I had given her one Christmas, years ago, when she was obsessed with the TV program *The X-Files*. She'd discovered the show when she was in middle school, and promptly began covering the walls of her room with posters related to aliens and the paranormal. "This is foolishness," Joe said to me one night, when he'd tried to get Dawn's attention during a commercial and she shushed him. "Hanna, we can't let her start believing this stuff."

"She's just having fun," I told him. "Shouldn't we be glad she has something to think about, besides how unhappy she is about her eye?" This was only a few months after he'd originally said no to the surgery, so he gave in without too much argument. What I didn't tell Joe (because I knew he'd consider it silly) was that I remembered my own days as a *Star Trek* worshiper, walking around giving the Vulcan salute to everyone, especially my father when I wanted to annoy him. I practiced the salute so much back then that I still find my fingers separating into that formation sometimes, all these years later; my brain trauma may have taken away the ability to add numbers, but the Vulcan salute remains intact.

THE TRUTH IS OUT THERE was printed across the front of Dawn's pajama top, and there was a small rip in the word *truth*. I expected her to say something about meeting her niece for the first time, but instead, when she plopped down next to me on the couch, she asked, "You don't think what Iris said is true, do you?"

I was startled she would bring it up so abruptly, when we had both been so careful to avoid talking about the attack in any kind of a direct way. "Of course not," I told her, though as I recall it took everything in me not to look away from her as I said it. "What are you talking about? I know you had nothing to do with that night."

"No," she said, shaking her head a little impatiently, as if *that night* were of no interest to her. "I don't mean that. I mean what she said about my eye. It's not really going out again, is it?"

I hesitated without wanting to let her see it. Her eye was indeed straying again; there was no doubt about it. But I saw that she needed me to tell her it was hardly noticeable, so I did. In my mind, I reasoned that she must know the answer—she looked in the mirror every day—but that for some reason, at that moment, she needed the comfort and relief of hearing from me that it wasn't so bad.

She pushed her hair away from her face, another old gesture that stirred a wave of nostalgia in me, and displayed the smile I hadn't seen in many years; probably I hadn't seen it, in fact, since she became a teenager. It was the smile I remembered most vividly from bath time when she was a child. Up until we rejected her bid for surgery before she began middle school, Dawn's favorite part of the day was after dinner and before bed, when she and I secluded ourselves in the bathroom the girls shared and spent an hour or more together, talking about things that were of no importance and, especially as she got older, about things that were. She was always careful to signal me when she wanted to bring up something more substantive than the sweet but relatively directionless chatter we often exchanged. "Can we have one of our discussions, Mom?" she'd ask, as I laid her pajamas on the bed while the bath water ran. When she was settled in the tub, she began talking, usually about her eyes.

"Why doesn't Daddy want me to get better?" she asked once, and I said, "Oh, honey, he does—it's just that he doesn't believe the operation is the best way to go about it."

The smile came when she stepped out of the tub, into the towel I held open for her, and looked up at me to say, "You're my favorite mother."

"I'm your *only* mother," I'd say, rubbing her wet hair and thinking—for some reason I never figured out—that I shouldn't let her know how good her words made me feel. Looking back, I realize it was superstition: I was afraid that if I showed her how much her love meant to me, she'd decide she didn't want to give it anymore.

Sitting with my coffee the next morning, Dawn still asleep, I was wondering if it was too early to call and apologize to Iris when my own phone rang. It was Peter Cifforelli, telling me that Iris had

207

contacted him to find out what the requirements would be for her to obtain a guardianship.

"Guardianship of who?" I asked, and when Peter didn't answer, I realized what he was saying. "Oh, my God! You can't be serious."

"She's concerned. She told me what happened at your house last night."

"What does she think that will accomplish?"

"I don't know. You'd have to ask her. Anyway, I told her you're not nearly far gone enough. I told her to call me when you take your clothes off at Price Chopper or stir your soup with the broom handle, that kind of thing."

He spoke of it lightly to make me feel better, but I didn't laugh. I thanked him, hung up, and dialed Iris. I could tell she was eating something, and although I had no way of knowing, I assumed it was some of Josie's Halloween candy from the night before. "Peter just called me. What do you think you're doing, asking him a question like that?"

"Mom, calm down." Of course, this only inflamed me further. "You're not making good decisions for yourself. Your focus needs to be on remembering what happened that night, and getting ready to testify."

"I *told* you I'm going to!"

There was a pause on the other end before she swallowed. "Gail Nazarian called me. She told me about the cell phone they found on Rud Petty. If you don't look out for yourself, somebody else has to."

"I don't need you to look out for me, Iris." I felt tempted to tell her my suspicions about Emmett, but I knew it would only make her more certain that I wasn't in my right mind.

"I think you do." Another wrapper got ripped open on the

other end of the line. "Listen, do you want to come out here and stay with us for a while? Josie would love it. So would I. And you could even come to San Francisco with all of us for Thanksgiving."

She had to know I would turn her down, and I felt sorry about the distress I heard in her voice. I told her I appreciated her concern, but that I was fine, and as I hung up I heard the sound of her exasperation. I knew I hadn't bought much time between now and whatever she would try next, but at least it was something.

My hands shaking, I rummaged through the junk drawer to find Gail Nazarian's phone number. It was seven thirty in the morning. "Don't you ever sleep?" I asked her when she picked up. Before she could answer, I said, "I don't want you calling my daughter again. She's off-limits to you."

"You don't get to decide that," she said.

"Look, I told you about Emmett Furth and the tattoo. I'm doing my best to be able to testify. So why are you making my life so difficult?"

"You won't do us any good if you're not available."

"What's that supposed to mean?" But I knew what she was saying. "Nothing's going to happen to me."

At that moment, Dawn stepped into the room, and the sight of her startled me so much that I hung up without saying anything further into the phone.

"Who was that so early?" she asked.

"Nobody. Iris," I said, feeling flustered because I sensed she'd been listening on the stairs before appearing in the kitchen.

"It didn't sound like her." Dawn went over to the cupboard and pulled out the Cap'n Crunch, which was all she would ever eat for breakfast despite my efforts to feed her something better.

"Who else would I be talking to at this hour?"

"I don't know." She ate noisily, and I looked away from the mouthful of cereal and milk. "I hope you don't think you have to keep any secrets from me, Mommy. You know that, right?"

"I'm not keeping any secrets." But my voice shook, and I knew it was giving me away.

I told her I had to be at work early, though that wasn't true, either. I did my best to ignore the strange, wide grin she gave me as I left the house, trying to figure out when I had begun feeling like a person who had something to hide.

Black Friday

I t wasn't just the fact that Iris had sought guardianship information that upset me about our call. The mention of Thanksgiving triggered the dismay I'd felt with each of the past two Novembers, when the anniversary looming at the end of the month had caused a fresh spout of grief in me as soon as I felt autumn's chill.

The first year, I'd hoped that Iris and Archie would spend Thanksgiving with me, but the holiday coincided with a big family reunion on his side, and I could see how difficult the conflict was for Iris, so in the end I told her not to worry about it, I'd find something to do, I'd be fine. And I *was* fine, or as close to fine as I could be: I spent the day with my friend Trudie, from Tough Birds, and we didn't make a big deal about it, because I had no inclination to celebrate and because, since she was British, the holiday meant nothing to her. We went to one movie in the late morning, ate turkey sandwiches at our favorite deli, then hit another movie in the afternoon. By evening, I had managed to distract myself from the anniversary, my eyes were glazed over from so much food and screen-gazing, and what I ended up being thankful for was the fact that it was then easy to fall asleep. The Thanksgiving after that, we'd done exactly the same thing.

This year, during Dawn's second week home, Trudie took me aside before group began and said she assumed I'd be spending the holiday with my daughter, but if that fell through, she'd be happy to do a movie marathon with me again. I thanked her and told her I probably would have plans, though Dawn and I hadn't even talked about the holiday. The truth was that I had allowed myself to put off thinking about it; I felt paralyzed by the approaching date, and by the memories I did have of the holiday three years before.

A month before the attack, Iris had told Joe and me that she'd be spending Thanksgiving with Archie's family in California. Though I felt disappointed, I knew it was only fair, because some of his relatives hadn't been able to make it to the wedding in the summer. The newlyweds would be guests of honor at a celebratory party out there.

A few days after Iris canceled, Dawn called to tell us she'd been invited to Nashville to meet Rud's parents. At first I felt bereft at the notion that it would only be Joe and me, mainly because it was *always* only Joe and me at the dinner table those days, and it would be hard to make it feel different from any other day.

But shortly after both our daughters notified us they wouldn't be there, Joe came home from work and handed me an envelope. Inside was a reservation confirmation for two nights—Thursday and Friday of Thanksgiving weekend—at a dog-friendly bed-and-breakfast in Vermont. "Oh," I breathed, recognizing immediately that I could think of no better gift he might have made me at that moment. It was the way he could always surprise me, when

I least expected to be surprised—here I'd been figuring that he couldn't have cared less what we did for Thanksgiving, and in the meantime he'd been thinking up something to make us both feel better about the prospect of being separated from our girls on the holiday.

But as it turned out, we never made it to the inn. On Monday of that week, Dawn called and asked if she and Rud could come to our house for the long weekend, after all; plans had fallen through, she said, with his parents in Tennessee. Though she didn't go into detail and seemed not to want me to guess, I hung up with the definite impression that the Petty family had disinvited Rud and his girlfriend guest from their Thanksgiving table. All Dawn murmured to me—nearly in a whisper, as if she didn't really want me to hear—was that in communicating about the visit, Rud and his father had "gotten their wires crossed." At the trial, of course, I learned the truth, which was that Rud's father, Hal Petty—who was not in fact a cardiac surgeon, but a slaughterhouse supervisor—had just been notified by the Mascoma Savings Bank in Lebanon, New Hampshire, that his son had forged his signature on a loan application. Apparently, it had not been the first time. He told his son not to come home that week, and he threatened to call the police. Somehow Rud convinced him not to do this, but he (and, by extension, Dawn) did not have a place to go for the holiday.

When Joe heard that I had canceled our bed-and-breakfast reservation and told Dawn to bring Rud for the weekend, he walked to the window without saying anything, and I could tell he was angry. "I know I should have asked you first," I said. "But you were in a meeting, and I didn't want to lose the deposit you put down."

"It's not about the deposit, Hanna," he said quietly.

"Then what? Aren't you glad Dawn's coming home?"

"Dawn is one thing. Of course I want to see her. But have you completely forgotten what happened at Iris's wedding? The poisoning of the dog?"

In fact, I *had* forgotten. Or maybe *forgotten* isn't the right word. But when he reminded me, I did experience the familiar sensation of *Oh, that's right*.

"We don't know that for sure," I told him. "It could have been Emmett. I don't think we have any choice but to give Rud the benefit of the doubt."

Joe let too long a silence pass between us before he said, "Well, you're going to have to be the nice one. I won't be able to fake it. And don't let him near the dog."

Dawn and Rud were coming on Wednesday, and planned to stay until Saturday; Joe bought four tickets for a production of *Hamlet* in Schenectady on Friday night. When he told me this, I said, "*Hamlet?* Don't you think that's kind of a downer on a holiday?"

He shrugged. "It's a downer anytime."

"You know what I mean," I said, though I couldn't help smiling. "You really think they'll want to go?"

He shrugged again. "I don't really care if they want to go. *I* don't really want to go." I looked at him, baffled, and waited; I knew enough after so many years that he'd tell me, in his own good time, what he meant. "The show is three hours long. That's three hours we don't have to talk to *him*."

"Oh, Joe." That it had come to this—his wanting to just get through the holiday, endure it, with as little discomfort at possible until our daughter and her boyfriend left—made me sadder than I would have been able to articulate. I know it made Joe sad, too, but not enough that he was willing to pretend he liked or trusted Rud, or enjoyed having him in our house.

Dawn and Rud arrived later on Wednesday than they'd told us, which I was beginning to identify as a pattern with them and, when she came home to live, with Dawn alone. Of course, their being late was fine with Joe. I wanted to hold dinner for them, but they hadn't called, and he saw no reason to let our food get cold if they couldn't be considerate enough to let us know they'd be delayed. We ate our share of the lasagna I'd made, and I put the pan back in the oven to keep it warm. Joe suggested watching a movie, but I said we'd only have to interrupt it when they arrived. When they hadn't come by eight o'clock, he persuaded me to pop in the DVD. I could only watch it with half my attention, because I kept expecting to hear a car pull in the driveway at any moment. Since they'd come for Iris's wedding during the summer in Dawn's Nova, I found myself wondering what kind of car Rud had. He only worked in a vet's office, I knew, but Dawn had also told us how well off his family was, so it occurred to me that maybe they had provided him with something expensive and sturdy—a Volvo or an SUV.

When they still hadn't arrived or called by eleven, Joe said he was going to bed. I didn't want them to come home to a sleeping house, but I had to admit that the fact that they hadn't let us know where they were, or when to expect them, was finally annoying me, too—assuming they hadn't had an accident, the prospect of which did worry me some even though it seemed less likely than mere thoughtlessness on their part (*on Rud's part* is how I said it to myself). It took me a while to fall asleep, and I was shocked when I woke up the next morning and realized I hadn't heard anyone come in. Joe was gone from the bed already, and when I pulled aside the curtain, I started when I saw Dawn's Nova parked in its usual place.

I'd slept later than usual. It was almost eight thirty when I went down, having hurriedly thrown on sweatpants and a flannel shirt and run a fast comb through my hair. Dawn and Rud sat at the table holding hands while Joe stood at the stove making eggs and bacon, throwing me a look that said, *It's about time.* Dawn stood to hug me, and I waited for Rud to do the same, but he merely stayed seated and held his face up to receive my kiss on his cheek. Joe watched this with an expression of blatant disbelief. Taking the turkey out of the fridge and beginning to get it ready for roasting, I asked them what time they'd gotten in.

"It was before midnight," Rud said. "I remember thinking we had to make it by then, or the car might turn into a pumpkin." He winked at me, but I pretended I didn't see it. I was on the verge of saying that it had to be later than that because I'd been awake until after twelve thirty, listening for them, but decided there was no point.

"I'm guessing you didn't choose that dog at the shelter because of his watchdog genes," Rud added, as Joe set the eggs down in front of him. "Thanks, Mr. S. I love them runny like that."

"It's a *she*," Joe said, looking at me over Rud's head. I knew what he was thinking: *This guy works in a vet's office, he's met the dog before, what kind of a moron is he?* Along with: *My eggs are* not *runny.*

Dawn, seeming to sense but not picking up on exactly what was passing between us, hurried to join the conversation. "It's just because she knows us that she didn't bark," she told Rud. The truth was that it was because Abby knew *Dawn* that she hadn't barked; if Rud had tried to enter the house on his own, surely she would have let us know.

Or would she? I found myself wondering. She hadn't been quite herself since the day she'd been poisoned. Under the table, Abby put her nose up as if she knew we were talking about her, and Dawn fed her a piece of bacon.

"Your car having trouble again, Rud?" I asked, reaching inside the turkey to dig out the giblets. I hadn't meant it to sound like an accusation, but Dawn took it as one even if Rud didn't.

"What's wrong with our using my car, Mom? Who says it always has to be the man who drives?"

I was surprised by the vehemence of her response. "Of course there's nothing wrong with it, honey. It's just that the Nova isn't the most reliable, that's all. And you're a student, while Rud works full time. So I thought his would probably be in better shape for a longer trip."

They looked at each other. "Mine's kind of loud," Rud said, as if that explained anything, and helped himself to the last three slices of bacon.

"Anyway, Happy Thanksgiving, everyone!" Dawn sent her brightest countenance across the table. "Nobody's said it yet." She looked up at me for help, and I set the giblets aside, washed my hands, and came to join the rest of them for breakfast.

"Yes. Happy Thanksgiving." I kissed the top of her head. "I'm glad you guys could come after all. I mean, I'm sorry it didn't work out at your family's, Rud, but it means we get to have you both for the holiday."

I knew I'd said the wrong thing even before I finished. Rud glared across the table at Dawn, and she said, "What? I didn't tell her anything!"

I rushed to say, "Oh, all I heard is that your parents didn't know you were coming, so they made other plans." It wasn't ex-

217

actly what Dawn had said to me on the phone earlier in the week, and it was the best I could come up with in the moment. Luckily, it seemed to be good enough, and Rud softened as he reached for Dawn's hand.

"Sorry, Kitten," he told her. "Mr. and Mrs. S., thanks for having us on such short notice. I know it isn't easy to just throw together Thanksgiving dinner at the last minute."

"We're glad you could come," I assured him, trying to figure out if I'd imagined the fact that I'd heard him start to say "ain't" before he corrected it to "isn't."

Maybe to make up for the fact that he sensed our misgivings about him, Rud was far more enthusiastic about everything that day than any of it warranted, including the meal. When Dawn asked if he wanted to watch the parade on TV with her, he acted as if it were an opportunity he'd been seeking all his life, settling down next to her on the couch and making a big deal out of every float and badly lip-synched musical act that went by. When Joe saw that I didn't need him as a bolster, he holed up in his study to prepare papers for the Marc Sedgwick embezzlement case, which was scheduled to be adjudicated in January. I would have liked to ask Dawn if she wanted to go for a long walk with me and Abby, but I knew she'd probably invite Rud along, and I felt uncomfortable enough around him, because of what Joe had said about the poison, that I took Abby out by myself as usual, giving her an extra circuit around the brook because she deserved something for the holiday, too.

We sat down to eat at two o'clock. In my own family we'd always said a Swedish grace before supper, but Joe wasn't religious, so we never brought up the girls that way. But as Joe and Dawn and I reached for dishes to begin passing, we saw that Rud had bowed his head, and then he asked permission to say the blessing. I nodded, not letting myself look at Joe. "Dear Lord, thank you for allowing us all to be together on this day we set aside for gratitude," Rud intoned, and then I couldn't help sneaking a glance at Joe, who rolled his eyes at me. "Thank you for bringing Kitten into my life this year, and for the graciousness shown by the Schutt family in inviting me to their table. May we all properly appreciate what you have made possible in our lives, and humbly offer up our gifts to you, our Lord and Savior. Amen." He paused an extra moment after speaking, as if saying a final private prayer.

When it was clear that he was finished, Joe forked some turkey onto his plate and said, "Rud, about this nickname you have for Dawn. *Kitten*. Don't you think that's a little—I don't know. What would you call it, Hanna? Precious?"

I hesitated, not appreciating his having put me on the spot. "It doesn't matter what *I* think, does it? As long as Dawn likes it, it's fine with me." I should have just said my real opinion—that it sounded demeaning and ridiculously out of date. But I hadn't allowed myself to feel convinced, yet, that Joe was right about Rud, and for all I knew, he'd end up in the family. I didn't want to alienate him.

"It just seems a little reductive," Joe said. "I mean, it's not very personal, the way her name would be, for instance."

"Daddy, you've got it wrong. It's *very* personal," Dawn said. "Don't you remember how we met to begin with?" She put her hand on Rud's arm; he hadn't been looking, and I tried not to notice that when she touched him, he twitched as if to shake her hand away. "When I brought my kitten into the vet?"

"It's just something I thought would be cute, Mr. Schutt," Rud said. "A term of endearment. And she seems to like it. But if you don't, then by all means I'll stop." He smeared a wad of butter onto a roll and took a bite. "Mrs. Schutt, this food is delicious. I may embarrass myself with my appetite here today."

"Embarrass away," I told him, feeling idiotic because it was such a dumb thing to say.

We ate in silence, except for the sound of silverware and chewing. "Everything's awesome, Mommy," Dawn said finally. After I brought the pie out, Dawn cut dessert short to announce that the football game was on. I knew she had no idea who was playing, but she made a point of saying how much Rud loved football, and loved to watch it on Thanksgiving, so we all took our plates into the living room and turned on the set, and watched two teams we couldn't have cared less about. Rud didn't seem all that interested, either, but he had no choice but to express a high measure of enthusiasm because Dawn had made such a big deal. I took Abby out for another walk, and when I returned, everyone was asleep in the same spots I'd left them. I cleaned up the kitchen, and by then it was dark. The rest of the night we passed watching whatever we could find on TV, because no one seemed to have the energy to do anything else.

Before Dawn headed upstairs to bed, I asked her if she wanted to go shopping with me the next day. I'd never been one of those Black Friday shoppers who get up before dawn and join the lines in front of the mall waiting for it to open, but I wanted some time with her alone and I figured Rud wouldn't want to come along on a women's shopping trip, especially in all those crowds. I was right; when Dawn asked him if he'd like to come, he said, "No, you guys go, do your lady thing. I'll hold down the fort at home." When he used the word *home* about our house, I saw Joe raise his eyebrows, and for a moment I thought he'd change the plan he told us he had for the morning, which was to go into the office to finish up some loose ends on the Sedgwick case. But he didn't, and we all agreed to go our separate ways in the morning and meet up again at lunchtime. Rud told us he would sleep in, and might not even be up when we all returned.

Upstairs, Dawn and Rud entered her room together and closed the door. Joe had already gone ahead to bed, and I debated telling him they were sharing the room, but figured that neither of us had the heart for a big scene, especially when we'd decided that we just wanted to get through the visit and say good-bye.

Joe left the house in the morning before Dawn and me. She and I had breakfast and then hit the mall, but it was more chaotic than either of us could stand, so after making a few purchases that had us waiting in line forever, we headed home.

It wasn't even eleven o'clock yet, and I expected that Rud would, as he'd predicted, still be in bed. But we found him asleep in the family room, the movie channel playing in the background. When he heard us entering, he woke up. I would have expected him to seem sheepish, having been discovered slack-jawed and almost drooling in front of the TV by his girlfriend and her mother, but instead he appeared irritated that we had interrupted his nap. At least, that was my first impression of his attitude. But then he adjusted quickly, jumping up to grab the packages Dawn and I carried, saying he hadn't realized he was so tired.

Joe came home within the half hour, carrying his briefcase and a stack of folders directly into his office on the first floor. That was when he discovered that we had been robbed.

Something looked wrong about the cabinet in his study, he told me later, and opening it, he saw that my expensive binoculars were gone. Immediately he checked the closet, where he kept his grandfather's telescope, but that shelf was empty as well. With a sick feeling in my throat, I rushed up to the bedroom to find that my mother's ring was missing from my jewelry box. The crystal obelisk Joe had received as an award at the previous year's accounting banquet had been taken, too.

Of course, the first person we turned to was Rud. Had he not noticed anything? Wouldn't he have heard someone come into the house? Wouldn't Abby have barked if someone tried? That was when he put on the embarrassed expression I'd expected earlier, and told us he was a hard sleeper: "My mother used to say they could test bombs in my bedroom without waking me up." I thought I saw Dawn startle and almost say something, but she seemed to think better of it and tightened her lips.

We called the Everton police and they sent over Kenneth Thornburgh, who took down a list of the missing items and listened as Joe described the cabinet doors in his office being slightly awry, which was what had tipped him off that someone had opened them. "But you're saying the doors were closed when you came in here, right?" the detective said. We didn't know what he was getting at until he added, "Why would a thief come in to steal things, then bother to close the doors behind him? If it was just a grab-and-run?" This made sense, and I could see that Joe thought so, too. Dawn had left us and gone into the bathroom—hiding from the conflict, most likely—but Rud was still standing behind us, his hands thrust deep in his jeans pockets as he looked down somberly at the floor. "Can I talk to you two for a minute?" Thornburgh said, nodding at Joe and me. Rud mumbled something that sounded like "Sure, sure" and backed out of the room, though I sensed reluctance in his movement. Thornburgh shut the door.

"How well do you know your daughter's boyfriend?" he asked, and though Joe understood immediately what he was implying, it took me longer.

"Not well," I admitted. "But she does, of course. They came for Thanksgiving. Why?"

Joe moved closer to me, as if he thought I might need to lean against him when I finally understood what he and the detective had already grasped. "He was the only one here, Hanna." In his face I saw relief, which at first I interpreted as a kind of gloating that his growing suspicions about Rud had been confirmed. It would take me a while to realize that he was relieved because if we knew who the thief was, we would likely recover what we had lost.

"But—why?" I looked from one man to the other. When neither of them could answer me, I said, "Isn't it possible it happened the way he said—that somebody came in and robbed us while he was asleep by the TV?"

"It's very unlikely." Thornburgh spoke in a low voice, and it occurred to me that he thought Rud might be listening outside the door. "There haven't been any reports of burglaries in this neighborhood, or the whole town lately, for that matter." He nodded in the direction of the hallway. "Do you know anything about his finances?"

We didn't. We knew only that he worked as a vet's assistant—a job that, I assumed, didn't pay very well. It hadn't occurred to me to wonder about how he supported himself. But even if I had wondered, I would have thought only that since he came from a successful family, his parents probably helped him out if he needed it.

"I'll want to talk to him," the detective said, and we followed him back into the hall. Dawn had come out of the bathroom and was standing behind Rud, biting the tip of her thumb into bloodlessness. It was one of her old habits I associated with her most anxious moments, and I thought she'd gotten rid of it in college—when she met Rud—so I winced when I saw her doing it again.

Thornburgh asked Rud to accompany him downstairs and into Joe's study, so they would be able to speak privately. Dawn asked if she could be there, too, but Rud turned and kissed her forehead and said, "Don't worry, Kitten—I've got nothing to hide." Though I tried to resist them, the words *con man* flashed through my mind.

While they sequestered themselves in the separate room, I made sandwiches from the leftover turkey. When I put plates down in front of Joe and Dawn, she said, "How can you guys even think about eating?" Joe had already taken a bite, and I could see that he considered feeling chagrined and decided against it.

"Maybe it's all for the best in the long run," he told her. "If this guy really is bad news, you want to know it sooner rather than later."

"He didn't steal those things. Honestly, Daddy, how can you think that?" She pushed her plate away, and nobody spoke for the next several minutes until we heard Rud and Thornburgh come out of the office.

The detective said quietly to Joe and me, "Apparently, there's some camera equipment missing, too. Mr. Petty said his camera was stolen along with all your property." His tone implied to me that he did not believe what Rud had told him, but Dawn didn't seem to notice.

"I don't remember seeing any camera," Joe said, as we watched Rud walk over to Dawn and put his hands on her shoulders from behind. She lifted a hand to pat his in a gesture of support, though I recognized confusion in her face.

"Really, Mr. Schutt? You didn't see me yesterday after dinner, taking pictures of the bird feeder out there?" Rud pointed to the yard, where behind the garden—which was essentially shut down for the winter—we kept suet and sunflower seeds in a contraption designed to let the birds get at the food while keeping squirrels out. "There was that gorgeous cardinal, don't you remember? And what's that other kind you said, Mrs. S.—nuthatches? There was a whole family of them." Same smile on his face, same charm in his voice as during the rehearsal dinner before Iris's wedding, when I fell for it all. Only this time, I was aware of the duplicity behind it. There had been no camera, no photographing of birds in the backyard. After dinner there was the football game and then a long evening of TV. I was the only one who had gone outside, to walk the dog. Rud had not left the house at all.

"That never happened." Joe was shaking his head, looking at Rud with a smile on his own face I'm sure he didn't even realize was there. Knowing my husband as I did, I could tell that as angry as he must be about Rud having robbed us, he also felt fascinated by the arrogance it took for him to lie about it.

"I set the camera right down there on top of the hutch," Rud continued, pointing to where we stored the good tableware in the dining room. "And now it's gone. They must have gotten that, too."

They. The fictitious burglars who, having noticed someone sleeping in front of a blaring TV, and probably a dog as well, still chose to enter the house in broad daylight and scope it out for valuables before removing those items and restoring order behind them. Of course it made no sense, and the fact that Rud was lying about the camera made me realize that he *had* to be the actual culprit.

Rud, still holding Dawn's shoulders, leaned down to her and said, "I know *you* remember, Kitten. You said you couldn't remember seeing anything so red as that little birdie."

I watched my daughter freeze for a moment under his hands—just a moment; no one but a mother would have caught it—before she turned her face up to him, willing her features to brighten along the way.

"Of course I remember," she agreed, but she could not look at Joe and me as she added, "Maybe you guys missed it when you were watching football."

"We were *all* watching football," Joe said. He spoke in his quietest voice, and I could see Dawn shrink, at hearing it.

It was clear that Detective Thornburgh understood what was going on. When he motioned for Joe and me to accompany him to the door, he told us as much. "But with him reporting himself a victim, too, and no other evidence, there's not much we can do but file a report," he said.

"You can't search his car?" Joe asked, as we stepped into the driveway and remembered that Rud and Dawn had driven up in her Nova. "I mean, our daughter's car?" Though it had started to snow, Emmett Furth was riding his motorbike down the street wearing only a tee-shirt and jeans. When he saw the uniformed officer outside our house, he gave Thornburgh the finger.

"Maybe *he* did it," I said, forgetting for a moment that all the evidence pointed to Rud.

"Oh, we're familiar with Emmett," the detective said. "But he's pretty small time. And he's smart enough not to rip off the people next door." Joe and I looked at each other, deciding between us not to mention the burning of the tree house. Thornburgh turned to Joe. "Do you own the Nova?"

Joe pursed his lips, shook his head. "No. It's in her name."

"Then she'd have to consent to it."

I would have tried to stop him, but Joe had turned back toward the house before I could do so. "Dawn! Would you come out here a minute, please?"

In a moment she appeared, trailing Rud behind her with her hand locked in his. "What now?" Something had changed in her expression even in the short time since we'd been in the house with them. Her features were hardened against Joe and me, as if Rud had whispered a promise she'd been waiting to hear.

"Would you let the officer take a look in your car?" Though I could see that Joe also felt shaken by the shift in our daughter's demeanor, he would not let it deter him from persisting in his inquiry. When she hesitated, he added, "After all, if there's nothing to hide, there's no reason not to allow a search, right?"

He was right, of course, and I saw that Dawn wanted to say yes, so that she would have the satisfaction of proving our suspicions wrong. But Rud stepped in front of her and said, "We are not going to stand here and listen to you accuse us like common criminals. I was taught not to talk back to my elders, but if you want to know the truth, Mr. and Mrs. Schutt, I think you should be ashamed of yourselves." He lifted his chin, and literally standing by her man, Dawn did the same.

I thought about reminding him that nobody was accusing *Dawn* of anything, but I recognized it as one of those cases that called for restraint of tongue. At that moment I wished Joe were the type of man who would just say the hell with it and pop the trunk himself before anyone could stop him, or that I had the

227

courage to do it myself, but neither was the case, and I knew it. A weighty silence followed, after which Thornburgh cleared his throat and told us that if anything changed we should call him, and he'd let us know if, on their end, the police had any news. "You have my number if that camera turns up," Rud said to him, and Thornburgh—also exercising restraint, it seemed—barely acknowledged the statement before getting into his car and pulling out of the driveway.

"What now?" I whispered to Joe as I followed him into the house, but he must not have heard me.

Dawn said to Rud, "Honey, Mom made you a sandwich." I hadn't done so, and she knew it, but she held out the plate I'd prepared for the detective.

Rud just looked at it, and then at her, before taking the plate from her and setting it back on the table with exaggerated delicacy, as if he considered it contaminated. "We won't be staying for lunch," he said, ostensibly answering Dawn but directing his words at Joe and me. "Get our things together, Kitten. We're obviously not welcome here."

"Dawn is most certainly welcome here," Joe said, unwilling to hold back what both of us wanted to say. Until then Dawn had only looked anxious as we all waited to see how the scene would unfold, but at her father's words, she erupted in tears.

"How can you *do* this," she said to him and me, pushing past us to run up the stairs. We heard her rummaging around in her bedroom, throwing clothes into bags, collecting things from the bathroom. The whole time, Rud did not move to help her, but pulled a chair out and sat down at the table. Despite his stated refusal to remain in our house for another meal, he picked up the detective's sandwich and finished it in a few bites, all the while ignoring Joe and me as we stood by watching him, stunned by his nerve. Then he got up, strolled to the hall closet, took out his leather jacket, and fitted his arms into the sleeves as if he were a model preparing for a shoot.

When they left a few minutes later, Dawn having slung their belongings into the Nova's backseat, it was without any further words among any of us. We listened to the car chug down the street, and across from me at the table, Joe put his face in his hands. "We shouldn't have let them leave," I told him. "It's snowing, they're angry, and we're not really sure what happened." I was pleading with him to agree with me. "Are we?"

"Oh, Hanna." I could see that it wearied him to have to insist, again, upon what we both knew. I was grateful that he didn't invoke our private expression: *lacy eye.* "Yes, we're sure." He rubbed at his temples. "This is my fault. I'm the one who left him alone in our house."

"We all did that," I told him, but I could tell it didn't get through.

Then there was another long stretch of silence before he stood, rinsed Rud's plate, and put it into the dishwasher, as if knowing that I would not want to touch it. (He was right; it was the kind of moment I loved him for.) Without even talking about it, we decided not to go to see *Hamlet* that night as we had planned. Our hearts were heavy, and we were in no mood to watch a tragedy. Instead, we stayed in and ordered a movie on cable.

I did not remember doing this; when Kenneth Thornburgh came to question me in the hospital, after I emerged from my coma nearly three weeks later, I could not tell him anything about the hours leading up to the attack. The last thing I remembered was turning the outside light on and watching the snow fall lightly in its track, then deciding to call Dawn to make sure she'd gotten back safely to her apartment. I resolved not to mention anything about the burglary, so that our conversation wouldn't disintegrate the way the Thanksgiving visit had; I would keep it short and sweet, a check-up call just to say, "I love you, no matter what."

But Dawn wasn't home. Opal answered and told me she hadn't seen Dawn since Tuesday night, and then she kept me on the phone for fifteen minutes, chattering away about anything and nothing; I sensed she was lonely, and I hoped for her sake as well as for Dawn's that it would not be long before Dawn returned to their apartment. I asked Opal to have my daughter call me when she got home. But if she did so, I could not remember.

I also didn't remember calling Claire to confirm our date to walk our dogs at Two Rivers the following morning, although she gave testimony that I did.

Opal maintained that Dawn was in their apartment from six o'clock on, when she returned after dropping Rud off at his place on the way home from our house. Our phone records showed that I made my call at five fifteen, so there was no reason for the grand jury not to believe her.

One of the investigators testified that our cable records showed that Joe and I had ordered a movie that Friday at 8:11 p.m. When Gail Nazarian asked the witness what the movie was, he answered in as matter-of-fact a manner as his position called for, yet Gail Nazarian allowed a pause before her next question, to ensure that the irony was not lost on anyone in the room. Just hours before someone came into our house and crushed our skulls with a croquet mallet, my husband and I selected—and presumably watched—*Catch Me If You Can*. Even the judge raised her eyebrows as a nervous titter bounced off the courtroom walls.

Affinity Fraud

I'd felt sure that once Warren removed the graffiti from Dawn's car, she would go out and try to find a job. It was what we had agreed on, one of the conditions for her coming home. But three days after Halloween the car still sat where it was, and still she did not leave the house except for the rare times I asked her to walk Abby, which both Dawn and Abby seemed to resent.

It annoyed me to come home from work every day and find her sitting in front of the TV. She'd made dinner only that one time, on Halloween—if you could call it dinner—and I found it more and more difficult to see any reason to cut her some slack. I knew Joe would never have stood for it. And frankly, I didn't feel very sympathetic, either, especially given the fact that I hadn't had much choice about going to work when I was younger than Dawn.

I still remember, all too well, the night during my junior year in high school that federal agents came for my father. It was during a blizzard, school had been canceled, and every radio and TV station was warning people not to go outside, let alone drive, if

231

they could avoid it. I was doing my homework in the living room as my mother sat across from me, working on a quilt. My father was playing solitaire at the dining room table, which I had just helped my mother clear after supper. In our old house on Humboldt Street, there had never been enough space for us to be very far away from one another. Manning Boulevard was a different story. Even though my mother and I were in the same room, it felt as if I watched from a distance when she jumped at the sound of the doorbell and murmured, "Aj!" as the quilting needle in her hand slipped and her finger began to bleed.

Sucking on the finger, she went to the door. There were two of them on the stoop, but only one spoke. He called my mother "ma'am" and asked if Carl Elkind was at home. I watched my mother freeze as she took her finger away from her mouth, and I could tell that for a moment she thought about lying, but then she called my father to come to the door, and he did. When he saw the uniformed officers, he let out a big sigh that still, even in my memory today, sounds more like relief than anxiety, as he understood why his name had been called.

"You couldn't wait until this was over?" he asked the men, nodding toward outside, where the wind whipped the snow in icy gusts. My mother was gripping the back of her chair, making a whimpering sound I had never heard before, which almost made my dinner come back up and spill from my throat. "Hanna, I will explain things," my father said to me as they led him out the door and down the slippery steps into the idling black car. My mother and I watched the headlights leave, and, too late, she thought to run to the closet to pull down my father's coat. She let out the whimper again, and it took me all night to calm her down.

Eight months after they took him away, my father was con-

232

victed of securities fraud, wire fraud, mail fraud, money laundering, and filing false statements about the investment accounts he handled, mainly for friends we knew from Trinity Lutheran. The newspapers made a big deal of the fact that he was accused of committing "affinity fraud" against so many people who had considered him a close friend. My mother insisted to anyone who would listen—though there weren't many by then—that they had the wrong man. I thought maybe she was just saying that in public in an effort to save face, but even when it was just the two of us, she told me the same thing. My father was "a victim of circumstance," she said, and though I wasn't quite sure what she meant by that, I didn't ask her to explain.

He had a good lawyer (and it wasn't until Joe's gentle suggestion, years later, that I realized there must have been a secret account somewhere, from which my father paid the guy) who, along with coming up with phrases such as "legal infelicities," managed to convince the court that my father's sentence should be on the minimal side. As it turned out, it didn't matter that he got only five years instead of fifteen, because he died of a stroke in prison before he was halfway through.

The judge had frozen all his assets; the only thing he allowed us to retain was the house on Manning Boulevard, where my mother and I continued to live. Even before my father was officially declared guilty, I knew my own plans would have to change. I'd always wanted to go to college and become a nurse, but after my father's conviction we didn't have the money. On top of that, my mother got diagnosed with uterine cancer two weeks after I graduated. I stayed home taking care of her until she went into the hospital. About an hour before she died, she made a sign for me to move closer, so I could hear her whisper. She was moving her

233

hands, and I didn't know what she was doing, until she tried to pull off the ring her own mother had given to her when *she* died. But she was too weak. "You do it," she said, and I shook my head. "*Yes*," she told me, more strongly, using all her energy, and afraid to send her into a tailspin, I did as she instructed and slid the ring off her finger. She wouldn't stop agitating in the bed until I put it on, and I felt that sting in my chest that goes deeper than crying.

I'd thought that was the worst of it, but no; the worst was reading her obituary in the Albany newspaper two days later. I didn't know why, but whoever handled it hadn't contacted me for details about my mother's life; instead, the brief "appreciation" was written with information provided by a neighbor, Estelle Graber, who was in my mother's monthly bridge group but otherwise didn't know her very well. Either Estelle wasn't aware of or she didn't tell the writer about my father's imprisonment, or (more likely) she did, and the newspaper decided, out of respect for the deceased or because of a space shortage, not to include it. In any case, I was grateful for my mother's sake that the notice said only that she was survived by her husband and daughter.

But the item was short, and the last sentence pierced me to the core: "She enjoyed playing bridge and was renowned for her oatmeal crinkles." Both were true (although "renowned" might have been a stretch), but reading those words evoked more grief in me than I'd felt in the moment my mother died as I held her hand. The fact that I knew it wouldn't have bothered *her* to have her legacy reduced to these two dubious notes made me all the sadder.

I began working for Kip Gunther, who hired me on the spot to be his receptionist and secretary when I answered his ad in the *Schenectady Gazette*. A lawyer specializing in divorces and contract disputes, Kip—who instructed me to call him that, never

Mr. Gunther—wore his hair long, tucked behind his ears, and his glasses dark, even inside the office. He had a way of talking out of the edge of his mouth as if he didn't really want you to understand what he was saying. I suspected even during our interview that there was something shady about him, but I didn't listen to myself until it was too late.

I tried not to pay attention to the questionable work tasks Kip had me do, because I didn't want to know that I was working for an unscrupulous person—after all, what would that say about *me*?—but I was pretty sure he was padding his billable hours, and more than once he had me type up double invoices, to two different clients for expenses on the same business trip. I told myself that I just didn't understand the law, and who was I to say anything? The man paid me well. Of course, he also said more than once that he gave me such a good salary because he could tell I was the type of girl who'd always be loyal. I wished he hadn't said that, because how else could I take it other than that he expected me to keep my mouth shut if anyone came around asking?

I'd be doing my work, typing up some document—he mostly handled little things, like people suing their contractors—and he'd come over and stand next to me, too close, waiting for me to take my fingers off the keyboard. Then he would ask me his raunchy riddles. "What do a Christmas tree and a priest have in common? Their balls are just for decoration." I always made a noise that I knew he took to be appreciation of his humor, because he got a satisfied look on his face and went back to his desk, whistling off-key.

I worked there for two years, during which time my father died in the New Jersey prison they'd sent him to. I sold the house on Manning Boulevard to pay off my mother's medical bills and rented a crappy apartment across the river. I could have gone to college then, but instead I kept spending my days doing what Kip told me to do, and my nights watching television and drinking cheap wine. I had thought I would start making a quilt, the way my mother taught me before she died, but all the squares came out uneven because I was drunk while making them, and eventually I put the fabric and needles away. I knew this wasn't how I should be living. A combination of grief and panic thrummed through me every waking moment, and years later, when I heard Opal Bremer say she had "the wim-wams," I understood she was describing what I had felt back then.

That was when I was in danger, I should have told Gail Nazarian when she tried to warn me about Rud Petty being in touch with Dawn. I fought the wim-wams every night by getting wasted—even then I knew that that word, *wasted*, was the most apt one I could have used—and felt sick every morning before I stumbled my way, usually late, to the law office.

Looking back, I realized I was waiting for something, though I had no idea what it might be.

What pushed things over the edge was the day I returned to the office after lunch and found Kip sitting behind his desk, smiling stupidly, looking more boldly at my breasts than he usually did. It took me a few minutes to realize he was drunk and he told me he'd had a fight with his wife that morning. I said I was sorry to hear that and sat down at my desk, hoping to ignore him, but he wouldn't leave me alone. He came over and began massaging my neck, even after I lied and told him that it tickled. He bent closer to my ear and whispered in it. "What do you call a virgin on a waterbed?" Usually he just delivered the punch line immediately, but this time he waited for me to guess.

"I don't know. What?" I said. I had never been so close to a man before, aside from my father. The idea of sex scared me.

"A cherry float," Kip said, and made a gurgling, giggling sound deep in his throat as he pulled me up out of my chair, turned me around to face him, and kissed me firmly as he slipped his hands under my blouse and up to my bra. I felt immobilized, not knowing what to do. (Years later, when I heard Iris use the word *clueless* for the first time, my mind flew me back to that moment, and my daughter had to ask me what was wrong.)

Even as naïve as I was, I knew I was supposed to slap his hands away and get out of there as fast as I could. But I didn't. I let his hands linger, and without wanting or intending to, I felt the quick shiver of a sexual itch rise up between my legs. He unbuckled his pants. I did say, "Stop," but at the same time, I didn't move away when he slid his hand down to my crotch.

Finally, my senses returned to me when he suggested we move out to his car, which, he told me with a wink, had fold-down seats. He tried to lead me to the door by the hand, and when he separated his body from mine, I got hold of myself, straightened my clothing, collected my purse from the bottom drawer of my desk, and walked out on my own, somewhere finding the courage to shake his hand off when he reached out to touch me again. I drove off trembling, the tires sputtering on gravel, leaving Kip literally standing in the dust.

The next day I went to the bank to take out a loan, and enrolled for the spring semester at the state university.

I'd never been a great student in high school, but I loved college right away—the classes themselves and feeling as if I were forging my own path in life, even if I couldn't envision where it might end. In April, a few thousand students gathered for Fountain Day, when the huge spray fountain in the center of the quad was finally turned on after the long winter. You could feel the excitement in the air as noon approached and people began to collect around the long rectangular pool, putting their books and backpacks aside, turning their faces up to the weak but oh-so-welcome spring sun.

I sat at the pool's edge, preparing with everyone else to make a big fuss when the fountain spouted for the first time. Most of the people around me on the quad that noontime wore casual clothes—tee-shirts and shorts, even though it wasn't nearly warm enough for bare legs. They were trying to fool spring into acting like summer. I had on jeans and a pink long-sleeve jersey I'd picked up at Goodwill, with FREE SPIRIT spelled out in sequins across the front. I'd bought it as a kind of joke with myself, because I was not a sequins kind of girl. But I grew to like wearing the shirt. Being able to glance down and see those words on my chest made me feel as if they might, someday, be true. Who wouldn't, after all, want to be a free spirit?

Well, Joe Schutt, as it turned out. When the fountain came on and I stood up with everyone else to cheer, I saw that the short, already balding guy standing a few feet away from me, who was wearing a tie with a blue Oxford and khaki slacks, had caught sight of my shirt's message, and he was smiling. I didn't know whether to feel complimented that he had noticed me, or annoyed that he appeared to be amused by what I was wearing. Out of the corner of my eye I watched him maneuver along the pool until we were standing next to each other. Then he turned and gave me a full-on grin.

I had never seen him before, but I felt a charge of something like recognition as I returned the smile. Otherwise I might have moved away from him, thinking that he could be a stalker (though in those days the word would have been *weirdo*). This is how I know what Dawn felt, so many years later, when Rud Petty turned his charms on her; I felt the same breathless rush at realizing a man had taken an interest in me.

"Why are you wearing that?" he asked, pointing at the glittery silver letters spelling out *free spirit*.

"What do you mean? Because I like it."

He shook his head. "No, you don't. You think you should, but you don't. It isn't you. Glitter? I don't think so." From someone else, the words would have come across as smug or arrogant. But I could tell that this man was neither of those things.

"You're right," I told him, and the relief I felt in admitting this to him astonished and energized me. I felt the surge of pleasure that comes from being recognized in return, when you are not expecting it.

Around us at the pool, people were jostling one another, throwing Frisbees, reaching into coolers for cans. Somebody had set up a boom box in front of the campus center, amplifying the sounds of The Who and Journey and Queen. "Are you available?" he asked, and I said, "What?" in order to figure out what he really wanted to know. I decided he must be inquiring whether I was seeing anybody, and since I wasn't, I told him, "I guess so."

"Want to go grab some coffee, then?" I liked this, too—that he suggested coffee instead of a beer at the Rat, which was where (despite the fact that it was only lunchtime) most of our classmates seemed to be headed, now that the show was over.

"I can't. I have Logic in ten minutes."

"But you just said you were available."

"Oh. I thought—sorry. Anyway, no. I have class." I could feel my face flushing.

"Well, what's after Logic?"

"Reason," I said, without knowing I was going to. My spontaneous answer surprised and delighted me, as it obviously did him.

"I'll be back here at four o'clock, right in this spot," he told me. "We can find a table somewhere and come up with some conclusions." It took me a moment to realize that he was following the thread of my joke, but when I got it, I smiled back at him and agreed.

I only half-expected him to be there when I showed up again after my class, and when I didn't see him at first, I was surprised by the plunge of disappointment I felt, as well as angry that I'd let myself become so hopeful. But then there he was, walking out of the student center, and although I wanted to chide myself for allowing the thrill I felt at the sight of him, I couldn't manage it.

"You don't know how completely unlike me it is to ask out someone I don't even know," he told me.

"And you don't know how completely unlike me it is to accept." I wasn't even sure this was true, because I hadn't dated very much up to that point, but it felt like the right thing to say.

He had in mind the Daily Grind, across the street, but he understood when I hesitated because I spent four afternoons a week there bussing tables. I lowered my eyes when I said it, feeling embarrassed, but when I raised them again, it seemed that he looked at me with even more respect than I had seen in his eyes before. "A working girl," he said, making it sound like something a person should aspire to. Then he added, "A girl after my own heart," and I felt blood rise to my face again.

Instead, we walked five blocks to the newer, fancier coffee-house I had never been to. Seated across from him, I felt both excited and anxious, not sure how I should act. I knew that people always advised, "Be yourself," but I wasn't at all sure of what *myself* actually was.

Because of this, it was much easier to ask Joe questions than to answer any. I learned that he was in the university's graduate accounting program, and worked twenty-five hours a week keeping the books for a local car dealership ("So, a working boy," I said, feeding his own line back to him but stopping short of adding that he was a man after my own heart); that he liked things in his life—from the balance sheets on his desk to the cabinets in his kitchen to the tools in his garage—to be in order, with everything in its place; and that eventually he wanted to become something called a certified fraud examiner.

Then, though I didn't ask, he told me about his family. How his father had been fired from the steel company, when Joe was in junior high, for showing up drunk for his shift one too many times. How his mother tried to support the family by working as a home health aide, but was forced to apply for government assistance because her salary wasn't enough. How his father had always made fun of Joe for being "more serious than a heart attack," even now, as he accepted the checks Joe sent home and spent them on cases of Genny Cream.

I appreciated his confiding in me. It should have made it easy for me to reciprocate and talk about the things that made me sad, the things I was ashamed of. Yet I held back because that's what we did in my family; it was the Swedish way.

Joe didn't press me. When we'd each drunk two cups of coffee and it was time for dinner, he suggested we walk even farther up the street, to Neillio's, so he could treat me to their veal parm. Though I warned myself against it, I knew I was falling for him.

"Enough about me," he said when we'd been seated in a cozy corner booth I assumed he'd requested in the murmur he exchanged with the hostess after she greeted us. I knew from TV that some men slip bills into the hands of hosts and hostesses and maître d's, as a way of getting what they want, so the fact that Joe accomplished the same thing with just his manner, his smile, and his words, attracted me to him all the more. "Tell me the Hanna Elkind Story."

He sat back in the booth and made a beckoning motion with both hands. I loved the sound of my name in his voice, and it seemed he could tell this. It made me unreasonably happy to see he was an ice chewer, like me.

I started to speak and immediately stumbled, realizing I didn't know where to begin. The waiter interrupted to ask if we wanted drinks, and I looked at Joe for his answer, somehow already knowing, because of what he'd told me about his father, that he wouldn't order something for himself. Part of me was tempted to order a glass of wine, but a bigger part knew it would be a mistake. I wanted my head to stay clear, this night. I knew I'd want to remember.

When our iced teas came, I managed to tell him the only things that seemed important: that my mother had died before she could have the garden she'd always dreamed of, and that I wanted to be a nurse.

"Is your father still living?" Joe asked after a moment, but the swift rise of warmth to my skin must have caused him to add, almost immediately, "Oh, I'm sorry. I didn't mean to be rude."

"It's not rude. I just don't talk about him much."

"You don't have to talk about him now."

"But I *want* to." And I did; suddenly, though I never would have expected it, I found myself eager to tell this man, whom I'd known only a few hours, everything that had happened to my family since that knock at our door on that stormy night. I began with telling him the name of the prison my father had died in a few months earlier, then my memories about the arrest itself. "It's still hard for me to accept that my father was a..." I hesitated over the next word.

"Criminal?" Joe said it calmly, and after a moment I nodded, then took my own sip of iced tea and crunched down on a cube.

"I guess there's no way around it," I said. "That's what he was. Even though he didn't exactly go around breaking people's legs." This was something I had always told myself as a way to feel better when I thought of what my father had done.

"What he did was worse than breaking legs, don't you think?" Though his message was blunt, Joe kept his voice gentle. "Or at least as bad. Taking advantage of people who trusted him."

"I guess." I coughed a little, nervous because I knew what I wanted to say next but wasn't sure I should. "I think I'm afraid of what that might make you think about me."

"It doesn't make me think anything." He shrugged. "Nothing your father did reflects on you."

"It doesn't?"

"Why should it? It wasn't *you* who stole your friends' money, was it?"

"No." That didn't seem strong enough, so I added, "I wouldn't do that."

"Well, then. When *you* start stealing people's money, ask me again." He held my gaze steady as he reached for the check, and

243

I was the first to look away. On the way out of the restaurant, he said, "It seems we have a lot in common, Hanna Elkind."

"How do you figure?"

"Weak fathers. Meek mothers." He seemed to startle himself with the poetry of it, which made us both smile.

"Lethal combo," I agreed. I said it in a joking tone, but in fact I meant what I said; I believed that my mother's illness and her death had been sped up, if not caused by, the stress of my father's trial.

When we walked out into the warm evening, Joe took my arm. By the time he kissed me at my car an hour or so later, I knew what it felt like to be on that precipice—the one jutting out over love.

Because I was ashamed of it, I'd never told either of my girls the story of Kip Gunther, and how indirectly it had led to my meeting their father. Now I considered mentioning it to Dawn, as a way of starting a discussion about work and where she might look for a job. But something stopped me. Sitting across from her at the kitchen table as I'd done so many nights before, I felt suddenly vulnerable, wanting to protect myself. I'd often felt that way with Iris when she was younger, because I sensed that she and her friends mocked their parents behind their backs, but I'd never experienced the same sensation with Dawn. I tried to set it aside, but it wouldn't let me.

Though it went against my instincts and against what Joe believed about raising self-sufficient children, I thought about how I might help Dawn find something to do. Trying to shut Joe's voice out of my head, I decided to ask Francine if she thought Bob Toussaint would go for the idea of hiring Dawn as a delivery person for our in-home meal service. We'd been down an employee since the end of summer, when one of the college kids who'd been working for us went back to school, and as much as I knew Joe would have hated for me to use an "in" to get one of our kids a job, I thought it might be a good match: the job didn't require a college degree, only a clean driving record and a car.

I made a point of getting to the office early, when Francine usually had the place to herself. When I asked what she thought about the idea of Dawn coming to work for us, I could see that the question startled her. Then I remembered I hadn't mentioned to her yet that Dawn was returning home. I tried not to notice that her enthusiasm, like everyone else's, was tepid at best. Cautiously, she said she didn't see why we couldn't hire Dawn, "as long as you can vouch for her." She tried to say this in a jokey way, and ostensibly she was only asking me to guarantee that Dawn would be reliable in the job.

But I knew that what she really wanted me to do was assure her that Dawn had had nothing to do with trying to kill me. Of course I couldn't do this, since Francine hadn't actually voiced the question. She said she'd speak to Bob about the possibility of hiring Dawn. Later in the day, I could see her trying to muster some happiness for my sake when she told me that Bob had approved it, and that I should let Dawn know she was hired.

Dawn showed little reaction when I got home and told her she could begin training the next day and delivering meals to our clients the day after that. "I thought you'd be happy about it," I said. "With your maxed-out credit cards and all." I didn't mention the money she'd borrowed from me the night we went to Pepito's.

She shrugged. "I guess." She was focusing on a rerun of *Three's Company*, and had made no effort that I could see to start any kind of dinner. "It's just that it's not very exciting," she added, following me into the kitchen where I began rummaging in the cupboards. The TV show had just ended. "Delivering food to old poor people. You know?"

I bit my lip, knowing how Joe would have responded: *You're a college dropout. You're lucky to get any job. Your mother and I didn't start out with jobs we liked, either.* Instead I said, "They're not 'old poor people.' Some of them are old, but some are laid up on crutches or just too busy to shop. And none of them are poor—they all live in Everton, for God's sake. And it's not charity; they pay for this service."

"Oh." She seemed to brighten at this information, then thanked me and told me she appreciated my help.

She began delivering meals to a reduced roster of six clients; once she proved she could handle that, Francine would increase it to ten. When I got home after work on her first day, Dawn was like a different person—energetic and cheerful, bustling around the kitchen preparing a meatloaf that ended up not tasting as good as it looked, but I was glad she'd tried.

"I love this job, Mommy," she said, setting the table. "Everybody's so nice, and one lady even tipped me. Mrs. Wing. Do you know her?"

I did, of course; Dottie Wing had been on my own delivery rounds list from the day we started the service. Since Francine had suggested I compile Dawn's route myself, Dottie was the first person I put on it, because she was friendly without demanding an undue amount of time, as some of the clients (lonely, shut in) did. I'd called her personally, to let her know my daughter was taking over, but that I'd stop in now and then to say hello.

I should have anticipated that she would offer Dawn a tip.

And I should have warned Dawn that accepting tips wasn't allowed, but I'd forgotten. I told her she'd have to give it back, and though she balked at first, I convinced her she had to if she wanted to keep the job.

On her third day, I got home early because our last two patients had canceled. I knew Dawn was home because the Corvette was in the driveway. But although the TV was on as usual, she wasn't in the family room. Following Abby, who seemed to want to lead me to another part of the house, I found Dawn in Joe's office, digging through his desk drawer. She was so intent that she didn't hear me approach, and when I said, "What are you doing?" from the doorway, she jumped, a sheaf of papers falling onto the desk.

"Jesus Christ! You scared the shit out of me," she said, and once again I felt startled by the profanity coming from my timid daughter's mouth.

I walked toward the desk, and she seemed to take a step back. "I was just looking for my birth certificate," she said, looking flushed. "I thought I might need it sometime."

"You could have just asked me," I told her, trying to keep the tone out of my voice that would have communicated what I was thinking: *What's the* matter *with you?* "Besides, you know we keep those papers with Tom Whitty. They're not here."

"Oh. Okay." She stacked the papers she'd been rifling through, and stuck them back in the drawer. "Thanks, Mommy. I knew I could count on you."

I managed to put the incident out of my mind, but two days later, when Tom Whitty called and said he needed to talk to me, I felt a flash of alarm. I was surprised he wanted to meet in person, because usually we conducted our business on the phone. We set a time during my lunch hour, at the coffee shop near the Stinson and Keyes office just outside the city. Though it had been three years and I'd never spent much time at Joe's office myself, I still didn't feel ready to go back to the place he had worked during most of our married life. I think I was afraid I would have been able to feel too much of his presence around me, at a time when it would have felt like a threat of some kind—in terms of the emotion it brought up—instead of a comfort.

Tom was sitting at a back table, and when I came over he rose to give me a kiss, turning over the piece of paper he'd been looking at. "Is everything okay?" I asked, trying not to betray my worry. I hadn't paid too much attention to the details of the financial crisis of the past few years, because Tom had assured me that though our account had taken a hit like everyone else's, Joe had built up a strong and smart portfolio over the years, and eventually it was sure to come back. But in those few moments before I sat down, I let my mind run to the what-if of having no money left to draw on, and conjured a childhood image of my mother sitting at the kitchen table on Humboldt Street with all our household bills open in front of her, putting her hand out to pick up one and then another, setting them down again with a dazed expression on her face. I had always chosen to believe it was because he couldn't stand this expression that my father resorted to the scheme that got him arrested and destroyed our family's name among the people who thought of him as a friend. "Blood from a stone," my mother would say at such times. "That's what they want from us."

When my girls were little, I used to tell them about what my father had done in such a way that they might feel sorry for him and understand why he'd turned to what I called "bad behavior" as a means of winning people's respect and admiration. I was careful to do this when Joe wasn't around, because he wouldn't have wanted me to sugarcoat the whole thing. But I didn't like the idea that Iris and Dawn wouldn't know anything about their dead grandfather other than the fact that he was a criminal who had died in a federal prison.

It never seemed to me that Dawn was listening all that intently when I talked about my father, or that she cared about the story at all. But one day Iris, who was sixteen at the time, said, "Bullshit," when I told them that their grandfather had never intended to mishandle the investments people had trusted him with; it had all just snowballed and gotten away from him. "You make it sound like he was the victim," Iris said, "when really what he did was pure evil." That was when I knew she had talked to Joe about what her grandfather did. "You get that people lost their entire bank accounts, right? They trusted him, and he pretended to be their friend, when the whole time he was stealing their money."

The way she put it made me wince, but I couldn't tell her she was wrong. But Dawn turned on her sister and said, "Shut up! He just made a mistake!" I told her I wouldn't call it a mistake, exactly. "Well, what, then?" she asked. When I hesitated, she said, "That's okay. I get it." But I'm not sure she ever did.

When I sat down at the table across from Tom Whitty, he told me, "Oh, no, you're fine. I didn't mean to scare you." His skin glistened—I remember Joe told me he had some condition that made him sweat constantly, regardless of the temperature—and he reached to grab another napkin from the dispenser at the side of the table.

We made small talk over coffee for a few minutes, because Tom seemed hesitant to tell me why he'd called. Finally, he asked if I'd heard from Dawn recently. "Actually, she's moved back home," I told him, steeling myself for the reaction I knew this news would receive. He managed to hide it after a moment, but it was there, as I'd known it would be. "Why?" When he said he wasn't sure where to start, I nodded at the piece of paper I'd seen him turn over on the table. "What's that?"

He picked it up, and I could see he was grateful I'd just come straight out and asked. "I'm really sorry about this, Hanna," he said, "but I think Dawn's trying to pull a fast one."

"What do you mean?" By the time he said it, I wasn't necessarily surprised, given his reticence. But a slow curl of dread wound its way through my stomach as I waited to hear the details.

He turned the paper over. "You didn't sign this, did you?" It was a computer printout of a loan agreement from a bank I'd never heard of. Dawn's name was signed over the line that said "Loan Applicant," and next to it, over "Co-signer," was scribbled "Hanna Elkind Schutt"—or something that looked like it. The handwriting of the first signature looked identical to the second, and I recognized it immediately.

For a moment, I admit, it occurred to me to lie and say I had signed it; my instinct to protect Dawn was still that strong. But only for a moment. Then I told Tom, "No. That's not even close to what my signature looks like."

"I didn't think so. I checked it against what I have on file. But I thought, well, maybe after the attack…" I could tell that part of him had been hoping my signature had changed as a result of my cognitive impairment. But the other part was, like Joe, a fraud examiner: he loved to sniff out when people were trying to get away with something, catch them in the act, and see them punished for it. Even if it was the daughter of an old family friend.

I looked at the paper more closely. Dawn had applied for a personal loan in the amount of thirty thousand dollars. Among other information, the form contained my Social Security and banking account numbers.

"Oh," I said, now understanding what Dawn had been looking for in Joe's desk drawer.

Tom said, "I'm sorry to have to tell you. But Dawn needs to know she could get in a lot of trouble for this."

"Do you have to report it?"

He shook his head. "No. That's up to you."

I leaned back in my chair and let the waitress refill my coffee. Tom sneaked a look at his watch, so I thanked him and said I'd take care of it. He left me the copy of the loan application, and I folded it to tuck into my purse. Then I sat and looked out the window at nothing until the coffee turned cold.

If I'd had a cell phone, I would have called Dawn. Instead, knowing that Dottie Wing was the last person on her meal delivery route, I got in my car and drove to Dottie's house, where I parked at the curb and waited. When I saw the Corvette pull into the driveway, I went to meet her at the trunk as she pulled out the tray containing Dottie's food.

"Goddamn it!" She practically dropped it when she saw me.

I was about to apologize when I remembered why I'd come. "I just saw Tom Whitty," I told her. When she shrugged to show that she didn't understand why I was telling her this, I added, "He handles my finances now."

Dawn just kept looking at me, with no acknowledgment of what I'd said, for a good ten seconds. Though it hadn't happened since she'd come home, I remembered this from her growing-up years—how could I have forgotten?—the way she'd stare at someone who'd addressed her, to the point that sometimes people had

251

to say, "Did you *hear* me?" I pulled from my purse the paper Tom had given me. I handed it to her, and when she didn't unfold it, I said, "Read it, Dawn," in a tone I had rarely if ever used with her, even when she was a child.

"Can't this wait until we get home?" But she saw from my expression that it couldn't. With a weary sigh, as if I were aggrieving her, she opened the paper and kept her eyes on it far longer than she should have needed to understand what it was. Then she closed it and murmured, "Mommy, I just wanted to have some money of my own, to start my life over. Is that so wrong? Here I am without a college degree, so what kind of job can I get? A real job, I mean. Not *this*." She gestured at the house's front window, behind which I knew Dottie Wing waited for her lunch. "I was never convicted of anything. Never even indicted. But all I can do is make eight bucks an hour delivering food." Right there, in Dottie's driveway, she began to cry.

I told myself not to soften. Actually, it was Joe I tried to channel: *She needs to take responsibility for her own life.* "You didn't even ask me if I'd sign," I said. "You didn't ask *me* for a loan. Why not?"

"I knew you wouldn't do either," she said. Of course, she was right.

"And how were you ever going to pay it back? Did you think about that?"

She shook her head, finally setting the tray down on the car.

"That's the problem with you, Dawn. You do things without ever thinking ahead about the consequences." Now she nodded, but I knew she was barely registering my words. This made me angry, so I drew on all the fuel that had been building up since she returned home.

"What's with this car, anyway?" I tapped the Corvette and

she flinched, as if I had made contact with her instead of the car's hood. "Why are you driving this? You could get some good money for that car." It had been something I'd wanted to say since the moment I saw her pull the Corvette into the driveway the night she arrived back home.

This did get through; I could tell from the way her eyes immediately began to narrow. "I like my car. I'm keeping it," she said, the way a child would insist she wanted to keep a toy. She added, "Can we not talk about this now, while I'm at work?"

I didn't want to hold Dottie Wing's food from her, waiting for an answer I was never going to get. I waved at the house, and Dawn took this as the signal I intended—that she was dismissed.

Back at the clinic, we were overrun suddenly by more than a dozen four-year-olds whose mothers worried they had strep throat. They all seemed to come at once, after their mothers had picked them up from preschool, so we were able to finish testing them in a shorter amount of time than if they'd had appointments. My head was aching; I kept seeing, in my mind's eye, the way Dawn had scrawled my name under the amount *Thirty thousand dollars* on the paper Tom had held out to me. As far as I could tell, she hadn't even tried to disguise her handwriting, or to imitate mine. When the last child had left with her certificate for an ice cream cone at Lickety Split, I told Francine I didn't feel well and left work an hour before my shift ended.

There was an unfamiliar car—one Iris would have referred to as a shitbox—parked behind Dawn's in the driveway when I returned. In the kitchen I found a young man sitting at the table eating chips while Dawn put pizza on two paper plates. She turned to me looking startled and said, "Mom! You're early!"

"I had to come home. My head is killing me." I was still upset over the loan forgery, but not enough to continue arguing with Dawn in front of a stranger. I said a tentative hello as I read the front of his jersey, which said I GET ENOUGH EXERCISE PUSHING MY LUCK. It made me smile, and he seemed to appreciate this.

Then I felt my mouth go stiff as I recognized him: it was the kid with the Cat in the Hat tee-shirt and auburn curls I'd felt watching me at the mall, the day Rud Petty's new trial was announced. "I know you," I said, seeing the look of further shock my words triggered in Dawn's face.

"You do not," she said to me. "How could you? This is my friend Stew."

Stew wiped crumbs across the top of his jeans and stuck his hand out to me. "I remember you from the mall," I told him.

"What mall?" Dawn said.

"Really? I don't remember." He gave a smile I was sure was supposed to charm me. "But I like their food court, so, yeah, maybe. I'm there a lot."

"What are you talking about?" Frustrated, Dawn pulled cheese off the side of the pizza box and rolled it between her fingers.

"I felt like you were watching me," I told him.

He laughed. "Me? Why would I do that?" His tone implied I should feel stupid for suggesting such a thing.

I turned to Dawn. "How do you two know each other?"

"Mom, what is this, the prom and you're my father?" Dawn flushed. "I'm allowed to have friends, you know."

"Of course you are. I just don't remember Stew from high school, that's all."

"I met him after that."

"When?" *At Lawlor?* I might have asked. He didn't look like the type who would have tried or wanted to belong to that kind of crowd. When would she have come across someone while the trial was going on, when she lived with Peter and Wendy? As far as I knew, she hadn't exactly been out socializing during that time. And surely he wasn't a friend from New Mexico who had followed her home to Everton.

But she was saved from having to answer when there was a rap at the back door and we all looked to see Warren Goldman standing there with a covered dish. He stuck his head in and said, "Anybody hungry? I made this big cassoulet."

"The fuck is that?" Stew said.

"Oh, Warren." I went over to the door. "Thanks, but right now I need to talk to Dawn. In fact, Stew, would you excuse us, too?"

Dawn's friend seemed only too happy to follow Warren outside. For a moment I entertained the cartoonish vision of them sitting down to dinner together, but Stew got in the shitbox and drove away as Warren crossed the street back to his house, dipping his head in chagrin. I called, "Thanks!" after him, but I could tell he felt he had intruded.

Dawn put the two plates of pizza down and said if she'd known I was going to be there for dinner, she would have gotten pepperoni. It was clear that she planned to pretend our conversation at Dottie Wing's had never happened, and to distract me into doing the same.

But I couldn't let her. "Are you *trying* to get me to kick you out of this house? It almost seems as if that's what you're hoping for."

She stopped mid-bite. "I don't know what you're talking about, Mommy."

"Do you understand that I could press charges about that loan signature? It's forgery. It's the same thing Rud did with his father. How could you be so—careless?" I'd been about to say "stupid," and we both knew it, but I changed my mind at the last minute.

"So are you going to have me arrested?" She looked down at her plate.

"No," I said, after letting a moment pass without speaking—not because I had to think about the answer, but because I didn't like the idea that she presumed she knew already what I would do.

"It was dumb of me, signing your name," she said, trying to appear contrite. "That was a mistake."

I didn't say what we both knew Joe would have said to that: *A mistake is adding up two and two and thinking five is the right answer. What you did was make a bad moral decision.*

"I'm sorry, Mommy," she added. I knew she was counting on her apology to end the conversation, and I let it be. My headache was starting to flare up again, and fighting would only make it worse.

No More Collateral Damage

I told Dawn I wasn't hungry and went straight up to my bed-room, where I popped a couple of aspirin and lay down to wait for my headache to go away. After a while I sat up and from under the pillow next to mine pulled out the folder Gail Nazarian had left with me at the office on Halloween. When I returned home that day I'd taken it out of my bag and left it on my dresser, but then I decided to hide it in case Dawn came into my room for some reason. I knew she wouldn't know what to make of it. Since I hadn't actually looked at the contents yet, I wasn't sure what to make of it myself.

The top page read "Transcript of Interrogation of Dawn Schutt," and was dated the day after the attack. I was relieved to see that Kenneth Thornburgh hadn't been the main interviewer, because I liked him and didn't want to find a reason to stop feeling that way.

The interrogation had been conducted by another detective, Stephen Peck, whom I remembered from the trial. He was younger than Thornburgh, and he always seemed arrogant to me.

He began by asking Dawn a bunch of simple questions—how old she was, where she went to college, how many siblings she had. He asked her if she understood that she was not under arrest—that he was just gathering information—and I imagined Dawn nodding dully, maybe apprehending what he was saying and maybe not.

DETECTIVE PECK: When were you at your house last?

MS. SCHUTT: Yesterday. My parents kicked us out. (Inaudible statement.) There was a misunderstanding about something, and they blamed Rud.

I expected that the detective would follow up to inquire about the "misunderstanding," but instead he shifted to another subject entirely. I noticed that he did that throughout—it was probably a technique designed, I thought, to catch people in lies before they could settle into a comfortable groove. He asked Dawn about the layout of our house, then abruptly said, "I imagine this is a shock to you, what happened?"

MS. SCHUTT: Yes. It hasn't sunk in yet.

DETECTIVE PECK: I haven't had a chance to talk to your mother yet, but I'm hoping we'll be able to do that soon.

MS. SCHUTT: Me, too.

DETECTIVE PECK: You want us to talk to her?

MS. SCHUTT: No, I mean *I'd* like to talk to her. Is she making sense? Are you telling me she can talk?

DETECTIVE PECK: I'm wondering why you ask that. Whether she can talk or not. Instead of if she's going to be okay.

MS. SCHUTT: (Inaudible statement.)

DETECTIVE PECK: I mean, do you have any idea what somebody did to her last night?

MS. SCHUTT: I know they said "bludgeoned." Exactly what that means, I don't know. But I assume it was—I assume it wasn't pretty.

Wasn't pretty? I could only think that she'd been in shock during the interview, and had no idea what she was saying. As it had in the newspaper accounts, the word *bludgeoned* made me wince. I tried to will myself to put the transcript aside, but it was no use—I felt compelled to keep reading, even as I recognized that my brain no longer processed the words as having anything to do with me, but had turned them into fiction.

DETECTIVE PECK: No. No, I would say it wasn't pretty, not pretty at all.

MS. SCHUTT: (Inaudible statement.)

DETECTIVE PECK: Listen, Mrs. Hinds over there is asking if you can speak up a little. I'm going to be honest with you, okay? Your mother was badly injured, but she's been able to communicate. And she indicated to us that you were involved in this.

MS. SCHUTT: That's impossible.

DETECTIVE PECK: I wouldn't lie about a thing like that. Now, I don't know what the situation was inside your family, but I want to try to work with you here. I really do.

MS. SCHUTT: M-m h-m-m.

DETECTIVE PECK: Why would she indicate a family member? (Indecipherable, two words.) One of her daughters?

MS. SCHUTT: I don't think she did.

DETECTIVE PECK: Well, I wish she hadn't, either, but it's the truth. Listen, trust me on this, this is going to get way out of hand fast if you don't start talking to us. If this goes to a grand jury, you're not going to have time after that to give your explanation.

MS. SCHUTT: (Inaudible statement.)

DETECTIVE PECK: Work with me here, okay? I'm telling you she's not dead. She's indicating what happened to her. (Inaudible three words.)

MS. SCHUTT: I don't think so.

DETECTIVE PECK: So you think I'm a liar? Or maybe your mother is?

MS. SCHUTT: (Inaudible statement.)

DETECTIVE PECK: Could you speak up? We need to get all this on the record. Now, put yourself in our shoes here. It looks to us like a family coming unraveled.

MS. SCHUTT: Unraveled. Ha! My father would never let that happen.

DETECTIVE PECK: But he did, didn't he? (Indecipherable two words.) You know what bothers me about all this? You're not really showing much of anything here. I get a *hangnail*, I show more emotion than what I'm seeing right now. We're talking about two people, your parents, beaten to a pulp. In their own bed.

MS. SCHUTT: I'm sorry if I'm not responding the way you want.

DETECTIVE PECK: I mean, I've been around this job long enough to know how people react, depending on whether they're guilty or not.

MS. SCHUTT: Yeah, I'm sure you deal with a lot of hard-core criminals around here. Tons of murderers in Everton, hunh?

I sat back on the bed, as astounded by this last statement attributed to Dawn as by anything that came before it. Of our daughters, Iris had always been the snarky one—in fact, it was *her* tone I read in this last remark, instead of anything I could imagine in Dawn's voice. Reading on, I saw that Stephen Peck seemed to keep his cool instead of reacting with anger to Dawn's sarcasm.

DETECTIVE PECK: Yeah, enough. One just a month ago, over on Grove Street—this one guy killed another guy in a lawn mower dispute; don't know if you heard about it. Anyway, I'm still interested in why your mother would have said you were involved in all this.

MS. SCHUTT: Ask my mother in front of me when the last time she saw me was.

DETECTIVE PECK: You think her answer's going to be different than when they asked her who did this to her?

MS. SCHUTT: I want to see my mother. I'd like to hear everything from her.

DETECTIVE PECK: Well, you can't see your mother, because we believe you're involved in this. The last

```
thing we want is for her to wake up and be in
fear for her life again. You can understand that,
right?
```

At this point, the transcript indicated that Dawn had said she'd be happy to keep answering their questions, but she wanted to call her lawyer—"Actually, he's more of a family friend"—first. Not for nothing, I thought, was she addicted to TV shows like *Law and Order*. When Peter Cifforelli showed up, he advised Dawn to stop talking to the police until he could meet with her in private, so there was nothing further for me to read. Not that I *wanted* more. Besides, with all the "inaudible" and "indecipherable" statements, who knew if the transcriptionist had gotten it right?

I wasn't sure what Gail Nazarian's real intention had been, in giving me these pages. Ostensibly, they were supposed to help me remember the attack, but the transcript had the opposite effect—the more I read, the more numb my body and brain became. I stuck the papers back in the folder, laid it on the bed beside me, and fell asleep.

I woke to a shock of electricity and the sensation of being shaken on the shoulder. When I opened my eyes and saw Dawn's face hovering over me, I gasped and threw my hands up, and she stepped back as if I'd struck her.

"Sorry," I said, sitting up and putting my hands to my temples, which thudded in rhythm to the panicked throb I felt in my gut. "I must have been dreaming," I told her, though I could not remember any dream.

"What's the matter?" She stepped back from me, asking the question warily from a distance. "Are you remembering something?"

"Nothing. Just give me a minute." I got up and went into the bathroom, where I covered my face with a warm cloth, hoping to slow down my pulse. When I came back, Dawn was sitting on the edge of the bed, looking at the transcript I'd forgotten was there.

"What's this?" She shook the folder in front of me as I sat down next to her.

My heart did a flip. "Well, you can see what it is," I told her, trying to keep my voice even and figure out how I was going to respond to what I knew would come next.

"I mean why do you have it?"

I shrugged, hoping she might take it as some kind of answer.

"How?" she persisted.

"Gail Nazarian."

"Why?"

I shrugged again. "She thought it would help me remember."

"Why would an interview with *me* help you remember anything?" Her questions came at me like bullets.

"I don't know, Dawn." It was the truth.

"Did it work?"

"No. It gave me a headache."

"Oh." She closed the folder and put it back beside me. "Well, I'm sorry." She opened and closed her fists at her sides, but then began peering at something under the bed. "What's that?" She got down on her hands and knees and pulled out the baseball bat. I'd forgotten it was there. "What the hell are you doing with this?"

"I don't know. It made sense when I got it. Sleeping alone— you know. I guess it's just silly." Her alarm made my head hurt more. "Did you need something?" I asked.

"What do you mean?"

"You came in and woke me up."

263

"Oh! Right. I came to tell you I'm leaving." She leaned the bat carefully against the wall next to my nightstand.

"Leaving? What do you mean?"

"Not *leaving* leaving. But Opal called while you were asleep, and she asked me to come down there. She's in trouble somehow. I think she had a fight with her mother—you know how they are. Anyway, she asked me to come and give her some moral support."

"But I thought you were the ones who were fighting."

"We weren't fighting, exactly. More like just not seeing eye to eye." She blushed, the way she always had at any expression containing the word *eye*. "Anyway, I'm taking off now. She sounded pretty upset. I'll call you tomorrow when I know what's going on."

"Are you sure you want to be driving all that way in the dark?" Dawn was the one who seemed upset to me, and I didn't like the idea of her making such a trip at night. "Can't you just wait till morning?"

She shook her head. "You know how Opal gets. She's impulsive. She doesn't always take care of herself. I'll be fine—like I said, I'll call you tomorrow." She leaned forward to kiss me, then seemed to think better of it and pulled me into a long hug. "I love you, Mommy."

"I love you, too." The words came automatically. "Be careful, okay?"

She promised and left the room. I heard her collecting things from the bathroom, zipping her suitcase shut, and lugging it downstairs. I waited a few minutes after I heard the Corvette glide down the street before I opened the folder and read the transcript again. My impulse was to call Iris, but I stopped myself, and instead tried Gail Nazarian again. This time I would have liked to

264

speak to her in person, but got her voice mail. "Have you followed up on Emmett Furth yet?" It was difficult to ignore the sound of my own desperation, but I did my best.

When I saw how early it was, not even eight o'clock yet, I threw on a jacket and crossed the street. After ringing Warren's doorbell, I thought for a moment about making a run for it, back to my house, before he could see who was on his stoop.

But even though I might have had the time to do so, I knew that I had left my own house for a reason, and I forced myself to stay put. When Warren opened the door, the pleasure I saw on his face made me know I had done the right thing.

"Hanna," he said. His voice broke a little saying my name, and I felt a reckless rush of warmth.

"I wanted to say I'm sorry about earlier," I told him. "I was rude about the cassoulet."

"Not at all! I shouldn't have just barged in like that." He ran a hand through his hair, and I wondered if he was worried about how he looked. "I know I must seem like a goof, running around offering people food all the time. But it keeps me out of trouble. By 'trouble,' I mean lonely. You know?"

"I do." Many times since Joe died, I had been tempted to take Warren up on one of his offers for us to eat together, instead of heating another meal in the microwave. But I'd always stopped myself before now, afraid of where it might lead. "I'm not really very hungry, but I wondered if you might have some coffee or something? Or tea? Anything. I'm not picky."

I smiled as if what I'd said had been funny, and felt grateful when he did the same.

He apologized for his manners and said he hadn't been expecting anyone, adding that it was a nice surprise as he put a hand

265

out to usher me inside. When he didn't move to take my coat, I stepped toward the hall closet, and he apologized again, yanking the door open to search for a hanger. Not finding an empty one, he shoved one of his own jackets onto the floor and hung up mine. In the closet's corner I saw a stack of Maxine's old protest signs: NO MORE COLLATERAL DAMAGE and MAKE LOVE NOT WAR.

Stepping into the living room, it occurred to me that for all the times Warren and I had spoken out on the sidewalk or in our driveways, I hadn't been inside his house since the last time Joe and I came over for dinner, more than three years earlier. Could it really have been that long? Everything looked exactly as I remembered it, down to the furniture that had seemed shabby but comfortable the first time I was invited in almost twenty years before. I remember thinking, that day, how different Warren and Maxine must have been from Joe and me, in terms of a sense of order: at our house nothing was out of place, even though the girls were little and it took exhausting vigilance on my part to keep their toys in the bins and baskets we'd set up in their rooms for storage.

At the Goldmans' house, you'd always had to move something aside if you wanted to sit down—a section of the newspaper, a sweater, one of Sam's drawings or a piece of one of the model airplanes he was always building. The night I went over for the party to celebrate Hillary Clinton's election, I figured they would have straightened up because they were expecting guests. But the rooms were no neater than usual, and though I knew Joe would have been uncomfortable in the disarray, I remember feeling a little envious. Because I was the one who was home with the girls most of the time, it had been largely my job to teach them to put things away as soon as they were done with them. Dawn never complained (because she was not one to put up a fuss about anything), but Iris made a big deal out of it every time we asked her to return something to its designated container. "I have better things to do than pick up Magic Markers," she'd say, even at the age of six or seven. And although of course I didn't let her get away with it, part of me admired the fact that she recognized her time as valuable, and that she had big ambitions for the things she would eventually accomplish in her life.

Even the candy on the Goldmans' coffee table seemed familiar; the dish contained the wrapped peppermints Maxine had taken to eating after she got sick because they alleviated her nausea from the chemo. I wondered if these were the same candies from that time, or whether Warren ate them out of nostalgia—as I recalled, he didn't like them himself—and kept replenishing the stock. I could see him doing such a thing.

"How about some wine?" he said, opening a cabinet as I followed him into the kitchen. As he spoke he was uncorking a bottle, and he'd poured two glasses before I decided, as tempting as it was with all that had been going on around me, not to indulge. "I don't usually drink," I told him as he held mine out to me.

"Oh. I'm sorry, I forgot. It's been too long." I had embarrassed him again, and it made me feel bad; here I was, just dropping in on him, expecting to be served. "How about some tea, then?"

As he turned the stove on to boil the water and took up a glass of wine for himself, I stood in front of the fridge to look at the pictures fastened by magnets in a casual collage. Most of the photos' edges curled up at the sides, making me think that the display had been Maxine's handiwork; leaning closer, I saw that the only one that looked remotely recent was a shot of Warren, Sam, and

Sam's bride posing in front of the synagogue on their wedding day. It reminded me of the photograph in Iris's house that had caused our argument about Rud, so to distract myself, I pointed to a picture of Warren and Maxine from when they were much younger, which looked as if it had been taken on a boat, and asked Warren about it.

"That was her father's yacht," he said, smacking his lips over the wine in a way I was sure would have dismayed a connoisseur. "Long Island. I worked at the marina, and you can imagine how thrilled her father was when his princess took up with a dock-hand."

I told him I was surprised to hear that Maxine had come from money, and said I'd always assumed they'd met at a rally or something. "I always thought of her as a little bit of a kook," I added. The words came out before I realized how they might sound, but before I could apologize, he smiled and told me, "Well, she was. But in a good way."

"Oh, I'm sorry." I accepted the mug he handed me. "I didn't mean it like that."

"It's okay." He led me into the living room and sat on one end of the sofa, leaving room for me to take the other end with plenty of space between us. "Now I can tell you that I always thought of Joe as a little bit of a stuffed shirt."

"Well, he was," I said, smiling back at him. "But in a good way."

A silence followed, but it didn't feel awkward anymore. Then he said, "I know what you mean. I miss Maxine like crazy. Little things, mostly. I even miss the things I couldn't stand when she was alive, like the way she cleared her throat all the time. You know?"

I nodded. "For me it's how much he expected of everybody—himself as much as everyone else. I used to feel like I couldn't live up to it. But now I miss having that kind of moral compass."

"Not living up to your own standards, Mrs. Schutt?" Warren laughed as he raised his glass again.

I tried to laugh, too. "I know that sounds silly."

"No, it doesn't. I know exactly what you mean. I liked having Maxine as a witness to how I lived my life." He took another sip and smacked his lips again, which made me laugh a little. It seemed to encourage him. "We were lucky," he went on. "Well, if you can call it that. But we had time—we knew she was dying, and we had the time to say things to each other. I don't think I left anything out." He lifted his glass to his mouth, but lowered it to add, "It wasn't like you and Joe. So sudden, such a shock. I can't even imagine."

Something about the sympathy in his voice, combined with the flush I felt in my cheeks from the tea, made me close my eyes. I knew I was about to tell Warren something I'd never told anyone before. Part of me wanted to stop myself, but it wasn't as big as the part that wanted, finally, to confess what I'd never had the courage to say to Joe.

It was our fifth wedding anniversary. Iris was four years old, Dawn a year and a half. Joe had said he'd be home early to give the girls their bath before we went out to dinner to celebrate while my friend Claire babysat. Around three o'clock Joe called and said something had come up—a last-minute audit he'd been assigned—and he was really sorry but we'd have to reschedule.

I knew I couldn't ask him to object to the audit, because he'd just gotten a promotion at Stinson and Keyes and was still working to prove himself in the new job. But I was far more disappointed than I let on to Joe. The whole week had been rainy, and I'd been playing Chutes and Ladders with the girls all day to the point of a boredom that made me think I might scream. After hanging up with Joe, I called Claire to see if she wanted to come over anyway, but she begged off, saying she was tired and that if I didn't need her to watch the girls, she thought she'd just go to bed early. I put Dawn and Iris in front of the TV, letting the sounds of cartoons and *Sesame Street* fill the house as I opened the cupboards to take out ingredients for a dinner I did not want to cook.

I stared at the shelves for a minute or so, then shut those doors and opened the one to the cabinet over the sink where we kept liquor, although we seldom had people to serve—most of the guests who came to our house, especially in those days, were Iris's playmates. Checking to make sure the girls couldn't see, I poured vodka in my coffee mug and added a jot of orange juice, then went in to join them by the TV, thinking, *Don't I deserve a break?* I had not allowed myself to have any alcohol since I'd met Joe, remembering the nights I'd soaked and erased myself in wine after my mother died. It was the one thing I hadn't told Joe before we married, because I was afraid of what he would think of me. Afterward, I was afraid of becoming that person again without being able to help it. I knew I'd lose everything if I let that happen.

But the night of our anniversary, my resolve flagged. I refilled the coffee mug three times before Iris said she was hungry, at which point I got up to make macaroni and cheese but forgot it was on the stovetop and burned it in the pan. Dawn cried, until I told them they could have cookies for dinner *and* dessert.

I could tell she needed her diaper changed, and I told myself I'd do it when she was finished. She was a slow eater, though, and as she dawdled over her cookies, I got impatient. I wanted to

270

put her and Iris back in front of the TV and pour myself another drink.

The glass of orange juice (which was how I thought of it) sat almost empty on the dresser in the nursery. I was in the middle of changing the messy diaper when Iris screamed from the bathroom, "Mom, come here!"

There was something in her voice I took to be panic. I don't think I ever even made the decision to run from the changing table; I just ran. In the bathroom, Iris stood in front of the toilet and pointed into the water. "Perfect poopy," she said to me, turning up a proud smile. She only wanted me to praise her, I realized, as she reached over to flush.

"Oh, God," I said with a groan, rushing back to Dawn's room. What I'd heard as a shriek of distress had only been my daughter exclaiming her admiration for herself. What was wrong with me, that I couldn't tell the difference?

When I returned to the room, Dawn wasn't on the table. My heart clutched, along with my breath. Then I saw her moving behind the toy chest, trying to sit up, getting herself tangled in the smeary diaper she'd pulled down with her when she rolled off. I sucked my breath in with a noise, and when I picked her up, I saw that she'd cut her forehead on the chest's edge; a slit of red bloomed over her left eye.

But she wasn't crying. She didn't seem to realize she'd been hurt. "Mommy," she said, reaching for me, "I falled." I set her back on the table and looked carefully at the cut. It didn't seem too deep, and it wasn't gushing. If I got ice on it right away, I thought, I could probably keep it from swelling. I slapped a clean diaper on her and, afraid to lay her down on the couch, put her on her back on the floor in the living room while I filled a bag-

271

gie with ice, then pulled her onto my lap and held it against the wound. At the touch of the coldness she began to struggle, and I remember thinking, *Good, at least she feels* that.

Iris came and stood in front of me as she watched me tend to her little sister. "She can't even do poopy right," she announced. That was the year she started announcing things, and she never stopped. She added, "Dawn is a dummy."

"She is not," I said. "You never say that, Iris. About anyone, but especially your sister."

She shrugged; it was also the year she seemed to stop being bothered anytime I said anything sharp to her. "Go play in your room," I told her, because I wanted to be as far away as possible from what she'd said.

Dawn had settled back and let me keep the ice on her forehead. In the back of my mind I knew I should call the doctor, but then I reasoned, *I'm a nurse. I know what the bad symptoms are—vomiting, drowsiness, bleeding that won't stop—and she's not showing any of those.*

It also occurred to me, distantly, that whoever I brought my daughter to for help might be able to tell I'd been drinking. I'd been alone with my children. I couldn't risk it.

I also didn't want Joe to know what had happened, of course. The vodka had made me sleepy, so I put the girls down early and went to bed myself around nine, before he got home, but the next morning at breakfast Iris told him about her sister's fall. I played it down behind my hangover headache, but he looked alarmed before he took Dawn's head between his hands, looked for the mark (which, thank God, had lessened instead of swollen overnight), and allowed me to assure him that she was fine. He told me he understood, but I couldn't help feeling that he blamed me. Which he should have; it was my fault. I kept apologizing, and he said more than once, "Hanna, accidents happen." But I couldn't tell him the whole truth, so from that day forward, even though I never took a drink again—and allowed him to believe I did it out of consideration for him, since he'd grown up in an alcoholic home—a wedge existed between us that softened and shrank over time, but never went away altogether. And only I knew about it, which made it worse.

I finished my monologue to Warren by saying it hadn't taken me long to realize I should have called the doctor, or just taken Dawn in to get examined, and not only for her sake. If I had taken her in and gotten official word that she was okay, or that she wasn't okay but here's how we'll fix it, I wouldn't still be torturing myself like this, wondering if my letting her fall that day might have contributed to her getting a lazy eye a few years later. Or to the "something missing" her teacher had mentioned. To other kids calling her Ding-Dong Dawn.

And to what happened to Joe and me in our bed nearly twenty years after the fall.

Warren listened intently the whole time I was speaking. The kind expression on his face did not waver. "I might have been able to save us—my family," I said, and this was when I couldn't sit on the couch any longer; I had to stand up from the force of my own guilt and grief. But I didn't know what to do once I'd stood up—which direction to turn—so I let Warren take my arm and guide me back to rejoin him.

"Listen to me," he said. "You're not responsible for anything Dawn did. You know that, right?"

"What she *did*?" I pulled away from him. "I was talking about how she *is*."

273

He looked stricken. "I didn't mean anything, Hanna."

"Yes, you did." But instead of feeling angry at him, I began to cry. I told him about the interrogation transcript, and how I hadn't recognized my own daughter in the things she was reported to have said. "It didn't sound like Dawn. But of course it was. I know that." Warren pulled an old-fashioned handkerchief from his back pocket and held it out to me, telling me not to worry, it was almost clean.

Despite myself, I laughed and took it from him. "I'm not worried." I wiped my tears and said, "What *happened* to her?" I didn't expect he would have an answer, but I'd needed to ask the question for longer than I realized until that moment.

Warren spoke so quietly that I wasn't sure, at first, what it was he'd said. "I really appreciate this, Hanna."

"What?"

"Your opening up like this. You're usually so—I don't know. Held in." He folded his arms across his chest to illustrate what he meant. "I thought maybe it was me."

"No," I told him. "It's the Swedish way." The words, my mother's, popped out before I could plan them. When the prison called to tell me that my father had died in his cell while playing solitaire, I remembered all those nights of watching him turn over cards as he sat beside my mother, who quilted silently beside him. "Why don't you guys ever talk to each other?" I'd asked her once, and she told me again that it was "the Swedish way." "We keep to ourselves," she said.

"Ah. 'The Swedish way.'" Warren smiled. "I'm glad to know there's a name for it." He leaned in, and I thought he meant to kiss me, but then I realized that the intention was my own.

He kissed me back—I thought I heard a small groan during

it—and then put his hand up to my temple. I couldn't help pulling back and drawing a piece of hair over my damaged eye.

"Don't," he said, pushing the hair back in its place. "I'd rather see you." He lifted his forefinger and traced it over my longest scar. The touch made me cry, and I reached out to clutch him close. "Hanna," he said, "Do you know what you're doing?"

I nodded, not trusting my voice, then shook my head.

"Have you been with anybody since—?" he said. I shook my head again. "Me, either," he said.

I began to unbutton his shirt and let him pull me down next to him on the couch. When he felt for my breasts, brushing my nipples lightly, I felt myself responding with a surge, suddenly remembering—as I had not before—that the last time Joe and I had made love was that Friday night after Thanksgiving three years earlier, only a few hours before we were attacked in the same bed. We were both upset by what had happened with Rud and Dawn that day, and the sex was more comfort than anything else, as well as a way to allow us both to sleep when otherwise we might not have been able to.

I had testified to the court that the last thing I remembered, before waking up in the hospital, was watching Dawn and Rud pull away in her Nova, which Joe and I believed contained the items he had stolen from our house. Now I was remembering something that had happened hours after that. The realization was almost strong enough to make me want to sit up, stop Warren, and tell him about it, but then the desire *not* to do so—and, perhaps, not to remember?—overtook me, and I began grinding against him in a way I hadn't felt myself move in years, since long before Joe died, since early on in our marriage. At first I thought I felt Warren wondering if he should keep going, but then he began moving with me,

275

and I found myself giving in to the impulse to express what it felt like to have this man touch me the way he did, to feel my body react in ways I hadn't been sure it still knew how to, until now.

When we lay against each other afterward, I felt my head drop forward in the way that meant I was almost asleep, and forced myself to sit up, grabbing hastily for my clothes in an effort to rearrange myself. Warren took his time, sitting up slowly and swinging his feet over the side of the couch next to mine, laying a hand on my knee before putting his shirt back on without refastening any of the buttons.

"Are you okay?" he said. I knew the polite thing to do was to say yes and ask him if he was, too, but the words stuck in my throat. I tried to nod, but then I was crying again, and I gave up and buried my face in his shoulder until we both ended up laughing, though I'm sure neither of us could have said why.

"Ah, Hanna," he said, hugging me close. We just listened to each other breathe for a few minutes, and though I tried hard not to because it seemed disloyal to Joe, I recognized how good it felt to be held again.

I dozed a little, then jerked awake to the sensation that I had forgotten something. "What time is it?"

He craned his neck to see the clock on the mantel. "Eleven twenty."

I swore and jumped up. "Abby. I've got to go."

He got up, too, bumping his shin on the coffee table. "Do you want me to come?"

"No. Why?" Then I realized I had been rude. "I mean, I don't think so. There's no need. But thanks for offering."

"I was doing it for my own sake," he said, reaching out again to brush my hair from my face.

I made what felt like a bold move myself, cupping his chin in my hand. "Warren. I mean it: thank you. Let's talk in the morning, okay?"

He agreed, walked me to the door, took my coat out of the closet, dropped it, laughed at himself, then helped me slip it on. "Be careful," he said as I went out, and I realized that they were the same words I'd said to Dawn when she left a few hours before.

Proud Participant

Abby met me at the door, whimpering, and I let her out into the backyard because I didn't like to walk her so late, even around the neighborhood. Besides, I had a voice-mail notification, and I thought I should listen in case it was Dawn.

I was relieved at first when I heard Peter Cifforelli's voice, but the feeling vanished as soon as I understood what he was saying. "Are you insane, Hanna?" the message began, and I wanted to cut it off, but I was stopped dead by the accusation in his voice. "How could you let her do something like that? Okay. Okay." In the background I thought I could hear Wendy urging him to calm down. "Listen, if you haven't done it already, go look up the *Bloody Glove* website. It'll be all over the news tomorrow. Call me." Then he hung up, the click so loud I could feel the anger in it.

I wished more than anything that I could ignore what I'd just heard. For a moment I considered just letting Abby in and going to bed. But I knew I wouldn't be able to sleep if I didn't find out what Peter had been talking about.

Reluctantly I went to my computer, which I'd used only a few times since reading the archived news stories about the attack. Feeling my stomach constrict, I searched for *The Bloody Glove* and, when the site came up, closed my eyes in something resembling prayer before I clicked. At the sight of the main headline— "Daughter Confesses in Brutal Dad-Slay"—I felt a collapsing sensation in my chest.

What had Cecilia done to Dawn now?

The following is an interview between *Bloody Glove* investigative reporter Cecilia Baugh and her childhood friend and former murder suspect Dawn Schutt, who escaped indictment after her parents were attacked in their bed in Everton, N.Y., on the night after Thanksgiving three years ago. The attack, committed with a croquet mallet taken from a set in the family's own garage, resulted in Joseph Schutt's death and severe injury and disfigurement to Dawn's mother, Hanna Schutt.

In previous statements, Dawn has always contended that neither she nor Rud Petty was present in the Schutt house that night. Last month Rud Petty won appeal of his conviction, and he will face a new trial in the spring.

Dawn Schutt requested two conditions for talking to our reporter: that the *Glove* pay her an undisclosed amount of money, and that nothing in it be printed or in any other way revealed until after Petty's trial is over, when Dawn believes her boyfriend will be acquitted and released, and they will resume their lives together under new identities.

Though the *Glove* did pay her a significant sum for this interview, which took place at a coffee shop in Everton, we decided in the public interest not to honor Dawn's request to withhold the information it contains.

BG: Thanks for sitting down with us today, Dawn. I'm sure this can't be easy.

DS: No, it isn't.

BG: Our readers might wonder if you feel like you're taking a risk here, talking to me.

DS: Well, I thought it through—all the things you said—and you're right, it's worth it. By the time people see this, Rud will be free. They can't put him on trial twice for the same thing. Like what happened to me. *(Ed. Note: Dawn Schutt is mistaken, here, about her own legal status; since she has never stood trial for the crime, she will not face double jeopardy if the district attorney chooses to bring charges at a later date.)*

BG: Okay, let's get to that night. What happened after you and Rud were questioned earlier in the day in connection with the burglary at your house? *(Ed. Note: The Everton police had been called to investigate the theft of several valuable items from the Schutt home when the only person present in the house was Rud Petty, who claimed he was asleep when the burglary took place.)*

280

DS: We drove back up to my house because Rud wanted to talk to my father. He didn't like the way Daddy treated him after that cop came—so suspicious, when there was no real evidence Rud had done anything at all. He said he just wanted to talk, though. Nothing more than that. I said to Rud something like, why don't we just wait until tomorrow, when everybody's cooled off? But he said he was too pissed, he had to get it out of his system. I didn't want to go with him, but he said he needed me. I always liked when he said that; it made me feel good. The whole ride, he talked about how it wasn't fair of my father to accuse him of burglary, and how humiliated he felt. I tuned him out after a while, because it's not like he wanted me to say anything. When we got there, of course, the house was dark, because it was after midnight. I knew they would be asleep. I asked him if we could just leave, and wait until tomorrow. Or just go in and go to sleep ourselves, wake up and see things fresher in the morning. Rud said, "No, I have a plan. It'll be fine. Trust me, Dawnie." He was the only one who ever called me that, and I liked it. My sister and other kids used to call me Ding-Dong—well, I don't have to tell you that. You remember. I hated it. But I liked when he called me Dawnie. It made me feel cool. I said we should ring the bell, but Rud said, "Don't wake them up." I thought he was being considerate. So I told him I knew where the spare key was, hidden in the flower

281

box at the front of the house, but when I took it out and turned around to show him, he wasn't there. I opened the front door with the key and pressed in the code for the alarm in the entryway.

   Then Rud came up behind me and I saw he had a croquet mallet from the garage. He had a pair of gloves on. "What are those for?" I asked him, and he just said, "Nothing."

BG: But what did you think when you saw him holding the croquet mallet? And why did his saying "Nothing" make sense to you?

DS:(shrugging) I don't know. I guess it sounds kind of stupid. I know, Ding-Dong, right? But sometimes he does things like that, for no reason. Anyway, Abby came in from the TV room—

BG: And Abby would be your dog?

DS: Yeah. We've had her since I was nine. She's named after Abigail Adams, because I was doing a project on her the weekend we went to the shelter and picked her out.

BG: I remember that project. Awesome Women of the World. I did mine on Mother Teresa. Go ahead.

DS: Well, Abby came in and she was yipping a little at first, but when she saw it was me, she started licking my hand. I said, "Good girl." Rud took her by the collar and began pulling her toward the basement. "What are you doing that for?" I asked. I told him to stop it. But he yanked her down the stairs, and I heard him closing the laundry room door to keep her in there.

BG: When the police entered the home the next morning, the dog had been severely injured. Probably with the same weapon that attacked your parents, they said—the croquet mallet.

DS: *(wincing)* That was an accident, Rud said. He loved animals. He would never hurt one on purpose.

BG: Dawn, no offense, but do you know how absurd that sounds? When he's accused of smashing your parents' skulls? Sorry—do you want to take a break?

DS: *(shaking head)* No. Let's just get it over with. So we went upstairs, where the bedrooms are. Rud made me go first. I was about to knock on my parents' door, but Rud pushed it open before I could. My mother's a heavy sleeper—it takes a lot to wake her up—but my father isn't.

BG: Do you realize you're referring to your father in the present tense?

DS: Really? God, Cecilia, you notice everything.

BG: Thanks. Okay, go ahead. So your father's a light sleeper—

DS: And he sat up right away in the bed and said, "Who is that?" I said, "It's me, Daddy," and he turned on the light. He was mad, I could tell. He likes his privacy, and he didn't want us there—especially Rud. He said, "What are you doing? It's the middle of the night." He threw his feet over the edge of the bed, but Rud got him sideways before I knew what was happening. The sound of the croquet mallet hitting my father's skull—I'll never forget that as long as I live. Sorry. (*Ed.*

283

Note: Here, Dawn Schutt presses fingers into her forehead.) I must have made a noise or something, because Rud told me to shut up. He went to swing the mallet again, and I saw my father look up at me. He expected me to catch Rud's arm and try to stop him. I could see that. But I couldn't move.

My mother, believe it or not, was just waking up. My father used to say she could have slept through Pearl Harbor. She didn't get what was going on, right away. She saw me standing there, and she said my name. Then she asked, "Are you okay, honey?"

My father was trying to get at his inhaler—he kept it on the nightstand in case he woke up in the night and couldn't breathe, because of his asthma. He was fishing around with his hand, but he knocked the inhaler onto the floor. I picked it up and gave it to him, but Rud saw me do it, smacked it away from my father, and stomped on it. Crushed it to pieces.

The look on my father's face then—I can't even begin to describe it. It made me freeze up, and I couldn't move. As soon as I heard him gasping, I started to have trouble breathing, myself. And that hadn't happened in, I don't know, six years.

BG: The newspaper accounts described you as requesting an inhaler in the police car that transported you to the hospital where your mother was. Was this a flare-up of the asthma you suffered when you were a child?

284

DS: I don't know. I think it would have been more psychological.

BG: Sorry for interrupting. You can go on.

DS: Rud hit him again, and this time my father went down on the floor with a funny kind of sound, like surprise. There was blood everywhere. I almost slipped in it. He gave a big groan and then he went quiet, lying there on the floor. I couldn't believe when I read in the papers that he wasn't actually dead then—that he got up and tried to do all that stuff, get dressed and unload the dishwasher, but on the other hand that was just like him. Routine. Order. I'm surprised he never joined the army, he loved that kind of thing.

BG: The investigators couldn't believe it, either. That he was able to move as much as he did, with the injuries he sustained.

DS: Well, that was my father. He was unusual.

BG: And your mother—

DS: My mother was trying to get up, and Rud swore and went toward her. I could see she was going to reach for the phone on the bed table, and I wanted her to get to it and call 911. Things were out of control, I wanted it to stop. But Rud pulled the cord out of the wall. My mother just looked at me, as if she didn't know who I was. "Dawn?" she said, like she'd made a mistake or something. As if I might have been someone else. That's when Rud pushed her down and then swung the mallet. I think I screamed, and he told me to shut up again.

285

He hit her and hit her, and blood flew all over the wall.

BG: You must have been hysterical.

DS: I was. Rud threw the mallet onto the bed and grabbed my arm and yanked me out of the room and down the stairs. He still hadn't said much of anything, the whole time, except those two words—*shut up*. When we got to the door, I wanted to go back in and check on Abby in the basement, make sure she was okay. I knew my parents were dead, or at least I thought so, but I wasn't really thinking. If that makes any sense. I thought I could still save Abby. *(Ed. Note: Here, Dawn Schutt closes her eyes.)*

But Rud was too strong. He pulled me to the front door and bashed the alarm pad against the wall, then put his arm around me—like we were on a date—and took me out to the car. I thought he would start talking like he always did, but instead he turned the music up loud. Bad music, stupid music, the heavy metal he listens to when nobody's around that he wants to impress. It always gave me a headache, but what could I say? He wanted it. Loud music made him horny, he said.

Once we got on the Thruway about twenty minutes downstate, he pulled the car over and we had sex. I can't say he made me do it—I wanted to. It felt like if we did something normal, maybe it meant what just happened hadn't really happened or something. That probably sounds like Ding-Dong Dawn to you. I don't know, Cecilia. *(Ed. Note: Dawn Schutt covers her face with her hands.)* I'm doing my best.

BG: You're doing fine.

DS: Thanks. After that we just kept driving; we didn't even stop to pee or for food or gas or anything. We got to his apartment and went inside, and Rud fell asleep right away. But first he took his clothes off, because there was blood all over them.

BG: You know the prosecution contended that because your boyfriend worked in a vet's office, he knew how to clean up blood. For instance, in his car. They didn't find any. Can you explain how that happened?

DS: Before we left, he grabbed my father's old down L.L.Bean jacket—we used to tease him whenever he wore it; we called him Puff Daddy—out of the closet, and went to put it on over his clothes. I said, "No, not that one," but he already had it on. He took his shoes off and told me to, too, and we stopped at the McDonald's on the way out of town and stuffed them in the trash.

I'd been aware of the sour panic rising in my throat as I read, and suddenly I had to pull myself away from the desk as my stomach heaved and I expected to vomit. For a few minutes I sat with my head almost in my lap, focusing on the nausea instead of on what I had just read. Then, when I realized it was a false alarm, I forced myself back to the screen.

When we got to his place, before he went to bed, he told me to take a shower and throw both our clothes away. I was happy to, because I was wearing the sweater my mother had bought for me when we were at the mall that morning—an early Christmas present, she said. I didn't like it, it wasn't my style, but I could tell she wanted to get it for me, so I let her. I threw the sweater in the trash with my jeans and socks and underwear. I figured, after what happened, she'd never know the difference.

I couldn't sleep, so I stayed up and watched those Hitchcock movies. In the morning, it was real early, Rud came out of the bedroom and said he was taking me home. I thought he meant home as in Wildwood Lane, and I said, "What are you *talking* about?" But he said no, he meant my apartment. "You were there all night," he told me. I said, "What?" He got all impatient like he usually did when I said something stupid, and told me, "That's your alibi. You were at home with dumb-ass Opal all night. You and I talked on the phone around midnight, and I said I was going to sleep. Got it?"

Then he farted. I know it's dumb but I always laughed when he did this, and this time he did, too. We got in the car and he dropped me off without kissing me, which I didn't like. He always kissed me when he dropped me off, if he wasn't coming in. But this time he just drove away. He didn't even look back.

BG: And what made you decide to come home now—move

288

back from New Mexico—in the wake of Rud Petty's being granted his appeal?

DS: Rud asked me to. He was worried my mother might remember something about that night, and he wanted me to find out if she was planning to testify.

Reeling, seeing the wall shimmer in front of me, I thought about the Friday afternoon a few weeks earlier, when Kenneth Thornburgh came to tell me what had happened in court. Then I remembered Dawn's two separate calls to me the following day, and her asking me, during the second one, if she could return home to live.

DS: Once I got here it became pretty clear right away that she didn't remember anything, and I told him that.

BG: How did you tell him? He was in prison. And records show you never visited him there.

DS: (shaking head) That's right, I didn't. But he has a cousin, Stew, who does visit him, and he's been kind of a go-between between me and Rud.

Stew. The boy who had been eating pizza with Dawn in my kitchen. The boy who'd followed and watched me at the mall even before Dawn moved back home. I put a hand to my stomach again.

DS: I told Stew my mother didn't remember anything, but he said Rud told him we couldn't take that chance. I said, "Whatever you're talking about, you can forget it."

289

BG: He was referring to removing your mother from the picture, so she couldn't testify, is that right?

DS: *(shaking head emphatically)* No. Not "removing." More like just scaring her. But there's no way I'd let him do something like that. She's been through enough.

BG: I see. Now, Dawn, here's a question I think anyone reading this story would want to ask. In light of what you've just told us, why would you want to spend the rest of your life with the man who attacked your parents in the way you've described?

DS: This is what I want people to understand. It wasn't really Rud who did it. I mean, something took over—rage, or something—and I know his *body* did those things, but he wasn't in his right head. His real head. It wasn't the Rud I know, or the Rud I love. *(A pause as she seems to reflect.)* And it never would have happened if my parents hadn't treated him the way they did.

BG: What about the dog? The dog didn't do anything.

DS: *(voice shaking)* I know. I told you, it was an accident. Collateral damage, Rud called it. I still don't know what that means. *(She appears to try to regain her composure.)* But I know he'd give anything if the whole thing hadn't happened. And when we get to start over together, he'll never do anything like this again.

BG: Okay. Do you mind if I just look at my notes for a minute?

DS: Take your time. Wow, this scone is good.

BG: Is it okay if I switch tracks for a sec?

DS: It's your interview. Shoot.

BG: Some people might assume that once you met Rud Petty, you became a victim yourself. That he held a power over you it was impossible to resist, leading you to do things you wouldn't normally have done. Most people who know you don't realize that your tendency toward violence—or destruction, anyway—precedes your time with him.

DS: What?

BG: I had an interesting conversation with your next-door neighbor, Emmett Furth. You might recall that the defense tried to implicate him in the attack against your parents.

DS: What does Emmett Furth have to do with anything?

BG: You remember the day your family's tree house burned down, in tenth grade?

DS: *(voice rising)* Of course I remember. Why are we talking about this?

BG: It's always been assumed that Emmett was responsible for that fire. But he says he actually saw *you* out there, standing on the ladder and lighting sticks before tossing them inside.

Now I thought I might choke on the hot shriek gathering in my throat. But I was afraid Abby would hear me from the yard and be alarmed, so I swallowed hard to keep it down.

DS: I have no idea what you're talking about. Of course he would say something like that! He doesn't want people to know what he did. Look, aren't we done here? Didn't I do what you wanted? Did you bring my check?

BG: I went back and looked at the date. The fire happened the morning after we had auditions at school for *A Chorus Line*.

DS: (nearly shouting) So?

BG: You didn't try out for a part, even though your name was on the list. You signed up, then changed your mind. *(Ed. Note: Dawn Schutt remains silent.)* You were upset by that, weren't you? I think you wanted to audition, and you were mad at yourself for pulling out.

DS: (attempting to regain her composure) That's completely crazy. I don't know what you're talking about. I'm sorry, Cecilia, but that has nothing to do with anything. I get that you want to "stir up interest," but you can't just make *(expletive deleted)* like that up out of thin air.

I'd read enough—in fact, I'd read too much. But every time I tried to force myself to click the *X* at the top of the website, I couldn't make myself do it. As with the transcript of Dawn's interrogation, I couldn't stop reading the next paragraph, and then the next. Finally, I forced myself to close the website's window and then, as if it meant anything, shut the computer down.

The first thing I did was walk to the hall closet and, taking a deep breath before pulling it open, saw that Joe's old "Puff

Daddy" jacket was not hanging where it always had, with our winter clothing. I'd never noticed it missing before. I went through the rack three times, hoping I'd just rummaged over it, but there was no mistaking—it was gone.

Numbly, I went to the back door and let Abby in. Usually she was calmer when she entered the house after being outside, but tonight she still seemed agitated. "Sorry, girl," I told her, assuming she hadn't appreciated my leaving her alone for so long while I was at Warren's house.

Then I said, "Come with me," and she panted up the stairs behind me. At the closed door to Dawn's room she paused and sniffed, giving a little yip, but I barely noticed because I was so intent on my mission.

It was true that I hadn't remembered anything significant when I'd gone into our old bedroom by myself a few weeks earlier, but somehow I believed that tonight might be different, especially given everything I'd just read. I felt a new resolve, though it contained a measure of dread I didn't recognize fully until later. And I planned to go further in my efforts to reenact that night.

Opening the door, I tried to focus on my breathing, as Barbara had taught us all in Tough Birds. But it didn't work. I swallowed hard and took a deep breath as I switched the light on and walked to the spot I'd stood in the first time, when I remembered the tattoo—at the foot of the bed, across from the bathroom.

This time, though, I took a step closer to the bed, feeling my breath catch in my throat. It came out in a sound that resembled a muffled scream.

I heard myself, but it was through a rushing in my ears. I was two places at once—the present and the past, this night and the one from three years earlier holding equal weight at either side of my pounding head.

Before I realized that I was doing it, I turned off the light and sat down on the bed, then swung my legs on top of it and settled down against one of the pillows where no head had ever lain. Abby came over and turned her face up, as if to ask, *Are you sure you want to do this?*

"It's okay," I told her, trying to soothe both of us.

I closed my eyes, and after a moment I could almost imagine the sound of Joe's breath next to me. Because of his asthma, he was never silent when he slept, and I had gotten used to the familiar noise over all the years of our marriage. Though part of me knew the sound was only an illusion, I listened to it for a minute or so, tempted to give in to the comfort it made me feel.

Then Abby whined at my side, and I sat back up and patted her on the head. "You were downstairs on your bed that night, next to the TV." Somehow, narrating my thoughts out loud put them at a distance I could bear. When I said this, I realized that now I actually *did* remember Abby settling into her big cushion in the family room after Joe turned off the movie, and I knew I had the right night in my head because, on our way up the stairs to the bedroom, I assumed Joe was thinking about the awful scene earlier in the day with Dawn and Rud, and I told him, "She'll probably call in the morning and apologize."

In the room where I sat trying to remember, Abby barked. And then it was all clear before me—so clear that it was as if it had always been there, and immediately I couldn't remember what it was like *not* to have it at the front of my consciousness. The sudden, vivid clarity felt like a kick in the forehead. It was the most disturbing sensation I'd ever known.

"You weren't barking that night," I whispered, allowing myself to return slowly to a lying position, knowing that if I didn't take care, when I sat up again everything would have changed in a way I wasn't prepared to face. "That means Dawn *was* here with him. Right?" In retrospect, I can almost feel amused to realize I was asking a dog for confirmation, though there was nothing remotely funny about it then.

The next thing I remembered was hearing Joe—not his strained breathing, but his voice. He was saying something, but not to me. He started wheezing, and he knocked his inhaler off the table when he tried to grab for it.

I reached up to turn on the light on my nightstand, but a voice said, "Leave it off," and I recognized it as Rud Petty's. Across the bed, I saw Joe sitting with his legs over the side, putting his head down to his knees. At the time, I thought he was only trying to catch his breath. After reading Dawn's interview, I understood that he had also been hit in the head already with the mallet.

Then I heard another sound—not a word but a more high-pitched, asthmatic gasp, the sound so familiar and chilling that I heard my own voice scale an octave when I asked, "Dawn?" Dimly, through the darkness, I thought I could make out the Fair Isle pattern on the blue sweater I'd bought her that morning. "It looks so pretty on you," I'd told her, when she tried it on for me. "It brings out the color in your eyes."

In the store, she told me she liked the sweater. I wouldn't have bought it for her otherwise.

In the bedroom, she raised her hand to touch the pattern on her chest, and I saw 768*—our alarm code—scribbled in black ink on the back of her wrist. *I must be dreaming*, I thought.

But she murmured, "Shit," and came toward me; I could see her face, now that my sight had readjusted in the dark. "Be quiet, Mommy," she said. I heard right away that her words were more of a command than an attempt to calm me.

"Are you okay, honey?" I reached my hand up toward her and opened my palm, as if she might lay the answer inside it. In the distance I heard Abby—not barking, but squealing in pain, and I thought I saw Dawn flinch at the sound.

Joe was standing now, though hunched over, still having trouble with his breath. He bent to pick up his inhaler from the floor, but Dawn beat him to it. Looking relieved, he reached out for her to give it to him, but instead she lifted a foot and squashed the inhaler with a force that made the floor shake.

I thought I heard Rud Petty laughing. Is it possible he would have laughed at a time like that? Then his tone turned quickly to alarm, as he must have noticed me trying to lift myself. "Shit, she up?" He made a movement in my direction, but then Joe made a sound like a sharply wounded animal.

"Get out of here," he gasped, and I watched Rud raise what I thought was a baseball bat above my husband's head. In the next instant, I saw him swing the thing through the air and heard Joe yelp as it hit him, sending him to the floor.

I shrieked as Joe fell beyond my sight, then grabbed for the phone on the night table. I managed to dial 9 and 1, but then Dawn darted over and pulled the cord out of the wall. "Dawn?" I said again, still thinking she might help me as I tried to get out of the bed, but then Rud pinned me back onto the mattress, and after a few moments I gave up struggling and collapsed. Looking up, I felt rather than saw something coming at me, being swung hard and fast. Then nothing until I heard Kenneth Thornburgh's voice as if he were speaking through cotton. He asked if I could hear him—if I knew who had done this to me.

Of course, it was Rud Petty who'd hit us, with what I learned later was a mallet from our own croquet set.

But it was Dawn, not Rud, who withheld Joe's inhaler from him and then crushed it to pieces. It was Dawn, not Rud, who pulled the phone cord out of the wall when I was trying to call for help. In the space where all this had happened three years before, I slumped onto the bed, once again feeling barely alive, although this time it was a psychic condition instead of a physical one. Then, shivering against the idea of lying there one moment longer, I forced myself to muster the energy to stand and leave, shutting the door behind me with an emphatic click that made Abby's ears rise.

She rustled along beside me, barely able to keep up as I pitched myself downstairs toward the kitchen. I found Dawn's cell phone number and dialed, but she didn't answer. Her recorded voice came on and told me, "Just wait for the ding-dong," followed by the sound of a ringing bell.

I started to leave a message, then stopped, realizing that I had no idea what it was I would say to her.

As if observing my own actions from a distance, I rummaged in my junk drawer to find my address book, where I knew I had the number for Opal Bremer's house in Glen Cove. When Opal's mother, Saffron, answered, I tried to keep my voice normal and my manner as pleasant as possible, even though Opal had told us stories that made me critical of her. I reminded her who I was and asked to speak to Dawn.

"Why would Dawn be here?" I heard Saffron reach for something, then the flick of a cigarette lighter.

"I—well, she was going to your house."

I couldn't tell if it was a laugh or a snort that came back at me.

"I don't know why she would come here." Now I realized that the voice sounded medicated and off-speed.

"She thought Opal might be upset." I felt the urge to hang up because I knew that whatever was coming, I did not want to hear it. But a mix of politeness and paralysis kept me on the line.

"Is this some sick kind of joke?" The laugh again, or the snort. I heard a long exhalation—either smoke or anxiety, or both. "Well, no, Dawn isn't here. And Opal isn't here, either, because she killed herself last month. After that D.A. came down and said she wanted her to testify again, at that asshole's new trial.

"No, don't say anything," she told me, hearing the noise I made. "I don't want to hear it, especially from you. She was never the same after all that shit with your family." In the background I heard a man's voice inquiring, and Opal's mother said, "Nobody."

"You know what I think?" she asked me, even though I understood that it was not actually a question but a preamble for whatever she already planned to say. "Your daughter got Opal to lie for her, the first time. She never told me in so many words, but a mother knows." Though I had used that same phrase— "A mother knows"—in defending Dawn to Claire, it carried no weight with me coming from this other woman. "I think my girl was afraid of Rud Petty. And she was too weak to say no. But she was never the same after that trial. The guilt got to her."

I knew I should tell her I was sorry and just hang up, but against my better judgment I said, "Opal was always depressed. Since before she met Dawn."

"I'm not talking about depressed. I'm talking about guilty. And scared. Because she perjured herself—that's a crime, right? And

298

the district attorney knows it. So now my daughter's dead, and I have you to thank for that. You and your degenerate daughter. Same thing." Another sucking sound, and she hung up before I could collect myself to do the same.

I sat for a moment just looking at the phone in my hand, feeling it vibrate as if Saffron Bremer's fury had been transmitted physically along with her words.

My head throbbed. My mind felt clogged, overloaded. As dazed as if I hadn't slept at all, I couldn't think how to clear it.

When Abby barked a warning, I almost didn't notice, but at the last minute I turned as I felt someone approaching behind me, from the stairs. I heard myself cry out, though I don't think it was an actual word. Instinctively I tried to move backward, but tripped over the dog. Squealing in panic, she caught me against her body before I could fall, and I righted myself by grabbing the kitchen counter to regain my balance.

I couldn't see him, but I knew that whoever came toward me held something high over his head and was preparing to hit me with it. Instead of closing my eyes and waiting for the impact, I swung wildly with both arms and knocked whatever he held to the floor, striking him on the wrist with the force of my resistance.

"Shit!" he spat out, grabbing his arm. "Son of a bitch!"

Through my shock and the thunder of my heart beating in my ears, I saw that it was Stew. The "go-between," Dawn had called him. "Oh, my God," I said, my voice sounding unfamiliar to myself.

He gave out what sounded like a growl and thrust himself toward the weapon he'd dropped, but I stepped on his hand, and we both heard something crunch before he began cursing loud enough to make Abby back away.

I leaned over to pick up what he'd been reaching for. It was the trophy Dawn had won in fifth grade for her participation in the egg-and-spoon race. "You've got to be kidding me," I said, and the absurdity of it made me feel like laughing, though my stomach still curled in alarm.

With the trophy in my hand I looked down at him writhing on the floor below me. "I know who you are, you know. You're the cousin. Right?"

"The fuck you know that?" He was still folded over his injured hand.

"It's online. It's out there for everybody to see." Emboldened at seeing the trepidation this raised in him, I went on. "They'll be looking for you. If you hurt me now, everyone will know who did it. It'll be a no-brainer." I picked up the phone and pressed the buttons for 911.

He turned and ran, almost tripping over himself in his rush toward the back door. As the operator answered on the other end of the line, I could have sworn I heard Dawn's voice in the driveway shouting, "You fucking wimp!" and the sound made my heart go cold. For a moment I couldn't speak into the phone, until the operator prompted me, and I said, "I want to report an intrusion," knowing that it was much, much more than that, but not having the courage to come up with the right word.

Kenneth Thornburgh arrived within seven minutes. I know because I watched the clock the whole time—he pulled in with a screech, his red light flashing, at 12:04. I told him what had happened, leaving out only the part about thinking that I'd heard Dawn's voice after Stew bolted from the house. I could have been wrong, couldn't I? In my confusion, couldn't I have hallucinated that sound?

"He must have been hiding in here, waiting," I said, putting it together only as I thought back to what had happened since I'd returned from Warren's house. "In Dawn's room. The dog was trying to tell me, but I didn't listen."

The detective cleared his throat in that nervous way he had, when he didn't want to say the next thing but knew he had to. "Do you have any idea where your daughter might be, Mrs. Schutt?"

I shook my head. "Why?"

Before he could answer, Warren stepped into the house and said, "Hanna? You all right?"

I told him I was fine, although of course he could see that I wasn't. He came over to put his arm around my shoulder, and I felt grateful for the support.

"They're trying to find Dawn," I whispered.

Thornburgh said, "We have a 'Be on the Lookout' issued for her, as of yesterday. Totally separate from this incident, but now, of course, we want to talk to her more than ever."

"Yesterday? What happened yesterday?" I could barely hear my own voice.

"Well, for one thing, your other daughter reported Dawn committed a fraud. Trying to secure a loan in your name." I closed my eyes, understanding that Iris was receiving reports not only from Peter, but from Tom Whitty, too.

"But more serious than that, it appears she tried to use a stolen credit card. It belonged to a woman named Dorothy Wing. Your daughter delivers meals to her, correct? She has access to Mrs. Wing's house and property? Apparently she stole the card and attempted to—use it." At the last minute he faltered.

"Use it how?" Though I knew I would not want to hear the

answer, I also had the distinct sense now that it was my next line in a script already written for me.

"She tried to pay for an attorney's services." A slight pause, the one a hangman might take before dropping the noose. "Rud Petty's attorney."

Warren said, "Oh, my God." At the same time, I said, "What?"

"I'm sorry, Mrs. Schutt. But it looks like when Rud's family paid for his defense the first time around, his mother was still alive, and she persuaded the father to take out another mortgage. But she died last year, and the father isn't about to cough it up for this new trial. Rud had to raise money somehow. That's why Dawn did that interview for *The Bloody Glove*. I'm not saying it was Rud's idea—he probably didn't even know about it. He's not that stupid." I could tell he said these last words before realizing how they would sound: *Rud's not that stupid, but Dawn is.* I was glad he didn't try to take it back or fix it. "I know Gail Nazarian's been in touch with you about this: it seems Dawn and Rud have been communicating for some time."

I nodded to indicate that, yes, Gail Nazarian had told me she suspected that. But I couldn't speak.

"Is there someplace you can stay tonight?" Ken Thornburgh looked not at me but at Warren as he said this.

Warren said, "Of course," and we walked outside with the detective. Abby cringed behind me, and I could tell how spooked she'd been by the whole thing. "It's okay, girl," I told her, rubbing the spot between her ears and doing my best to sound as if I believed it. For the second time that night I entered Warren's house, and before he went to sleep down the hall in the room that had been his son's, he tucked me into his own bed the way you would a child who'd suffered a bad dream.

Inquiry Above All

In the morning, I called Iris's house from Warren's phone, intending to ask her to come to me. Archie answered and told me she was already on her way. He said that Peter had called the night before to tell Iris about the website interview, and though her impulse was to get in the car immediately, Archie convinced her to wait. I asked him to let her know I was across the street, instead of at my own house.

"Thank God," I said to Warren, as he made us toast. "What if she'd come and found out I wasn't home? She'd have no way of knowing I was here."

"She would have called the police. Thornburgh would have told her." He spoke calmly, but I could tell he was just trying to assuage my anxiety; the sleepless look in his face told me how upset he'd also been by the events of the night before.

When Iris arrived, she pulled me close and murmured, "Oh, Mommy," so fervently it surprised me. I could feel her shaking. Warren set down a plate for her, but she waved it away and said she was too upset to eat. "They could have killed you," she kept saying to me, so many times that I thought she must be in shock. "I should have known better than to leave you alone in that house."

"It wasn't anything like that, Iris. It was just a little boy with a plastic trophy. He was more scared than I was."

I'd hoped she might smile at that, but I could see what a strain she'd been through. "I'm sorry," I told her, hating how distraught she looked, and feeling responsible. "I'm sorry to put you through all this."

"It wasn't you," she said. "Don't you know that? None of this is *you*."

Before we left the breakfast table, Thornburgh came to tell us that they had apprehended Stew and Dawn in northern New York State, near the border, "attempting to flee."

"They were together?" I said, closing my eyes against the realization that what I had heard in the driveway must have been Dawn's voice after all. "Why?"

"We can only assume they thought you were going to testify against Rud Petty in his new trial. And they were trying to— dissuade you." He appeared to stumble in choosing the last words, then added, "Most likely at Rud's command."

"Oh, God. I told you, Mom." Iris emitted a violent whistle between her teeth.

"We don't have all the facts yet," Thornburgh said. "I'm sure it will all come out."

I asked if I could see Dawn, and he told me she wouldn't be back in Everton, for questioning, for another few hours. He coughed slightly and added, "I should prepare you for the fact that there may be more charges pending than just the credit card fraud." As the detective and I spoke, Iris and Warren had moved away slightly, as if to give Thornburgh and me privacy, though of course they could still hear it all.

"What charges?" The memory of Gail Nazarian's threat to try to indict Dawn again stirred in my stomach.

"I shouldn't say, because I don't really know yet. It isn't for me to decide." He put a hand across the space between us to touch my shoulder. "Mrs. Schutt—*Hanna*—I'm sorry about all this." And I knew he was, just as I knew he'd been sorry to have to tell me, a few weeks earlier, that Rud Petty had won his appeal.

Around noon, after calling to confirm that Dawn was there and that they would allow me to speak to her, I asked Iris to drive me to the police station. Warren stayed behind to take care of Abby, who still hadn't been able to settle down.

Despite all the contact I'd had with the Everton officers during the past three years, these encounters had always taken place either at my home, in the hospital, or at the courthouse. The only time I'd been inside the station before was back when the girls were little and the town ran an antitheft campaign by asking kids to register their bicycles. Remembering how proud Dawn had been to put that neon orange ID sticker onto her little bike with the white wicker basket, I had to reach out and clasp the railing along the steps for a moment. Iris looked concerned, so to distract her I said, "Was that always there?" nodding at the row of oakleaf hydrangeas lining the walkway.

"I think so. Why?"

"I would think I'd have remembered." Feeling slightly more stable, I took my hand off the railing to test myself.

Iris came closer, putting an arm out to spot me. "People don't tend to remember things unless they have to."

"Well, that's a dim view."

"Maybe. But do you think it's not true?"

To avoid answering, I told her I was fine now, and said we should go inside.

Peter Cifforelli was already there, waiting on the bench outside Kenneth Thornburgh's office. I hadn't seen him since the trial, when I was used to him sitting in the courtroom in dark, well-fitting suits, newly shined shoes, and ties in bold colors like magenta and deep yellow. In the friendship between him and Joe, Peter had always been the flashy one, the one who seemed to want to call attention to himself. I think that quality in his best friend amused Joe and also piqued his interest, because it was so unlike his own personality.

But today, a Saturday morning, he had on corduroys and a Buf State sweatshirt, with muddy sneakers and socks that didn't match. As Iris and I approached, I saw that he was scribbling notes on a pad. He jumped up when he saw me. "Hanna, what were you thinking? Letting her be in touch with Rud Petty, for God's sake?" He pushed his hair back on his forehead as if it might help him understand.

Trying to contain myself—not for his sake but for my own—I struggled to keep my voice calm as I told him, "I don't know they *were* in touch."

"Trust me. There's a warrant out for her arrest in New Mexico. Credit card fraud. Apparently she was cleaning houses and stealing people's account numbers while she worked. It took them a while to catch up to it because out there she wasn't Dawn Schutt; she was using a different name." He consulted his notes. "Cecilia Devereaux." I did my best to hold in the gasp I felt, and he didn't seem to notice. "You think she'd be doing that if Rud Petty weren't behind it?"

He was on a roll, not about to let me get a word in, which was fine with me because I had none. "And you think Gail Nazarian doesn't have all the records she needs to make a jury believe they've been in contact? What do you think that moron Stew Jerome was doing in your house? Maybe he was even supposed to kill you—finish the job Rud botched the first time. How do we know?" Peter threw his hands high in a gesture I had seen often over the years. It was meant to lend dramatic effect to whatever words it accompanied, but to me it always just looked silly.

"Look, I know you've always been protective of Dawn," he went on. "And I understand why you wouldn't want to see what's going on here. No parent would." He tapped his sneaker for emphasis on the gray tile floor. "But she was in trouble even before she met Rud Petty. If you refuse to accept that, you're putting yourself in danger."

That word again: *danger*. Now both Peter and Gail Nazarian had used it in referring to my daughter. I felt the anger sweep through me as I said, "You've never liked me, have you, Peter?" Suddenly it occurred to me that it hardly mattered, anymore, what I said to my dead husband's best friend. I couldn't see a reason anymore to pretend *we* were friends. "You've always thought I was stupid—too stupid to be with Joe. Well, maybe I am. Was. But I'm not stupid enough to have known Dawn was talking to Rud Petty and not done anything about it. I mean, really—what do you take me for?"

He looked away, and it enraged me even further to see the pity in his eyes. "Hanna," he said, "I don't think I can help her this time. That interview, the cousin—" He shrugged, as if to say, *What more can you expect from me?* When I didn't try to persuade him otherwise, he turned on his sneaker heel, squeaking down the

307

corridor and out of my life. As good a friend as he had always been to Joe, I wasn't sorry to see him go.

Iris and I were heading to Kenneth Thornburgh's office when he came out of a room next to it, and instinctively I knew that Dawn was behind the door he'd just shut. "You can go in now," he told me. "We just got through talking with her, and she's a little—confused, might be the best way to put it." He hesitated, and I understood that for my sake he had chosen a more neutral word to describe Dawn's state than he'd originally intended. "Do you want me to fill you in, at all, on what she told us? Or—" He waved as if he knew I'd understand how to finish his sentence; we'd always had that shorthand between us.

"No, I just want to talk to her." He nodded as if that was what he'd expected.

"Go ahead, Mom." Iris sat down heavily on the bench and clutched her bag close, as if grateful she had something to hold on to. "If you need me, I'll be right here."

I took a deep breath as Thornburgh opened the door, and I followed him into the room. I felt far away from both my mind and my body, which in many ways was a relief. It wasn't the same kind of feeling as being drunk—that hazy, floating sensation you know will end in a headache you already dread. This was more of a numb suspension I would have been perfectly happy to sign up for if someone had been able to offer it to me as a steady state for the rest of my life.

Now, more than a year later, I am glad it wasn't an option. But at that moment, I wanted more than anything not to acknowledge all that was in my head and heart.

Though the room was only a small rectangle, it seemed to swallow Dawn up the way she sat in the metal chair on the other

308

side of the table, slumped into herself. How many times, after Iris had gone away to college and Joe began working late on the Marc Sedgwick case—and even since she had returned home only two weeks earlier—had she and I sat in front of TV crime shows featuring police station interview rooms? On TV, the rooms were completely stark, and the cops and the district attorney observed from behind the one-way window. It didn't look to me as if this room in the Everton station had a one-way window, but I might have been wrong. I was beginning to understand that I couldn't trust my own perceptions.

On the wall behind Dawn was a mural-size map featuring an aerial view of Everton's territory bordered by the Hudson on one side and the conservation land on the other, along with the town's motto, INQUIRY ABOVE ALL, which had been coined by its founder, Josiah Everton, an inventor and scientist. The police map was not framed, but taped to the wall. After a moment I realized that this was not because the cops were cheap, but because the glass in a frame could have been used as a weapon in the wrong hands.

Dawn stood when she saw it was me. She let me come toward her, and Thornburgh stayed in the room to supervise our hug. "I'm going to leave you two to talk, but I'll be right outside, okay?" he said, and when the door closed behind him, I could see his head through the window at the door's top, his face tilted just enough that although he wasn't staring, he'd be aware of everything that went on in the room.

When I sat down across from her, Dawn tried to smile. At first I couldn't look at her, but when I did, I was astonished to see how far her bad eye had wandered. Could it have happened since we'd last seen each other the night before? Or was it possible it had been like that since she'd come home, and I hadn't recognized it

309

for what it was? I understood now that this had to be the case, but the idea that I could see things so wrong made me breathless, and my heart skipped a beat.

"How are you, Mommy?" Dawn asked.

I tried not to look as shocked as I felt. Even Ding-Dong Dawn couldn't be that *clueless*, could she? "This isn't a social visit, Dawn," I said, and immediately she plunged her glance down at the floor in the familiar attitude that announced she felt ashamed.

"Peter was just here," I added. "He said he can't be your lawyer anymore."

She nodded, and I couldn't tell whether this turn of events surprised her. Then she frowned. "Lawyer for what?"

I clucked my tongue in impatience, and then she did look up surprised; it was a sound she had heard often from Iris over the years, but never, I was sure, from me. We sat there looking at each other, each waiting for the other to speak. In thinking about it since, it has occurred to me that this was the moment we both understood there was no going back for us, however much we might have wished to.

"How could you?" I asked finally. I was referring to all of it, but couldn't bring myself to ask her specifically about what I'd read in the website interview. I was still hoping there was some explanation I hadn't yet figured out.

"How could I what?" She let her good eye dart toward me. But when I didn't answer, she looked away and murmured, "It was nothing personal."

I made a noise that could have sounded like laughter, feeling a twist in my gut. " 'Nothing personal'? What could be more personal than trying to kill someone?"

She shrugged, but her shoulders were trembling. "Nobody

310

tried to kill anybody." She wanted me to believe her, but it was too late for that. "He was just going to scare you," she said, and I realized she thought I was only talking about what had happened with Stew.

My mind played out, in all its panicked silliness, the bungled assault in my kitchen from the night before. "With that stupid trophy?"

Dawn winced at the word *stupid*. "He's an idiot. He was supposed to use the bat by your bed." When I caught my breath sharply, she said, "To *scare* you, I said. He wouldn't have hit you with it."

"I guess I'm lucky he's an idiot, then." I didn't want to ask where in the house Stew had been hiding before he came at me, even though I was sure she knew. I assumed he'd been in her room, where the trophy was displayed so prominently that he decided to grab it instead of risking a trip to my bedroom for the bat.

"Where were you last night, anyway?" she said. "Shtupping Mr. Goldman?"

Her words—and the fact that they emerged from the mouth of the daughter I'd always felt so close to—made me feel physically ill. I took a breath and didn't answer. I didn't ask her whether she'd been waiting for Stew in the driveway, or where they had parked, away from the house, to make their getaway. I knew it was her voice I'd heard when I chased him out. But I couldn't bear to hear her admit it just then.

I didn't answer her question, instead asking one of my own. "So you *have* been in touch with Rud all this time?"

She shook her head vehemently. "Not until he won his appeal. I wrote him every single day before that, but he never got my letters, because the guards hated his guts."

It was hard for me to believe that after all that had happened, she was still gullible enough to fall for what he'd told her. I wasn't sure I did believe it.

"When the appeal came through, he called me on a cell phone somebody gave him. I was so happy—I hadn't heard his voice since the end of the trial." She smiled at the memory, and I felt another rise of nausea. When she spoke her next words, I couldn't tell whether it was with shame or pride. "He thought it would be a good idea for me to come home and test the waters."

"Test the waters? As in, was I going to take the stand against him?"

"As in, did you remember anything."

"You told me at Pepito's that night you believed Rud was guilty. So that was to trick me into thinking you'd turned on him?"

"I had to say that." She shifted in the hard chair. "You wouldn't have wanted me home if I told the truth, which is that Emmett did it." She began picking at her cuticles, not looking at me.

"Stop that," I said, and immediately her hand jumped as if I had slapped it. "What are you talking about—*Emmett*? I just read the interview you did with Cecilia. You confessed to the whole thing."

Her face drained—of color, expression, the appearance of life. "What?"

"What do you mean, *What*? It's on that website. *The Bloody Glove*."

She seemed taken aback, and for a moment I tried to believe that there had been some mistake.

"She said she wouldn't put it out until the trial was over. She promised." Her words came out slowly, as if she were speaking a language she wasn't sure of. "So she did trick me."

"Why would you think she would do anything else?"

312

"I don't know. I keep thinking people are going to be different than they are." Even now I find myself turning that line over and over in my head, particularly when I'm trying to fall asleep. "She kept saying this would be her big break, I was doing her a favor, she'd be forever grateful, all that bullshit." At first I thought she spoke with anger, but then she gave another smile, this one more sinister, and my stomach lurched. "Well, it doesn't matter. I tricked her back."

"Tricked her? How?"

"I made the whole thing up. Don't you get it, Mommy?" A different kind of energy entered her face and body, some creative force I'd never seen there before. She looked excited about something, for once, and I had to turn my head. "That's the beauty of it. They paid me all that money, and it was all a lie."

I would have given everything I had to be able to believe her. Now, I am glad no one offered me that choice.

"Why would anybody believe you made up a story implicating yourself?"

"But I'm not doing that." Her expression was smug, as if she'd just been waiting for my question. "I looked it up online, and it would be hearsay. They couldn't allow it in court, even if they did think it was true."

"But why make up a story at all?"

The look she gave me made me think for a moment that she was going to say, 'Duh'—the word she herself had been the victim of, so many times before. "What else? For the money. Cecilia said nothing sells better than kids killing their parents, except parents killing their kids."

I felt my breath leave me, and shut my eyes. "How much money?"

"You'll never believe it. Guess. Okay, I'll tell you." She paused for effect before adding, "Fifty thousand! Can you believe that?" She said it as if she'd just received a salary raise she knew would make me proud.

I remembered Dottie Wing's stolen credit card and the fraud warrant for Dawn in New Mexico. "You were going to give it to Rud for his defense, weren't you?"

"Yes." She lifted her chin, daring me to defy her. "I still am. I want him to get a good lawyer, like Grandpa had." *Grandpa.* She had never met the man, and my father had never been known by that name to anyone. What she knew of him was that he'd been able to pay a lawyer to get him the lightest sentence possible. Some of my father's victims had said he got away with murder, though of course he hadn't actually killed anyone. This was the legacy Dawn aspired to.

"When he gets out, we're moving to Alaska. He has some friend up there who helps people start over. We'll get new identities. Nobody will know who we are. Who we *were*." She waited for me to challenge her, and when I didn't, she said, "He isn't guilty. Mommy, trust me on this."

I almost laughed—a blast of misery at how absurd a request that was—but managed to contain it at the last moment.

"He dropped me off that night, after we all had that fight about the burglary, and then he went home to his own apartment," she went on. "He called me from there. I was with Opal when you and Daddy were attacked—you know that."

"No. I don't." The words came out faint, because it hurt to say them, but I could tell she heard me loud and clear; her eyes darted in panic she tried to hide. I forced myself to raise my voice. "You weren't with her last night, either."

On the table between us her hands closed in fists. "I was so."

"Dawn, I called Opal's house." The fists grew tighter, the knuckles white. "She killed herself." I couldn't tell from her reaction, or lack of it, whether she had known this before I told her. And if it was news to her, I couldn't tell if she felt upset. "But not before her mother told me she lied for you on the stand."

The look she gave me then was one of shocked indignation. "She said that? That bitch."

I was still unaccustomed to hearing her curse. But then, everything about this scene felt unfamiliar and surreal.

At least she wasn't trying to tell me Opal's mother had lied, I told myself. At least she had sense enough not to do that.

"Daddy's jacket," I said. I expected her to pretend she had no idea what I was talking about, but she was smart enough not to do that, either. "'Puff Daddy.' That wasn't part of the trial, either. In fact, I never realized that jacket was missing, until I read the interview."

She looked at me steadily. "You gave it away the other day when you were collecting things for Goodwill."

For a moment, my heart stumbled. *Had* I put the jacket in with the other clothes?

But no; I knew better. I'd only brought one bag to the collection bin, and the jacket would not have fit in it along with everything else I discarded. Now my own daughter was gaslighting me, doing her best to make me think I was losing my mind and that my memory couldn't be trusted.

"You should understand something, Dawn." Her fear emanated toward me as I said this; I could smell its tang, sour and hot, in the air between us. If I reached out, it might have been solid enough to touch. "I *do* remember. I was remembering all

315

along, I think. But I didn't know it was real until I read what you said to Cecilia." I waited, half-hoping she might have something to say that would divert me, even momentarily, from where I was headed. But she just let her head hang as she twirled her hair around her finger and slumped in the metal chair.

"The inhaler," I said. The word caused her to look up, and for the first time since she'd come home, it almost seemed that both eyes focused on the same spot. "That was never part of the testimony. The police found it, but they assumed it just got broken in the struggle, and they didn't put any importance on it. It wasn't brought up at the trial.

"But when I read what you said about Daddy having trouble breathing, and reaching for it on the nightstand, it all came back to me. *You* were the one who stepped on it. And who pulled the phone out. I can see it, Dawn, in my head." She looked away again. "You couldn't have known about any of that unless you were there."

She mumbled something.

"What?" I said.

"That inhaler thing only happened because I remembered how he embarrassed me when I tried to use it on Abby. At Iris's wedding. I was so humiliated, and in front of Rud."

"Are you trying to justify that as an excuse?"

"No." She said it quietly, into her collar, and I wished I could believe her at least about this. "It's just that I felt like I could either crumble or get mad, and mad was safer. It just happened—I didn't plan it, but then all the pieces were on the floor."

"What about cutting the phone off, when I was trying to call for help?"

She slid further down in her chair. "Part of me wanted you

to get through. I swear to God, Mommy. I wanted the police to come and stop what was happening."

"Then why—"

"Because I'm stupid, okay? Is that what you want from me?" She folded her arms on the table and threw her head down on top of them, giving the impression that she was crying, but I could tell there were no tears.

I was starting to get a headache, a monster one, and I wanted nothing more than to stop talking. But there were still things I needed to get out. "How you could just stand there and let him do what he did? You never tried to stop him." I almost choked on my own words. "You let him *kill* Daddy. Kill both of us, really. You didn't know I wasn't dead until the next morning. Right?"

When she didn't answer or raise her head, I kept going. "The tree house," I whispered, dropping my voice because this subject had always seemed sacred somehow. "That *was* you, wasn't it? Not Emmett." When I'd read the *Bloody Glove* story, I realized I'd always known it, which was why I must have hidden the matches when the police came. And why I encouraged Joe not to press charges. But I hadn't realized that Emmett also knew Dawn was responsible, and for some reason—the same secret decency that caused him to offer me help, the day I saw his tattoo?—he kept it to himself, even knowing that Joe and others continued to suspect him. "I should have said something back then."

Dawn's shoulders had stopped their fake shaking. She lifted her head from the table slowly. "Well," she said, and a peculiar smile I'd never seen before played at her lips. I still see that smile in my mind, sometimes; it can wake me out of a sound sleep, and I find myself covered with sweat. "I guess you're not as out of it as I thought you were, Mom." For a moment I tried to believe she felt as shocked by her own words as I felt hearing them. But I knew it wasn't the case.

"'Out of it'?" The phrase ignited a rage inside me that made everything go white before my eyes. Though I never would have expected it of myself, I said, "*I'm* not the one they called Ding-Dong." *I'm not the one who got duped by Rud Petty*, I could have added. *Who gave that interview. Who's lying right now, thinking there might be some way out of this.*

Yet even as I spoke, I knew it went deeper than "out of it." That part had always been there. She was in police custody because of some other part.

"Do I even know you, Dawn? Did I ever?" The dull hammer I recognized as fresh grief began tapping inside my chest. "What kind of a person *are* you?"

She let the air out of her mouth slowly, then leaned across the table. Through the window at the top of the door, I could see Kenneth Thornburgh's head turn slightly as he made sure she was not making a move he would have to interrupt. In a voice that let me know she'd been wanting to ask this question for a long time, Dawn said, "It was never just about my eye, was it?"

Of course it had never been just about her eye. But I wasn't about to give her this satisfaction. "I hope you're not telling me that you think being teased, or being a little different from other people, justifies killing someone," I said. "Least of all your own parents. I hope you're not saying that, Dawn."

She was so intent on her own vision of things that I don't think she registered my words. "If you and Daddy had just let it go that day and not made a federal case out of the burglary—if you had just let things be the way they were—none of this would have happened. Daddy dying, the trial, any of it." The smile again, stronger; it twisted her face into a degree of asymmetry I had never seen there before. It would not have been a stretch to call it grotesque, and it had nothing to do with her amblyopia. "But you couldn't leave it alone, could you? You just couldn't let me be happy."

The knocking inside my chest grew stronger, threatening to steal my breath. "Are you really going to sit there and tell me that what happened to us—what you did—was *our* fault?"

For a moment she looked sorry—looked, even, as if she might give in to grief. Or did she? It's another thing I can't be sure of. Maybe it was just the look of someone who was upset because she hadn't gotten her way. Abruptly she sat up straight, the way she would have if a puppeteer had snapped a string up sharply through her spine.

Though I sensed it was futile, I tried one last time to get through. "Don't you understand that if you really had the money he thought you had, he would have killed you, too? He would have married you, yes. But then he would have killed you."

She murmured something I didn't quite catch, and against my better judgment, I asked her to repeat it.

"I said, you can believe whatever you want about Rud. I know the truth. And I'm the only one who does." I understood then that she was too far away for me to reach. "He'll be totally psyched when he finds out I got him a Corvette."

Lacy eye, I heard Joe saying in my head as I used my last strength to push back from the table and stand up. I made my way to the door, feeling Dawn watch my every move. Halfway across the room, I paused, stilled in my steps by what I thought I heard in a low voice behind me. The words Dawn knew made me cry—and the same ones I'd witnessed by accident years ago, so briefly, in her unexpectedly stunning voice. Was it possible that in these circumstances she could really be singing "Wish me luck, the same to you?"

But when I turned to see if it was a private message, calling me back, I realized I must have hallucinated the music. She was looking beyond, not at me. I knocked, and the detective opened the door from the other side. Without taking a last look back at my daughter, I told him I was finished and walked out of the room.

A Dissimulation of Birds

All this happened more than a year ago, though it seems much more distant in time, maybe because it's so far away in place. I'm in California now, in a cozy carriage house only a few yards away from where Iris, Archie, and Josie live with the new baby, Max. There's room enough for a small garden, where I like to sit with Josie in the afternoons after I pick her up from school. We watch the birds that come to the feeder we made together, and although sometimes I feel a jolt of nostalgia for when Dawn and I did the same thing when she was Josie's age, my granddaughter's presence always soothes me. She keeps away the wim-wams. And on the best days, there is a measure of joy I thought would be impossible for me to feel again.

I planted a bed of irises as a memorial to my mother. After everything that happened with Dawn, I found my thoughts returning often to the night the agents came to arrest my father. I remembered the way he said, "Hanna, I will explain things," and the impulse I'd recognized in my mother not to answer the doorbell when it rang. It had never occurred to me to wonder, before, why he wouldn't have needed to explain things to her, too. I thought she really believed what she'd always told me, up until the day she died: that the police had made a mistake.

Joe asked me only once if I thought my mother knew anything about what my father had been up to, all those years before he got caught. It was later the same day we'd taken Dawn to the doctor so he could tell her she had a lazy eye. "Of course not," I said to Joe. "Why are you asking?" He gave me a look that told me my response was just what he'd expected, but he loved me anyway. He never brought it up again, and I forgot he had ever asked.

Having learned it in the most painful way possible, I know better now. The irises are a reminder that as much as I loved my mother, I can't afford to be like her anymore.

Holding my grandson for the first time, a few months back, made me think about the day Dawn was born. I'd had Iris at Albany Medical Center, and we planned to go there for the second baby, too. When I started having contractions at four in the morning, we called Claire to come over and babysit for Iris, and she said she'd be right there. She arrived within fifteen minutes, but it wasn't soon enough. For some reason even my obstetrician couldn't explain afterward, my labor slipped into high gear—went from zero to eighty, she said, trying to hide her nervousness about how things might have gone—in only ten minutes, and by the time Joe said, "Forget it. We're taking her with us," and went in to wake up Iris, the baby had begun to push herself out. With Iris I'd had a lot of pain and an epidural, but Dawn's birth was fast and simple, with only a slight pressure below my abdomen. For a few moments, I was worried that she wasn't getting the oxygen she needed, but then Joe slid her out. It was so easy I thought she might have been stillborn, but then I heard her noises and began to cry. I think Joe thought the tears came from happiness, and of course some of them did, but mainly it was relief I felt; I'd expected the same excruciating experience I'd had three years earlier, and then, almost before I realized it, it was over and I had nothing more to dread.

When Claire arrived she called Bob Toussaint, and after cutting the umbilical cord, she took Dawn into the bathroom to sponge her off. When Bob came to examine the baby and me, saying I should take things slowly but we should both be fine, I asked him how it was possible that I hadn't felt any pain. He shrugged and smiled. "It happens," he told me. "Not often, but it happens. Maybe she felt like doing you a favor. You owe her one."

"And you're sure she's okay? I thought she might not have gotten enough air."

He assured me that she seemed fine and smiled down at Dawn, who lay next to me asleep. I looked out the window and saw what a perfect morning it was—the sun was just arcing over the garden, making the scarlet-orange blooms on my Oriental poppies brighter and more vivid than I could remember ever seeing before. I wanted to cry again. I knew it was only a surplus of hormones, but I felt as if I couldn't bear how beautiful the flowers were—it was that sharp, that piercing. Though Joe and Claire kept urging me to go back to bed, I asked them to set me up outside, and I spent the day lying with a light blanket over my legs, holding my new baby and listening to the sounds of my family and best friend moving happily around me. Joe set up a plastic pool for Iris, and she entertained herself by splashing around and singing. Claire went out to buy food and came home with cold cuts from the deli, sweets I saw Joe wanted to scold her for but didn't, and a stuffed animal for Iris. Halfway between sun and shade, I drowsed in and out of consciousness, waking every time to the delicious surprise of not being pregnant anymore, and profound relief that my baby was in the world.

Since we hadn't wanted to know the gender, we'd chosen names for both. For another girl we'd settled on Matilda, in memory of Joe's mother. But even though I'd been the one to pick Iris's name after my own mother, I pressed Joe to reconsider, once I had our second daughter in my arms. "She's Dawn," I told Joe, because the first thing I'd seen when I turned my head to the window, after she emerged, was the sun coming up. It wasn't like Joe to be spontaneous, or to give up something we'd already planned together, but to my surprise he agreed quickly, bending to kiss both the baby and me.

For years, that moment was one of the happiest of my life. But I hardly ever let myself think about that day now. What would be the point?

I spend my weekday mornings at a mammography center in the next town. The women who come in for their tests are more or less my own age, and I enjoy trying to make the experience as comfortable as possible for them.

One of the patients who came into the office this morning told me she'd considered not keeping her appointment. "I was sitting there with my coffee and I thought, *What if there is something in there, that does want to kill me?*" she said, gesturing at her right breast as I lifted it onto the Plexiglas paddle, then compressed it in the optimum position for the film. She was nervous, and had been babbling a bit since I handed her the gown, and I had to ask her to stop breathing, and talking, while I stepped into the next room to activate the machine.

"I thought, *Am I ready to hear something like that?*" she went on, when I returned to switch to the other breast.

I knew she had reason to be concerned—they'd seen a shadow on the first film, which was why she was sent to us for a second look. But I like to remain as neutral as I can with patients, and there was no way I was about to engage in any worst-case talk with her, especially when we didn't have any results yet.

"Do you know what I mean?" she persisted, reaching to stop my hand on its way up. I could tell she needed an answer before she would let me put her other breast in that vise grip and tell her not to move. "I know it probably sounds irresponsible. Crazy, even. But can you see why I thought about canceling this morning? If there's something in there, it would give me more time to not know."

She wasn't looking at my face as she asked her questions. I don't know whether it's because she was ashamed of them, or whether it had more to do with the fact that despite all the corrective surgeries I've had, it's still not easy to look at my face.

I knew I should have just given a supportive murmur—it probably would have been enough. But I made a point of moving my head to where her glance fell, so she couldn't avoid my eyes. I wanted her to see that I meant it when I said, "That makes sense to me."

In the last year, a lot's happened aside from our move west and Max's birth. For one thing, Gail Nazarian got the promotion I knew she wanted. CROQUET KILLER VERDICT PUTS D.A. ON FAST TRACK, the headline in the newspaper said. When I'd called that day after returning from the police station, to tell her I remembered what had happened the night of the attack and that—as

325

she already knew—it had nothing to do with Emmett Furth, she asked if I could testify in Rud Petty's retrial, and I told her yes. I heard her hesitate on the phone, and then she asked if there was any chance I'd testify against Dawn as well. I think she was shocked when I agreed to this, too; I believe I heard her gasp on the other end of the line, though I'm sure she wouldn't have wanted me to hear it.

She was more sympathetic with me on the stand than I'd seen her be with anyone in the first trial against Rud. The public defenders working for Rud and Dawn tried to shake my story, but they had to be careful, because I was the victim, after all. Rud was convicted of murder and attempted murder, and also of conspiracy to commit murder, in arranging for Dawn to let his cousin into my house to lie in wait for me. The second trial was much shorter than the first, and didn't come close to living up to the theatrics Cecilia Baugh tried to create on *The Bloody Glove*. The jury deliberated less than a full day before returning its verdict of guilty.

The jury in Dawn's trial had no trouble convicting her, in light of my testimony, the communications they found in Dawn's cell phone records between her and Stew Jerome, and Cecilia's interview. Dawn's court-appointed lawyer did try to get the interview thrown out as hearsay, but the court allowed it because she had made admissions against her own interest, which is an exception to the hearsay rule.

I can't pretend, as I might have once, not to understand why Dawn did what seemed on the face of it so stupid—giving that interview, then trying to disavow it to me as fiction. Why she believed that Cecilia would honor the request to withhold the information until after the trial; why she believed that she could say all those things with immunity, collect the money they paid her, and go off to spend the rest of her life in happiness with Rud Petty. It dismays me to say that I *do* understand it, and all too well: she believed those things because they were more appealing than the truth. She believed them because she wanted to. How can I, of all people, fault her for that?

The whole time I sat in that same witness box—in both trials—I didn't look at my daughter. I didn't look at her when the forewoman announced she was guilty, or six weeks later, when she was sentenced to life in prison. Our last conversation was the one in which she admitted she helped someone attack me two separate times.

Shortly after Iris and Archie brought Max home, I was still staying with them before the carriage house was ready to be moved into. I woke up in the middle of the night and found Iris sitting in the dark in the living room, nursing her son. Without switching on the light, I sat down beside them on the couch, and something about how quiet it was—and how moved I was by the nearness of my grandson's newborn head—made me whisper, without realizing I was going to, "You don't think badness runs in families, do you?" I couldn't bring myself to say the word *evil*— the word Iris had used about my father all those years ago.

"'Badness.'" She laughed softly. "Okay, Mom, if that's what you want to call it. No, of course not. You don't inherit that." I could barely hear her, but it was obvious how much vehemence was behind her words, and I realized it was a subject she had given a lot of thought. "If people inherited a gene for moral behavior, then you could never blame anybody or praise them for what they do. Right?" I was a little slow catching up to what she'd said, but when I did, I nodded. "And I want at least some of the credit for who I am."

"You sound like your father," I said, because she did, and it made us both smile.

Then she added, "She didn't get that way from anything you or Dad did, either. From your not letting her have the surgery or anything else." She adjusted the baby against her breast. "And she certainly didn't get that way from being dropped on her head."

I sucked in my breath, and Max turned his eyes toward me. "He *told* you that?" Warren had never mentioned he'd been in touch with Iris, and neither had she. I felt angry for a moment, and then ashamed, but Iris reached over to touch my shoulder, and I lowered my face to hide the fact that I wanted to cry. "He was worried about you, when you went to see Dawn at the police station that day. I was, too. Thank God you saw through her and did the right thing." She cupped Max's socked feet with her hand, and I cupped the top of his head with mine.

"I just don't understand how I didn't see it sooner," I murmured. I was thinking of the notebook I'd found when Dawn was in sixth grade, containing her fantasies about the life she wanted to have someday; about how I hadn't pushed further to find out how she was supporting herself all that time after the trial; about the fact that she'd been trading messages with someone the whole time she'd been home, and I had just let it drop. Though the knowledge about the tree house had always been there—that it was Dawn, not Emmett, who started that fire—I hadn't allowed it to come to the fore. There were so many other clues along the way. If I had intervened in just one of these circumstances, couldn't I have kept things from turning out the way they had?

"I know." Iris lifted the baby over her shoulder for a burp. "Just because something looks a certain way doesn't mean it *is*."

When I heard her say these words an image occurred to me

that seemed to come out of nowhere, and hit me with such force that I had to sit back. In a video display at the state museum about 9/11, one of the surviving FDNY firefighters talked about what he encountered when he managed to escape one of the towers. He turned a corner and saw dozens of cows piled on top of each other. Later he realized that of course they weren't cows—they were human bodies. "My counselor says that my mind is being helpful by not letting me recognize what it actually was," he told the camera. At this point, the firefighter started crying, and I'd had to turn away from the video because I couldn't see it through my own tears.

"Sometimes I worry I'm not a whole person," I whispered to Iris, half-hoping she might miss what I said.

"What does *that* mean?" For a moment I thought she was putting her hand over Max's ear so he couldn't hear our conversation, until I saw she was just caressing him.

"I mean, I'm not sure who I am, really. I'm not sure I have a core. You know? The thing that makes people who they are." I'd never articulated it to anyone before, but it was something I'd felt as long as I could remember. By the time I was old enough to wonder about such a thing, I was the girl whose father had gone to jail. Then I'd been Joe's wife and the girls' mother—a "meek mother," to use Joe's term from our first date, although I never saw it until now. After that, I was the victim of a savage attack. Now that I've moved to a new place where no one knows me, I feel safe enough to understand that I don't want to die, whenever it happens, without finding out more.

I want my obituary to include more than the fact that I make a good oatmeal crinkle. And I don't want to keep to myself any longer. The Swedish way is going out the window, at least for me.

"Of course you have a core, Mom. How can you not know that?" With the hand not touching the baby, Iris reached out to cover mine.

"Remember when Dawn used to wear a patch?" I gestured at my own left eye. "Remember how they called it 'occlusion'? You cover up the strong side of something so the weak one will have to work harder." I'd never realized that all these years, I'd been carrying around the weight of this analogy. "I feel like I've only had a weak side. It's been working; it's been trying. But it'll never be as strong as the part that's covered up."

Iris nodded. "I can understand how you would feel that way."

"You can?"

"Of course. With Dad around. He was strong enough for two people, but sometimes it was too much." As shocked as I was to hear her say this because she and Joe were always such a tight pair, her next words surprised me even more. "I know you never knew how much I loved you. You never got that you were, like, home free." Hearing her say this, I felt that sharp pull in my chest I remembered only from the time my mother died. "I was always jealous of Dawn because she was your favorite."

"But that's because you were Dad's!" It came out before I had a chance to check it. She tilted her head at the drowsing Max, asking me to keep my voice down. In another whisper I added, "*You* were jealous of *Dawn*? I'm sure she never knew that."

"I'm sure she didn't. But it's true." Pausing for a moment to look down at her son and then in the direction of the room where Josie slept, she said, "If there's one thing I'm going to watch out for with these two, it's that we're not going to divvy up the love."

Being out here, in a new place, has been good for Iris, too. She's eating better and she started exercising again, though not in the same way as before Joe died, which I'm glad to see, because it always seemed compulsive to me. She's almost back to her old self, both physically and in her spirits. When Max is a little older, she's planning to go back to medical school, and she wants to switch her concentration to psychiatry.

Becoming closer to her has been a balm, especially since I've lost Dawn. I keep remembering something I heard Claire say once: "You can only be as happy as your unhappiest child." For a long time, that was true of me; my psyche was intertwined with Dawn's, my feelings linked to hers. All that time, and without really thinking about it, I thought this said something positive about our relationship—that we were cut from the same cloth, marched to the same drummer, shared a soul. Most of all, that we understood each other. Now I don't know if I ever understood anything about her at all.

She's going to be in prison until long after I've died. It doesn't matter (I keep telling myself), because I won't ever see her again, even to visit her at Bedford Hills. Not ever seeing Dawn again is the deal I made with Iris when we moved out here. I'm just as relieved that she put that condition on it, because otherwise I might have made the trip back east once a year out of guilt, even though Dawn has not tried to be in touch with me since she was sentenced, and for all I know, she'd refuse to see me if I tried.

I do feel guilt. And a sadness I can't even bear to acknowledge, most days. But being out here, on a different coast and in a different climate, makes it easier somehow. And when I stumble in my resolution about letting Dawn go from my life, I force myself to remember the things she told Cecilia in her interview, and the things she said to me in the police station that last day. I force myself to remember the night of the attack, because once that memory returned in Joe's and my bedroom, it's never left me again—not even on the days I wish it would.

Since I've moved, I've spent a lot of time trying to figure out what happened to my family. Well, not just *what*, because that seems all too obvious, but *why*. Would Dawn have turned out to be a different person without the amblyopia? Was it possible that during her birth she lost a single, crucial breath of oxygen, as I'd feared that day? What was it that made her so nervous and vacant, so distasteful to other kids, and ultimately so vulnerable to the spell Rud Petty cast on her?

And *did* Rud cast a spell? Or was there something in her that recognized the part of him that would hurt anybody to get what he wanted? Maybe she was a bird without a flock until she found him, or he found her. I imagine him spotting a tiny seed of corruption inside her, spitting on it, then helping it grow until, like a weed gone wild, it choked and strangled whatever had once been beautiful underneath.

Originally I hoped that putting it all down here, in a notebook identical to the one Dawn used to record the names for the identities she might want to claim someday, would help me make sense of the whole thing.

Instead, what I've discovered is that it doesn't make sense, and I expect it never will. The best I can do is acknowledge this, and hope that someday I find a form of peace.

Now I'm glad to be out of the house I once thought I would never leave. Despite the "psychological impact" I'd been told it was tainted by, I managed to sell it, after all. In fact, it was a friend of the Tough Birds leader, Barbara, who bought it— another frizzy-haired, kind but disorganized therapist, named Patsy, who told me at the closing that she'd take good care of my memories, and make sure that the house didn't forget me. It was the kind of New Age talk Joe always hated, but I appreciated her saying it. I left the lawyer's office feeling that 17 Wildwood Lane would be in good hands.

When it came time to pack up the things in the attic, I was surprised to find I had no trouble throwing away most of what was up there. The only memento I couldn't bear to leave behind was a tattered handmade scroll I'd forgotten about entirely, with two little handprints in blue paint over a poem rendered in faux-calligraphic script:

> These are prints you've seen before
> On bathroom towels and kitchen door.
> Those you removed so graciously;
> These you may keep for memory.

I kept the scroll and brought it out here with me, though I haven't hung it up, and won't, because I know I couldn't bear to look at it every day.

I also brought Iris's old trophies, taking a chance that she would be happy to have them back, and I was glad when she seemed so grateful. They're not on display in the new house, but at least she knows they're there.

Claire helped me with the task of packing and cleaning out; maybe because she was relieved to know I was moving and there wouldn't be that strain anymore of living in the same town but not seeing each other, or maybe because she felt, as I did, that this was really the end of a friendship we had both valued so much, she offered to come over and assist me in packing up what I would take to California and deciding what things I would dispose of or give away. We hugged, and cried, but probably neither as much as we each expected to. Though I knew she was relieved to see me go, I also knew she felt the same pain I did. I don't believe I'll ever be able to have a friend like her again.

When Pam Furth saw that I wasn't taking my TV with me because there wasn't room in the truck, she asked if she could have it. Remembering something I had heard Emmett say on more than one occasion, I told her to knock herself out.

The day before I left, a card arrived bearing Art Cahill's return address on the envelope. On the front of the card was a picture of Emily Dickinson, and inside, Dawn's old English teacher had copied one of her poems, which begins "I felt my life with both my hands / To see if it was there." I wasn't sure why he had sent it to me, unless it was to communicate some lines from the final stanza: "I told myself, 'Take Courage, Friend— / That was a former time.'" Or maybe he wanted to make sure he was on my good side, because he was afraid I'd tell somebody what he'd confessed that night at Pepito's about tampering with Dawn's first grand jury. He must have heard that I was moving, because he had signed the card, "With all best wishes for your new life." My first thought was to throw it away, but at the last minute I tucked it in a flap of my suitcase, where I'd already saved the note Dottie Wing had sent to me after Dawn's conviction. "I know it wasn't any of your fault," she wrote. "I have one son a deadbeat and the other that never calls." She's still in the meal delivery program; I had Tom Whitty arrange to pay for the service for the rest of her life.

I also had him set up a scholarship fund at Lawlor College, in Opal Bremer's name. Though Dawn was tried in connection with only one death, as far as I'm concerned she was in large part, if not entirely, responsible for Opal's, too.

It was harder than I thought it would be to say good-bye to the Tough Birds. For three years, every time I went to one of those sessions, I grumbled in my head about it, wishing I didn't have to make the drive, listen to all the complaints, put up with the crazies, and, especially, talk about the things that made me feel the most vulnerable. But on my last night there, I started to say what I had rehearsed in my mind—that I'd miss them, and that I appreciated all they'd done to help me—and found myself crying, because all of it was true. Trudie had brought me a gift-wrapped can of Hawaiian Punch as a going-away present, and I gave her a tin of oatmeal crinkles. During the session, she reached over and held my hand, despite the No Physical Contact rule, and Barbara ignored it. Nelson said, "Just be careful out there," and we all laughed because this time it sounded like what any normal person might say.

On the last walk I took with Abby around the conservation land, I cried the whole way. She didn't seem surprised, and I thought maybe she understood that we were leaving—that we would never see that place again. I kept her out there a long time, pausing to look at every tree, every slice of sky and sun through the branches, every piece of the path I'd walked almost daily for more than twenty years. At first I thought I might take some pictures, along the route, to bring with me to California. But then I decided I'd rather just remember. It's more alive that way.

As the taxi pulled away from my house to take me to the airport, something caused me to look up to the left, and I saw Emmett watching me from the window of his bedroom. There was a movement behind the shade, making me think he was waving, and automatically I raised my own hand back. Then he disappeared. I wondered again why he had never told anyone, at the time of the tree house fire, that he'd seen Dawn out there that morning. Had he felt some instinct to protect her, some compassion, despite all the distress he'd subjected her to over the years? I choose to believe this, rather than that he thought no one would take his word over ours.

And it makes me feel more remorse than I would, otherwise, about letting myself believe he could have been our attacker. Seeing his tattoo that day allowed me to start down a path I'd glimpsed and wanted to follow, without realizing it, since Dawn called, returned home, and began acting in ways that raised old questions in my mind—along with new ones—that I had trouble ignoring until suspecting Emmett gave me a way. When I look back on the years we lived next door to him, I remember all the times he teased Dawn, but I also remember the time he called to ask if she wanted to be his date for the junior prom. At the time, we all assumed he was playing a cruel joke. But now I wonder if he meant it—if it had been a gesture on his part to say he wanted a do-over.

Kenneth Thornburgh left Everton and returned to Massachusetts. The last I knew, he was still working on the case of the murdered teenager that had haunted him before he pulled up stakes in his old town and moved to ours. He sent me a note after the verdicts, expressing condolences, as if Dawn had died. And I guess, in every way that matters, she did.

Cecilia Baugh is on one of those tabloid TV shows now; I see her by accident sometimes, when I turn the set on to watch with my microwave dinner. She specializes in reporting on grisly murders, and I usually change the channel as soon as I recognize her, because I know she got that job by exploiting what happened in my family—and exploiting the fact that Dawn always wanted to be her friend, no matter (as it turned out) what it might cost. Of course, she tried to get an interview with me after the verdicts. I told her, "Over my dead body," and even though I hadn't meant it to sound the way it did, I laughed when I saw the look it put on her face.

Warren and I talk every couple of days on the phone and by e-mail, and around New Year's, he's coming out here to visit for the first time. He tells me he's thinking of selling his house, especially since I told him what a good price I got for mine. He didn't say where he'd move, if he did sell. I get the impression that if he likes it out here when he comes to visit, we might talk about something more serious than what we have now, which is already pretty good.

On weekdays, after I'm done doing mammograms, I pick Josie up from nursery school and bring her back to my house. On nice days, I like to take her to Lake Merritt, not far from where we all live, to feed the birds in the wildlife sanctuary. It reminds me a little of Two Rivers, though I realize it's probably only because I want it to. Josie always asks me to recite the names of the birds; she especially enjoys hearing her grandmother say "bufflehead" and "American coot."

We used to take Abby with us for walks by the water, but she'd been slowing down lately. And in the past couple of days, I noticed a glaze over her eyes. She'd never really been the same since we made the move out here; I think the plane ride, and the new surroundings, were too much for her. It also seemed she might be going deaf. None of this was too surprising, given not only what she'd been through, but the fact that she was almost fourteen now.

I knew when she wouldn't eat any breakfast this morning, or

get up from her bed, that I needed to call the vet again. During the past two months, I've had to take her in almost once a week, though before today I always did it on my own time, because I didn't want to upset Josie. But today there was no choice but to make the appointment for early afternoon, and when I picked up my granddaughter, I told her we were going to take Abby to the animal doctor. "You can be my helper," I told her, and the expression on her face—excited to have been chosen, solemn in her resolve to do a good job—was so similar to her mother's expression as a child that it clamped my heart.

"I'll hold your hand if you need a shot," Josie said to Abby, patting the dog's head on her lap in the backseat. While we waited to be called into the examining room, I read Josie the names of all the animal groups from the illustrated poster on the wall. I wanted to distract myself from what I was afraid I'd hear when they took us into the room. Like some of the bird names at the sanctuary, the animal categories made Josie giggle, especially when she heard, "A drove of asses."

I continued reading the list: "A nuisance of cats. A shrewdness of apes. An obstinacy of buffalo. An exaltation of larks." The only one I skipped was "A murder of crows," but because she can't read yet, she didn't notice.

"What do all those words mean?" she asked, and I said, "Pest, smart, stubborn, and happy."

"A dissimulation of birds," I added, seeing I'd missed one.

"What's that mean?"

"Well, if you dissimulate, it means you're pretending. Say you're a mommy bird and you leave the nest to get some food for your babies, and when you come back to the nest, you see that another bird is about to swoop down on it. You could make a noise

338

and pretend you're hurt or something, so the bird that's about to go after your children will come after you instead."

Josie looked thoughtful, imagining the scene. "All those words are too big," she said finally. "You should just say you're pretending."

"You're a smart girl," I told her, as Abby's name was called and we stood up to lead her in. The vet lifted her onto the examining table, and I could tell just from the way he touched her—a soft, regretful pat that the news wasn't good. As she had promised she would do when the needle came, Josie reached out to take the dog's paw. And I knew that even as young as she is, she understood the same thing I did: our trip here had been Abby's last car ride, and we wouldn't be bringing her home.

Still, I could tell it made us both feel better when the vet said he'd done everything he could to try to save her.

Acknowledgements

Many thanks to the following people, among others, for their support and good cheer during the writing of this book: Elizabeth Searle, Nancy Zafris, Lori Ostlund, Anne Raeff, Christine Sneed, Dawn Tripp, Elisa Bronfman, Deb Fanton, friends and colleagues at Emerson College, Laura Treadway Gergel, Jack and Katie Gergel, Sadie Johnson, and the rest of my generous, faithful family on both sides.

For their specific contributions to the manuscript and its publication, I am indebted to Ann Treadway, Molly Treadway Johnson, Lauren Richman, Monika Woods, Dianne Choie, and especially the dream team of Kimberly Witherspoon and Deb Futter.

Finally and foremost, deep gratitude to my husband, Philip Holland, for asking the right questions and listening to mine.